SEVEN KINGS

Death waited for him in the jungle. There was nothing else to find here. No refuge, no escape, no safety or comfort. This place offered none of those, only a savage end to suffering and a blinding slip into eternity. Tong expected to die here, and he welcomed it. He would die a free man, his knees no longer bent in slavery. He ran barefoot and bleeding through the bloodshot wilderness.

Yes, he would die soon. But not yet. He would take more of their worthless lives with him. This was why he fled the scene of his first murder and entered the poison wilderness. It was not to save himself from the retribution of his oppressors. He fled so they would chase him into this scarlet realm of death. The dense jungle and its dangers gave him precious time. Time to steal the lives of the men who chased him. He would survive just long enough to kill them all; then he would give his life gladly to the jungle and its cruel mercy . . .

BY JOHN R. FULTZ

Books of the Shaper
Seven Princes
Seven Kings

BOOKS OF THE SHAPER: VOLUME II

SEVEN KINGS

JOHN R. FULTZ

www.orbitbooks.net

ORBIT

First published in Great Britain in 2013 by Orbit

A CIP catalogue record for this book
is available from the British Library.

ISBN 978-0-356-50082-9

Typeset in Garamond by M Rules
Printed and bound by CPI Group (UK) Ltd, Croydon, CR0 4YY

Papers used by Orbit are from well-managed forests
and other responsible sources.

MIX
Paper from
responsible sources
FSC
www.fsc.org   FSC® C104740

Orbit
An imprint of
Little, Brown Book Group
100 Victoria Embankment
London EC4Y 0DY

An Hachette UK Company
www.hachette.co.uk

www.orbitbooks.net

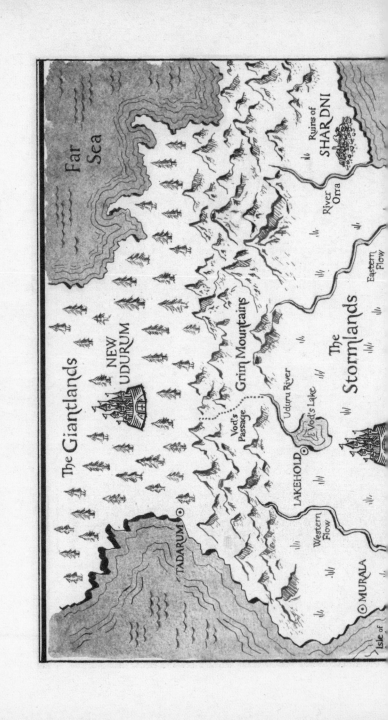

Dramatis Personae

Vod the Giant-King – Former ruler and rebuilder of New Udurum, City of Men and Giants; slayer of Omagh the Serpent-Father; sorcerer and legend; also known as Vod of the Storms

Gammir the Reborn (formerly Fangodrel of Udurum) – Vod's adopted bastard son; his true father was Gammir the Second, Prince of Khyrei, who was slain by Vod; also known as Gammir the Bloody and the Undying One; currently Emperor of Khyrei

Ianthe the Claw – Former Empress of Khyrei; grandmother of Gammir; an ageless sorceress; slain by Vireon and Alua at the fall of Shar-Dni

King Vireon of Udurum – Son of Vod; ruler of New Udurum; father of Maelthyn; all the power and strength of a Giant in the body of a Man; also known as Vireon Vodson and Vireon the Slayer

Queen Alua of Udurum – Ageless sorceress married to Vireon; mother of Maelthyn; known for her mastery of the white flame magic

Maelthyn of Udurum – Seven-year-old daughter of King Vireon and Queen Alua

Dahrima the Axe – Blonde-haired Uduri (giantess) who once served Vod the Giant-King; now she serves as one of the Ninety-Nine, King Vireon's personal guard

King D'zan of Yaskatha – Ruler of Yaskatha; reborn from a state of living death by the sorcery of Iardu and Sharadza after reclaiming his father's usurped throne; also known as the Sun Bringer

Queen Sharadza of Yaskatha – Vod's only daughter; disciple of Iardu the Shaper; married to King D'zan of Yaskatha; also known as Sharadza Vodsdaughter

King Tyro of Uurz – Twin brother of Lyrilan; swordsman of renown; also known as the Sword King; co-ruler of Uurz

King Lyrilan of Uurz – Twin brother of Tyro; scholar and scribe; also known as the Scholar King; co-ruler of Uurz

Queen Ramiyah of Uurz – Wife of King Lyrilan; born in Yaskatha

Queen Talondra of Uurz – Wife of King Tyro; born in Shar Dni and survived its fall

Lord Mendices – Warlord of Uurz; King Tyro's chief advisor; hawkish warmonger eager to lead Uurz into war against Khyrei

King Undutu of Mumbaza – Nineteen-year-old ruler of Mumbaza; also known as the King on the Cliffs and Son of the Feathered Serpent

Khama the Feathered Serpent – Ageless sorcerer whose true form is that of a great feathered serpent; involved with the founding of Mumbaza, advisor to its Kings, and protector of its long peace

King Angrid of the Icelands – Lord of the Frozen North; ruler of the Udvorg clans (blue-skinned Giants)

Varda of the Keen Eyes – Shamaness in service to King Angrid

Tong of Khyrei – An escaped slave

Iardu the Shaper – Master of Shapes; an ageless sorcerer reputed to live on an island in the Cryptic Sea

Prologue

Stories

The Storytellers of Uurz say that Man lived in the sea until the Gods taught him to walk on land, but Giants were born whole from the great stones of the earth. That is why the sea always draws Men back to its maternal depths, and why Giants are stronger and more durable than Men.

Those same Storytellers, for the price of a copper or a bowl of fermented grape, will speak of an era a thousand years ago when the land was ruled by Serpents. These monsters crawled among the hills and woodlands like colossal centipedes, breathing fire and devouring all that lived. Once the lands about Uurz were thick with forests, these raconteurs will insist, until the monsters burned the trees to dust, leaving the land parched and barren.

This was the Age of Serpents.

Nine human tribes roamed the wilds in those days, so the story goes, and the Serpents feasted on them all. Each of these Serpents could swallow a Man whole, and they often did, one right after another, until only four tribes were left. This was long before the walls of Uurz were raised; long before the secrets of smelting bronze and tilling the earth gave rise to civilization. Long before Men spread the first of their fragile empires across the earth.

If you return the next evening to that same corner of the bustling bazaar or mud-walled tavern of the night before, the Storyteller will continue the famous tale. He will sip wine gratefully from a clay bowl and tell how the four surviving tribes of Man fled into the heights of the Grim Mountains, there to accidentally rouse the race of Giants from their long sleep. The teller might even claim that the Gods had placed these Giants inside the mountain stones for Man to awake during such a crisis, but there are not many who believe this. He will surely tell you how the Giants chased the human tribes out of the mountains and so came upon the horde of Serpents whose breath had charred the lowlands.

The Giants took up boulders and fallen trees as weapons. They poured from the crevices and clefts of the mountain heights, thundering across the blackened earth. They fell upon the Serpents like an angry storm, smashing skulls and ripping legs from bodies. They crafted shields and armor from the scales of the dead beasts, used the great fangs as the heads of their spears. While the four tribes of Man took shelter in caves and remote ravines, the war between Giant and Serpent raged. The earth shook and rolled for eighty nights; some Storytellers will say a thousand nights, but Storytellers often exaggerate.

If you are willing to come back a third night, and if you have yet coppers or drink to bribe this narrator you have chosen, he will surely tell you how the Age of Serpents ended. The Giants destroyed all the Serpents but one, whom they called Omagh the Serpent-Father, greatest of all the scaly behemoths. Most Storytellers agree that the beast had one hundred and twelve legs, and all will tell you how the Serpent-Father swallowed five hundred Giants before the one called Hreeg wounded him deeply with a great spear carved from the heart of a mountain pine. The Serpent-Father slunk into a chasm in the Grim Mountains and fell into slumber at the heart of the world.

Some Storytellers here might pause to mention Vod the Giant-King, who was both Giant and Man, and how he finally slew the Serpent-Father when it awoke a thousand years later. Yet the Legend of Vod is too new a tale to join this story of ancient days. Vod's tale, they will say, must be told some other night. You see, there is always another story to tell.

After Hreeg's mighty battle, the four tribes of Man came from their sanctuary to beg mercy. The Giants chose Hreeg as their chieftain, and Hreeg said, "Your lands are burned and scalded. Your forests are gone. You tiny Men may keep the lands south of the mountains. We Giants will live north of the peaks, where the land is green and the water runs fresh and clear beneath the sky. We also claim these mountains. So if you want to live in peace, keep to your blackened lands. If we find any of you in the mountains, we will kill you and eat you."

The four tribes followed the advice of Hreeg the Stoneborn. They came out of the mountains and wandered across the black sands. They went in four directions searching for water. The Magnahin Tribe found an underground river that had survived the firestorms of the Serpents, and they named it Uurz. They built a great city of green and gold above the river, with many wells and flowering gardens to replace the lost beauty of their forests. For ten centuries Uurz thrived, a golden oasis amid the Desert of Many Thunders, until Vod's sorcery brought the green earth to life again. That is how Uurz went from jewel of the desert to capital of the Stormlands.

The remaining tribes founded other cities in distant climes, where they developed their own languages and cultures: Yaskatha, Shar Dni, and Khyrei. The unity of the four tribes was lost forever. That is why the race of Men often goes to war against itself.

Now the good Storyteller, having finished his tale, will rise and go to find another paying customer. Such Storytellers will often voice the same legends again and again, but only a few of them actually believe what they tell.

I am such a one, for I know my words are truth.

I tell only of true things, even those that never happened. I know tales drawn from lost ages and dim epochs. I know secrets and terrors, and the names of heroes and tyrants long forgotten.

I know the great Tale of the World that weaves the bright towers of Uurz into its dark fabric even as we speak.

Would you care to hear it?

1

Three Lives

The colors of the jungle were bloody red and midnight black.

Whispers of fog rustled the scarlet fronds, and the poison juices of orchids glistened on vine and petal. Red ferns grew in clusters about the roots of colossal carmine trees. Patches of russet moss hid the nests of red vipers and coral spiders. Black shadows danced beneath a canopy of branches that denied both sun and moon. Toads dark as ravens croaked songs of death among the florid mushrooms. Clouds of hungry insects filled the air, and red tigers prowled silent as dreams.

Death waited for him in the jungle. There was nothing else to find here. No refuge, no escape, no safety or comfort. This place offered none of those, only a savage end to suffering and a blinding slip into eternity. Tong expected to die here, and he welcomed it. He would die a free man, his knees no longer bent in slavery. He ran barefoot and bleeding through the bloodshot wilderness.

Yes, he would die soon. But not yet. He would take more of their worthless lives with him. This was why he fled the scene of his first murder and entered the poison wilderness. It was not to save himself from the retribution of his oppressors. He fled so they would chase him into this scarlet realm of death. The dense jungle and its dangers gave him precious time. Time to steal the lives of the men who chased him. He would survive just long enough to kill them all; then he would give his life gladly to the jungle and its cruel mercy.

Only then would he allow himself to seek Matay in the green fields of the Deathlands.

Already he had claimed a second life, leaping from the trees like a wild ape, plunging the blade of his stolen knife into a soldier's throat. That first night the company of nine Onyx Guards had been foolish enough to sleep about a small fire. They had assumed their prey would be sleeping as well, somewhere ahead of them on the crude trail Tong's passing had created. Some had stripped the plates of black bronze from their chests, arms, and shins. They had even removed the demon-face masks that hid their humanity. For the first time in his young life, Tong saw the raw sweat-stained faces of his oppressors, the masters of whip and spear and disemboweling blade.

Their flesh was as pale as his own, their eyes and hair the same black. As far as he could see, there was nothing that physically separated him, a slave, from these tormentors of slaves. Nothing except their actions. Far more than enough to damn them all. While the night watcher's back was turned, Tong pounced. His short blade ripped the life from a sleeper's chest as his hand clamped over the dying man's mouth. His entire weight pressed against his victim's chest, he watched the man die slowly. When his twitching eyes closed forever, Tong stole his curved sabre and a bag of rations. He slipped back into the night, ignoring the winged vermin that gnawed his skin and stung at his blood-smeared hands. He ran south, toward the mountains of fire at the edge of the world, making sure to leave an obvious and clumsy trail.

In the morning they found the dead soldier and followed Tong deeper into the jungle. He ran as he ate from the stolen food bag. Salted pork and dried apricots. The vegetation of the jungle was poisonous, as were most of the creatures who lived here. So finding anything edible was next to impossible. After days of starvation and pain, the meal sent waves of fresh energy coursing through his limbs. The fire of his hatred burned hotter, and he laughed as he leaped over a coiled viper that bared its dripping fangs at him.

O merciless Gods, let them follow me, he thought. *I will lead them all into death.*

He ran until exhaustion fell upon him like a black cloud. He slept in a hollow between two great tree roots, on a bed of ruddy lichen. He called Matay's name in his sleep, and he dreamed she was near, reaching for him like she did on the day of her death. Rising from the jungle filth, he reached out and grabbed only a fistful of lichen. A colony of red ants crawled across his body, feasting on the dried blood coating his lacerated skin. His chest and back were a maze of fresh welts, the work of razor-edged fronds, biting insects, and patches of sharpgrass. He uprooted a fern and used it to brush the ants from his body, wincing at the pain of beating his own wounds.

Pain was good, he decided. Pain would keep him from sleep . . . keep him wary . . . keep him ready to kill.

He climbed a tree as high as he dared, not far enough to breach the lofty canopy, but high enough to see a great distance across the leagues of crimson undergrowth. He waited there until he saw his pursuers, just at the edge of his vision, cutting their way through the jungle. They reminded him of the marching ants he had wiped away, except these black ants were far more vicious and cruel.

The upper mass of the tree's branches rattled. A great black bird flew from its nest and burst through the canopy. A ray of orange sunlight fell through the hole the bird's passing had made.

It warmed Tong's face and shoulders. He recalled Matay's love of the golden sun, how she watched it sink beyond the fields every evening. Sometimes she even halted her work, forgetting the harvest as the glory of sunset burned across the sky, amber and scarlet sinking into purple. More than once her sun-gazing had drawn the whip of the Overseer. Yet it was her daily ritual to watch the sun sink beyond the walls of the black city and into the Golden Sea, where ships sailed to and from mysterious lands. Somewhere in that walled hive of barbed towers the Undying One sat on his throne of blood and tears, dreaming new tortures for his people.

Matay's eyes saw well beyond the ramparts of oppression. She discovered freedom in the splendors of dawn and dusk.

Tong recalled the morning after their first night together. She had awoken wrapped in his arms inside the wooden shack, only to slip away from him into the chill of dawn. He lay on his side on the woven sleeping mat and stared at her sleek body as she pulled on the rough-spun colorless garment that all female slaves wore. The blackness of her hair shimmered with silver as the first rays of morning peeked through the ragged window.

"Where are you going?" he asked. "We can sleep a while longer before the work horn blows."

She paused before the door curtain and looked back at him with sparkling eyes. Her smile was the one she would wear in all his future memories. "I want to watch the sun rise," she said. She held out her small hand, soft and warm. "Come with me . . ."

He joined her that day and nearly every day after for six growing seasons, staring into the gray sky as the face of the sun set it on fire, burning away the last shades of night and making way for the brilliant blue of morning. They sat on a log outside his narrow hut, enjoying the most precious part of the day, the part when they were not yet driven to toil and sweat in the fields, when the whips and clubs of the Onyx Guard and the Overseers had yet to appear between the rows of windswept corn. It did not take him long to understand why she valued the beauty of the sunrise, and why she stopped every evening to watch the sunset. Dawn and dusk. These were the only two things she possessed that slavery could never take or destroy. This awareness was a gift she had given to him, long before she gave him the more precious gift that grew inside her belly.

I wish I could see Matay's sunrise one more time. Tong stared at the ray of light slicing through the red shadows. He climbed down to a lower position in his tree. The path he had so carefully laid would lead them directly below his perch. He need only wait. He may never feel the warm glow of sunrise on his skin again, but he would know the hot blood of his enemies on fists and fingers. He drew the long sabre from its scabbard and crouched like a panther on a wide branch above the trail.

Soon the noise of the masked ones rang through the glade, the swishing of blades, the falling of stem and branch, the tramp of metal-shod boots through mud and moss and rotting leaves. Tong's own boots were mud-caked leather, torn in places by thorn and brush and stone. The boots of a slave. His feet were cold and his toes tingled against the red bark of the tree. He decided it would be good to meet his death in a pair of soldiers' boots. Eight such pairs drew nearer to the tree that sheltered him.

He would wait until the last one passed below, then drop and kill the man, drag him into the undergrowth and steal his boots. Then he would march out to face the remaining seven at once and kill as many as he could before they brought him down. He was no swordsman, but his arms were big and powerful, the arms of a man used to laboring all day every day for twenty-three years. The masked ones had their armor, but they were frightened of him. They were cowards, impotent beneath their shells of black metal. Only black ants, marching.

His time in the jungle had made him wild and desperate, hungry for blood like the vipers and the tigers and the flying insects. All things here were hungry for blood. He was becoming one of them.

He could wait no longer.

Dropping from the wide branch, he fell directly toward the last soldier in line, sabre pointed down, hilt grasped in his clutched fists. His knees hit the man's back, knocking him forward. He drove the sword's point into that familiar soft spot between corselet and helmet, the same vulnerability his knife had discovered earlier. Half the blade's length sank into the man's body with a crunching of bones and a vertical spray of hot blood. The soldier cried out as he died, but his masked face was pressed into the mud. In the constant melange of jungle noises – crying birds, whirring insects, the cutting of foliage and tramping of armored feet – the sounds of this man's death were lost to his companions. The last of them disappeared among the fronds as Tong twisted the heavy blade.

Dragging the body into the undergrowth, he exchanged his footwear as he had planned. The new boots were tight yet warm on his aching feet. He lifted the bronze helmet with its welded mask from the dead man's head and placed it on his own. Let one of their own demon faces be the last thing they see as they die. He took what else he could from the body (a few more bits of dried food) and rolled it into a stagnant pool. A viper glided through the black water and wrapped itself around the corpse. Tong caught a glimpse of himself in the surface of the water. A pale broad-chested devil with a leering face of black death, twin horns growing from his temples. His mouth was a fanged grin and his eyes were invisible behind narrow slits. He grinned beneath the mask and walked back to the trail, the bloody sabre in one hand, his knife in the other.

He stalked after them in resolute calm, ready to face the triumph of his death. To find a better place among the spirits, where surely she waited for him. As for these Onyx Guards, they were city dwellers. Those who dwelled inside the walls of the black city did not share the beliefs of their slaves, who could only stare from afar at the ebony towers. The men Tong killed today, their souls would sink into the Hundred Hells that the city's priests venerated, there to feed the ranks of true demons or be judged and made into demons themselves. Tong did not care what they believed. He only knew they would not be in the bright meadows of the Deathlands, where milk and honey fed the spirits of earth-born slaves.

There, in the glow of a new sunrise, he would meet her again. Matay. And the one she carried in her soft round belly. His son, who was never born into a slave's life as his father was. At least he was spared that. Yet his son had also never breathed the fresh air of morning, never held the sweetness of the sun in his eyes, never known the touch of his father's hands, his mother's breast, the lips of a girl he would one day love. A slave's life was not much, but even that mean gift had been stolen from Tong's unborn son.

The Overseer on that day had been a youth himself. Tong heard it in the quavering voice that came through the mouth slit of the fanged mask. Perhaps nobody had told him that pregnant slaves should be given extra periods of rest in the latter half of their term. Tong was working on the far side of the field when he saw the glittering of the black-lacquered club rising and falling in the sunlight. He raced through the rows, kicking dirt behind him, ignoring the whips of other Overseers who tried to shout him down. He even knocked one of them over in his headlong rush to reach Matay before the fifth and sixth blows fell.

There was no sixth blow, however. The youth in the devil mask stood over Matay's bloodied body. She lay still among the rows of green and yellow plants, lines of scarlet spilled like whip marks across her white frock. Her skull had been split open, the bones of her face shattered. A clump of her beautiful hair hung from the end of the dirty club. All these things fell starkly into Tong's vision as he threw himself to the ground and took her in his arms. She was still warm then, though her heartbeat was fading. Her sweet face blurred as his eyes welled, and he called her name. Suddenly, as if she had turned to weightless mist in his arms, he knew that life had left her completely.

"Up, slave!" cried the young voice, ripe with nervous power. "Get back!" Now he applied the whip, striking Tong across the back. One, two, three times. Tong never knew how many more times it fell, leaving red trails across his back and shoulders. He stared into the slate eyes peering from within the mask. There must have been other Overseers, other soldiers, other slaves rushing toward them at that point. Yet Tong never knew.

His fist grabbed the whip that plied his flesh and he pulled the armored youth off his feet. The Overseer fell against the dirt with a heavy sound, his body squirming next to Matay's still one. Tong did not remember climbing on the man's back, or wrapping the leather whip about his exposed throat. He only remembered pulling, twisting, tightening. The sound of the youth's gagging filled his ears. The metal helmet was knocked away in the struggle, but Tong's weight held the Overseer against the earth. Pulling, gnashing teeth, squeezing, and snapping. The flesh of the neck gave way as boiled leather bit into it. Finally, an expulsion of breath as the Overseer died.

The next thing he remembered was the terrified face of his cousin Olmai, standing over him with arms full of green corn husks. His mouth was an open cave of darkness, like a tomb. "Run!" he begged Tong. "Run now! They are coming!"

He would have stayed there and taken Matay's body in his arms again, but Olmai kicked at him, pushed him into the corn stalks. "Run, fool! Make for the treeline! Go!"

After that, there was only running . . . panting . . . bleeding . . . hunger.

Rage.

And the deep red jungle whose poisons were nothing compared to the venom in his heart.

Now he marched after the seven masked soldiers wearing one of their own fanged faces, carrying two of their own blades, wearing the solid boots of a man no longer a slave. He had killed three of them now, but it was not enough. He marched toward Vengeance and its smiling sister, Death.

The whir of a black arrow caught his ear and the shaft took him in the right breast, just below the collarbone. If he had run into a wall of stone head first, he could not have been more stunned. Two more shafts followed from the left and right, one taking him in the left leg, the other piercing his side. Now the masked ones came screaming toward him, sabres raised, horned helms grimacing in the red gloom. He fell on his knees in the muck as the rushing forms surrounded him. The blades of swords and spears gleamed dully as they pressed near to his skin, and a fourth arrow clanged off his stolen helm. The Onyx Guards laughed while Tong gasped for air inside his mask.

They had fooled him. They let him take their rearguard, then circled about to pin him down with arrows. The chase was over. He had thought he was stalking them, but they had snared him instead. Already he felt the poison of the arrowheads rushing into his blood, making his arms heavy. The sabre and knife fell from his numb fingers, dropping like useless stones into the mud. The weight of the helm was terrible, so that he could no longer keep his head up. He fell backwards to a chorus of metallic laughter. The circle of blades moved closer about him, sneering devil faces hovering behind.

One guard barked an order, and another reached down and plucked the stolen helmet from his head. A high-ranking Overseer stood above Tong, marked by the black whip with a golden handle that hung from his belt. "Stupid, stupid slave," he said, though the demon lips did not move. His eyes blinked through the slits of the mask. "What did you gain from all this? A few more days of misery and starvation?" He kicked hard at Tong's belly with a filthy boot. "Eh? What did you gain?"

Tong's voice was a rasping groan, like the ripping of a delicate fabric.

"Three . . . "

"Eh? Speak up, slave!" said the Overseer. He kicked Tong again, striking near the arrow protruding from his side. A wave of agony made Tong shiver. The poison froze his blood and his limbs.

"Three . . . " he moaned again.

"Three? Three what?" The demon mask hung low before his face now, the Overseer kneeling to mock his prisoner.

"Three lives."

Tong used the last of his strength to force his lips into a smile. He would die a happy man, knowing he had taken three of the Onyx Guard with him.

The demon face stared down at him, saying nothing. The Overseer rose and uncoiled his whip. "Tie him to that tree," he ordered. "I'll flay the life from him piece by piece. We'll carry his carcass back in pieces to fertilize the fields."

Hands gripped his arms and legs, hauling him up from the earth. They rustled him toward a crimson tree bole thick with russet moss. He had seen slaves whipped to death. He knew his demise would be a long and lingering process. Yet he wept with joy as the soldiers dragged him across the glade. Death was coming to greet him. He need only cross a river of boiling pain and she would welcome him into her domain.

Matay . . .

He wanted to call out her name, but his tongue would no longer move.

They slammed him chest first against the tree, rattling the three arrows still in his flesh. His cry of pain was a gagging moan. One man got some rope from a shoulder pack while the other two pulled Tong's arms about the tree trunk.

Behind him, the Overseer cracked his whip, warming up his arm for a slow execution.

Now the men stopped, the rope gone slack in their hands. Masked heads turned to the left and right, and the sound of the whip fell into silence. The soldiers stared at something behind Tong. Something had come out of the jungle. No, there must have been several things, though they did not make a sound. The Onyx Guards were silent, but the sound of their metal blades sliding from scabbards filled the glade. The three archers, who had come into the glade after Tong's capture, nocked fresh shafts and drew taut their bowstrings. Tong's limp body dropped into the muck, his head fell back across his shoulders, and he saw the beasts.

They might have been hunched apes, long of arm and squat of haunch, yet they were entirely without hair or fur. They ringed the glade, at least thirty of them, though perhaps more lurked in the scarlet foliage. Their skins were white as bone, supple as leather. They crouched atop clumps of rock or fallen trees, lifting great flat hands that ended in claws, working silently in the air as if speaking with their fingers.

Most shocking of all, their heads were lizardine ovals with no eyes at all. Where eye sockets should have been grew instead a pair of white curling horns like those of a ram, tapering to points on either side of their skulls. Their mouths were impossibly wide and full of sharp teeth. Above the mouths sat slitted noses like those of bats, flaring and pulsing as they sniffed the jungle air. The beasts' arms and legs were mightily muscled, their bellies lean and flat. It was not clear if they had dropped down from the trees, risen up from the ground, or simply lumbered into the glade. They moved quickly, silent as white mists.

The seven masked soldiers stood wrapped in a precarious calm before this strange audience. From his place among the gnarled roots, Tong saw a white blur leap across the glade, then another, and another. A helmeted head rolled across the ground like a melon and bumped against his shoulder. The men behind the masks were screaming. At first they bellowed rage and warnings. In a matter of moments, as clouds of warm red mist erupted into the air, raining down upon Tong's face, their screams turned to cries of terror and pain. Soon a heavy silence replaced them.

Tong managed to raise his head a bit. He moaned softly at the pain of his pierced flesh. The white creatures crouched among the bodies of the dead men. Scarlet stained their long claws and bony chests. Tongues descended from their fanged maws to lick at the bronze faces of corpses. At first he thought they were lapping up the blood, that they would devour the dead men and himself. He only hoped they would kill him before eating him. Yet the eyeless ones seemed only to explore the men's faces and armor with their weird pink tongues like curling tendrils. Their tongues moved more like curious fingers than organs made for tasting.

Now they gathered about Tong, sniffing at him and sliding their tongues across his skin. Tongues wrapped about each of the arrow shafts and pulled them from his body in quick, painful jerks. Fresh blood welled from the ragged holes. The eyeless faces drew near to his own, and he heard them sniffing. He must smell like a wild animal dying of infected wounds. Perhaps his stink would drive them away, and he would lie here and die at last.

The shadows of the jungle converged to flood his brain, and the beasts lifted his useless body. He hung weightless in the grip of their powerful hands, and their claws unavoidably pricked his skin. Blood spilled from his poisoned wounds as awareness spilled from his mind.

The creatures raced in bounding, graceful strides through the scarlet wilderness.

He did not believe they were carrying him toward the green fields of the Deathlands.

2

Sword and Scholar

Drought had come to the Stormlands. It lay dusty in the gutters like a dying beggar, parched and cackling. It crouched in the waves of heat rising from the stones of Uurz, while the green-gold city baked in the sun's glory. The few clouds that dared the blue sky were wisps of memory, impotent ghosts gliding toward oblivion. After thirty-three years of daily rains, the earth had remembered its barren legacy.

In the roof gardens beneath the cool shade of palms the city's noble elders spoke of the desert's return. "The season of Vod's magic is done," they whispered, sipping at their gilded cups. "Eight years now the Giant-King has been dead. Vod of the Storms is gone and so is his power." Even the meanest of wines was terribly expensive in those days.

The youngest of these privileged folk, confident in their robes of silk and silver, rolled their eyes and laughed at such talk. "The Desert of Many Thunders is little more than fable," they said wrongly. "The old ones fear changing times. No season can last forever. We will learn to live in these dry times, as our ancestors did before us." These young ones had never known the great expanse of black sand or the terrible heat and dust storms of the great wasteland.

In the marketplace at the city's center, merchants grew rich on casks of water hauled up from the Sacred River still running strong beneath Uurz's golden palace. The subterranean stream was the source of Uurz's founding, and it had sustained the city for twelve hundred years. Uurz was a legend unto itself, a thriving paradise in the heart of the black wastes, until Vod cracked open land and sky with his power.

Vod, who slew the Father of Serpents three decades ago and changed the mighty desert into a verdant plain between two rivers. Vod, who was both Giant and Man, made the Stormlands an agricultural empire, with the City of Sacred Waters rising bright and proud at its heart. Then he turned his attentions across the Grim Mountains and rebuilt New Udurum, the City of Men and Giants, leaving Uurz to reap the profits of his world-altering sorcery.

Minstrels in the wine shops and brothels of Uurz still sang of colossal Vod's journey south. Yet now they also sang of his madness, his death, and the fading of his magic. None sang of his return. Generous Vod was long dead, his mad bones swallowed by the Cryptic Sea.

The Giant-King had not truly destroyed the Desert of Many Thunders. It only slumbered beneath the emerald leagues of long grass and the twisting courses of new-made rivers. Like the Serpent-Father had done a millennium ago, the desert slept, dreaming of the heaps of dried bones it would one day rise to reclaim.

Uurz would suffer, but it would not perish. In this, the young dilettantes were correct. The Sacred River would sustain the City of Wine and Song as it always had. It was the newer settlements, the farming communities, the outlying hamlets and vineyards, the riverside villages, and the lone plains dwellers who would lose everything as the rivers sank low and the tall grass went from yellow to brown to blackened husks. Vod's Lake sank in its immense crater until it stood no deeper than a stagnant pond, and the great waterfall that fed it with melting mountain snows diminished to a trickle.

From far and wide came the thirsty, the ruined, and the doomed to seek refuge behind the gates of Uurz. In the catacombs beneath the great palace, the Sacred River flowed steadily as ever, hidden from the sun's burning vengeance. Far above the city's burnished pinnacles and fortified walls, dry thunder rolled on hot winds.

Yes, the Desert of Many Thunders was returning.

And the Twin Kings of Uurz could do nothing to prevent it.

In the warm shade of his study Lyrilan awaited the sage's arrival. His watery eyes stared past the rim of his goblet toward the final page of the manuscript. His right hand ached between thumb and forefinger, and the stains of ink marred his fingers like bruises. It was finished. His most important work and certainly the closest to his heart. For ten months he had lovingly crafted every word, every phrase, turning the threads of memory and the flavor of language into official history. Now it lay complete before him, a testament of love for his dead father.

A single window he kept uncurtained, and from the heights of his balcony the gardens and orchards of Uurz sparkled with evening light. A hot wind fell at times through the portal, raking his bare chest like the touch of a desperate woman. He had no time for such passions. Not yet. He missed the rain, the coolness of its breath, yet these dry days reminded him of the manuscript's early chapters, which chronicled the desert years before his father had gained the title of Emperor. Long before Lyrilan or his brother were born.

In those days the Great Desert lay just beyond the city gates.

Dairon was a soldier who survived two wars, a dozen battles, the Whelming of the Giants, and still he rose to sit upon the throne by public acclaim. He was the inaugural Emperor of a new blood-line, the old one having been destroyed to the last man by the enraged Giants before Vod calmed their savagery. There would never be another Man like Dairon the Liberator, Friend to Giants, Savior of Uurz.

All this and more lay within the scrawled pages Lyrilan had labored over for so long. The book had taken possession of his life while he was writing it, excluding practically everything else. Even sweet Ramiyah he had ignored, but he would soon make up for that. Now that the manuscript was finished, it was time to start a family. She had waited for him, and she would be pleased.

To compose the biography Lyrilan had interviewed every man still living who had known his father: grizzled soldiers who'd shared Dairon's early years in the legions, brawny captains who had served beneath him in latter years, diplomats and legislators, merchants and chefs, sages and stable hands, dignitaries and dilet-tantes, venerable priests and powdered courtesans, even a pair of solemn magicians. The result was a thousand diverse views of the humble soldier who eventually became Lord of the Sacred Waters, Emperor of Uurz. To these accounts were added the intimate blessings of Dairon's personal journals, the keystones of Lyrilan's inheritance. These were the raw tools he used to sculpt a monu-ment to his father's existence, a memorial of ink and paper built on the foundation of a son's most poignant memories.

He hoped the truth of his father's life lay revealed among these scrawled pages.

The Life of Dairon, First Emperor of the New Blood was complete. Yet was it worthy?

Volomses entered the study in the company of Lyrilan's per-sonal servant. The purple of the sage's robe matched the tapestries that rippled along the walls. The old man's head was bald but for a few wisps of white hair, and his white beard was triple-braided with bands of bronze, like a trio of silent asps grown from his chin. His black eyes were keen in their wrinkled sockets, and his gnarled fingers anxious upon his walking staff. From his kneeling position, he greeted Lyrilan in the formal courtly manner. During the past year Lyrilan had grown accustomed to such enforced formality. The very air had grown thick with it.

"Rise, Volomses," said Lyrilan. "The book is done." The breath went out of his lungs as he said this, and he slipped down onto a cushioned divan. The sage's eyes turned toward the writing table of ebony wood with its racks of ink and quills, and the thick pile of vellum pages stacked neatly at its center. Like a priest approaching a holy relic, he walked forward. His fingers extended to touch the papers, as if to verify their physical existence. He read the title aloud, and it sounded like a holy benediction.

"Majesty," whispered the sage. "This is ... outstanding."

Lyrilan frowned, rubbing his sore quill hand. "How can you say this to me, old friend?" he asked. "You haven't read a word of it yet."

Volomses turned to stare at him, and his face swiveled into the look of a tutor addressing a student. It was a look he would never dare cast upon Lyrilan's brother. Yet Tyro had not spent the better part of his youth lost in the lessons and riddles of Volomses' scholarship. To Lyrilan the old sage was practically a second father. Even more so since the passing of Dairon thirteen months ago. For the first time Lyrilan wondered if Tyro had anyone who served this role for him. Someone who could ease the pain of losing a father simply by his presence. The thought troubled Lyrilan deeply. He did not know his twin brother. Not really. They shared the throne and a vast kingdom, yet they barely spoke these days.

Only in the midst of court duties, each on his high seat

responding to civil cases and foreign diplomats, did they converse at all. Lyrilan had made the rift greater by cloistering himself in this lofty tower for the better part of a year to work on this book. Yet surely Tyro understood that this was Lyrilan's tribute to the life of their father. Tyro had ordered a golden statue of Dairon erected in the palace courtyard, and another of bronze in the Great Marketplace. Yet Tyro did not create these works himself. Lyrilan's ode to Dairon's greatness was something he had created out of raw love, stubborn dedication, and blood-dark ink. Both of Tyro's sculptures had been completed months before Lyrilan's manuscript.

"One does not need to stare at the sun to understand its brightness, Majesty," said the sage, tugging at a single braid of his white beard. "Have I not read your previous tomes, and every line of your inconstant poetry? I have no reason to believe that this volume will not be a masterwork. Your father would be very proud of you."

Lyrilan shrugged his shoulders and poured wine into a crystal goblet for his guest. He refilled his own cup with more of the Uurzian vintage. Now that his head need no longer be clear, he could afford to get good and drunk. Then would come sleep, long and deep. After that, he would take his wife in the way he had so long denied himself.

Ramiyah, he prayed, *please be able to forgive my long absence. Now I will give you children, as many as you desire.* He knew there would come a day when another unwritten book would call out to him, possess his body and spirit, and demand that he write it into existence. Someday he would creep from his bed and find himself chained to the writing desk again, obsessed with some new work. Yet now he put the thought from his head. He must find a balance between this solitary work and his duties as husband, as King, and eventually as a father.

"Stay here," he told Volomses. "The chamber is yours. Read it. It needs your eyes. Only when I have gained your studied endorsement will I have it bound and passed to the scribes for duplication." Lyrilan waved to his servant, who opened a wall closet and brought fine new robes for the King as he shed his sweat-stained tunic.

Volomses gave a solemn half-bow. "I will not leave this chamber until I have done so," he swore. Servants would bring the sage meals and wine, and even courtesans if he wished, while he inhabited the study and perused Lyrilan's pages. This was a ritual Lyrilan had enacted with every book he had written for the past seven years. His first volume, *The Perilous Quest of Prince D'zan, Scion of Yaskatha*, was one of five such tomes to grace the shelves of the Royal Library of Uurz. Each of those volumes had benefited from the editorship of Volomses. This book of Dairon's life would be the sixth. Lyrilan wondered if, someday when the old sage had passed away, he could ever write another book or have the courage to put it on public display. He put the thought from his mind.

"Thank you," he said, embracing the sage as an uncle or cousin. "They are never finished until you read them."

Volomses nodded. His gaze wandered to the manuscript as he drank from the goblet, then his head turned back to Lyrilan, who had donned a robe of green and gold, a cape of liquid-blue silk, and hose of black velvet. His wiry legs were far too thin for going bare, even in the long heat of the drought.

"Your brother expects you at the feasting," said the sage, as if he muttered a warning.

Lyrilan nodded. "I will not disappoint him. In fact, I may drink more wine than he does this night." The servant handed him a thin coronet of gold with a single emerald set at the center of the forehead. Lyrilan slipped it on to fit tightly about his brow and arranged the long, oiled curls of his black hair. "Tell my wife I await her in the Grand Hall," he said. The page rushed off to summon his mistress.

Volomses still had not looked away from his King. "You know there will be gladiators? Khyrein spies in a duel of death."

Lyrilan nodded, took a deep breath, and drained his cup of its red refreshment. Already he felt the pleasant sting of the wine between his temples. He sighed.

"I did not," he admitted. "My brother's command?"

Volomses stared out the window at the falling gloom of evening. Stars winked in the deep twilight. The sun was nearly lost beneath the flat horizon, and golden towers stood purple as wounds. "More than likely the idea came from Lord Mendices," spat Volomses. "That one has a hunger for blood that is never quenched. Would that he were not so close in your brother's affections."

Lyrilan pulled on tall boots of black oxen leather. He felt as stiff and formal as he looked. The sundown had brought little relief from the day's heat, and he looked forward to the great fan bearers at the feast, if not the blood sport.

"Or perhaps it was Talondra?" he asked. His brother's wife was an olive-skinned Sharrian. Her vicious beauty was exceeded only by her absolute hatred of Khyrei, the nation that had reduced Shar Dni to rubble in a single day of sorcery and slaughter. Her presence fueled Tyro's lust for war as oil fed a brazier's flames. Perhaps it was that dark passion, that very eagerness to spill Khyrein blood, that so attracted Tyro to her above all other courtesans. Perhaps it was her keen ambition to revenge the dead of Shar Dni that had impressed Tyro enough to make her his Queen. Dairon would not have approved, but Lyrilan had never said this to his brother. It was not his place.

Lyrilan must be the Peace Speaker. He must provide the balance to his brother's glory-seeking war lust. Dairon had refused to initiate or participate in a war of vengeance. Lyrilan understood why. At one time he had thought that Tyro also understood. Perhaps it did not matter anymore now that Dairon was gone. His influence over Tyro was no more.

Would Tyro deign to read the book his brother had written? Would he rediscover the principles and philosophies that had made their father a great soldier and a great ruler?

That is why you really wrote this book, a voice inside him whispered. *You wrote it for Tyro. You hope it will reach him.*

Lyrilan shook his head. The wine was strong.

He strapped a jeweled dagger to his belt, strictly for the sake of formality. Now he descended the spiral stairs toward the opulent heart of the Palace of Sacred Waters. A pair of wing-helmed guards accompanied him, mute but for the clatter of their boots and the jangling of scabbards.

He braced himself for the sight of tonight's bloodshed, a gaudy entertainment staged in the guise of justice. Normally he would never attend such an event, and would even argue its legitimacy with his brother. But he had learned one thing above all others in his thirteen months of being a King. He had learned to choose his battles carefully.

Though he must endure watching a man die during the feast, at least he would know the comfort of Ramiyah's presence. They might even finish the dining and depart before the combat began. This would no doubt irk Tyro, but Lyrilan enjoyed sending such subtle signals of disapproval. Where Tyro was blunt, Lyrilan was understated.

The Scholar King and the Sword King, they were called. While two Kings ruled Uurz, there could be no Emperor, for that was a single title, meant for only one man to bear.

Always in the back of his mind, Lyrilan knew what this meant.

One of them must eventually die before Uurz would again have an Emperor.

It was a sobering fact that he had taught himself to utterly ignore.

The Feasting Hall was a hive of activity. A hundred barefoot servants rushed about in white togas serving platters of roasted meat, towers of sliced fruits, brown loaves and steaming broth. The royal board lay heavy with delicacies contrived by a squad of clever cooks, and vintages dark as ruby from the palace cellars sat along the table in crystal decanters. Already a few dozen noble couples and lacy courtesans had arranged themselves along the board, sipping at sparkling goblets, toying with powdered curls, whispering heresies into bejeweled ears, and chewing the flesh of plump black grapes plucked from jade bowls.

Squat pillars of white marble veined with violet lined the sides of the hall, and high windows admitted the evening breezes. The flames of torches dances in their sconces. The smells of steaming provender and wafting perfumes filled the high chamber. The walls lay hidden behind tapestries of ancient weave set with scenes of past Emperors leading their armies to victory or battling fiery Serpents in apocalyptic scenes that probably never happened. Yet the jewel eyes of the tapestry heroes gleamed bright as stars in the hall.

The floor was inlaid with a mosaic representing all the great ages of the world, from the Time of Walking Gods to the Age of Serpents, on to the Scattering of Tribes, the Age of Heroes, and many others, ending with the Age of the Five Cities. Four of those great cities still stood in this the Modern Age, yet there were no depictions of New Udurum. That titanic capital of black stone lay north of the Grim Mountains and was not founded by the Tribes of Man, but by the fickle northern Giants. It was Vod of the Storms who had opened Udurum's gates to Men, and the thousands of refugees from fallen Shar Dni. One city was annihilated by darkest sorcery; another was transformed by similar powers.

The people of Uurz were close allies with Vireon, Son of the Giant-King, who now ruled Udurum. Yet in their hearts they did not fully trust the Tall Ones; many living still in Uurz remembered the day when Giants conquered their city and crushed the bloodline of their aged Emperor. Those survivors of Shar Dni's destruction who had not fled to the City of Men and Giants fled instead to Uurz.

In recent years, rumors of the Giants' departure from Udurum had spread to the green-gold city. Merchants from Udurum said the Uduru went farther north to find a new home in the Icelands. Still, there were many in Uurz who never forgot the sight of a Giant host thundering against the city walls, and they half expected the Uduru to return one day and take back the city they had conquered then abandoned.

At the far end of the great table, on a raised dais of glassy marble, Tyro the Sword King sat staring into the eyes of his wife and lover, Talondra. She lounged at his side in her own gilded chair of velvet and silk, her ring-heavy hands caressing Tyro's chest. Tyro was everything his scholarly twin was not: broad of shoulder, dusky of skin, heavily muscled, and radiant with royal power. His long black hair hung wild about his shoulders, but his heavy beard was tied into a single braid with hoops of golden wire. His scarred chest was bare in the heat, glimmering with a necklace of topaz and opals. He wore a plaited bronze kilt in the manner of a legionnaire, underscoring his status as the realm's chief soldier, his strapping legs bare, jeweled sandals resting on a lush carpet. Bracers of silver and onyx sheathed the Sword King's forearms, and a slim crown of gold and emerald (identical to Lyrilan's own) sat upon his brow.

Tyro did not need the crown to evoke a majestic aura, yet he wore it as custom dictated. Against the right arm of his high seat leaned a broadsword in a scabbard crusted with emerald and jade, the Emperor's final gift to his warrior son. Dairon had left his journals to Lyrilan, his sword to Tyro. The man knew his sons well.

The eastern wing of the hall was covered with black sand, forming a small arena where tonight's combatants would shed one another's blood. Four flaming braziers sat about the sandy area, each of them fronting two spearmen in polished breastplates. These eight guards would ensure the gladiators did not flee. It would be a fight to the death, the winner gifted with the Kings' mercy. An ancient rite of justice, one that Tyro had revived only recently. Lyrilan's protests had been powerless to prevent it. Now he must endure the blood spectacle.

Ramiyah waited between two pillars, standing apart from the mass of courtesans and revelers who streamed into the hall in their best satins and gemstones. A trio of serving girls stood at her back, having dressed her in a slim gown of crimson trimmed with amber thread. Her golden hair fell like a mantle of silk to the middle of her back, and her neck bore a collar of emerald and jet, a gift from Lyrilan on their wedding night two years ago. Diamonds hung from her seashell ears, and the nails of her fingers were perfect as red almonds.

She was Yaskathan, born and bred in that southern kingdom of tall ships, vast orchards, and year-long heat. The closeness of the drought did not bother her, only the dry spell of her husband's attention. Yet that long season was over. Her eyes fell upon Lyrilan, blue as northern ice, yet warm as sunrays. She rushed toward him as he entered through the grand arch. The guards slowed their pace so as not to intrude upon the happy reunion.

Lyrilan wrapped his arms about Ramiyah with a sigh of relief. Her first look had said, *I waited for you in perfect faith*. Twice now he had abandoned her for his scrolls and inks and quills. Two books written and two periods of loneliness that his wife had borne with the patience of a Goddess. He inhaled the lilac scent of her hair, the jasmine sweetness of her neck. He kissed pink lips, caressed warm brown skin.

"Gods of Earth and Sky – how I've missed you," Lyrilan told her.

"Is it finished?" she asked.

He nodded. "Volomses is reading it now. I am returned to the land of the living." He smiled, and she caught his joy in her own face, sending it back to him like a reflection in silvered glass.

He looked beyond the bobbing heads and bared shoulders of the assembled courtiers. His brother had noticed his arrival. Tyro raised his right hand in greeting, while his left lay firmly in the grip of the Lady Talondra. The Brother Kings sent their smiles across the hall like messengers' arrows aimed at one another.

"Let us dine," said Lyrilan, leading Ramiyah toward the board. The horde of courtesans and fools spread apart like rainbow-hued water, and the royal couple walked between two aisles of bowing and kneeling nobles. Servants stopped in their tracks, food steaming on great oval trays, wine sloshing in fresh decanters, until Lyrilan approached his seat.

At the opposite end of the table, much farther from his brother than he would have liked, a second dais rose to support Lyrilan's throne and its companion seat. He assisted his wife as she ascended the three steps to her chair. When she was safely nestled on a velvet cushion there, he sat himself unceremoniously upon the throne. Now he stared across the heaped board and the two hundred guests directly at Tyro. The Twin Kings sat above their courtiers on platforms of equal height. Like the identical crowns, the twin thrones showed the equality of the two monarchs. Pairs of servants cooled both of the royal couples by wafting great feathered fans made from the feathers of Mumbazan ostriches.

Talondra stared with tigerish eyes at Ramiyah. The two women were nothing alike. Talondra's raven-black hair set her apart, as did her unrestrained curls. Her eyes, like Ramiyah's, were blue, yet Talondra's eyes were cold. They reminded Lyrilan of the glistening snowdrifts between the Grim Mountains, and the perilous crossing he and Tyro had made eight years ago.

Talondra was a child of Shar Dni, yet her family had sent her here a year before that city fell to horror and war. Her loathing of Khyrei and its pale peoples was already a legend among the court. Rumors said that she had tortured to death with her own hands a Khyrein spy found in the palace three years ago. Her constant influence had utterly ruined any Uurzian merchant families who claimed a trace of Khyrein blood. No matter that most of those hapless fools had never set foot in Khyrei themselves. Talondra would never be satisfied until Tyro led the Legions of Uurz south to conquer the jungle kingdom.

Tyro wanted war with Khyrei as a matter of honor; Talondra wanted vengeance, raw and bloody and bitter on the tongue. This made her far more dangerous than he. Lyrilan was not the only member of the court to recognize this uncomfortable truth.

The Brother Kings were seated just far enough apart that conversation would be impossible. If they wished to discuss some matter, they must send servants to carry their words around the table like honeyed pastries. Lyrilan noted the presence of Lord Mendices without surprise. The tall hawk-nosed warrior with the shaven skull and oiled beard was not dressed in his customary bronze mail and plate, but wore instead a nobleman's green-gold toga, a wreath of grape leaves twined about his narrow skull. His dark eyes scanned the board, making mental note of all those present, assessing each personality for its usefulness in his palace schemes. Rubies glimmered on his fingers like drops of blood. Of all the courtiers at table, Mendices sat closest to Tyro, as he loomed large in the Sword King's private councils.

A trio of musicians began to play on harp, pipe, and lute, signifying the start of the festivities. The assembled People of the Court fell to feasting with hearty abandon, staining their lips with red wine and greasy gooseflesh. Only the unmarried women held back, nibbling at dainty bits of food, filling their slim bellies with drink that made them lightheaded and prone to bouts of giggling. Servants brought Lyrilan and Ramiyah platters of food and goblets of wine, holding them steady as living tables while the Scholar King and his wife dined. Across the mass of feasters, Talondra fed Tyro strips of pink meat with her own supple fingers.

Ramiyah spoke of a trip to Murala, possibly a sea cruise to Mumbaza. Like Lyrilan's mother, she loved to sail on the great Uurzian galleys. Lyrilan made no promises, but nodded. Perhaps it was time for a few days away from this court with its stifling formalities and increasingly barbaric entertainments. A page boy approached and brought him word from the table's far end.

"Majesty," the page bowed, "your brother bids you welcome. King Tyro rejoices to see you come down from your lonesome tower. His love for you has turned to worry over your well-being."

Lyrilan smiled. "Tell my brother that I missed him too. But this night belongs to my Ramiyah. I will speak with him tomorrow, if he will, in the Garden of Memory."

The servant bowed again and carried his message around the teeming table to the seat of Tyro. Tyro nodded and turned to share his thoughts with Talondra. The dark-haired Queen looked not in Lyrilan's direction, but focused only on Tyro. She could exert an iron influence over his deeds. Lyrilan had learned this the hard way, as she pulled his brother further and further away from him during the last four years.

In some way the brotherly bond had been shattered on the day of Tyro's wedding. Was this only natural for brothers? As twins, the two boys had shared a special intimacy while growing, one that endured despite their separate natures. Each supplied strength where the other displayed weakness. Lyrilan often prayed to the Four Gods that the bond of twins was not broken, only muted. Yet he, too, had often pulled away from his brother. When he was consumed in the research and composition of a new book, he turned away from all companions. Even his wife. He squeezed Ramiyah's hand and silently swore to find a greater balance between his writing, his relationships, and his Kingship.

The servant returned with another swift bow, bringing the words of Tyro: "Majesty. King Tyro wills it. He bids you enjoy the evening's spectacle." Lyrilan frowned and offered no response. He waved the servant away, and the boy was gone, lost in the flurry of attendants hefting full salvers and porcelain dishes to and from the table.

Lyrilan enjoyed the touch of Ramiyah's fingers, the taste of her lips flavored with dark berries, the warmth of her smile, and her soft words slipped into his ear. He soon forgot about the feast, the courtiers, and even his brother's presence. Ramiyah had this effect on him: hers was the ability to consume his attention as nothing but a Great Idea could ever do. It was those Great Ideas that were her only competition as Queen and wife. They were the only things that could break the spell of her charms and draw him away from her. Now he reveled in her presence. The music of the feast, the voices of the celebrants, all sank to a dull roar. The sparkling wine sang in his blood, swam between his ears like dancing motes of starlight, and he found himself smiling and content for a timeless moment. That contentment was shattered by the voice of Lord Mendices.

The gaunt Warlord rose from his place at the table and with a gesture caused the musicians to cease their playing. All eyes turned upon the lord, and his lean face smiled in the manner of a wolf or jackal contemplating easy prey. Such was Lyrilan's imagination, yet he knew himself to be drunk, or close to it, so he ignored his fancies.

Lord Mendices raised his cup. "A toast to the Twin Kings of Uurz, Lords of the Sacred Waters. Long may they run!" Every man and woman in the hall joined him. "In his grace and wisdom," said Mendices, "King Tyro has revived our ancestors' tradition of blood justice. Tonight we bring before the Brother Kings not one but two known spies from the poisonous realm of the south. Two Khyreins, marked not only by their pale skin and dark eyes, but by their own words, spoken during a righteous interrogation. They have confessed to being agents of Gammir the Reborn, whom they have the gall to call Emperor. Yet no spy can stalk the streets of Uurz for long. Our legions are vigilant! Our swords are sharp! Our walls are strong!" Another round of cheering, unasked for but triggered by the traditional evocation of Uurz's triple strength. Mendices paused to bask in the effect of his words, and calm returned to the hall.

"As our ancestors knew, a warrior's worth can be proven in battle by strength of arm and swiftness of foot. So that ancient principle lives again. Rather than face the headsman bound in mortal unity, these Khyreins have chosen to fight to the death so that one may be granted the Kings' mercy. A stain of wickedness pervades the entire Khyrein race, which knows nothing of brotherhood. You will see it on display this evening, as one man of Khyrei willingly strikes down another. Let this combat remind you of what separates us from these fiends of the crimson jungles."

Mendices turned to signal a guard. "The prisoners."

Lyrilan's stomach sank, sobriety returning like a lead weight upon his chest as the guard walked off to retrieve the captive Khyreins. Ramiyah's hand squeezed his own, a silent message of support. He took a deep slow breath. It reeked of brazier smoke and greasy bones.

The points of naked spears herded the two Khyreins into the

hall and onto the circle of black sand. The eight spearmen arranged themselves in a ring about the makeshift arena. The courtiers at the Kings' table stood to have a better view beyond the guards' bronze shoulders. Only the two Kings and their Queens would have an unobstructed view of the combat, sitting safely atop their platforms.

The Khyreins were nude but for loincloths of crimson silk. Their skin was pale as marble, their narrow eyes and unwashed hair black as kohl. The half-healed marks of torture and bondage were visible as crimson welts upon their wrists and feet. One was barely a man, little more than shaving age, his arms thin and chest sunken. The other was a man of middle age, with beefy arms and squat legs, a warrior who had seen pain and taken men's lives. It was obvious who would win this combat. Unless the younger man proved far quicker than his elder.

A guard removed first the young man's shackles, then the elder's. They stood at the far ends of the ring. Two shortblades were tossed into the middle of the arena, hitting the sand with dull thumps. They were common blades, wide and honed to deadly sharpness, but without any flourish of design or jeweled accent. These were tools made only for one purpose: killing at an arm's length. Both of the prisoners eyed the blades, rubbing their wrists that had suffered so long under the shackles' bite.

Perhaps they thought of taking up those blades and cutting their way through the spearmen, maybe even leaping upon one of the Twin Kings' platforms and spilling royal blood across the steps. Yet the spearmen were chosen for their size and ferocity. Any step toward the outside of the ring would bring an immediate impaling. There was no choice now but to fight one another. Lyrilan wondered if he would make the same choice in a similar situation. What if he were forced to choose between killing his brother or sacrificing his own life? He chose to think he would not fight Tyro, no matter the consequences. Yet he did not truly know the answer.

No man truly knows himself until he faces death. The words of Pericles, greatest philosopher of Yaskatha. These two Khyreins were on the verge of an ultimate self-knowledge.

The younger man leaped toward the blades, followed a half-second later by his countryman. The younger had barely wrapped his hand about the sword's grip when the elder's bare heel slammed into his skull. The elder grabbed up his own weapon. He stabbed down with both hands wrapped about the grip. The blade sank into sand as the younger rolled to his side and jumped to his feet. They squared off like crouching panthers.

The elder waited patiently, and the younger lunged, stabbing forward. The elder brought his knee up and cracked a rib or two, then felled his opponent with a stabbing blow from his elbow. Again the younger went down to the sand. But he did not lose the grip on his shortblade. He sliced it casually across the back of the older's calf, just missing the great tendon that would have crippled him. The elder howled and leaped away. The courtiers cheered at the sight of first blood. Lyrilan's stomach churned. He must not vomit. Not in front of all these eyes.

Once again the two Khryeins faced each other, the one clutching his ribs, the other streaming crimson from the back of his lower leg. The moment lingered, and the pale panthers circled. Someone yelled a curse upon them both from the table. As if incensed by this verbal abuse, the elder swept forward with his blade, keeping his body well back from the younger's thrusting motion. A red weal appeared across the younger's chest from nipple to nipple. The elder wasted no time, sweeping a leg beneath the younger and bringing him to the ground once more.

The older thrust his blade deep into the younger's side. The younger's blade fell from his fingers as he howled. It was not a killing blow, but he would not rise again. Scarlet streamed from both chest and side wounds into the black sand, where it became invisible among the grains. Now the older raised his sword again in both hands, blade pointed down and aimed at the younger's heart. This would be the death stroke, the final mercy. He would put the gasping, quivering youth out of his misery at last.

A bronze spear snaked forward and dashed the sword from the older's hands before the killing blow fell. Guards surrounded him as he stood panting and bleeding from the calf, a desperate hope burning in his black eyes. The guards removed both shortblades, and their captain carried the bloodied sword across the hall toward Lyrilan's dais. Wordlessly he held the killing tool in both hands, arms outstretched toward the Scholar King. Lyrilan swallowed the dryness in his throat. He did not know what to do. As much as he knew the intricacies of courtly protocol, this was a situation entirely new to him. It was a custom that died out long ago, and it should have been left dead.

The wounded man gasped for air on the sand, grasping at his punctured flesh.

Lyrilan became aware of all eyes focused on him now. Lord Mendices threw his voice across the hall again. "Majesty. It is customary for the Emperor ... or King ... to claim the right of final execution." He paused, and when there came no reply from Lyrilan, he added, "The death blow is yours if you wish it, King Lyrilan."

Lyrilan shook his head. He waved the sword away with distaste, as if it were a platter of overripe cheese. His eyes turned toward Tyro, who watched without expression from across the long table. Did his brother enjoy seeing him squirm like this? Or did he feel Lyrilan's pain? Was it Tyro's idea to offer Lyrilan the killing sword first?

The guard walked about the table and offered the red blade to

Tyro. The Sword King wrapped his hand about the grip and stood before the audience gathered about him. All there knew he would do the deed. There was no question. Tyro had no qualms about killing his enemies, as no warrior should.

Lyrilan avoided his eyes, and the eyes of the nobles that flickered back and forth between the two Kings. He stared at his own hands, cursing the jeweled rings on his fingers. He could not even look at Ramiyah, though her presence beside him was hot as flame.

Tyro stepped down from his dais while Talondra stood to watch him go. He approached the ring of sand, stood over the dying man, and said something in a low voice. Only the bleeding Khyrein could hear him. As easily as slicing a melon, he drew the keen blade across the young Khyrein's throat, pressing it deep to sever the great vein. A fresh gout of red spilled among the black sand, and in a few moments the prisoner was dead.

The older prisoner stood nearby, still the focus of an octet of spears. Tyro would grant him freedom according to the custom of blood justice.

"I beg the Great King's mercy," said the prisoner in perfect Uurzian. He fell upon his knees before Tyro. Tears glittered in his eyes, perhaps shed for the man he'd killed, perhaps for himself, perhaps only a show to secure the King's pity.

Tyro kept his own dark eyes focused on the face of the victorious prisoner. Yet his voice spoke to the assembled courtiers and to his brother behind him. "This man has won the trial of blood justice. By slaying his own cousin he has proven his worth as a soldier. Yet the Kings of Uurz will allow no mercy for the devils of Khyrei."

The Sword King's fist moved quick as a shadow, a dance of silver in the smoky air. The blade sank deep into the older Khyrein's heart, stopped only by the curve of the bronze hilt. Tyro released the blade and stood quiet as the prisoner keeled over. Now both captives lay dead on the sand.

Lyrilan blinked and realized he had forgotten to breathe. Ramiyah whimpered softly once beside him.

Tyro turned to address his shocked audience. "No mercy for the devils of Khyrei!"

Now the crowd fell from shock to applause, and Tyro's cry was repeated from many drunken throats. Even the guards of the hall joined in the chant. "No mercy! No mercy! No mercy!"

During the cacophony of applause Tyro walked back to his dais, sat himself upon the throne, and met Talondra's lips with his own.

Lyrilan, sitting silently as the two dead men were dragged away, saw the faces of a half-dozen nobles staring at him. These were the sensible ones, the ones who feared war and supported his talk of peace. They expected him to balance his brother's martial sensibilities. They looked to him now, deafened by the cheers of their fellows. But he could do nothing to stop the rising tide of Tyro's bloodlust. It spread through the court like a virus, a contagion that could not be stopped.

This had all been planned. Tyro had called him out.

The true spectacle this night was not the slaughter of two Khyrein spies.

It was the weakness of the Scholar King.

Lyrilan rose from his chair and descended the platform, drawing Ramiyah after him by her hand. A quartet of legionnaires followed as they left the Feasting Hall, where the reek of spilled blood overpowered now the scents of meat and smoke and spices. To his surprise a half-dozen noblemen followed him as he exited. He only wanted to be alone with Ramiyah, to think. To figure out this problem dropped into his life like a bead of poison into a cup of wine.

He was not the only Peace Speaker among the court. Yet he was their leader, their Scholar King, their only chance. They did not want a war any more than he did. They feared Tyro the Sword King and the voices who guided him toward savage glory.

This was the beginning of something new and terrible.

Factions. The Sword and the Scholar.

Before there was war with Khyrei, there would be war in Uurz.

O Father, what have you done to us?

3

Born Into Shadow

It began with a dream of blood.

Vireon sank into a red sea, rich and warm as the ocean that had drowned his father. His great arms, his mighty thews, the Giant strength of his body, all these things were worthless as he sank deeper into the crimson depths. His iron-hard skin that no blade or arrow could break ... useless. His limbs flailed like a child as the bloody tide invaded his mouth and lungs. At times he broke the surface, where a black sky sparkled with icy stars. He pulled against the current, yet always it pulled him back under, until he lost the stars completely. All was red and molten and weighty as a mountain collapsed on his broad chest.

The red sea turned to burning flame, and he awoke. The bedchamber was warm with orange torchlight, and his sweat drenched the silken bedding. Alua lay peacefully next to him, her arms wrapped about tiny Maelthyn. Vireon breathed the night air into his lungs, pulling the covers back. He stalked to the open window where the breezes would cool his dreaming fever. The King's Chamber lay at the top of the palace's highest tower, and the window opened on a view of Udurum's northern quarter. The City of Men and Giants slept quietly beneath a harvest moon, only a few pale fires and flickering street lamps alive at this late hour.

Beyond the encircling wall of black stone stretched the wild forests of Uduria, ancestral land of Giants. The great Uyga trees rivaled the height of the city wall, which stood higher than even the tallest Giant. Vireon gripped the window-sill, and his thoughts turned to the stones of the palace itself. His father and the Uduri had rebuilt the palace when they rebuilt the shattered city some thirty years ago. Vod the Man-Giant had slept in this very bed-chamber with Vireon's human mother for more than twenty years. At times he could still smell his father's scent upon the very walls. Could the curse have taken root deep within these very stones? No, he must not consider such a thing. He knew where the curse came from, and it was not his father's doing.

He thrust his shaggy head out the window, breathing in the scents of the distant forest: pine, leaf, bark, soil, night blossoms, animal scents. It called to him, a balm for his troubled mind. Such thoughts of doom never assailed him in the depths of the wood-land. He must escape his own palace to find peace in the hunt. And he must do so now, before the sun came up to remind him he was a King, no longer a boy who could run away and lose him-self in the forest. How long had it been since he ran the Long Hunt? Too many years.

He returned to the great bed, moving silently across the carpet on the balls of his feet. Alua's face lay beneath a tangle of golden hair; he brushed the locks aside and put his lips lightly upon hers. She moaned but did not wake. He would not leave his wife a scrawled message. She would know where he had gone and why. She always knew.

He turned to the curled form of his daughter, a miniature ver-sion of Alua, yet with hair black as his own. When her eyes were open they gleamed a fierce blue, another mark of her father's blood. She was seven now and had her own room in the King's Tower, yet every night this month she had climbed into bed between her father and mother. Vireon did not mind this. He loved Maelthyn as deeply as he loved her mother. Perhaps even more. He placed a rough hand on her small cheek, kissed her pale forehead. Lost in some pleasant dream, she took no notice of these things.

He stepped away from the bed and gathered up his tall boots, his buckskin leggings, a wide belt hung with a broad-bladed hunting knife, and a shirt of black ringmail. As he dressed in the glow of the brazier's fading embers, his eyes caught the gleam of his greatsword where it hung upon the wall. Blue and silver hues danced across the length of *steel,* the metal of Giants. The blade was slightly longer than he was tall. He would not take it with him; it was a tool of war, not the hunt. It had taken the life of his own brother. Fangodrel leaped unwanted into his memory. Fangodrel with his sneering mouth, arrogant eyes, weak shoulders, and Khyrein-pale skin.

Vireon hesitated as he lifted the light crown of silver and onyx. It was little more than a tight-fitting circlet, a traveling crown, an alternative to the great crown he must wear when sitting on the throne. He placed the circlet upon his head, settling it snugly over his black locks. The charred face of Fangodrel floated before him in the gloom. Flesh curled back from a grinning skull, ruined lips flapping over yellow fangs, spitting words like poison: *I curse you! Your children will be born into shadow . . .*

Vireon had interrupted that curse with the sharp blade of the greatsword. So he had avenged his true brother, Tadarus, when he cut the head off his false one. His skin crawled as he recalled the crunch of the blackened skull beneath his boot.

He had rejected Fangodrel's curse. It was no more than the raving of a dying man, a soul poisoned with obscene sorcery. Yet never could he forget the words hurled from those scorched lips. He looked once more at his sleeping daughter, admiring her small limbs, the rising and falling of her tiny stomach, the little pointed chin that so reminded him of his wife. Maelthyn had not been born into shadow, whatever that might mean. She was perfect and healthy and beautiful. Instead, it was Vireon who bore the curse. As his father had endured nightmares in this chamber that should offer a King his rest, so did Vireon. Was this dream of blood, this sense of unease, this constant worry for his daughter and his kingdom . . . was this the curse? Or was it simply the burden of being a King? He could not say.

In the heady embrace of the forest he would think more clearly. He could run and leap and climb until the earth itself gave him the answer to his question. The Long Hunt called to him as sweet water calls to a man dying of thirst. Stealing a last glance at his wife and child, he took a long spear from the wall and crept out of the chamber.

A cloak of black and violet flapped about his ankles as he departed. The door was guarded, as always, by two Uduri, the stern Giantesses who remained in Udurum. All of the city's male Giants had marched north years ago to inhabit the realm of the Ice King. Vireon had been responsible for the uniting of these two Giant tribes, and for the emigration of the male Giants. Often he felt the sting of guilt over this, usually when he examined the face of a lonely Giantess standing guard in some corner of his palace. He had never asked the Uduri to dedicate themselves to his service. In fact, he had urged them to follow their menfolk northward, to find a new life together in the White Mountains.

Yet the Ninety-Nine Uduri chose to remain in the city. Barren, they could bear no children for the Uduru, unlike the blue-skinned Giantesses of the north, the women of the Udvorg. The Uduri had claimed their place here, inside the walls of New

Udurum. "Let the Uduru go forth and spread their seed," they told Vireon. "We do not condemn them. This is for the good of all Giants. We are Uduri. We will endure. We will serve."

So they served, and Vireon appointed most of them as official palace guards. The rest of the world knew that the bulk of Giantkind had abandoned the City of Men and Giants, but Vireon made sure that word of the Ninety-Nine's loyalty also spread far and wide. An army of twelve hundred Giants had once conquered Uurz in a few days. Even this small number of Uduri was enough to secure Udurum against any foe. In fact, tales of Uduri ferocity in battle helped keep any potential aggressors from the city's walls. Even the brazen hordes of Khyrei dared not assault the Rebuilt City where Giantesses walked the earth.

Now he found himself accompanied by a pair of Uduri as he strode the broad corridors and descended to the palace grounds. Each Giantess stood nearly three times his height, greatspears in their fists, axes and greatswords buckled to their harnesses. Uduri hair was either sun-yellow or night-black, bound into a waist-length war braid by leather thongs. Their sun-browned legs were bare but for tall sandals, and their breastplates were black-lacquered bronze. Headbands of gold set with orbs of jet marked them as the King's Guard, though not as overtly as their monolithic statures. The two Giantesses paced behind him like great, silent cats as he entered the palace courtyard and spoke with the Night Captain. He explained three times that no escort was necessary, but the captain insisted on sending a squad of horsemen to accompany his hunt.

Vireon shook his head. "The smell of the horses will drive away any game within three leagues of us," he explained. "Let alone the scents of the Men themselves. No, I hunt alone."

The flummoxed captain bowed and ordered the palace's outer gate flung open. Even so, Vireon's "alone" meant in the company of the two Uduri. They offered more protection than a platoon of human soldiers. The Uduri followed Vireon into the lantern-lined street leading toward the city gates.

Few citizens were about at this dark hour to note their King's passing: a few restless youths well into their cups, a weaponsmith working late in his shop, harlots returning to their brothel after a discreet engagement. Folk from all over the continent came to Udurum seeking wealth and prosperity, and most of them found it. The forests of Uduria provided endless game, and the Grim Mountains to the south offered mining opportunities that industrious merchants had learned to exploit. After a flood of Sharrian refuges came to replace the missing Uduru, the City of Men and Giants had become one of the most culturally diverse cities in the world. Trade routes extended south through the mountains to Uurz and Murala, as well as west to the coastline, where the new settlement of Tadarum provided a harbor for southern merchant ships. It was Vireon's decision to name the port after his murdered brother. Tadarus would have been the rightful King of Udurum if not for Fangodrel's treachery.

Vireon gave a sign to the Gatekeeper. Seeing his King practically alone in the night, he scurried to rouse his wheelmen from their slumber. Soon he had them working at the main winches, and the mighty gates of Udurum swung open with a low thunder.

Vireon stepped forth onto the Giants' Road. It ran west from the city into a vast green grassland, turning at length toward the south, where it ran to meet the misty peaks of the Grim. He took a last look back at the walls of sable stone and turned his eyes north to the deep forest. In that direction he ran, the massive gates shuddering to a close behind him, and the two Uduri ran after him. A pale mist wandered above the tall grass, and the dark sky glowed purple beyond the walls and pinnacles of Udurum. Dawn was still hours away. A golden moon splashed its glow across the leaping braids of the Giantesses.

In his man-sized body Vireon possessed all the terrible strength of an Uduru and three times the speed. He ran, legs pumping, feet pounding the damp earth, relishing the cool wind on his face, and the Uduri grew smaller behind him. They struggled to keep up with him because it was their duty. He did not grin at or mock their slowness, for it gave him no pleasure to abandon them. Yet he needed to be alone this morning. They would of course follow his trail without eating or sleeping until they found him. Eventually they would catch up, but by running he could put a day or two between himself and his escorts. He hurdled the massive roots of Uyga trees and plunged into the green hollows of the Giantwood.

His senses came alive to the perfumes of loam, leaf, and blossom. Nightbirds fled their branches when he passed below like a racing wolf. He leaped shallow streams and crested craggy tors, pounced from stone to stone across a rushing river, and lost himself in the maze of gargantuan tree trunks.

When the sun rose bright and fierce above the forest canopy, green-gold rays fell between the mossy boles and lit the secret glades full of cobflower, snowberry, and thornwhistle. He soon caught the scent of game, a herd of great elk. The odor filled him with renewed energy, and he followed the tracks of their hooves for league after league. North and west, then north again. The torn earth told him the herd was on the run, moving fast from some predator or threat. He planned to overtake them when they paused to drink from pond or stream.

Now a second set of tracks mingled with the great hoofprints. Another smell, pungent, laced with fury and desperation. The mud bore the imprints of an Udhog, one of the great boars that dwelled in the darkest thickets of the forest. They never preyed on the big elk, preferring to feed on grass, roots, leaves, or rodents. However, they were known to take down a young deer on occasion. For the

Udhog to chase a herd of great elk this far was something entirely unheard of. And for the elk bulls to actually fear such a predator when their great numbers could most certainly bring it down . . . This was a mystery.

Vireon moved on, following the crude trail until he topped a low ridge lined with gnarled Uyga. Some distance below the ridgeline, near the ford of a shallow river, a black Udhog feasted on a fallen carcass. Vireon crept closer, using the tree roots to cover his approach. He smelled the blood and offal of the fallen elk, and the stink of the boar's flesh. But there was something else here too. Something smelled unnatural. A nameless odor on the edge of his awareness.

The boar dug its tremendous head into the split belly of the great elk. Its tusks had ripped the flesh open and its front quarters were slathered in gore. Now and again it raised its pink snout from feeding and squeal-howled at the sky, as if challenging whatever spirits lived among the branches to come down and share its kill. Its flanks quivered, and its head jerked back and forth painfully as it devoured the fresh meat. Something was definitely wrong with the beast.

Across the shallow river the torn ground led Vireon's eyes up a hill where the last of the elk herd were already galloping away from their tusked pursuer. Vireon might have followed them, taken down one for his own dinner, and brought its great spread of horns back to mount on the wall of his palace. But something about the Udhog's strange behavior commanded his attention.

He crept nearer to the beast and halted when its bloody head swiveled about in his direction. He ducked behind an Uyga root as the Udhog squealed a challenge. A terrible quiet fell across the glade. Vireon wondered where the birds had gone.

A thunder of hooves drew his head above the root. The Udhog had forgotten its kill and raced directly toward him. Its spearhead tusks gleamed yellow beneath smears of gore and strings of dripping flesh. It stood larger than an ox at the shoulder, and either one of those mighty tusks might pierce his bronze-hard skin to impale him, or split him from groin to collar. Each of its cloven hooves was as large as Vireon's head, which they would crack open like a melon. His head was harder than that of a Man, as was his skin, but he had no desire to test the density of his skull bone.

He bounded atop the root as the beast charged. Its tiny eyes were black with malevolence. It slammed tusks first into the barky flesh, knocking him back. He tumbled along the ground and found his feet in an instant. It charged again. Now he saw the white foam bubbling from its mouth, leaving a trail along the ground. It squeal-howled at him, tusks quivering as it galloped. The tiny eyes rolled back in its head; its tongue lolled green and spotted. The beast was mad. Some disease must have fallen upon it.

He sprang above the tusks and drove the point of his greatspear into its back. The *steel* head scraped bone and sank deep between the shoulder blades. At the zenith of his leap Vireon pulled the spear free and landed catlike behind the beast. It swirled around gracelessly with a reckless speed, spouting black blood. Its left tusk came near to ripping his belly open. Again Vireon leaped and again his spear found entry in Udhog flesh. Twelve times he stabbed it deep, and still it took no notice of the wounds. Any Udhog was difficult to kill, but half this many strikes should have done the trick. The madness made it strong. Oblivious to death.

It sprang forward, spilling scarlet from its terrible wounds, and mauled him with its front hooves. One struck his chest, one caught him a glancing blow to the forehead. He fell flat on his back in the mud, witchlights flashing before his eyes, thunder in his ears. He could no longer feel his hands or feet. Darkness fell upon him as the beast stamped across his body. The mighty tusks rose and the Udhog squeal-howled its triumph. Now it would finish him, either by crushing his skull beneath its hooves or by slashing open his stubborn flesh with fang and tusk.

Vireon struggled to raise his spear but found that he had dropped it. Where was the knife at his belt? His arm sought to find it, but hooves kicked at him relentlessly. The great bristly head lowered itself to stare at him, pale froth dripping across his black ringmail. For a moment that seemed forever, he stared into the depths of its brutish close-set eyes. A sea of torment and hunger boiled in the beast's tiny mind. The stink of insanity filled Vireon's lungs as the tusks lunged for his belly.

A sound like that of an axe chopping wood met his ears, followed by another exactly like it. Two meaty blows struck nearly at once. The black bulk fell away from him, squealing and spouting fresh gore as it toppled. Two hurled greatspears had found the beast's neck and heart. The shafts quivered now like saplings grown from its dying bulk. Vireon rose to his feet as the two Uduri came forward with axes to finish the beast. He found his own spear lying an arm's reach away. His knife was still in its scabbard on his belt. He simply could not reach it while the boar squatted atop him. He had come very close to death.

He shook his head as the Uduri quartered the beast, hacking it into four pieces. He watched, admiring their grisly precision.

"We'll eat well this evening, eh, Majesty?" asked a Giantess.

"No," said Vireon. He pointed to the white froth about the boar's severed head. "See? This beast carried some kind of sickness. Go to the river and wash its blood from your skin." He joined the Uduri as they followed his command, wading into the cold current. The chill of mountain-born water revived his numb limbs and cleared his head.

"Dahrima the Axe, Chygara the Windcaller," he addressed them by name, "you have my gratitude."

"Unnecessary, my King," said Dahrima. "We have sworn. Even your great speed cannot outrun our vows." She smiled at him, a warrior's smile. It reminded him of his uncle, the Giant Fangodrim, who taught him the ways of the hunt.

They were not unpleasant to look at, these Uduri. Their lean faces were softer than those of male Giants, yet the line of their jaws was as firm. Their bodies, while carrying all the curves of a human woman, were tightly corded with muscle, and they were lithe as southern tigers. In fact their slimmer frames and lesser bulk made them quicker than male Giants, and thus often more deadly in battle. Hence the old saying: *Uduru will crush your bones to dust; Uduri will hang them on her wall.*

Vireon returned the smile and waded back onto the riverbank. He studied the split carcass of the great elk. Its heart was gone. The mad Udhog had burrowed through its belly into its chest specifically to eat that organ. Odd behavior for any animal.

"What could make such a beast mad?" asked Chygara, studying the segmented boar.

Vireon shook his head.

Mad, something whispered. *Like my father.*

He didn't want to think this, but could not help it. Vod of the Storms had gone mad just like this boar, and that madness had driven him to his death. The first King of Men and Giants had walked into the Cryptic Sea and drowned himself. Vireon's mother claimed it was the Sorceress of Khyrei, Ianthe the Claw, who sent the madness. Ianthe had also perverted Fangodrel's jealousy and stolen his humanity. During Vireon's confrontation with Fangodrel, Alua had unleashed the power of her white flame, consuming Ianthe utterly. So had Vod been avenged by Alua, even as Vireon avenged Tadarus by killing Fangodrel on that same day.

Vengeance had not been a sweet flavor in the mouth. It tasted like bitter tears. Even now, eight years later, he missed Tadarus as much as he had before killing their traitorous sibling. He missed his true brother even more with each passing year. And his father, too. Vengeance, Vireon had learned, was not a cure for grief. It was only a kind of madness. He rejected it as he had rejected his dying brother's curse.

Yet what if a taint of that madness remained? Growing in him like some hidden disease, until one day it would emerge and poison him as this great beast had been poisoned. He hoped that, if this happened, there would be enough Uduri there to cut him down. Such mad things should not be allowed to live. They would only spread their sickness to others.

"Shall we follow the herd?" asked Dahrima, pointing toward the elk trail. "We still might take some good meat for tonight's fire."

"Yes," said Vireon. "Go and take your kill. I will not go; I wish to be alone. You will find my trail and catch up with me again. Allow me some little portion of the solitude that Uduria can provide."

They must have seen the ache in his eyes because they agreed without protest. After burning the diseased Udhog carcass along with the slain elk, Dahrima and Chygara ran north after the elk herd. Vireon walked west toward the deep glades, leaving the stench of the beast's madness behind him. After a while he climbed a steep hillock and sat upon a fallen log. He gazed across the green roof of the forest, spreading like a carpet all the way to the black walls of Udurum. In the light of day the city's towers seemed tiny as toothpicks. Far beyond them sunlight glittered upon the white crests of purple mountains. Birds sang baroque melodies, and the breezes played with his thoughts.

What did it mean to find such a mad beast so near to his home? He was no shaman or sorcerer to interpret such omens. He might ask Alua. Her magic was great, her wisdom deep. She often read messages in the subtle movements of nature. The pattern of fallen leaves in the courtyard told her the coming weather, and the shapes of clouds sometimes showed her the future. Yet he could not speak of his fears with her, his thoughts of this nameless curse that may or may not exist. She would only worry. Seeing her fret, Maelthyn would cry, for the girl was sensitive to her mother's moods. He must remain aloof, silent, strong ... ever the King ... ever the Giant-Lord, the Son of Vod.

All day he sat upon the high rock, so deep in his own thoughts that he did not notice the sun eventually setting at his back. Elbows on his knees, chin on his crossed forearms, he sat well into the evening until the white fox came. It scrabbled up the hillside noisily so that he heard its coming. He knew its perfume before he ever saw it. The jasmine scent reminded him of cold snow and hot skin.

Starlight shimmered on the fox's pale coat as it loped near to him, pink tongue lolling, black nose steaming in the night. Its dark eyes blinked as it rubbed its cheek across his outstretched hand. It licked his face and whimpered. A sudden mist rose from the hilltop and Alua leaned against him now in her true form. His lips met hers in a deep kiss, followed by a flurry of lesser ones. Freed from the prying eyes of the royal court, their passion danced like a flame stoked by burning winds. They spoke no words; their bodies said everything of importance. After the lovemaking they lay together in the moonlight, arms and legs tangled, blades of torn grass across their thighs.

"Why did you seek me here?" he asked.

She rested her head upon his brawny chest. "Why did you leave in the middle of the night?"

He sighed. What to tell her? "I was troubled," he said. "I dreamed ... a sea of blood."

She stiffened against him.

"What have you come to tell me?" he asked.

She hesitated, pulling away from him, running hands through her thick blonde hair.

Suddenly his thoughts fell to their daughter. "Where is Maelthyn?"

Alua turned her narrow black eyes to him. "She is safe – six Uduri guard her chamber."

He nodded, glad of it. Yet there was something she had not told him yet. Something that drew her from the child's side and across the deep forest to this lonely crag. He felt it in his bones. He waited for her to say what it was.

"Your dream was true," she said, staring at the silver disk of moon. Her voice was heavy with concern. "Last night in a tavern on the Street of Vines, eleven legionnaires were slain. They were off duty and enjoying themselves. Three serving girls and the taverner were also killed."

Vireon's brow knotted. Street violence was rare in Udurum. In such a prosperous city the citizens had little reason to kill one another. And the presence of the Ninety-Nine Uduri kept most Men in line.

"A quarrel with the sellswords of some foreign merchant?"

Alua shook her head. "No. They were slaughtered by some kind of beast."

Vireon stood and pulled on his mail shirt.

The madness spreads . . .

"What beast could enter my city?" he asked. "Do we have witnesses?"

"None," said Alua. She rose to stare at him, her hand on his bare chest. "Somehow . . . nobody saw the killing."

"Then how can you be sure it was a beast?"

"Or beasts," she said. "I saw the remains. Nothing human could have . . . Their *hearts* were missing. Torn from out of their breasts." She looked away to the south. The towers of Udurum were lost in deepening night. "Some new sorcery has arrived. I *feel* it."

He wrapped his arms around her. "So do I."

He said nothing of the Curse of Fangodrel, though he was sure it had begun.

They came down and met the Uduri camped at the foot of the hill. Vireon ran with the Giantesses while Alua kept pace as the white fox. Before sunrise they reached the gates of the city. Early crowds of laborers shuffled aside to make way for Vireon and his tall escorts. He went directly to the Street of Vines to inspect the scene of the massacre. The hinged sign hanging above the tavern's wooden door depicted three white horses prancing on a green background. A squad of human sentinels stood about the wooden building in black bronze corselets and pointed helms gilded by the new day's sun. The soldiers were haggard, having been on guard all night.

The torn bodies of the victims had already been removed for burning, yet the tavern still smelled like an abattoir. Blood and viscera stained the walls and floorboards. The marks of great claws were sunk deep into the brown wood. From the look of things, each talon was as long as Vireon's finger.

Definitely more than one beast. A wild pack of gray wolves set loose in the drinking house would do less damage than this. If these had been wolves, they were large as Udhogs. Only the snow wolves in the Icelands grew to such a size, yet they never came south of the White Mountains. There was no trace of fur, or spittle, or any spoor that a forest creature might leave. These were unnatural beasts that killed in his city. Stolen or devoured fifteen human hearts and then disappeared. He found no tracks on the streets outside, and no drops of blood spilled by the slayers as they fled.

The Night Captain told him no more than Alua had. Nobody had heard screams or any sounds of slaughter inside the shop. Instead, the tavern had grown strangely silent. Eleven off-duty soldiers and no bawdy songs, no roaring voices. On a noisy street filled with crowded establishments, it took a while for anyone to notice. Sometime well after midnight a thirsty blacksmith wandered into the Three Stallions and found the mangled bodies. He reported it to the nearest constable and sought another ale-house to drown the memory of his discovery. The captain offered up a curled piece of parchment with the blacksmith's name scrawled above the names of the fifteen victims.

Vireon dismissed the tired soldiers. There was little left to protect here. No one would ever drink or eat in this shop again. The stench of death would never leave its walls. Some new owner would burn it down and start anew.

The two Uduri waited patiently outside the scarred door. This was not one of those establishments sized for Giant patrons, although Giant-friendly taverns were once as common as fruit stands in the city. Since the departing of the Uduru for the Icelands, most of the "tall shops" had gone out of business. Only three such alehouses were left, and they catered to the Ninety-Nine Uduri. An exclusive clientele.

Dahrima and Chygara paced behind Vireon as he strolled down the street with parchment in hand. The air was bright and fragrant with morning smoke. The aroma of roasting sausage and baking bread filled his nostrils. Roof gardens in the Uurzian style were common in this quarter, and small trees grew at each corner in squat urns full of black earth. Tavern signs hung from a succession of doors. Foreign faces come to trade in the Central Market peered curiously from open windows. Vireon ignored the babble that followed him along the lanes and the random shouts of "Hail the King!" His thoughts were his own.

He avoided the sprawling market because the crowds would mill about him when he passed there, eager for a touch of his hand or a spoken blessing. The people loved their Giant-King even more than they had loved his father. Unlike Vod, this King carried actual human blood in his veins. Vod had often stood at his true Giant's height when he walked about the city. And why not when his city was full of Giants? Vireon stood slightly taller than the brawniest laborer or legionnaire. He carried the power and density of a Giant in the body of a Man, and they loved him for that as well. His strength was their own. New Udurum was built by the hands of Giants, but it belonged wholly to Men now.

Vireon passed along the Avenue of Idols, where bronze effigies of Vod and a hundred other Giant heroes stood between columns of red marble smothered in ivy. The hulking statues were life-sized, forged by the world's finest artisans. Passing by, he glanced up at the face of his father, as he had done a thousand times. The brazen stare was impassive as ever, offering no guidance to future Kings. Dead fathers gave little advice to their sons. He walked on toward the palace, the street traffic spreading again and again to let him pass.

Alua awaited him in the council chamber. She sat at a table of polished oak and studied an ancient text. Vireon dismissed Dahrima and Chygara, ordering them to seek rest. Four of their spear-bearing sisters stood at attention between the sculpted columns. A crowd of royal advisors dawdled beneath the stares of the towering Uduri, discussing in hushed tones the strange affair of the Three Stallions. Vireon always found their ornate robes, golden chains, and jeweled fingers quite distracting. Better to have the advice of plainspoken Giants than the prattling indecision of Learned Men. Yet he had learned to endure the counsel of such advisors, as well as the sages who visited the palace to discuss art and philosophy with Alua. He had even learned to enjoy such lofty discussions at times. But he was in no mood for conversation. The mystery of the curse lay heavy upon him. It gnawed at his gut, a black worm tunneling toward his heart.

A wave of his hand dismissed the courtiers. They left a cloud of cologne and exasperation in their wake. Vireon bent to kiss his wife's lips. She offered him a platter of cheese and pastries. He found no stomach for such a breakfast, so he settled instead for a goblet of tart purple wine. The drink brought him a sense of calm. He sat brooding beside Alua, staring at the Night Captain's list of names while she scanned the pages of the great book. He sent a guard to summon the blacksmith Trevius for questioning. An Uurzian name, not uncommon in the city.

A fire crackled in the hearth and sunlight slanted through open casements. At last Alua looked up from her study with a sigh.

"I've found nothing," she said. "No mention of night prowlers who crave human hearts."

"What is this tome?" he asked.

She flipped back to the book's cover, showing him the engraved script. "*A Thousand Beastly Shapes*," she answered. "One of many works by Iardu the Shaper."

"My sister's counselor," said Vireon. Iardu was nothing less than the wizard who had taught Sharadza the art of sorcery. He thought of her now, so far away from him, no longer a precocious girl, but the Queen of Yaskatha. She dwelled in a fine palace near the wild southern sea. Four years since her last visit. Too long. She had been happy to marry D'zan, eager to leave her dreams of sorcery behind for a ring and a husband. Vireon liked the young Prince, had even helped him regain his ancestral throne. Yet in the end D'zan had fought his own battle and won it by himself. His first act as King of Yaskatha was to make Sharadza his bride.

No answers lay within the pages of the Shaper's book. Alua would have found them. He wished Sharadza were here to help solve this riddle of blood. His sister was learned and clever in the arts of sorcery.

Alua closed the book. "There are several more volumes like this," she said. "Perhaps I will find something in one of them. If not, I will ask the Spirits."

Vireon nodded. He knew she would find nothing. This was all Fangodrel's doing. He sensed it as surely as he sensed the sickness of the mad boar. His brother had learned to call the shadows ... feasted on the blood of the living ... took his power from it. Poor Tadarus had been the first to fall beneath Fangodrel's blood magic.

A scream pierced the silence, echoing along the halls from some high chamber. Vireon ran with Alua beside him. He was certain the scream had fallen from the King's Tower. Rushing guards darted aside as their King bounded up the stairs two and three at a time. When he passed by the King's Chamber, sobbing sounds came from the next archway along the hall. The door to Maelthyn's chamber stood open and without guards. He came near and looked inside. The two Giantesses stationed at the door were on their knees amid carnage and weeping.

The black marble floor and white pillars were drenched in crimson. The stench of blood lingered heavy in the air. The blood of Giantesses. The bodies of six Uduri lay torn and scattered about the chamber. Six Uduri lying dead on the rugs of his daughter's room. The scream had come from a human serving maid who cowered in the corner and sobbed along with the Giantesses. Their big hands were bathed in the blood of their sisters. Their faces were pallid masks of horror.

"Maelthyn!" Vireon called her name as he stalked between the corpses. Stomachs and chests were torn open. He knew without even looking that every one of their hearts was missing. His own heart threatened to burst out of his chest.

Where is she? Where—

He found her sitting calmly near the open window, forgotten by the grieving Uduri. Her tiny face was dark with blood. It dripped from her fingers. She wore a fine little gown of green and yellow silks, now gone black and sticky with gore. Maelthyn stared at her father, as unblinking as Vod's effigy of bronze.

"Maelthyn . . ."

She said nothing, as if she had momentarily forgotten that name altogether.

Vireon grabbed her in his arms, checking her skin for cuts or bruises. There were none. She stared at him with eyes blank as stones, dark blue and sparkling. Her soft little body was intact, despite the bloody baptism.

The wails of the two Uduri guards filled the chamber. How long had it been since one of them had perished? Centuries at least. And now six were slain in a single night. But by what power?

He squeezed Maelthyn close to his chest and whispered comfort in her ear.

The curse had reached its claws into his house, into the very bosom of his family.

Alua ran wide-eyed and fierce into the bloodstained room. She wrapped her arms about Maelthyn as a squad of guardsmen flooded into the chamber. Mother, father, and daughter stood for a while, locked in a terrified embrace, while Giantess tears fell to mingle with the expanding pools of crimson.

"We stood outside while our sisters died," moaned a Giantess. "We saw nothing. The door would not open . . . " Their dark eyes pleaded at Vireon for justice, or vengeance, or both.

Only when the Uduri ceased their wailing and began to gather up the bodies of their sisters did little Maelthyn begin to blink her eyes again. Alua removed her daughter's bloody dress and carried her to a basin of water for washing. Vireon stayed close. Guards rushed about the chamber and the palace looking for signs of intruders that they would never find.

Alua looked at Vireon as she rubbed Maelthyn's cheek with a wet cloth. He had never seen that look in his wife's eyes before. Terror it was, but also accusation. *You failed to keep our daughter safe. You, the Giant-King! Son of Vod! You failed!* She said none of these things, but he heard them anyway. They echoed louder in his skull than the wailing of the Uduri.

"Father?" Maelthyn's tiny voice broke the silence between King and Queen. Vireon lowered his face to hers, took her petite hands in his massive ones.

"Yes, Little One, I'm here," he said. "You are safe now."

How could he lie to her? He had no choice.

"The shadows . . . " said Maelthyn, turning her sapphire eyes at him. "The shadows came to play."

Once more he took her in his arms. He squeezed her as tightly as he dared. She was so small and so very frail, his little Maelthyn. Alua wept then, but still her daughter shed no tears.

"They came for *me*, Father," Maelthyn whispered in his ear. "I let them in."

4

Wings

At night she was an owl, flying high above the tangled swamp. The full moon stared at itself in the pools and fens of black water. Darkness swelled and writhed in the morass of weed, mud, and moss. The great mire was thick with vipers, slippery and venomous. If she were a true owl, she might swoop and grab one or two of them in her talons and feast on the sour flesh. In the back of her mind such owl-thoughts swam like tiny fish in the murky marsh pools. Yet she only stopped her flight when her wings grew tired, resting for a while among the clawed branches of a dead tree.

She marveled that anything at all could live in such a stagnant bog. The sheer multitudes of swimming, crawling, thriving beasts infesting the marshland amazed her. At times she spied great lizards plodding through the swamp, pulling their scaled bulk along on fat, muscular legs, dragging tails thick as trees. She stayed well above their snapping jaws.

During the day she was an eagle, gray-feathered and keen-eyed, soaring across the blue, bathed in the sun's warm gold. It was difficult not to miss the green fields and ripe orchards of Yaskatha. The winds above the Eastern Marshes were cold and reeked of rot.

She recalled the warm ocean breezes that caressed the seaside kingdom. The forest of colored sails rising from a bay filled with trade ships, lean galleys, tall freighters, and pavilioned pleasure barges. Every morning for the past seven years she had greeted the day on the palace veranda overlooking that blue-green expanse of ocean. Every day she dined on the fruits and vegetables cultivated in royal orchards, and sipped elder wines from the finest crystal. Every day, every night, she and D'zan, together. The Southern King and his northborn Queen. Now, below her, lay only a sodden wasteland, a realm with no solid foundation, where the fertility of nature had turned to rot and decay. So it was with her marriage.

She put such thoughts from her mind as she plied the sky, gliding through low clouds and skirting the tops of swamp fogs. East and north she flew, across lands where no man ventured to travel. The great fens were the dividing line between the outlying territories of Yaskatha and Khyrei. Although Khyrei claimed the marshes, there was no sign of settlement, fortress, or habitation. The marshland was not a place for humankind. It offered a thousand deaths and very little in the way of resources or sustenance. Yet, in its own way, this gloomy land was a blessing for both kingdoms. Surely there would have been war after war over this middle territory if living here were not so impossible. A range of impassable mountains could not have divided Yaskatha from Khyrei so effectively.

On the third day the land itself rose higher and the marshes gave way to a dense crimson jungle. The great trees stood like towers of blood, blossoming with vermilion leaves and scarlet fronds. Now the eagle sailed above the poison jungles of Khyrei proper, and there was no denying it. A black tower, spiked and thorny, dominated a high hill. It rose from the livid undergrowth to rival the blood oaks, a testament to the power of the city-state that built it. Her eagle eyes watched sentinels walking the parapets of that tower, figures in black armor and fanged masks. Their spears were tall with curved blades of gleaming bronze. A black pennon flew from the tower's summit, and she could not guess what purpose the outpost might serve this far from the center of Khyrei's walls. Then it dawned on her: As unlikely as an attack from the marshes would be, Khyrei remained vigilant along its western border. Another such tower rose several leagues to the north, so that no force of arms could emerge from the sucking grip of the marshes without being sighted. The Khyreins did not trust their neighbors across the great swampland. How many more watchtowers stood along the border between marsh and jungle?

By midday she found the winding green ribbon of the River Tah. It glimmered like the back of a colossal viper winding through the scarlet wilderness. Its waters were sluggish and full of black serpentine creatures. They rose at times from the rank flow to display fin, fang, or tendril, perhaps to grab a stray bird or water lizard, then sink back into the deeper waters. Flocks of copper-colored bats flitted from bank to bank. Once she saw a great crimson tiger drinking from the river, a gorgeous beast as large as a pony. It fled into the shadows as she soared past, following the river's course directly northward.

In late afternoon she spotted the spires of the black city on the horizon. It rose from the jungle like a gleaming mountain of jet, dominating the western banks of the river delta. Here the Tah flowed into the Golden Sea, dropping its green life into those depthless waters. There were few riverboats that dared to plumb the jungle's interior, yet beyond the massive walls of Khyrei City the harbor was filled with black-sailed war galleons. They outnumbered the bright sails of trading vessels ten to one. She did not wonder at the sight, for there were few countries now that would actively trade with Khyrei. Its reputation as a haven for pirates and sea raiders had traveled the length of the continent. These triple-sailed warships with blood-trimmed hulls would as often sink a merchant vessel as allow it passage on the trade routes.

Most of the traders moored in the harbor flew the orange and yellow standards of the Jade Isles. She could not readily identify any other sails among the black fleet. Yet she did notice the image stitched onto every one of the black sails, the insignia of a scarlet crown bearing seven points. Years ago, when this fleet sailed north to lay waste the city of Shar Dni, these ships had flown the sign of the white panther, sigil of their sorceress Queen. The red crown had replaced the pale panther on the same field of black.

The sight of this new standard lent credence to rumors that the city's old Emperor had returned from death. Gammir the Bloody. The Undying One. These were the names they called him, if Yaskathan spies were to be heeded. Ianthe the Claw was no more, annihilated at the Fall of Shar Dni by Queen Alua's white flame. Just as Fangodrel the Kinslayer, heir to Ianthe's dark power, was slain by the sword of his own brother Vireon. So Khyrei's forces had retreated, and the wicked nation had lain quiet for years. Sharadza's three brothers had finally stopped killing one another, leaving only one still alive. Unless . . .

Now an Emperor from decades past had returned to revive the power of the black city. Or had he? She had flown a long way to discover the truth for herself. She hoped it was indeed the Gammir of old returned from death, for if what she suspected was instead the truth . . . Best not to consider it until proof emerged.

The jungle subsided below her, replaced by a swathe of orderly fields. Thousands of pale slaves labored among the rows of crops. Green plantations encircled the city except on the north and east, which were claimed instead by river and ocean. Narrow roads ran among the sprawling farmlands, often busy with slave-drawn carts and yoked oxen pulling loads of produce. Unlike Yaskatha, where most growing lands were lined with fruiting trees, nearly every crop nurtured here grew close to the ground. She wondered if citrus trees would take root and thrive in this place, or only be poisoned by the sour soil. Then the black walls of the city reared before her, and she glided between the peaks of barbed towers.

The city walked in fear, moving in slumped clusters between buildings of low black stone. Even among the sprawling garden estates of noble families there was no single structure to rival the palace of onyx and obsidian. Its central spire rose above all into a vaulted crest surmounted by seven curving spikes, a manifestation in stone of the seven-pointed crown woven into the sails of the black warships.

Clusters of huge bats hung from the eaves and battlements of the tower. The beating of her eagle wings disturbed them, sent clouds of them flapping into the sky like dark fogs screeching with thirst. Fearing they might swarm her, she dived low into the heart of the city, gliding along a wide street where pallid laborers traded with gray-robed shopkeepers. A squad of demon-masked soldiers cut a path through the milling crowds. She flew into the shadows of an alley and settled there among the filth and debris.

She took the shape of a Khyrein woman, middle-aged, whose long dark hair had started to turn gray. Her feathers became a drab shift tied with a black sash, and her feet stood upon the wet flagstones in sandals of worn leather. Grabbing a crooked stick to serve as a support, she walked from the stinking alley into the crowds of Khyrein peasants. There was nary a smile to be seen or laugh to be heard among the shuffling multitude. The wrinkles of deprivation and exhaustion were etched deeply on these people's faces. Even their clothing reflected this lack of vitality, wrapped as they were in tunics and togas of gray or faded black homespun. Their hems were worn, the soles of their sandals thin, and a few wore jewelry of copper, bronze, or tarnished silver rings on bony fingers. They smelled of sweat and fear and denial.

There were no beasts of burden allowed in the city other than soldiers' horses, so workers from the fields carried baskets of produce on their shoulders or balanced atop their heads. There were no public musicians here, no great works of art lining broad thoroughfares, no poets spouting verse in the dismal dugouts that served as taverns. There was only a hushed murmur of voices, tinged with worry and suffering. She also sensed an urgency to conclude the day's business as the sun sank beyond the city's western wall. These people feared the night.

The clomping of soldiers' boots drowned out the wheedling voices of merchants, and the black-armored squad strode by. Their captain kicked a small boy into the mud. In the dullness of his youth, the sickly lad had failed to yield the right of way. She feared to next see one of their curving spearheads pointed at the boy's heart, yet the masked ones continued on their way. A starving child was obviously beneath the notice of their spears or their charity. She tossed the child a jewel from her purse as she followed the group of soldiers, a tiny yellow topaz. Drenched in mud, he snatched up the stone and ran like a frightened hare into the maze of booths and vendors.

Now she walked behind the guards as one of their own. Her body had grown tall, sheathed itself in blackened plates of bronze; her shoulders broadened and a mask rose like a black vapor to obscure her face in the manner of all Khyrein warriors. Her walking stick became a tall barbed spear like those of the soldiers she followed. The squad entered a great plaza ringed by more open booths and vendor stalls, yet dominated at its center by a single great effigy.

The statue was carved of black basalt, like most of the city's structures. A man with broad shoulders and long legs, draped in a flowing robe flecked with tiny sprays of quartz. The effect was an imitation of the night sky itself, hanging about the figure's body, shimmering against the purple of early dusk.

As she marched closer, safe in her disguise at the rear of the squad, she saw better the head and face of the idol. A lean wolfish face, its eyes represented by rubies set like bloody almonds in the sockets of the dark skull. A seven-pointed crown rising from its brow. One arm extended toward the west, a globe of crystal in its palm clutched by clawed fingers. The symbolism of the sphere was lost on her. The other hand was high above the crown, lifting a gigantic version of the Khyrein spear. This was an image of Gammir himself, there could be no doubt. It radiated an aura of conquest, war, and sheer defiance. An arrogant Godling giving challenge to the world.

She studied the stony face as well as she could without tripping over her feet as she marched. Could it be? The resemblance was . . . Yes, it was there. Distorted perhaps, or exaggerated to evoke the lupine qualities, the ferocious grace. Her heart sank. A quickening in her belly that was the first fluttering of genuine fear. Suddenly she understood the folk of Khyrei. She knew what they feared.

Still, she must see him with her own eyes to be sure. She would know if it were truly him. She could not fail to know her own half-brother.

On the plaza's far side lay the disgusting spectacle of the slave block. Such brazen cruelty amazed and appalled her. Khyreins selling Khyreins to the highest bidder. Frail children in rags stood upon the platform, linked neck to neck by an iron chain. A crowd of nobles, merchants, and foreign traders cast their bids with raised hands as the slavemaster touted the physical features and beauty of his stock. A line of waiting slaves cowered behind the platform in the shadow of masked guards. Farther back among those unfortunates she saw darker skins, prisoners taken in sea raids from the galleons of peaceful kingdoms. Every sailor knew it was better to die spitted on a Khyrein blade than to be taken alive for torture and servitude.

A handful of gold changed hands and a small boy was led away by a tall slaver She turned her face from the scene. She was not here to confront this injustice now. That time would come, but it was not today. Swallowing her revulsion, she bent her mind to the march, focusing on the armored backs of the men she followed.

The gates of the palace lay open before the Onyx Guards. She entered as one of them into a splendid courtyard. Here in the shadow of the black towers a tiny paradise thrived and bloomed in every shade of red. Blood oaks from the distant jungle grew here, surrounded by lesser vegetation of every kind, including several Yaskathan pomegranate trees. She thrilled to see them heavy with fruit, and knew her theory about poison soil had been foolish. Earth was earth, and growing things did not discriminate. The petals of gargantuan flowers lined a path of black stones, and she followed the squad toward the nearest of the guardhouses skirting the lush grounds. Some distance to her left stood the main doors of the palace proper.

The heavy iron portals were open wide, a quintet of legionnaires standing at attention before the opening. On the broad steps before them lay two black and scarlet tigers, each chained by the throat and anchored to the gauntlet of a guard. The beasts licked their paws and drowsed upon the marble, but she guessed they would tear apart anyone who sought to mount those steps unasked.

She slipped away from the marchers and entered a close group of trees where the foliage would hide her from prying eyes. The guards marched on until they disappeared through the portal of their barracks hall. A few seconds later, an identical squad marched out of the same building. It wound back down the court-yard path to begin its evening rounds in the city. In the ruddy glow of twilight, the palace towers seemed darker and more terrible. A few orange lights sprang up in scattered windows low and high.

Discarding the warrior shape, she stepped through a curtain of green ivy. A secluded grove lay beyond, rife with long-stemmed flowers the color of amethysts. She drank water from a stone fountain and sat in her true form on a tangle of mossy roots. She sighed as night coalesced above the blood oaks. She should have been thinking about what lay ahead of her, but instead her mind went back to Yaskatha. Back to D'zan. She lifted a palm to her eye and wiped away the moisture before it could escape to flee down her cheek.

Their first two years together were bliss, a heady blend of passion and splendor. Since the time Sharadza was a small girl reading the histories and tales of elder kingdoms, she had dreamed of a Prince who would one day become her husband and King. D'zan was everything she had imagined. When she first met the determined lad striving to regain his kingdom from the Usurper Elhathym, her heart had recognized him. Months later, when he gave his life to regain that lost throne, it was her magic that helped forge a new body for his undying spirit. D'zan's first act as King of Yaskatha was to ask for her hand. How could she refuse the love in his reborn eyes, the culmination of all her secret hopes?

The wedding was a grand affair, high point of Yaskatha's victory celebrations. The False King, a grave-robbing necromancer, was vanquished, and the Crown Prince annointed King at last. Only days later she became his Queen before a cheering multitude of sun-browned Yaskathans. She recalled with fondness the brace of doves set free at the zenith of the ceremony, the hundred musicians, the ranks of nobles draped in silk and jewels, the thousand bright sails gleaming in the harbor beyond D'zan's city. From a balcony high atop the palace, King and Queen had waved to the masses, their hands tied by a golden chain in symbolic union. This was no political marriage. It was love, deep and soul-stirring.

The months that followed were full of banquets, feasting, parades, and quiet moments stolen by the young lovers for their own private pleasures. They lay together in secluded orchard groves while legionnaires stood guard beyond the trees, or they frolicked in forgotten alcoves behind gilt tapestries. The royal bedchamber was full of golden daylight, salty sea breezes, and the urgent moans of love. Man and woman learned together the mysteries of their bodies as they shared the deepest precincts of their souls. D'zan's presence consumed her every moment, even when duties called him from her for a day of kingly concerns. Always he returned to her, as the moon returns to the sky at the close of day. Always she received him as the ocean received the weary sun at twilight.

All the pomp and jewelry, the adoration of commoner and noble alike, the manifold luxuries of the palace and its expansive gardens ... all of these things meant very little. She had been raised in the great castle of her father in Udurum, and the ways of a Queen were not far removed from those of a Princess. She relished exploring the great library at the heart of Yaskatha's palace, yet even that treasure trove of knowledge could not keep her from D'zan's side for long. She craved the smell of his skin, the power of his arms, the weight of his chest against her own, the heat of his lips. She even misplaced her passion for sorcery. She had discovered a far more potent magic.

Her joy was magnified when her mother sailed from Udurum to visit the Kingdom of Orchards. The aging Shaira found peace in the warm climate and opulence of Yaskathan high society, so she decided to stay. She had left the ruling of the City of Men and Giants to Vireon, and she seemed to come alive again with the blessings of the southern sun.

Late in the second year of the marriage D'zan had changed. Something restless and irksome had grown within him like a slow fever. Eventually he confronted her with anger. The morning was like any other, yet their lovemaking had lacked fervor. He was distracted, preoccupied, and eventually pulled away from her to pace between the pillars of rosy marble. A cool wind blew in through the harbor window, chilling her skin. She gathered the silken sheets about her and waited for him to speak. Outside, seagulls cried out strange alarms.

At last she could take no more of his silence. "What is it?" she asked.

He stopped, hands behind his back, and turned to face her. She could not tell if it were anger or heartbreak on his face. His eyes, as green as her own, sparkled like wet emeralds.

"Why have you given me no heir?" he asked. The words were a slap across her cheek.

She had no answer for him. She swallowed a lump in her throat.

"For two years now we have lain together, nearly every day and every night," he reminded her. It sounded like an accusation. "Yet your belly grows no rounder ... Your womb rejects my seed. Have you ... have you prevented this through some sorcerous means?"

The slap was now a whip scourging her back. Though he did not touch her, he could not have wounded her more deeply.

"I ..." she stammered, unable to breathe. "I ... never thought—"

"What?" he asked, stepping nearer to the bed. "You never thought a King might need an heir? A son to wear his crown when he dies? Or at the very least a daughter to indicate that a son might later be born? How can I believe this from you?"

"You must believe it," she said, wrapping the sheet closer about her naked body. "Because I say it is true!" Despite her efforts not to do so, she wept. How long had this quiet storm been building inside him? How long had he doubted her intentions?

"Then why?" he demanded. It was frustration that ignited his anger, not her actions. "Why has my seed not taken root?"

She looked away from him, casting her attention beyond the window toward the wild blue sea. She could not tell him. She feared it might destroy him. She remembered the words of Iardu the Shaper on the day she had woven a new body for D'zan's stubborn soul to inhabit.

He will live as other men, said the Shaper, *and feel as other men. But he will not be as other men. We have given him a gift that carries its own price, for his body will not age as does one born of woman. If he is not slain he may live far beyond his desire to do so. Neither will he sire any sons, or daughters, for the mortal body that could produce such seeds has perished. Yet he loves you, and this he may do without impediment, just as he may freely rule his kingdom. We have shaped a vessel for the soul, but it is an imperfect one. This is the best we can do.*

Knowing this, she had still chosen to work the Great Spell. Not to do so would have left D'zan's spirit trapped inside a decaying body. The act of sorcery saved him from becoming a monster, yet could not restore him to full manhood. She could never tell him this. For all other purposes, he *was* a man, with a man's hungers, desires, and emotions. The man she loved above all others. He might become the greatest King that Yaskatha had ever known, if he chose to pursue the goal. He might bring a new age of prosperity and peace to his nation. But never would he be able to father a child. The body that could have done so was destroyed by the Usurper Elhathym.

"I am barren." The lie fell from her lips, heavy as a stone wrenched from her gut. "I was afraid to tell you." Her tears fell to stain the bedsheets.

D'zan sighed. He wrapped his arms about her. He said nothing, and his touch was tender. Yet she had confirmed his fear. Her lie had preserved his pride.

He said nothing more about it after that day. He still lay with her, still smothered her with his passion, though not as often. He claimed pressing royal duties. Often she did not see him for days at a time. Yet always he returned to ravish her in the darkness of their chamber, as if she were some secret love rather than his ordained Queen and wife.

She renewed her interest in the study of history, philosophy, and sorcery. She spent most of her days in the library, or on the stone benches of the palace gardens, a book nestled on her lap. She dined frequently with her mother and those ladies of noble personage whose presence she could tolerate. She preferred the company of books and scrolls. Twice Iardu visted her in the form of a great eagle. He spoke of strange spirits, forgotten spells, and distant worlds. Some impending doom seemed always to worry him, but he was evasive. Always he flew from her at dawn, back to his lonely island, she supposed. The ageless wizard said many things she did not understand, or would not understand until years later. She learned not to forget a word that he mumbled.

In the fourth year of the marriage, the first of many black rumors floated across the marshes like poison vapors. The lost Emperor of Khyrei had returned. Gammir the Bloody. Now they called him Gammir the Reborn. It was Vod, Sharadza's own father, who had killed Gammir nearly four decades ago. Yet the word of his return brought nightmares. Yaskathan mariners, as well as merchants from the Jade Isles and Mumbazan traders, spoke once more of Khyrein piracy. The marauding of the black-and-crimson ships had ceased for years, but now they plied the waves again, preying on any vessels in their path.

D'zan sat in long meetings with his advisors. Many who shared his confidence urged him toward war on the returned Emperor of Khyrei, yet there were no facts to prove Gammir's return. Sorcerers could defy death a thousand times, so it was quite possible. Yet it was just as likely that some new lord, hungry for greatness and power, had taken the name of the old Emperor and used it to secure the throne. D'zan asked her to join a council meeting, against the wishes of his advisors. They did not care for what she had to say, or for her pleas for caution and diplomacy. They wanted war. That day she realized that these were the same advisors who had turned D'zan away from her, whispering in his ear the necessity for an heir. They were the ones who had ruined her marriage.

She had worked her magic on a garden pool, looking across the world as if through a mirror. Although she could spy the frosty peaks of the northlands and the Giant forests of Uduria, even the dry streets of parched Uurz, she could not bring the capital of Khyrei into focus. There was indeed some great power there, something that blocked her magical vision. It could be that Gammir the Undying had actually returned. She called for Iardu on the night winds, but he did not come.

D'zan was unsurprised at the failure of her sorcery, as if her lack of childbearing had proved her ineffectiveness in all areas. Yet he did not chastise her when she stood powerless to confirm the Khyrein rumors. He only kissed her forehead and stalked off for another conference with his generals.

She heard them speak of an embassy to Mumbaza. They would draw the Boy-King to their war by exploiting his eagerness to prove himself a man. Undutu was about to claim the throne from his mother the Queen-Regent. The Son of the Feathered Serpent would be a Boy-King no more. Now he would be the King on the Cliffs, the Jeweled One, as his fathers were before him. She had little doubt that Undutu's young ego could be stroked enough to end Mumbaza's long peace. An ambassador from Uurz had already pledged King Tyro's allegiance to Yaskatha, supporting whatever action they might take against the Khyrein pirates. For the second time in her young life, Sharadza sensed the reek of war rising on the air, the scent of warm blood flowing through street and gutter, dripping from the gnarled fingers of dead men.

So it went for months on end. Squabbling ambassadors and rumors of sea battles. It seemed Uurz could not commit itself to war after all, for the Twin Kings were in disagreement. Lyrilan the Scholar checked the martial ambitions of his brother Tyro the Sword. The King of Mumbaza was not as eager to prove his war prowess as expected. He was a thinker, this dark-skinned youth, raised by his Queen-Mother to be cautious, and counseled by Khama the Feathered Serpent to maintain the harmony of the Pearl Kingdom. Meanwhile the depradations of the Khyrein pirates continued, and ships were lost in every season. Perhaps it was these frustrations with political matters, added to his fears of remaining heirless, that drove D'zan into the arms of Lady Cymetha.

At first she was only a whiff of perfume, a sweet odor that lingered on D'zan's skin when Sharadza came near him. The scent of another woman's lust. The reek of betrayal. She followed him one night in the form of a black cat, gliding between the columns of the great hall and skirting the hems of tapestries. Earlier, he had claimed that a meeting with his advisors would keep him late into the night. He told her not to wait up for him. Several times now he had done this, slipping into the royal bed much later with that strange scent lingering on him.

She followed D'zan into the domain of the courtesans, directly to Cymetha's chamber. She listened at the door with her feline ears pricked, and heard the sounds of their passion. It was the sound of what she had lost. Something precious gone forever. A sparkling diamond dropped into the ocean's dark abyss.

She did not confront him the next day, or the next. Yet no longer did she let him touch her. He would never touch her again; not until he admitted what he had done. What he continued to do. So months passed in icy silence, as politics and infidelity claimed the King's attentions, and the pages of ancient tomes wrapped a protective sheath about her heart. Everyone at the court knew of D'zan's affair; yet he would not insult her by speaking of it directly. Likewise, she uttered not a word to spoil her mother's happy existence among the courtly idylls of Yaskatha. Yet even Shaira must have wondered why her daughter would give her no grandchild to coddle. Sharadza evaded her mother's deft questions on the matter.

Three months ago she saw Cymetha's round belly for the first time. The pregnant courtesan was roaming the halls outside her newly appointed private suite in the company of seven serving maids. Cymetha's status had improved greatly. And why not? She carried the King's only heir inside her ambitious womb.

Sharadza confronted D'zan that night, marching openly into a meeting of his advisors. She brushed aside their blather of war and justice, sweeping them bodily from their chairs with a great wind. Sensing her anger, fearing her power, they fled the room. D'zan was outraged and fuming. He rose from the table, yellowed maps rustling in the air like mad Yaskathan pigeons.

She slapped him. One of her jeweled rings left a tiny cut across his cheek. It gleamed scarlet, a mark of shame. He said nothing, protests dying in his mouth. She stared at him, and again her eyes betrayed her with tears.

"I must have an heir," he said. His voice was ragged with arguing, weary as that of an old man, though he looked not a day older than when they had married. Golden hair fell about his shoulders as her magic winds died away, and the gems in his crown sparkled. "A King *must* have an heir, Sharadza."

"She is a *whore*," Sharadza whispered. The child in Cymetha's belly could not be D'zan's, would never be his. She wanted to tell him now, to shatter his illusion and strip away his arrogance. But she could not. She could not tell him plainly that Cymetha had lain with some dozen other men. That one of them had substituted his own potency for D'zan's powerless seed. Of course Cymetha knew this. Of course she had ensured her pregnancy. Such was her path to Queenhood. The child would be an imposter, raised to be the next King of Yaskatha, with only its mother to know it was a fraud. A bastard, like Sharadza's own brother Fangodrel.

Bitter, unhappy, wicked Fangodrel. The thought of him stung her like the point of a dagger. Suddenly a flame lit inside her skull. A fear blossomed in her stomach where D'zan's seed could not. She turned and walked away.

"I'm sorry," he said. She pretended not to hear.

She spent that night in the library, reading by the light of a dozen fat candles. She studied the ancient accounts of sorcerers rebirthing themselves, forming new bodies from vapor, ice, earth, or shadow. The spirit was eternal ... Sorcerers could not die because they had embraced this truth. In fact, many sages claimed that a sorcerer could not truly rise to power until he had shed his earthly body as a moth sheds the cocoon. The new body, the one built of sorcery and raw elements, that was the sorcerer's true self. As such, it could never be destroyed, only created and re-created. She knew this firsthand, as Elhathym had re-formed himself upon the stolen throne of Yaskatha after falling to D'zan on the field of battle. Yet she had helped Iardu capture Elhathym's life force. A dark vapor trapped inside a crystal prison.

Seven short years ago she had watched in a reflecting pool the scene of slaughter that destroyed Shar Dni. She saw one brother slay another to gain revenge for the death of a third. Vireon cut the head from Fangodrel's withered body. Poor Tadarus, her oldest brother, was avenged. She watched as Vireon the Slayer wept over the corpse, realizing himself now as much a kinslayer as Fangodrel. She had seen, and yet she had not realized.

Fangodrel had inherited the sorcery of his true bloodline. The son of Gammir the First, the Prince known as Gammir the Second, was Fangodrel's true father. Thirty years ago Shaira had been raped by the Khyrein Prince, and Vod had repaid the offense with death for both the Emperor and his son. Yet a seed of darkness had been planted in Shaira that grew into Fangodrel. A viper curling in the bosom of the north until one day it struck, delivering its poison to the heart of her family. Tadarus had been the first to die.

Could Fangodrel truly be dead? Or could this new Khyrein Emperor be her depraved brother reborn via sorcery? If Vireon had freed him from his earthly body, Fangodrel might have formed a new one. He might have taken on the name of his true father and grandfather, neither of whom he had ever known.

He might be this new Gammir. The Undying One.

She brooded on the possibility for weeks, cloistering herself in the library or her bedchamber. D'zan no longer joined her there. He took a separate chamber for himself and his other Queen, the one who would bear his child. Perhaps he hoped Sharadza would eventually forgive him and accept her place as Second Wife. She cared nothing about losing the title of Queen, although it would surely happen. It was the loss of D'zan that pierced her heart. But she put that aside during the researching of her new theory.

On the night of the bastard child's birth, she went into the gardens alone. She breathed deeply of the citrus air tinged with a salty breeze. The labor cries of Cymetha rang from an upper window where torches guttered and midwives worked to preserve the bloodline of Yaskatha.

It's all a lie, she realized. *All of this ... the riches ... the power ...
the world that Men build to hide themselves from the touch of Reality.
Honor ... loyalty ... love.*
All lies.

She needed Truth. It was the only antidote for the poisoning of
her soul. She wiped her eyes. The sounds of a squawling newborn
drifted through the tower window.

She bent her head and grew smaller, sprouted black and gray
feathers from her flesh, flexed her sharp talons, and flapped her
owlish wings. The palace and its gardens grew small beneath her.
She flew into the dim east, toward the festering marshlands where
loneliness was but one of many dangers.

A gardener found her sitting there among the roots. It was a
young Khyrein slave girl carrying a pitcher of water to feed the
blossoms. The slave gasped, clutching the container to the breast
of her white tunic. Her dark eyes were full of fear below her
shaved pate. She had obviously never seen a stranger in this place.
Certainly not a green-eyed maiden with northern skin dressed in
robes of Yaskathan purple.

Sharadza calmed her with a smile. With a wave of her hand she
left the girl sleeping on a bed of moss. Taking now the girl's form,
she wandered toward the wide marble steps where the scarlet
tigers lay purring between rigid sentries. Carrying the water
vessel, she walked timidly up the steps, and the guards did not
spare her a glance. The tigers, too, paid her no attention. No beast
would, unless she willed it.

Inside the vaulted hall of the palace she walked on thick carpets
between rows of onyx pillars. Mosaics and tapestries adorned the
walls, inlaid with blood-red rubies, sky-blue sapphires, and
starlight diamonds. The patterns were mostly arcane, abstract.
Khyrei's artisans did not celebrate their great thinkers, warriors,

and sages inside the palace. Instead they carved and sculpted only images of the Emperors and Empresses that had reigned over the jungle kingdom throughout the centuries. She entered a colonnade where the statues of past tyrants and their imperious wives stared down at her with eyes of obsidian. She supposed Gammir the First and Ianthe the Claw must stand among them, but she did not scan the graven pedestals for their names.

Arched corridors led in every direction from the central chamber, and the skylights glittered with brilliant stars. Night lay heavy over Khyrei now, and the palace interior was thick with dancing shadows. She felt unseen eyes at her back, but turned to see nothing. She picked a corridor at random and fled down it as a tiny black rat. The water pitcher sat unnoticed on the flagstones behind her.

Rodent senses came alive; she smelled blood and sweat and roasting meat. Hunger swelled in her tiny belly, but she denied it. Skittering through frescoed galleries and winding passages of polished jet, she found a black stair spiraling up. From its position she guessed this was the central tower, the thorn-crowned immensity that dominated the entire structure. She took the stairs one at a time, staying close to the wall. Now she smelled what she was looking for ... an odor of the foulest sorcery. It called her upward, toward its secret source.

As a rat she passed demon-faced guards standing before doors of archaic iron. A quintet of slaves came rushing down the stairs carrying the body of a sixth one, a pale youth with a red gouge in his throat, like a dripping blossom that had opened in the flesh. It reeked of the sorcery she scented. Yet the stronger odor came from above ...

She climbed past floor after floor of arched entries and locked chambers. At last she found the great iron door at the top of the winding stair. It stood wide open, and a bloody glow flickered into the stairwell, staining the black basalt to crimson.

There, in the doorway, limned in scarlet torchlight, stood a tall and thin figure. A long robe hung about the gaunt frame, glittering like a shroud of dark jewels. Here was the man-sized version of the great stone effigy that towered over the plaza. A spiked crown of onyx and rubies sat upon his brow.

In the lean face a pair of eyes gleamed like specks of tarnished gold touched by moonlight. They peered down the stairs at her, and she stood once more in her true form, one hand against the cold wall to support herself. The yellow eyes burned.

She had no voice. She wanted to become an eagle again, to fly from this place. She should never have come here.

"Sister," spoke the voice, "I had almost forgotten your great beauty." It flowed into her ears like honey, sweet and laced with clear venom.

She studied those cruel wolf-eyes. It could not be him. This . . . *thing* . . . was too different. Too inhuman. Too beautiful and deadly.

"Fangodrel?" she whispered.

The shadowy King shook his head.

"Gammir," he corrected her. "I've always been Gammir."

A wide grin showed white fangs.

She turned and leaped down the stairs, body melting, feathers sprouting, heart pounding. But it was too late.

Spreading leathery pinions, he struck like a great jungle bat, a sable wind wrapping her in darkness.

5

Among the Eyeless Ones

A strange aroma raised him from the brink of oblivion. It was not unpleasant. No more offensive than the sweat of workhorses he had known in the cornfields. For a moment, right before opening his eyes, he imagined himself lying in such a field surrounded by green stalks. Yet his back lay against hard, uneven stone, not the soft and rich earth of the plantations. His eyes fluttered open stubbornly. He stared at the rough granite ceiling awash with firelight and shadows.

That he lay somewhere deep beneath the ground was immediately apparent. Although he had never seen a cave or cavern, he had been told such hollows in the earth existed. Where were the Deathlands, the fruiting meadows, and the wide-open sky of Eternity? Where were Matay and his unborn son? Some fiery underground had claimed him instead of the blessed afterlife promised to slaves by their own desperate faith.

He groaned at the discovery, twitching his anguished muscles. Invisible flames seared his chest, left leg, and side. He recalled the bite of the poison arrows. The demon visages of his pursuers. The pale beasts that had spilled the blood of the Onyx Guards across the jungle. Lastly, he remembered their claws upon his skin.

He forced himself to sit upright. Gritting his teeth and peering through a curtain of pain, he examined the place that was not Death. A hole in the earth's bowels no bigger than a slave's hut. A single round exit with only flickering darkness beyond. A tiny fire of twigs and moss gleaming near the wall of the threshold. Carmine furs and animal skins hung from the crude walls, along with implements of wood made for cooking and tools of stone wrapped in sturdy vine. Shuffling toward him from the far recesses of the cave, a hunched figure entered the fireglow. One of the pale beasts, long of arm and leg, fantastically clawed, with curling horns instead of eyes, and a horribly wide mouth full of fangs. There was no sign of the great tongue that lay coiled inside that maw. The creature's gaping nostrils sniffed at him, pink and flaring. Instinct ignited, and he tensed, ready to leap away from the beast.

The cave swirled about him and he fell hard upon a mat of woven reeds. The arrows had been removed from his body, yet his wounds were still fresh. And they were deep. The venom sang its painful melody in the current of his blood. He could not sit up again, let alone stand. He lay at the mercy of the quiet creature. His eyes swelled, dripping salty excretions onto the cave floor, and his reopened wounds seeped.

The squatting beast loomed over him. The stockyard smell of its flesh had awakened him. It filled the entire cave ... a tang of loamy musk. In the firelight its smooth white skin took on a golden sheen. Unlike the others he had seen, a pair of pendulous breasts hung from its chest. The pink nipples reminded him of Matay's body, and his stomach churned. He might have retched then, but there was nothing in his stomach to expel. The creature placed a single hand upon his heaving chest. Its touch was gentle, the palm of the hand soft as a human woman's. Its other hand went to his forehead, where a second tender caress calmed his spasms.

As he fell again into lonesome darkness, the beast opened her mouth and *sang*.

Matay waited for him beyond the living world.

Perhaps now he would die and join her.

Yet he failed to see Matay, not even in his poisoned dreams. He wandered lost in the crimson jungle, swam through pits of ruby-eyed cobras, swam dark waters that clutched and drowned him. He ran from the laughing heads of demons that hung from the branches of dead trees. There was no rest in his sleep. He fought to survive the poison, and something deep inside him decided to win that fight.

He opened his eyes again, no way of telling how much later, and stared once more at the glimmering cave roof. The female beastling squatted near him already, spooning a hot broth into his mouth. It ran down his cheeks and her long pointed tongue extended to lick it from his face. The flavor was a mix of root vegetables and mushrooms. His odd caregiver cradled his head in one massive hand as the other spooned the broth from a broad steaming bowl. Why could he not die? Despite this grim thought, he lapped hungrily at the soup. His wounds were cleaned, wrapped in mud and ruddy leaves ... a poultice resembling the earth medicine of his own folk. He did not resist the feeding; his belly ached with hunger. He sipped from the big wooden spoon, and the she-beast cooed, then trilled a weird melody. Somehow he knew these were the sounds of approval.

He recognized now another figure, one of the male creatures, crouching in the cave. It sat near the entrance, as if watching the feeding with its eyeless head. Its nostrils twitched and its round skull nodded. He marveled at its ivory horns, thick as the hafts of spears and coiled into points at either side of its jutting chin. It placed a handful of brown moss on the fire without turning its head, and the flames danced brighter.

Whatever they were, they wanted him alive. He did not have time to wonder why, as sleep claimed him again. His belly groaned contentedly, and the she-beast laid his head back upon the reed mat. Again she sang a strange lullaby as he faded.

Several more times he awoke to such a feeding. Helpless, he had no choice but to submit to the she-beast's nurturing. After a while the blackness of his wounds faded, and the venom worked its way through his system. The she-beast had taken his urine often in a hollow gourd, and when necessary she helped him void his bowels into a stone bowl. These she emptied immediately somewhere beyond the cave.

She kept the cave immaculate, despite its dirt floor and chaos of hanging tools and hides. Finally he found himself able to sit up. He accepted from the cave dweller an unknown fruit shaped like an egg but covered in fuzzy amber flesh that faded to pink at the tips. She licked her lips with a viperish tongue and raised a second fruit to her own maw. He followed her lead, biting into the fruit. It was sweet, delicious, and substantial. It tasted like sunlight, whose warmth he had almost forgotten in this deep place. He devoured it, examining his wounds one by one.

The poultice had worked well. His scarred flesh was pink and new. A few more days and he might even run again.

Run.

The thought hit him like a bolt of sky-fire. He wiped the sticky juice from his mouth with the back of his hand. There could be only one reason why these beasts had saved him from death at the hands of the Onyx Guards. He had only one value to anyone in this cruel and vicious world. He was a slave. A strong one, when healthy. He could outwork ten other men in the fields, and often had done so.

These earth dwellers were keeping him alive, nursing him back to health, for one purpose. So he would be of value to them as a slave. This was the same reason that wounded or diseased slaves were treated in Khyrei. They were property, nearly as valuable as well-bred horses to the Overseers and noble houses of the city.

Tong had fled into the jungle seeking vengeance and death. He had found the first goal, but had stumbled back into slavery. His eyes combed the walls of the cave, looking for something sharp. Now that he had some strength back, he might draw a blade across his wrists, or pierce his heart. He would not serve these inhuman masters, as kindly as they had treated him. He would die and find the long-promised happiness that was impossible for his kind in this world.

The she-beast offered him another fruit. He took it but nibbled slowly. Her usual visitor, the male, had not come today. So Tong sat alone with his nurse and savior. No doubt when she gave the word validating his strength, the male would take him out into whatever field or workyard required the labor of slaves. That day would not be much longer in coming. He did not intend for it to arrive.

His heart beat faster as his eyes spotted the Khyrein sabre hanging on the wall. A sheathed longknife hung from the same wooden peg. These must be the weapons he had stolen from his pursuers and used to take his vengeance. The pale beasts had brought them along as souvenirs. There were no other signs of weapons, although a few small stone cooking knives lay farther back in the cave. They were tossed amid reed baskets full of green leafy produce.

Now. She would not expect it. He was not fully recovered. If he waited until his health was normal again, it might be too difficult to cut his own throat or impale his willing heart. He might only wound himself, and therefore play out this extended drama all over again.

The sabre was his passage into the Deathlands, his second escape from slavery. He must strike fast and true.

For Matay.

Without warning he kicked the she-beast away from him and lunged toward the cave wall. His limbs were heavy and stiff. He could not move as fast as he wished. Yet his clumsy hands grasped the sabre and pulled it free of the scabbard. A white blur leaped into the cave mouth as Tong wrapped his hands about the hilt and turned the blade inward. He pressed the blade's tip against his chest, aimed directly at his heart. It would take all his strength, but he would do it by falling forward and using the cave floor to drive the sword deep. He had no more use for any strength beyond that last lunge. He squeezed the hilt and flexed his biceps.

A pale arm slammed against his own. The blade flew from his numb fingers. He lost his balance and fell among the bowlfuls of harvested roots. The male beastling stood above him now, sniffing, clawing at the air. Tong coughed and writhed against the stone. Again, death eluded him. He cursed at the creature and its mate behind him. She grabbed the sabre and the knife, hanging them back on the wall with care. The male picked Tong up as if he weighed no more than a child and carried him back to his sleeping mat.

"Why?" he asked. The blind beasts stared at him, nostrils pulsing, claws gesticulating unknown ciphers. "Why don't you let me die?"

But he already knew the answer. He was a slave.

Slaves did not choose the hour of their death.

That honor must go to their masters.

"Matay . . ." He wept, and curled himself upon the mat.

Sleep came fast upon him, a shallow imitation of the greater peace for which he longed.

There was no day or night in the subterranean realm where he lay and failed to die. Always the little fire glowed, always the orange light shuddered on the rocky walls, and always the darkness beyond the cave mouth seethed. What lay out there? These were his thoughts as he woke and gave himself to the ministrations of his inhuman nurse. He was a shell, drained of hope, emptied of the urge for revenge, absent of the need for life. Yet life he had. Like an obstinate weed thriving in a ruined garden, he endured.

Today the she-beast brought him a new kind of broth. He watched her crumble in her taloned fingers a great crimson butterfly from the jungle above (it must be above) and add its remains to the steaming pot. Then a pair of tiny crystals she crushed, dropping them into the brew. Unlike her other soups and stews, this one was bitter, tangy, hard to swallow. He pushed away the bowl, but she insisted, grabbing his hands and forcing him to take it. When he refused a second time she took the spoon and was ready to force-feed him. He was too strong for that now, and he thought she knew it. To avoid a confrontation he took the bowl and drank the foul concoction in a single quaff. It burned his throat but settled into his stomach nicely.

She sang again, gathering up the bowl and offering him a gourd full of cold water. He drank greedily, washing down the butterfly broth. A new strength spread along his arms and legs, dancing like a flame in his skull. He licked his lips. In the cave mouth now appeared the male creature, obviously the mate of his caregiver. He had guessed that days ago. He heard them nuzzling and cooing together often in the back of the cave. He could not bear to watch so he made a point not to observe their displays of affection. They seemed to communicate by a language of touch, smell, and some hidden sense that he could not identify.

The male motioned at Tong. His movements were unmistakable. The great clawed hands waved him forward, calling him out of the cave. The outer darkness pulled him onward. He leaped from the reed mat, feeling better than he could ever remember.

The broth of butterfly and crystal had done this. He looked about the cave as he stood. The sabre and knife were missing from the wall. He sighed. This must be the day they would call him to his work. His new slavery was to begin soon.

He looked back at the she-beast, but she was busy cleaning and ordering the cave. He did not know how to say goodbye, or he might have done so. She had not been cruel to keep him alive. She was kind. It was not her fault that the world was run by the strong who preyed on the weak and enslaved them. Although he might succeed in killing himself at some later date, he would not have tried it in her presence again. She ignored Tong as he left the cave in the company of her mate.

A sudden wave of dizziness fell upon him as he exited the cave mouth and stood to his full height. The dwelling where he had lain was little more than a niche in the face of a great rock wall inside a cavern of unknown proportions. The cave of his caregiver was only one of a thousand such grottoes dug into its high walls. Narrow stone ledges ran from each of these caves, criss-crossing and slanting from one to the other. In places crudely chiseled stairwells linked together the rows of wall dwellings. Dozens of the eyeless ones scampered along the ledges with uncanny grace, crawling and leaping like white spiders.

Dim firelight flowed from the mouths of the caves, yet it was not enough to illuminate the greater cavern floor far below. The wall of caves simply fell into darkness, yet down in that darkness a few fires gleamed like red and yellow stars. The male beast tugged upon Tong's arm. He followed it down a jagged stair and across a succession of ledges. Always they went downward, toward the hidden floor that had to exist somewhere in the lower darkness. Other eyeless beasts moved aside to let them pass, sniffing at Tong with their bat-like snouts.

From the ceiling hung great columns of black and green rock, tapering to narrow points. Raw nuggets of yellow and purple crystal gleamed along their surfaces in wild patterns, refracting the fireglow into a flux of glimmering lights. The smell of deep earth was stronger here, yet a cool breeze blew from somewhere. Tong could almost smell the sweetly sour scent of the jungle, but he was unsure if it was only his imagination.

As he descended with his silent guide, the lights from below grew brighter. Now the floor of the massive vault came into view. Some of the depending rock columns fed into the ground here, massive columns linking floor to ceiling. Others rose from the stony floor like miniature mountains, pointed and gleaming with crystalline essence. Now he smelled water, and the air was damp with its presence. It was cooler down here, and the sweat on his bare chest and legs turned chill. He still wore only the stained loincloth of a slave. The eyeless ones wore no clothing at all. His feet, like theirs, were bare on the cold stone. Yet the heat of the butterfly broth in his belly kept him from shivering.

Now Tong stepped onto the floor of the vault, where a forest of the stone columns rose into glimmering shadow. He followed his guide through a world of bizarre beauty, past rock formations carved into the shapes of strange beasts, among outcrops of purple fungi taller than cornstalks and harvested by eyeless females. He saw no fellow humans among these harvesters. To what unknown labor could they be taking him?

Great mushrooms grew high as trees, dripping with moss and alive with crawling black beetles. His guide paused momentarily to snatch a few of these insects from a thick stalk and pop them into his maw. He crunched them hungrily between his fangs. He motioned for Tong to do the same, but Tong declined. As on the wall paths, other male beastlings passed about them, but they only sniffed in Tong's direction or ignored him completely.

Here and there great fire pits opened in the earth. Flames

leaped high from these deep fissures. Near to these flaming holes the cavern's heat became great. The eyeless ones had no use for light, but they obviously valued fire for warmth and cooking. Among all the living things in this strange underworld, Tong might be the only one who benefited from the light of the natural flames. He silently thanked the Earth God for them. He could not imagine the horror of this experience if he had to endure it in complete darkness. How long he had lain in the high cave he could not say, but his wounds had all healed nicely.

Now he came upon another high wall of uneven granite lined with grottoes and ledges. By the light of nearby fire pits he saw that this new structure was actually a single great column of rock rising from the floor to be lost in the upper darkness. At ground level it was thicker than a Khyrein watchtower, with firelit caverns visible inside the carved arches. As it rose higher into the vault, it expanded, growing impossibly wider, home to a thousand more caves and cavelings. Suddenly he realized that the entire structure must be grown from the cavern roof into the floor itself. Otherwise its upper weight would surely collapse.

Ledges and stairwells were more numerous here, and they spiraled about the great city-column where cookfires danced and the children of beastlings capered. Whole families of the creatures moved about the place. Tong watched without words as the true scale of this subterranean tribe dawned upon him.

Beyond the great city-column, lights glimmered on an expanse of black water. The subterranean lake ran as far as he could see in three directions, rippled by constant drippings from the unseen cavern roof. Tong's guide stood before the arches of the city-column and raised his apish arms high. He sang in a loud sonorous voice, his song deeper and harsher than that of his mate. His voice carried through the great underworld, ran along the maze of ledges and stairwells, penetrated the heart of the great vertical cityscape.

Tong's blood rushed in his veins as clusters of the pale beasts came lurching from their holes, crawling and shuffling along the narrow routes toward the cavern floor. From the great arches marched two lines of eyeless ones wearing crimson robes, garments woven from plucked jungle foliage. Jewels and panther fangs hung upon their chests. Identical to the rest of the beastlings save for their ostentatious garments and clicking talismans, they approached Tong and formed a neat circle about him. They sniffed and gesticulated while Tong's guide replied in some obscure manner. Before long an entire herd of the creatures gathered about Tong: male, female, young, adult, even tiny infants scuttling like crabs between the legs of their mothers.

Now the robed ones began singing, and a procession began. The mass of beastlings walked toward the dark lake. Caught in their midst, Tong had no choice but to follow. If he refused, they would only pick him up and carry him. He was well aware of their great strength, and the power of their great claws to rend flesh. Yet they seemed a peaceful people, if people they were at all. No sword, knife, or spear was to be seen among the masses. Of course, they did not need such tools to work slaughter upon men. Their whip-quick claws had dispatched a band of Onyx Guards in seconds.

A new idea came to him as the black waters glimmered. The sound of waves beating against a rocky shore filled his ears. He might leap into the lake and drown himself. But he must wait until this strange ritual was at its apex, when the beastlings would be too involved with their ceremonies to stop him. Now at last he might secure his own death. Not even such a horde of beasts could keep him from joining Matay a second time.

The black waters stretched into darkness, and a cold wind blew from the gulf beyond. A sense of vastness fell upon Tong as he approached the beach, surrounded by the singing priests. The lake was in truth an underground sea. How far did it extend under the earth's crust, and how many weird kingdoms lay beyond it? The eyeless ones bowed low before the sunless sea.

He had no doubt of their religion now. They must worship this night-dark sea and the demons that haunted its depths. To either side of him along the rocky strand worshippers dropped to their knees, sniffing at the glimmering wavelets. The red-robed priests were the only ones who remained standing. Tong lost sight of his guide among the crowd of identical beastlings. There were hundreds, perhaps thousands gathering by the black waters. Understanding washed over him like a warm rain.

They mean to call up some blind Water God and offer my flesh to appease it.

So death would find him quick enough. He would not be a slave after all, but a sacrifice.

He smiled at the thought.

"Rise up, God of Beasts," he said, voice lost beneath the cadences of the eyeless priests. "Come and devour me! I give myself freely!"

Matay . . . At last I come to be with you.

He spread his arms wide, raised his face to the cool wet breath of the underground sea. The ceremony went on for some time, and the dark tide rose to lick at his feet. The water was cold and numbing. The song of the red priests continued, unbroken, swirling, and maddening.

Perhaps there was no beast-god. Perhaps they were simply mad, these blind cave dwellers. How long would their wordless rites continue? Were they waiting for him to do something? He walked forward, up to his waist in the chilling water. Nobody stopped him. He would let the nameless sea freeze and drown him. The eyeless ones would have their sacrifice either way.

Suddenly the black surface erupted, sending a spray of chill

mist across the multitude. The force of displaced water knocked
Tong back, and he struggled to keep his footing. Now a cold rain
fell upon him. The sound of falling water replaced the song of the
eyeless ones. They had fallen mute upon the instant. Something
huge rose from the black depths, shedding water and glistening
in the reflected light of fire pits.

The breath fled from Tong's lungs as he stared up at the God
of Beasts. It rose like a colossal viper from the waves, its flesh as
pale as the skin of the eyeless ones. Its body was as thick as one of
the cavern's stone columns, lined with gleaming scales. It had no
arms or legs, but two great gills spread behind its triangular head
like transparent bat wings. Unlike its worshippers, it stared ahead
with a pair of bulging oval eyes, scintillant with shifting colors.
Its open mouth was full of fangs, with two incisors dominating
the upper jaw, two more on the lower. A pair of convulsing nostrils mimicked the snouts of the eyeless ones, and its red, pointed
tongue was akin to theirs, though many times longer and thicker.
The massive head reared dripping above Tong, mystical eyes shedding their own subtle light upon him.

It might have swallowed him whole, so great was its size. Yet
it only swirled and coiled about him, hissing softly to rival the
sounds of the rushing water. Tong stood stiff and terrified in its
presence. He closed his eyes again, ready to feel the sting of those
great fangs as they impaled his body. Yet the pain never came. The
beast glided about him and slithered up onto the beach. There it
slithered among the eyeless worshippers, who bowed and sang to
it. They came forward to caress its chromatic scales and lick the
translucent slime from its back. Tong watched the culmination of
the rite and recognized it as a ceremony of adoration. The great
White Serpent flowed among its people and licked at them, but
it did not crush, rend, or bite. The red-robed ones kneeled before
it and began a new melody.

Childhood tales of Serpents and the Ancient World danced in the back of Tong's memory. Such beasts once ruled the world, breathing fire that scorched the northlands to ash. The Gods had sent Giants to battle the monsters. He had never truly believed such stories until this great Serpent reared before him. Yet there was no fire in this beast's gullet, or surely the waters would have quenched it. Neither did it have dozens of clawed legs like the mythical Serpents. Yet what else could it be?

For the first time in many years, Tong thought of old Trissus, who used to tell his fellow slaves outlandish tales and legends by the light of the evening fires. He had taught Tong everything he knew about the world beyond the fields, until the day he was whipped to death for some offense against an Overseer. Such deaths were common among Tong's people. He had only been a boy when Trissus died, but the old man's stories lingered in the fields long after his death. They were retold by his sons, his brothers, and his cousins, who taught others to tell them in turn. Legends, unlike Men, never seemed to die.

The Serpent's body was as long as a Khyrein tower was tall. In the gentle atmosphere of its presence Tong realized that he would not die today. He fell to his knees in the cold water. He should drown himself now, while the eyeless ones worshipped their scaly God.

The utter strangeness of his situation was broken by the even stranger sound of a human voice. It spoke his native tongue.

"Welcome to Sydathus, Tong of Khyrei."

Tong raised his face from the black water. An old man stood before him on the shore. No, it was a man whose true age was unknowable. He stood ankle-deep in the foam, wearing an orange-red robe of finely stitched silk. His hair was long and silvery gray, his short beard and mustache that same color. A thin band of gold sat upon his high forehead, and a dancing blue flame on a silver chain burned upon his chest. His skin was brown in the sun-kissed manner of a trader from the eastern or northern lands. No matter how long Khyreins spent under the hot sun, their pale flesh never darkened. So this man was definitely not one of Tong's countrymen. The jewels upon his fingers glowed less brightly than his eyes. He had the eyes of the White Serpent: a shifting blend of scarlet, emerald, violet, azure, and pearl. They gleamed and sparkled with an alert calm. He smiled at Tong with perfectly white teeth and offered his hand.

The Serpent was gone. The horde of beastlings stood tranquil about them, even the children holding still in the presence of the one who had come. The one who spoke now with the voice of a Man. Tong accepted his hand and met his curious gaze.

"Who are you?" Tong asked. "What are you?"

The ageless man grinned. "I am a Man, like you," he said. "And so much more . . . also like you."

He led Tong from the beach, back toward the great city-column. The eyeless ones walked about them, sniffing and prancing. The priests formed a broad ring about the two Men as they moved. The scents of roasting vegetables filled the cave air as they approached the settlement.

"How do you know me?" asked Tong.

"I know many things," said the ageless one, "and have forgotten many more. Such are the perils of old age."

"What is this place?"

"I told you," said the stranger. He lifted his arms to indicate the stupendous network of cave dwellings carved into the monolith. "This is Sydathus, one of the world's oldest cities."

The priests led the two men up a flight of stairs between the city-column and the beach, where a crudely carved stone chair sat overlooking the black ocean. A smattering of crystals gleamed along the seat's back and arms. The eyeless ones gathered about the rough throne and the ageless stranger sat himself in the chair with a sigh. He turned his prismatic eyes upon Tong once again.

"I apologize that there is no chair for you upon this dais," he said. "Please . . . sit." He motioned to the stone platform, which was covered by a mass of reed carpets.

Tong could think of nothing else to do, so he sat before the chair, crossing his legs. He groaned a little at the slight pain in his side.

"Are you healing well?" asked the stranger.

Tong nodded. "Well enough."

"The Sydathians are quite skilled at medicine. You would have lain helpless much longer if not for their good care. Are you hungry?"

Tong shook his head. The stranger smiled. "So they have fed you well. Once you accept their uncommon appearance, their benevolent nature becomes plain."

Tong rubbed his face with hands still wet from the freshwater sea.

"Please . . . " he said. "I don't understand any of this. Why must you torment me so?"

The stranger gave him a quizzical look, his eyebrows knotting. "Torment?" he repeated Tong's word. "I've saved your life. Or rather . . . *they* did."

"But why? Tell me why."

The stranger raised his head and took a long breath. He nodded, as if recognizing some forgotten need, or remembering some lost detail.

"Forgive me," he said. "Your confusion must be great. I have been remiss."

Tong waited. The silent Sydathians about the throne mirrored his calm.

"You were a slave," said the stranger. "But you are free now. A *free man*. Your life is your own."

Tong leaped to his feet. "I do not want it," he said. The eyeless ones moved uneasily as his voice echoed about the cavern and was lost in the darkness. He clenched his fists at his sides.

"You only long for death because you have not tasted life," said the stranger.

"I have!" said Tong. "I have tasted it enough to know its sweetness. And now she is gone."

The stranger nodded. "A great loss. You have known agony and pain and a lifetime of suffering. Yet these things are behind you now. Believe me—"

"Who are you?" shouted Tong. Anger boiled in his blood now, making his scars throb, his head ache.

"Men call me Iardu," said the stranger. "And other names. Yet Iardu will do."

Tong looked at the Sydathians basking in the glory of this Man who was also Serpent.

"Are you their God?"

Iardu rubbed his pointed beard and considered the question. "You might say that," he said. "I am an old friend to Sydathus."

"A sorcerer," said Tong, remembering the tales of Trissus. "A *warlock* . . ."

Iardu smiled, white teeth gleaming. "As good a term as any."

"You know me. Somehow you made them find me in the jungle and save me when all I wanted was vengeance and a quick death."

Iardu leaned forward, placing an elbow on the arm of the stone seat. "I sought you because you sought vengeance. Your desire for your own death is of no concern to me."

"I've had my vengeance."

"Have you?"

Tong wondered now if the warlock was mocking him. "I killed three Onyx Guards. I killed an Overseer."

"A mere handful of wicked lives."

"They are enough," said Tong.

"Tell me," said Iardu, leaning back in his chair. "How many soldiers guard the walls of Khyrei? How many legions walk its streets? How many innocents suffer and die at their whim? How many ships carry fresh slaves into the city from distant lands? How many generations have passed since your own ancestors were stripped of their holdings and sent into the fields to work and die like animals?"

"You mock me," Tong said. But his rage had subsided.

"No," said Iardu. "Consider all these things and answer one more question: have you truly had your vengeance?"

Tong stood silent for a while, listening to the sound of the waves beating upon the stone shore. Iardu's eyes glimmered red, blue, and golden, while the blue flame on his chest burned low.

"No," Tong grunted.

Iardu nodded. "How much longer will it stand, this empire of blood and cruelty? How many more generations must live and die under the yoke of the Khyrein Emperors? The one who reigns now is called the Undying One . . . Gammir the Bloody. They call him this because he subsists on the blood of his own people, treads upon their bent backs like the flagstones of his filthy streets. He, too, is what you would call a warlock. And, like me, he is far more."

"I know these things," said Tong. "Why do you remind me?"

"Because you are going to bring it all down. The tyranny of Khyrei will crumble, the blood-hungry Gammir will be deposed, and your people set free to discover the joy of living. All this will happen . . . if only *you* desire it."

Tong stared into the prismatic eyes. They dazzled him with brilliant depths. They were deep as oceans. Oceans of power.

"Do you desire it?" asked Iardu.

The face of Matay flickered like a dream in Tong's mind. The morning sun glittered in her eyes the way Iardu's power gleamed in his. Tong thought of the men and women, thousands upon thousands, working in the fields even now. Year in and year out, always the same pain and tragedy. Suffering in the streets beyond the black walls . . . dying beneath the heels of the Onyx Guard. He thought of the hopeless children pulling weeds, shucking crops with their tiny hands, raised in a world of endless toil and boundless brutality. He thought of all the children not yet born, and of his own son who would never see Matay's beloved sunrise. All the future generations of slaves with no hope and no savior.

"Yes," he told the sorcerer. "I desire it."

"Good," said Iardu, eyes blazing. "Very good."

One of the Sydathians brought the Khyrein sabre and offered it to Tong. Its blade and hilt had been cleaned and polished. Tong wrapped his right hand about the grip. It felt solid and dangerous in his fist. Something reckless leaped into his chest, a jungle tiger raging to break free and carve a bloody path. A path to freedom.

"There is always time for death," said Iardu. "All Men find it eventually."

Tong slid the weapon into its bronze sheath.

He could not die yet. But Matay would wait for him.

"Where is my knife?" he asked.

6

Two Hearts, One Kingdom

The bloodletting started with a slit throat in a Palm Street brothel. The son of a lord from House Burillus fell to squabbling with the cousin of a lord from House Tyllisca. The two lads had been fast friends until the discord between the Twin Kings divided the royal house into factions. Too much wine and too many hot words led to the drawing of blades and the spilling of Uurzian blood across the cobbles. The lords of House Burillus supported Tyro's drive toward war, while Tyllisca stood behind the Scholar King. It was unclear who struck the first blow, but a Son of Burillus was the first man to die in the argument for peace.

The killing set houses against one another, each lord calling upon his private legions and fortifying his estates as if the Khyreins were about to march out of the south and lay siege to the city. Twelve houses claimed allegiance to Lyrilan, fifteen to Tyro. In three weeks of waggling tongues, raised fists, and logical stalemates the unity of Uurz had been shattered. In the days since the Burillus lad's death, two skirmishes had broken out in the Central Market and six servants had been found dead in gutters or stuffed into dry wells. The city's commoners began to reflect this unrest, so that companies of city guards marched on constant alert. Fights broke out every night in taverns, gambling dens, and even on the steps of temples. Men died for poorly chosen words or careless bravado.

The long dry nights brought no relief from the heat of the day. In the torrid lack of rain, the Uurzians had begun to water their city with the blood of their fellows.

The specter of disunity brought palace life to a standstill. Lyrilan stayed sequestered in the western wing with Ramiyah and his chief advisors. The Green Legions paced along his towers and walls, while the Gold Legions fortified Tyro's apartments in the eastern wing. The two sides had not yet come to blows, yet there was little love between the commanders of the divided army.

Lyrilan sat most days in his high tower and discussed ways to mend the broken court. He missed the Royal Library, where he usually went to do his best thinking. Now, if he dared enter the middle precincts of the palace, he must take a cadre of legionnaires with him. How could he possibly think with all those clattering spears and tromping boots surrounding him like a pack of snuffling hounds? At least here he could keep the guards outside the doors of his quarters. He could send for the books he needed, but that was no substitute for walking among the forest of bindings and scrolls and shelves. It was his own private temple, and he resented being driven from it.

"This is not what my father wanted," he complained to Ramiyah. "It is everything he feared for his empire." She listened patiently, as she always did. She smiled sadly and rubbed a hand across his back. The sunlight through the casements of their bedchamber glittered on her golden hair.

Ramiyah took a green and silver robe from a servant and bade her husband stand while she helped drape it about his shoulders. "Tell them," she said.

"I have told them," he said. "They listen, they nod, they

sympathize. But what can they do? What one of them can reach my brother's ear, let alone his heart?"

She placed a necklace of opals, centered with an eight-sided topaz, about his neck. "Your brother surrounds himself with wicked men, hawks eager for blood and glory. He listens to their flattery and their lies. And *she* is the worst of them . . . "

Lyrilan nodded, adjusting his slim crown. He raised his feet one at a time while the servant slid tall boots onto them.

"Talondra wants vengeance, that is all," he agreed. "I understand that. Who would not want it? Her entire family died when Shar Dni fell . . . along with thousands of others. The tragedy of her loss blinds her to everything else, sweeps aside all other considerations."

"As it blinds your brother," said Ramiyah. He watched as attendants finished dressing her in a gown of green silk trimmed with white roses. She added silver accoutrements chosen carefully from a coffer of jade. She would not wear gold while the division lasted. Nor would any of the Scholar King's followers. Gold was the color of Tyro's legions, and therefore the color of war. Lyrilan hated this random assignation of pigment and metals. For twelve centuries Uurz had been the green-gold city. Now its colors were split, as were its people.

He gazed upon his beautiful wife in all her glory. He reached out to stroke her soft hair, drew her close to him in a rustle of royal silks. Her blue eyes locked onto his, and he wished he could dive into those pools of azure. It was the color of love, undiluted by ceremony or guile.

He had known so many women, and they had all been as one to him. Until the day he met Ramiyah in the palace of Yaskatha while visiting the court of King D'zan. Lyrilan's extended visit became a months-long affair, and he brought her back to Uurz for a wedding that sent the city into a week of celebration. Already

Emperor Dairon had grown ill, but the marriage of his son revived
him for a while, and he had whispered to Lyrilan that he liked
Ramiyah. Soon afterward, perhaps not to be outdone, Tyro had
married Talondra. It seemed a hasty decision, but perhaps Tyro felt
the same about Lyrilan's choice. The brothers had congratulated
each other and made fabulous gifts to their new sisters-in-law. All
under the eyes of Dairon, who would not live to see the year's end.

I chose well in you, Lyrilan thought. *Your love is as bright as sunlight. How can I ever tell you what it means to me?*

She was the most lovely thing he had ever seen, but he had
learned enough of women not to tell her so. At least, not too often.
So he had tried instead to show her, in a thousand different ways:
jewels, gowns, pearls, parties, celebrations. After a year of such
indulgence, she had taught him that the best way to show his love
was simply to *listen* to her. So he listened.

*Does this same devotion consume my brother's attention? If Ramiyah
spoke of war to me, would I listen to her as Tyro listens to Talondra?*

Ramiyah kissed his lips as gently as a drop of dew. "If the lords
cannot reach your brother, then *you* must do it."

Lyrilan's eyes fell across the room to his new book. Volomses
had finished his proofing and had only good things to say about
it. Now Lyrilan might present it to Tyro as a gift. A reminder of
their common heritage ... a testament to their father's legacy.
Perhaps it would remind Tyro that unity is more important than
glory. Or perhaps he would only dismiss it as he dismissed so
many of Lyrilan's interests. Yet this was their *father*. How could
even the Sword King deny the life and vision of his own progen-
itor?

Lyrilan nodded and kissed his wife's smooth cheek. "I will try,"
he said. "If they will let me, I will try." Lyrilan's advisors' concern
for his well-being had trumped all his efforts at a personal meeting with Tyro thus far. The twelve lords in service to Lyrilan, the

Green Lords as they were now called, represented him at all assemblies, conferences, and summits with their nemeses the Gold Lords. Similarly, Tyro's advisors bade him stay away from such parleys. So the two brothers had not exchanged a single word since the night when Tyro slew the Khyrein spy and split the houses.

Lyrilan approached the double doors that led to the hallway and turned to look at Ramiyah once more. She planned to enter the Western Gardens today with a coterie of noble ladies, under heavy guard of course. He would see her again at the sun's zenith, when they would dine on the terrace overlooking western Uurz. She blew him a kiss as a servant opened the doors. Three mailed guards paced at his back when he crossed the tower's middle and entered the carpeted stateroom. There the Green Lords sat gathered about a table of black marble.

Volomses was there too, seated next to the King's Chair. A pile of massive tomes lay before him. He had gathered whatever books Lyrilan had requested these past weeks, seeing them safely brought into the Western Tower. Yet Lyrilan had requested no books today. He did not recognize the topmost of the leather-bound volumes, though he could tell their great age by the yellowed parchment and cracked bindings.

The Green Lords stood and bowed as the Scholar King entered. Twenty guardsmen in green tabards over bronze mail stood about the room. The shafts of their upraised spears spoiled the view from the tall windows that opened on the city's northern quarter and the fortified wall beyond. Past the massive ramparts lay a grassy plain segmented by the northern road and a few muddy rivers in the distance. Portraits hung between the windows, the bearded visages of Emperors long dead, scions of the Old Blood. Their dead eyes seemed to mock Lyrilan as they gazed upon his predicament.

Lyrilan sat and the lords followed his lead. Undroth was the first to speak.

"Good morning, Majesty," he offered politely, striving to sound jovial. His heavy black beard was woven into a mass of braids set with jeweled bands, and his massive fingers were thick-set with emerald and ruby. His eyes were gray and his face kindly. Undroth was a longtime friend of Lyrilan's father, a veteran of the Island Wars, and a trusted counselor. Lyrilan found it easy to place faith in the man. Since his father had no brothers, he had long thought of Undroth as an uncle.

Lyrilan nodded to all the assembled lords, careful not to show favoritism. "What news?"

Undroth frowned. "None but two more deaths," he said. "Both of them nobles, boys barely out of school."

Lord Vaduli sighed. "Young fools eager to prove themselves, as is usually the case." Silver beads sparkled on the chest of his gray-green robe. Vaduli could easily pass for a sage, so long was his beard and so bright his eyes. He often displayed a sage's wisdom in these councils.

A moment of quietude settled upon the council chamber. Servants brought platters of black grapes and yellow cheese. They poured wine from crystal decanters. Some of the lords drank deeply, while others barely sipped. Lyrilan ignored his own cup. It was still morning, and the heat of the day had not yet awakened his thirst.

"I will wait no longer," he announced. "I must speak with my brother."

A chorus of protests broke forth. He silenced the lords with a raised hand.

"Negotiations have proved useless," he reminded them. "This is a family matter, a dispute between brothers ... and what's more ... it is what my father would want."

Most of the lords looked to their cups, but Undroth looked Lyrilan in the eye. "My Lord." His voice was soft, almost a whisper.

Lyrilan often felt his dead father advised him through the words of this living man. "It is not safe. The Gold Legions have their zealots, and Tyro's loyalists are eager for blood. Give us more time to reach an accord."

"No," said Lyrilan. "I've waited too long already. No more Uurzians will die because the Brother Kings cannot see eye to eye. I have decided."

Undroth pulled at his braided beard. He nodded, but said nothing more.

Vaduli drank deeply from his cup, then set it down and looked at Lyrilan. "Majesty, as much as I fear this course of action, I commend your bravery. Your escort shall be thirty of the finest blades. I feel it best that you too carry a sword. It will send a message to your brother that mere words may not."

"I will carry no sword," said Lyrilan. "I take a gift to my brother. I will not enter his presence equipped as if ready to spar. In any case, we both know it would be an empty gesture."

The twelve lords shifted nervously in their seats, some gnawing at grapes, others inspecting the polished surface of the table. Lyrilan could not tell what most of them thought. They were closed books to him, all except Undroth and Vaduli. Perhaps it was because these two spoke most freely with him. Were the others afraid to disagree? Or were they relieved to hear the King make his own decision?

Old Volomses broke the silence. "Majesty . . . may I?"

"Speak," said Lyrilan. Volomses normally left the discourse to the lords at these meetings. Yet Lyrilan's newfound determination seemed to make the sage's tongue grow bold.

Volomses gestured to the pile of heavy books lying before him. They were six in number. "Your Majesty's strength has always been one of mind, whereas King Tyro's is of the arm and thew. Yet here in these ancient pages lies another kind of strength. One that will make the Sword King tremble. Or at the very least . . . make him listen."

"What is this, Volomses? What have you discovered?" Lyrilan eyed the topmost volume as the sage wiped a layer of dust from its embossed cover with his napkin.

"*The Books of Imvek the Silent*," said the sage. His bony fingers caressed the pile nervously.

Lyrilan's eyes narrowed. "Sorcery?" He nearly laughed. But the situation was too dire for any humor. "Would you have me learn some spell of peace to secure the kingdom? Some charm of brotherhood to mend this rift?"

The Green Lords sat quiet, not a single outraged stare or protest among them. By this Lyrilan knew that they had asked Volomses to gather these books.

"So you all would have a sorcerer as your King."

Volomses spoke for them all. "Sorcery is simply a form of knowledge, My Lord. It is known to the wise that true sorcerers are born into magic. Yet a wise man may learn the secrets of those who master universal forces. A wise man like Imvek, who traded his own tongue for such wisdom. He ruled the City of Sacred Waters for sixty years. His reign was a prosperous one."

Lyrilan could not account for this silent conspiracy. How long had the lords discussed this? How many of them were secretly studying such ancient tomes, hoping to unleash some dread magic to aid his cause? Or were they all too frightened by the potential of such power to even try? No, they were foisting the dark duty onto him. After all, he was their King. Here was an advantage he might secure for himself and for their interests. The interests of peace. But it was ludicrous.

"And how did Imvek's golden reign end?" Lyrilan asked, already knowing the answer.

Volomses lowered his head. "Imvek died, as all Men must."

"Yet he left behind a strong kingdom," interrupted Undroth, "and he wrote all his wisdom down on these pages. They've been kept hidden here since the day his third son took the throne."

"If Imvek's own sons could not master his writings, what hope have I?"

"They were warriors like Tyro . . . not scholars," offered Vaduli.

Lyrilan crossed his arms, leaned back in his padded chair. He stared at the moldering pile of leather and parchment. It was tempting. The books were priceless, if only for their historical value. Had it really come to this? Was his case so weak that only this ancient wizard's scribblings offered any hope?

No. There was still the book about his father. There was still a chance to reach Tyro and remind him of his family honor. To rekindle their father's dreams of lasting peace. Dairon had refused to go to war unless Khyrei showed direct aggression toward Uurz. This had not come to pass, save for a few missing merchant ships. And there was no actual proof that Khyrein pirates were involved. There were only swirling rumors at the time. Yet the owners of those lost ships were firmly in the camp of Tyro, Gold Lords who made their fortunes from trading with the Jade Isles. Of course they supported Tyro's vendetta; they had everything to gain from it.

Lyrilan could not let economic interests and personal wealth outweigh the cost in human lives that war would surely bring. It was worth any chance to avoid the blood debts of such a conflict. These were the words of Dairon, himself a student of history, who had written such thoughts in his own journals.

If only Tyro would read those words. That would be the true sorcery.

"I have no time for this foolishness," said Lyrilan. He rose from the table. "Undroth, send a herald to arrange a meeting with my brother in the Great Hall. I will take your suggested thirty guards.

Make the same offer to my brother. Be sure that he understands I have something of great worth to give him. And be sure that no advisors, no Gold Lords, are present in the hall."

"And no wives, My Lord?" asked Vaduli.

Lyrilan nodded. *My one chance to get Tyro away from Talondra's tongue.* "Make this clear as well. Today the two brothers must meet alone."

Lord Undroth stood, one hand on the hilt of his sheathed greatsword. "It shall be done."

Volomses followed Lyrilan out the door, a servant carrying the six ancient books for him. Lyrilan paused before entering his study. He turned to face the sage but had no words to chastise him.

"They were hidden *beneath* the library, Majesty," said Volomses. "In a secret vault built just for the purpose. Waiting all these centuries for your eyes to scan their pages ... "

Volomses knew the way to his heart.

Lyrilan sighed. "Bring them in," he said, entering the study. The tables and shelves were thick with more recent volumes ferried up from the library. "I'm sure I have a place for them somewhere."

Lyrilan sat before his desk and stared across a clutter of scrolls through the triangular window. Below, the city was still green and gold. Its towers still gleamed in the sunlight, its walls still stood strong. Its people, though thirsty, and angry, and at one anothers' throats, endured. They filled the dusty streets and teeming plazas where the day's commerce was enacted in a million tiny transactions.

If only some cool rain would fall, he thought. *It might change everything.*

As the servant arranged the *Books of Imvek* carefully upon his desk, Lyrilan asked Volomses to retrieve *The Life of Dairon, First*

Emperor of the New Blood from his bedchamber. He stared at Imvek's sextet of tomes.

These books supposedly contain magic, he mused. *Yet the book I have written must contain the most powerful magic of all. The magic of a son's love for his father. If that should fail, what hope is there in a thousand such volumes of sorcery? And here we have only six.*

He walked to the window and looked down, surveying the green expanse of the royal courtyards. He could not see clearly the gardens where Ramiyah and her ladies were walking. Yet he knew she was down there somewhere, beneath the vine-woven bowers and the tangled canopies of fruit trees. Knowing this gave him the strength to face Tyro alone.

The heat of the day was growing sharp, and the sky was absent of clouds, an endless expanse of blue above the sweltering, smoking city. Perhaps there was something in Imvek's books that might bring the rains back to Uurz? He walked back to his desk and studied the cover of the first volume. The scaled leather had once been olive-green, the hide of some great lizard no doubt, but it had faded to gray over the ages.

The Empire of Uurz was well over a thousand years old. How many Emperors had lived and died, conquered and lost, breathed and bled before the Giants came and ended the Old Bloodline? He had studied their histories, but never actually counted their number. The Old Bloodline might have gone on forever if the Uduru had not squashed it and set Dairon upon the throne. Or had there been other coups over the ages, other shifts in the royal blood? Other fresh starts? Other squabbling Brother Kings? The written histories only went back seven hundred years, so nobody really knew. Not even the wisest of sages.

We are all history unfolding, he told himself. *There is a book waiting to be written about what is happening right now. Yet I am stuck within its pages and cannot break myself free to write it.* He remembered feeling this way before, when D'zan's quest had drawn him far from the comforts of Uurz. He missed the Yaskathan King. When all of this was settled, he must arrange a trip to visit his southern friend.

Lord Undroth arrived, winged helm in hand. "My Lord," he reported, "your brother agrees to the terms. He wishes to meet upon the hour."

"Good," said Lyrilan. His midday lunch with Ramiyah would have to wait. She would understand. If his errand succeeded, if his creation could truly reach Tyro's heart, they would have something to celebrate.

Thirty guards with silver spears awaited him outside the study. He took up the book that contained his father's life and held it to his chest like a talisman.

The Scholar King and his green-clad retinue descended the tower steps and streamed through the vaulted portico of the Great Hall.

Gods of Sun and Sky, Lyrilan prayed, *let him be moved.*

In the eastern courtyard the flag of Uurz billowed atop Tyro's pavilion, a golden sun on a green field. The canvas walls of the tent were raised to admit the breezes of morning. Orderly rows of pomegranate trees stretched from the base of the palace to the foot of its eastern wall, where soldiers in golden helms and bronze mail walked the battlements. Attendants moved about the orchard bearing large urns of water hauled up from the cavern of the Sacred River. They poured the holy liquid generously among the tree roots. Thus did the royal orchards thrive, even in the midst of the long drought. The branches hung thick with swollen purple fruit.

Inside the tent the Sword King gathered with Lord Mendices and three captains of the Gold Legions. Daggers and jeweled goblets served as paperweights securing a series of dog-eared maps to the oval table. Tyro leaned forward in his chair to better view the markers and notations scrawled upon the maps. From the center of his chairback a pair of gilded wings spread from a central sun of inlaid opals. His broad chest was already bare against the heat of the day, and he wore a kilt of scarlet silk in lieu of his usual bronze girdle. Golden bracers hid the dueling scars upon his thick forearms. The emerald at the forepoint of his light crown glinted dully in the shade of the tent.

"Here . . ." Lord Mendices stabbed at the map with a pointed finger. "Where the marshes meet the Golden Sea. That is the route for our legions."

"Treacherous territory," said Tyro, tugging at his thick braid of beard. "Infested with vipers, lizards, and worse. Some say more dangerous than the jungles beyond it."

"'Tis true, Majesty," responded Lord Aeldryn. The man was the oldest of the captains, having fought with Dairon in his younger days. Tyro trusted his word, if not the strength of his now-unsteady arm. Aeldryn's gray hair was still thick, but the deepset lines on his face spoke of a weary soul. "The dangers of the lands west of Khyrei cannot be overstated. Massive beasts wander those swamps, the kind that no longer live in the northlands. Throwbacks to the Age of Serpents."

"Nonsense," said Lord Mendices. "Superstition, Your Majesty. I am certain there will be some resistance, but Serpents? We may lose a few men, I'll concede, but what beast can stand against an entire army? This route through the swamps is the only way to flank the Khyrein forces. They will never expect it because no one has ever dared to try it."

Lord Rolfus harrumphed. "None have ever tried it because it is so dangerous. You make Aeldryn's point for him. I say we approach entirely by sea. With the aid of Yaskatha's navy we'll cut round the southern horn—"

"No," said Mendices. "You revisit an argument already proven false. The Khyrein navy is formidable, perhaps the greatest in the world. Our allies' ships will serve as a diversion, while our land legions move in to sack the city from the east. The Crab Strategem. Rolfus, do not undo these last days' work by taking us backward."

Rolfus chose not to face the accusing eyes of Mendices. Few men could. Tyro watched as Rolfus chose instead the goblet of wine sitting before him, letting the red vintage fill his mouth instead of rash words. Tyro considered the advice of Mendices. There was much battle wisdom there ... and a great sense of reckless courage. He admired Mendices for both qualities. It was partly the reason he had made the bald Warlord his chief advisor. That and Mendices' hunger for destroying the threat of Khyrei once and for all. Nothing could be more important.

"Very well, Mendices," said Tyro. He glared at the three captains. "'In the midst of battle, the best choice is often the least sane choice'," he quoted. "Your advice hearkens to the words of Quorances the Fourth. His ability to surprise and confuse his enemy led Uurz to victory in the Campaign of the Southern Isles. I see no reason why the same approach will not serve us here."

"Well quoted, Majesty," said Mendices.

"The strategy is decided," said Tyro. "Now let us speak of alliances. What news from Mumbaza?"

The taciturn Captain Dorocles spoke for the first time this morning. "The King on the Cliffs remains indecisive. Undutu neither refuses nor denies our entreaties. Yet I believe we can bring him to our cause. We must remain persistent."

Tyro nodded. The Mumbazans were known for their long love of neutrality. Yet eight years ago they had marched against the Usurper of Yaskatha. Tyro had ridden with them. At that time Undutu had still been called Boy-King. Now he was a man, and must be eager to prove the might of his nation. Tyro decided that a generous gift of gold and precious stones would likely sway the balance. He would send Dorocles with a sizable amount of treasure for the ruler of the Pearl Kingdom, as soon as the business of unifying Uurz was settled.

"What of Yaskatha? Does good D'zan join us? Surely he wishes to avenge the death of his father."

Rolfus put down his wine cup. "The signs are excellent, My Lord. D'zan has sired an heir, soon to be born. He will wish to secure the safety of his kingdom now, so that his son can inherit his throne during peacetime. He awaits the birth of the child before committing his forces."

Tyro smiled. "Sharadza is pregnant? I thought her too wild and independent to settle into the role of Royal Mother."

Rolfus coughed. "Your perception is keen, Majesty. The mother of D'zan's heir is not the daughter of Vod. It seems she has ... gone missing."

Tyro sat up straighter in his chair. "Vireon will be displeased," he mused. "What is the word from Udurum?"

Mendices handled that ambassadorship. "Our envoys have yet to return, Sire. Surely your close relationship with the Slayer will bring him to our side. Although he can offer little in the way of Giant forces, his kingdom boasts a sizable army of Men these days. At least twelve legions, if my sources are correct. And there is no enemy to fight north of the Grim."

Tyro looked at him. "Do not be so quick to discount the Ninety-Nine Uduri," he said. "Yes, they are Giantesses, but they are not like human females. They are every bit as dangerous as male Giants. Perhaps even more so. Look to your history books, Mendices."

"Yes, Majesty." Mendices bristled. Tyro knew he hated being talked down to like this, even by his King. Tyro was but half his age, yet he was still the ruler of Uurz. Mendices occasionally needed reminding of the fact. The Warlord was wise in military matters, but Tyro's father had forced his sons to endure a broader education. Only now that he sat upon the throne did he value Dairon's insistence. *The sword alone is not enough*, Dairon had told his son. *The arm wields the sword, but the mind wields the arm.*

Tyro paused to sample the morning wine. Not a bad vintage, though not the sweet fruit of the deep cellars. He stood to stretch his arms while the lords picked at the fruits and bread offered by servants.

"These matters of strategies and alliances are of secondary concern to me," Tyro said. He walked into the sunlight and let it warm his face. The lords ate and drank at his back. "My mind dwells most on our local troubles. How can we set our plans in motion without the twelve legions allied to my brother? We must end the division of the Royal Court. Ideas?" The lords were silent behind him.

"I've an idea, Lord," said a feminine voice. "And a message." He turned to see Talondra approaching along the garden path. Her loose gown of black silk rippled in the slight winds. Her arms and neck were lined with jewels, and a mass of black hair fell unrestrained past her slim shoulders. Her brown skin was splendid in the sunlight, and she lost none of her glow when she stepped into the shadow of the pavilion. He walked around the table to take her in his arms, kissed her red lips. She was his lioness, an exquisite creature of dangerous grace. He feared no sword or spear, nor the wrath of any man, but her words could wound him worse than a length of *steel* in the gut. For this reason, and because he loved her so, he went to great lengths to keep her happy.

It took a woman like her, a firebrand, to make him give up his many concubines. Talondra was every bit the warrior he was, yet she fought in the ways that were available to women. She crushed her enemies by manipulating them. Before she came to him from Shar Dni, he had never thought to find a woman who could tame his wild heart. She was born to be his Queen. Her onyx eyes captivated him. He forgot all about Mendices and the three lords as her fingers danced along his bare chest. He would take her right now if she wished. Let them run like timid servants from the sight of their King's passion.

"You speak in riddles," he said, biting her ear.

She smiled. He inhaled the ripe petal fragrance of her skin. "Not at all, My Lord. Which would you hear first, my solution to your problem or the message from your brother?"

He pulled away from her, but kept his arms about her waist. "Lyrilan sends a message?"

She glided from his grasp like a viper. "Your eyes make your choice evident. Always the brother before the wife . . . "

He frowned at her. She knew that was not true. It was a little game she played for his attention. Attention he would give her in great detail tonight in their bedchamber. "Tell it, woman," he said.

"The Scholar King wishes to meet with you today. Alone. In the Great Hall he will present you with a gift. His messenger did not say what it might be."

Mendices stood, suspicion growing on his narrow face. "A ruse, My Lord?"

Tyro shook his black mane. "No, that is not Lyrilan's way. He is honest to a fault. I think he wishes to apologize and restore our shattered unity. He must be tired of the bloodshed our feud has caused."

"Would he give in so easily?" Aeldryn asked.

Tyro considered the question. He loved Lyrilan, but hated sharing the throne with someone so weak. Often he wondered why his father had not simply named him Emperor instead of endorsing this ridiculous dichotomy of state. The Stormlands empire needed an Emperor. Perhaps Lyrilan had realized this and would step down, finally letting Tyro rule. Lyrilan was not a King, not truly. He was a scribe, a quill, a haunter of libraries. He would make a fine chief advisor, but he would never be a King. At least not the one that Uurz deserved. Lyrilan did not even understand the need to rid the world of Khyrei's wicked influence.

"My spies among the Green tell me he still refuses to march on Khyrei," said Talondra. "Do not expect this to change, Lord. No doubt this is some pitiful effort to make you see the error of your ways."

Tyro drained his goblet. "Mendices, see to the arrangements."

"I'll accompany you myself," said the bald lord.

"No," said Talondra, not bothering to look at Mendices. "Speak with the messenger. He has a list of demands set by Lyrilan. He obviously fears you, Tyro. He will allow no advisors. Not even your beloved wife."

Mendices laughed. "He must fear you as well, My Queen."

She gave the lord a quick look, driving him out of the tent. The three captains rose and followed. They had grown adept at sensing when their Queen demanded privacy.

"What is this idea of yours, Sweetling?" Tyro asked. "Have you some answer to the dilemma of the Twin Kings? One that Mendices and I could not design ourselves?"

Talondra playfully avoided his grasping hands and placed herself across the table from him. He loved it when she made him chase her. He was the hunter, she was the deadliest of prey. Her eyes fell upon the war maps.

"All this," she waved a hand, "will never come to pass while your legions are divided. Yet you have the power to bring them together. You must only be strong enough to wield it."

Tyro grabbed his empty goblet and crushed it in his fist. "I *am* strong."

"Strong of arm, yes," she said. "But are you strong of heart?"

"How can you ask me this?"

"Because I know the love you bear your brother. You forbid me to speak of killing him, although it would solve all your problems and make you Emperor. Yet you forbid it, so I will not speak of it. There is, however, another way to remove this obstacle in your path to glory."

"Speak," he said. Let her come out with it. He was no Sharrian to murder his own blood kin. That course could only bring the wrath of the Sky God upon his head, a curse to any throne won by murder. The proof of his belief was the Doom of Shar Dni. The Khyreins wiped it off the map, but surely the Gods had allowed them to do so. It must have been for the sins of its rulers . . . the feuding families and the blood-soaked throne. Generations of infighting and scheming for power. He would not reduce Uurz to such a state. The Gods had set him here to cleanse the earth of Khyrei, not to fall its victim. Not to perish by his own moral weakness, as had Talondra's home. He had never spoken such thoughts aloud to her.

"*Banishment*," she whispered. A breeze blew through the tent and rustled her black locks. "Send him into exile. Someplace safe, someplace far away, where his will can no longer trouble your own."

Tyro frowned. "Do you think I have not considered this? It is impossible. I have no legal grounds. He has done nothing wrong."

"But what if he did?"

Tyro stared into her narrow eyes, pools of dark beauty. A keen wisdom swam there.

"Lyrilan is a King, like me," he reminded her. "What could he do?"

She rounded the table and curled herself about him like a purring tiger cub. "What if he went mad? Proved himself to be unworthy of the throne?"

Tyro shook his head. "But he is *not* mad. He would never do anything to warrant exile."

She raised her wet lips to his ear and let her hot breath slide into it with her words.

"He can be made to *seem* mad," she whispered. "Such an easy thing to do. Both his life and your kingdom are then spared."

He grabbed her wrists and kissed her again.

A servant came forward and kneeled a respectful distance from their embrace. "Majesty, Lord Mendices sends me to inform you: King Lyrilan approaches the Great Hall."

Tyro nodded and released Talondra. Her cleverness never ceased to amaze him. There was much to think about here. But first, he must speak with Lyrilan. His brother could also be surprising.

"Let us see what the day brings," he said.

Talondra bowed her head. "As you wish, Lord."

He left her among the trees, picking the choicest of pomegranates from the branches.

The sculpted pillars of the Great Hall stood thick as the bodies of Giants. Rays of amber sunlight streamed in through the ceiling oriels. The history of Uurz hung about the walls on tapestries of spun gold and wool. Blood-bright rubies lay scattered across the stitched fields of ancient battles, and schools of sapphires glimmered beneath the prows of woven war galleons. The marble statues of past Emperors stood upon bronze pedestals, displaying sword, spear, and crown for generations who barely knew their names. No flames burned in the golden braziers hanging about the twin thrones, for the heat of the day had found its way inside the hall. The lower casements looked out upon the emerald gardens of noonday. If one were to awake in this place with no memory of coming to Uurz, one might believe oneself in some lofty temple at the heart of a verdant forest, so deep and tall were the encircling gardens.

Lyrilan entered the hall first, thirty men of the Green Legions at his back. They placed themselves in a half-circle about his side of the royal dais, and two of them came to stand at the arms of his throne. He sat himself uncomfortably on the high seat. A pair of twin opals, each larger than a man's head, served as centerpieces for the identical thrones. Patterns of green tourmaline ran along the seatbacks and down the legs, which ended in tigerish claws bright as gold. The armrests were carved into long-bodied eagles with backspread wings. Lyrilan leaned his book against the high seat and rested his nervous hands on the skulls of the eagles.

Tyro did not keep him waiting long. Soon the Sword King entered, trailing a scarlet cloak to match his kilt, sandals gleaming with golden shinguards, a string of sapphires sparkling across his brown chest. How different he seemed now, this King of Uurz, yet how much he remained the same. His face was Lyrilan's own, yet sun-hardened, perhaps firmer of jaw. The unruly curls of his long black mane were identical to Lyrilan's own. Tyro's healthy beard, plaited by the customary gold rings, distinguished his face from that of his brother, who preferred to remain clean-shaven.

Thirty legionnaires with eagle helms and golden corselets followed Tyro into the hall. Their flapping cloaks were, of course, spun from golden silk. These soldiers formed their own arc about the dais, completing the circle begun by the Green Legionnaires. Two of Tyro's warriors stood at the back of his throne to match Lyrilan's personal guards.

Tyro climbed the five steps of the dais and sat himself on the second throne, turning sideways to look his brother in the face. A cautious smile greeted Lyrilan.

"At last, he comes down from his tower," said Tyro. "Good to see you, Brother."

Lyrilan returned the smile, though his heart was not in it. "Men die while we do not speak," he said. "This has gone on long enough."

Tyro nodded. "I agree. Are you ready to listen?"

Lyrilan raised a hand. "I have heard your arguments and found them wanting. I did not come to discuss what we have already discussed."

"Then why come at all?" said Tyro, his voice rising.

Ever the impatient one. Quick with a blade, slow of wit. *Make him listen . . . make him understand.* Lyrilan shifted in the hard seat. Perhaps thrones were meant to be uncomfortable to emphasize the pain of rulership. It seemed likely.

"I admit, I have been distracted this past year," said Lyrilan. "I have not always been available to make the hard decisions. I have dropped the burden of rulership onto your shoulders too many times. For that I am sorry."

Tyro laughed. "No need to apologize," he said. "Simply abdicate, and I'll save you the trouble of running a kingdom. You'll be free to pursue your studies and write your books. Things will be as they should always have been. You weren't meant to rule, Lyrilan. You're a sage, not a King. It's time to accept that."

Lyrilan chose not to take the bait for an endless argument. "My studies are what bring me here." He lifted the book from his side and stood. A rustling of fabric came from the Gold Legionnaires, who would have sprung to murder him if he had raised a knife or dagger instead. "This is what I have labored on since Father died. You loved him. You commissioned his statues, made by the hands of the finest sculptors in the city. This . . . is my sculpture."

Lyrilan offered him the book of Dairon's life, and Tyro accepted it. He read the title aloud, his voice barely a whisper. He laid it across the arms of his throne and flipped idly through the fresh white pages lined with dark new ink. Lyrilan sat back in his own throne, letting the weight of the volume impress itself on Tyro's hands, on his mind, on his heart.

Tyro sat quiet as he closed the volume. He ran a hand across the stiff leather of the surface. His eyes glimmered and the hardness of his jaw softened. He must have been at a loss for words. He said nothing.

"Our father's life is on these pages," Lyrilan said. "His thoughts, his philosophies, his advice. His triumphs and tragedies ... his dreams for his sons and his Empire. Read it, Tyro. Read it and tell me if you still believe he would want this war. You owe it to him, if not me. *Read it*."

Tyro glared at him. The tears welling in his sable eyes refused to fall. He was too mighty for tears, this iron-hearted warrior. He raised a hand from the book and touched Lyrilan's shoulder. He wore a smile that reminded Lyrilan of his younger self.

The brothers stood and embraced. Tyro pulled away and held Lyrilan gently by the shoulders. "No matter what happens, you are always my brother. Remember that I love you, as our father loved us both."

"Never will I forget that," said Lyrilan. "Uurz is a single kingdom with two beating hearts. This is the way our father wanted it ... green and gold together. The explanation is on these pages. I swear it."

"Then I will read them," said Tyro. "You honor his memory with this work."

Tyro called for wine, a deep vintage. The sons drank to the memory of their father.

"We will speak again soon," said the Sword King, and he departed with his gift.

Lyrilan sat upon his throne for a moment. How different this hall had seemed when he was a child chasing Tyro between the pillars. While their mother still lived, they had seen little of Dairon. He sat up here on a single massive throne in those days, dispensing wisdom and justice. Lyrilan had thought him some kind of bejeweled Giant until he came down the steps and caught both his boys in a warm bearhug. Later, years after his mother's passing, Lyrilan realized that Dairon the Emperor, Lord of the Sacred Waters, was only a Man. A frail and sad man who had lost everyone he loved but for his two young sons.

Even the greatest of Kings and Emperors were only human.

And yet, he supposed, *all fathers are Giants in the eyes of their sons.*

Talondra found Lord Mendices waiting for her, deep beneath the palace where the Sacred River flowed through a grotto lined with potted palms. The cavern's stairwells were hewn from naked limestone, and clever aqueducts used the river's own momentum to drive water toward adjoining wells and reservoirs. The river's rushing thunder filled the grotto with a dull roar, and spume wafted from its worn banks like wisps of fog. The smells here were deep earth and the clean scent of fresh water. This was the priceless treasure upon which Uurz had built its foundations; while the Desert of Many Thunders had ruled the world above, this river had sustained the City of Sacred Waters for twelve hundred years. This was the Eighth Cavern, frequented only by the lowest level of palace functionaries who filled vats of river water for domestic purposes above. There would be no one of importance here to see the Warlord meet with his Queen.

Mendices lowered his bald head as Talondra trod carefully down the slick steps. His golden breastplate glittered beneath a sable cloak and, when he bowed, only his prodigious nose showed through its hood. As she reached the bottom step his glittering black eyes raised toward her own. A strange blend of duty, honor, and lust mingled in his curious expression. She motioned for her handmaidens to linger upon the lowest stair as she approached the Warlord. His fist rested on the pommel of his sheathed sword, as if to remind her that despite this secrecy he was foremost a warrior. How deep did his infatuation with her go? Would he kill his own King to have her? Did such thoughts ever run through his hairless head? Such musing mattered little; he was only another man that her beauty had enslaved. Reflecting upon this truth, she offered him a coy smile and the back of her hand for his lips.

"Majesty, what would you have me do?" Mendices said. He released her hand as if it pained him to do so. "You need only ask."

Talondra turned her face toward the underground river. Cool air excited the skin of her naked arms. In a matter of minutes her gown would be entirely damp from the mist, yet it was not an unpleasant sensation. Sometimes she came down here to find release from Uurz's great heat. She missed the cool breezes of Shar Dni's river valley.

"Why do you ask questions to which you already know the answer?" she asked. "Tyro is too soft-hearted for what must be done."

Mendices nodded, his eyes falling upon the rough stone at her feet. Or perhaps he stared at her painted toes. She had come barefoot down the slick stairwell, the carven rock cold against her soles. "Must we do this thing, then? Without the King's approval?"

She turned her eyes to him, imagined his heart beating faster as she stepped near. Her voice was calm and low. "Often a King does not know what is best for his realm," she said. "That is what Queens are for."

Mendices rubbed his smooth head. The golden rings on his fingers glinted in the wet gloom. He nodded. "Once you give this order there is no turning back. You must be *certain*."

"I am," she said, keeping her anger in check. Often it rose like a viper from deep within her breast to sour her demeanor with its venom. She had learned to control that poison; she had made a weapon of it. "I am certain that Khyrei has no right to exist. I am certain that Uurz and its allies will wipe it off the map. And I am certain that *this* tragedy must occur first. Tyro's greatness must no longer be stymied by his brother's weak resolve. For the Sword King to rise, the Scholar King must fall."

"I could not agree with you more," Mendices said. "Yet it is Tyro who will feel the bite of this pain."

"He is a warrior," she said. "Tyro will endure this as he has endured all other wounds."

"Are you so sure of it?"

Talondra gritted her teeth and looked again toward the river. It ran black and deep with secrets. The current was fierce and relentless.

"When I was fifteen the Khyreins came to Shar Dni," she said. "A horde of bloodthirsty shadows came before them. Ianthe the Claw and Gammir the Bloody led an armada of reavers across the Golden Sea. My three little sisters and I stood upon the wall with our parents and watched the Sharrian fleet sail out to meet the cloud of darkness. You know the slaughter that followed. The bloodshadows reached our gates well before the warships. They swam through the air like smoke, falling like great bats upon man, woman, and child. I will never forget the sound of my family's screams." She offered a sidelong glance to the Warlord. "Have you ever heard an entire city scream, Mendices?"

Mendices lowered his head again. "No, Majesty." A raw whisper.

"We fled into the cellars, but the shadows followed us. My mother and father died as we watched, helpless. Their lives were torn away by dark, wolvish things. They stared at me with eyes like flames hungry enough to burn the world to a cinder. They were the servants of Death itself . . . things never meant for our world. We hid in empty wine barrels but still the creeping shadows found us. My sisters . . . "

Her voice betrayed her. She cleared her throat. Her eyes welled. She must not weep. It was not becoming for a Queen to weep.

"My sisters were torn from me. Sashai, Elymna, Tehroti . . . they were only three, five, and seven. The shadows carried them away. I heard them howling in pain as I ran. What could I do? The devils would come for me next . . . I had no protection to offer the little ones. The entire city was dying. I found my way into the bloodied streets, where the bodies of Sharrians lay like trampled flowers. The flagstones were red as rubies . . . pools of blood reflected the light of great fires. The shadows swirled, and I stood there waiting for them to take me. I had no hope left: my family was gone, and I would soon join them. Yet the shadows lingered, bloated on the feast of blood perhaps.

"Then the soldiers came with their iron-masked faces, the faces of grinning demons, and they plundered the city. You've been to war, Mendices. I don't have to tell you of the cruelties they inflicted on me.

"Then the white flame arrived. Vireon the Slayer had come to liberate us. The Khyreins fled like frightened hares. Yet the Lord of Udurum had come too late. I might well have perished that day. In some ways, I did die. Yet someone found me in the street among the corpses and nursed me back to health. When my torrid fever finally passed, I awoke days later, already on the trail to New Udurum with the survivors. I did not speak for weeks, though I wept often. Many times I considered taking my own life. But I made a choice. I would make the pale ones pay for what they had done. This was my vow, and it has brought me to Uurz and delivered me to the Sword King.

"I love Tyro as I could love no other man. He is the key to my vengeance. Now is the time to turn that key. Tyro will survive this wound . . . as I survived all of mine."

The Warlord's face was pale. If the tale of her past had moved him, he did not show it. He only nodded and raised his dark hood.

"So be it," said Mendices.

He marched up the gleaming stairwell to set their plan in motion. Talondra stared at the rushing waters, so like a flood of hungry shadows surging through the dark, penetrating the earth with its violence. Like the Sacred River itself, she would carve away all obstacles between herself and her satisfaction.

Alone now in the grotto, standing well apart from her maidens, she wept freely. The sounds of her sobs were drowned beneath the thundering river. Then she splashed river water against her face and ascended to pace the resplendent halls.

Lyrilan dined with Ramiyah on the balcony of the Western Tower. They watched the lights of the city emerge from purple twilight as the sun sank beyond the horizon, a ball of orange fire. She had brought her favorite blossoms up here from the courtyards. Their table sat surrounded by painted vases ripe with flowers, heady with the scents of tarnflower, elderleaf, jasmine, and mistblossom.

He told her about the meeting with Tyro. She shared his hopes. If the book changed Tyro's mind about Lyrilan, about Dairon, about war itself, then all would fall into place. The strife would end and the blood would cease to spill.

"Lyrilan," said Ramiyah, grasping his hands, "you must be prepared for the worst. Your brother may be beyond your reach."

Lyrilan groaned, stared across the city where evening caravans were streaming through the northern gate. A parade of camels, horses, men, and goods from north, west, and south. Eight years ago there would have been Sharrians among those traders. Yet Shar Dni was only a pile of haunted ruins now. The result of war with Khyrei.

"I *must* reach him," he told Ramiyah. "If I don't, who will?"

She wrapped her arms about him and laid her head against his chest. "Only the Gods can say. Only the Gods . . ."

He kissed her and led her into their bedchamber. In the final glow of evening they made love. "I want sons," he told her. "I have waited long enough." She breathed satisfaction in his ear.

"You . . . will have . . . many sons . . ." she promised. She sang it to him as their bodies merged in the ancient dance of man and woman.

He did his best to ensure she kept that promise. He had been too careful for too long. Too involved with his books to start a family. He would deny his wife no longer. No matter what happened with Sword King and Scholar King, a man must have sons. This was something else he had learned while writing the book of his father's life. Let the world be filled with the joy of children and the laughter of family. Let blood spill, let the Gods cast Uurz into ruin. Let Tyro march off to war if he must. Lyrilan would rule his family here, and it began on this night, in this room, in the arms of the woman he loved.

The winds of passion cast him headlong into dream. He slept deeply and fully. Dairon spoke to him from the lips of a marble statue. *Two hearts . . . one kingdom.* The voices of his unborn sons sang to him a distant melody. Lyrilan's dream-self walked alone in a garden of fruiting vines, an old man full of wisdom precious as magic. He followed the sweet song of innocence, seeking its source among the green opulence. He found the shore of a river flowing bright as silver beneath the sun. Ramiyah beckoned to him from the distant bank. She was not old like him, but young. Young as she had been on this night of nights. The night he would never forget.

The cool breath of early morning wafted through the windows. The sun rose on the far side of the palace, so that shadows lingered about the western wing. Lyrilan's eyes fluttered open in the silver gloom. A sensation of wetness came to him through the sheets. He pulled them back and discovered a world gone red.

Blood smeared his naked body, sinking into the bedding, staining it from purest white to violent crimson. The breath fell from his slack mouth as he found her lying next to him.

Ramiyah lay still. Her flesh was pale as marble but for the obscene scarlet spray on chest, arms, and shoulders.

He raised his hands. His fingers dripped a thick, congealing red.

He cradled her close to his breast and moaned. Her body was already cold as a stone.

The legionnaires found him shouting and weeping as he dragged her body about the chamber. He searched and searched, and carelessly kicked aside the bloody dagger on the carpet.

Where is it?

Where is her head?

When they carried him away, kicking and screaming, he still had not found it.

7

The Night of White Flame

Fear ran unleashed through the broad streets of Udurum. The invisible chain that normally held it far from the necks of the populace had been broken. The fear itself wore many faces: the towering forms of Uduri in plates of blackened bronze, the fourteen legions of Men who marched beneath the banner of the Fist and Hammer, the great black wall that encircled the city, and the massive gates that were locked and impervious from either side. In a single morning the city was sealed, and a forest of gleaming spears stood on every corner.

In the Merchant Quarter all commerce was halted by order of the City General, Ryvun Ctholl, a strong-jawed veteran whose green eyes spoke of Sharrian blood. Drunken caravan drivers, mercenary guards, and the most vehement of the merchants were arrested and hauled away to dank cells beneath Vireon's palace. All traffic in and out of the city halted, swelling the inns and boarding houses with travelers bound for Uurz, Tadarum, or Murala. Wagons and cartloads of produce from surrounding villages piled up outside the gates, where a dozen Uduri stood with grim faces and spears of polished *steel*. Incoming merchant trains were halted on the road. For leagues along the Western Way there sprang up makeshift merchant camps and hastily erected tents as the sun sank closer to the horizon.

Squads of legionnaires on strong southern-bred horses carried word along the road: *Udurum is closed to friends and strangers until further notice.*

Ryvun's legions quelled three riots on the first day alone. Foreign visitors did not like being told where to stay, what do do, or when they might expect to leave. The less diplomatic of these outlanders grew determined after a few hours to fight their way out. A small mêlée had ensued, and Ryvun's Palatines handled it well. Twelve foreigners dead, thirty-two more in custody, and not a single merchant willing to admit to employing any of them. Not that any seller of southern goods could truly control the ruffians he hired to guard his train. Such hirelings were men of the road, little better than thieves and scoundrels, sometimes worse. They were sellswords, not soldiers. When the Uduri showed themselves in the crowded street, the fight went out of the mercenaries, and when the first of their mighty axes cleaved a man in two, those who saw it were eager to throw down their swords. More guests for the King's dungeons.

Vireon's grip fell strongest upon those rumored or proved to be wizards, soothsayers, seers, somnambulists, or magicians. Anyone whose name was associated with sorcery in any way had been gathered up by the Palatines or the Uduri. It fell worst upon those who resisted. The Uduri brought down two whole houses with their axes and hammers, picking the inhabitants out of the wreckage and carrying them senseless to cells deep in the earth. One self-avowed wizard fought back with a few meager spells of his own, throwing naked flames from his hands. The Uduri laughed at his antics, then sliced off both his hands. They tossed him bandaged and howling behind a set of iron bars.

The sound of the city had become a constant roar. The streets resounded with chattering peasants, outraged citizens, shouting fruit-sellers, rollicking children, and strumming bards. The Uduri stood above the chaos like pillars of dark stone. Their golden braids spilled from helms of iron wrought into the shapes of black Serpents. Each Giantess remained a resolute center of calm in the swirling sea of gossip, confusion, fear, and indignation. By the eighth hour of the city's lockdown, no one dared risk the drawing of those great *steel* swords or the casting of spears tall as flagpoles. Ryvun's legionnaires patrolled the streets promoting calm, dissuading any further violence. As the sun disappeared beyond the western wall, the City General turned his coal-black charger toward the palace gates.

In the violet blush of evening, a white flame blossomed from the palace's high tower. Ryvun hailed the gate guards as the miniature sun sprang to brilliant life. In the streets surrounding the palace grounds the anxious crowd drew its breath sharply and marveled at the wondrous light. The tower was not burning, anyone could see that. Yet it flamed like a star newly born. It was the King's Tower, and all who looked upon it knew the source of that flame.

Alua the Queen, Mistress of the White Flame, worked her sorcery.

Ryvun gave the reins of his horse to the stablemaster as he watched the white flame grow. It ran down the smooth black walls of the tower like water, then spread leaping across the domes and turrets of every palace wing and spire. From every vantage point in the city people must be looking toward the white glow of the palace, amazed at the lack of smoke and the pure glow of this fire that blazed yet did not burn. The City General removed his silver helm and placed it in the crook of his arm, while the white flames spread like an intricate spiderweb, invading the courtyards and gardens that surrounded the palace proper.

Cats howled, horses bucked, and dogs ran to hide themselves as the web of white flame spread through the trees and hedges. It gave no heat, this flame, nor did it consume. It danced along paths made for human feet, leaving not a single scorched leaf or singed blade of grass. It brought light, and something else. Something that could not be named. It was fascination.

The net of flames reached the inside of the palace wall and climbed up its smooth surface. Now white fires danced atop the encircling wall, between and among the feet of patrolling legionnaires. In the bustling taverns nervous Men discussed over their cups what the Queen's white flame must mean. Women huddled their children into cellars and attics, certain of a coming apocalypse. Merchants bristled and complained among themselves, fingering their jewels at neck and wrist. Even the King's legionnaires muttered questions here and there, though none was bold enough to demand an answer from Ryvun himself.

Only the Uduri remained silent. The gravity of their charge, blended with the weight of their sorrow, made them silent, brooding icons of power. This was Vireon's city, and today he had reminded everyone of that fact. He would not let the deaths of six Uduri or the infiltration of his palace go unanswered. In the search for truth and justice, Ryvun Ctholl was the King's right hand. Since Vireon had taken the throne from his mother seven years ago, Ryvun had served him with pride, just as he had served Vireon's father for a decade previous. He carried Vireon's trust, which was a stronger weapon than sword or spear could ever be.

As for the blacksmith Trevius, the unfortunate who had discovered the massacre at the Three Stallions, Ryvun himself had dragged the man before the King earlier in the day. Trevius had not put up a fight when the Palatines invaded the sleeping room behind his smithy and clasped irons about his wrists. He was still half-drunk from the night before and in no mood to argue. He walked between the warriors like a timid child, looking about with anxious twitching eyes.

Vireon sat on his throne that day in uncomfortable silence. His orders were given in close whispers, to Ryvun, to Dahrima the Axe, and to a handful of chancellors. Most of the time he spent staring at a tapestry that showed his father Vod battling the Father of Serpents. His thoughts were unknowable. The King took no wine and refused a fine lunch of roasted pork. It was just after midday when Ryvun presented the blacksmith on his knees before the throne.

"Tell me what you saw," Vireon commanded.

Trevius did not pretend ignorance. He knew why he had been called here. Vireon made him tell his story five times before rising from the throne. He came down to stand before the trembling blacksmith. "You saw no man outside the tavern? No man living inside it?"

"No, My Lord," stammered the blacksmith. "As I said . . . I am a man of few friends. I hoped to find Finney the Cobbler at the Three Stallions. We sometimes drink together. Thank the Sky God he was not there or he would have . . . " Trevius's voice trailed off. His eyes rolled up at Vireon, who towered over him like an Uduri over a turnip stand.

Vireon crouched then to look Trevius in the eyes. His hands reached out to grasp the blacksmith's shoulders. The man's face was pockmarked, etched by a half-hundred little scars made by flying embers and pieces of cinder. His arms were likewise covered in miniscule wounds, and one great scar ran across his left forearm. This was a working man, not a weaver of deadly sorcery. The King knew this as much as Ryvun did.

"Tell me something I can use, Trevius," Vireon asked. "*Anything*. All those men and women torn to pieces . . . their hearts stolen. And now it happens to Uduri in my own house."

Shock and horror fell across Trevius' craggy face. His chains rattled as he wiped the sweat from his sweaty beard. "Oh, My King ... " Tears welled in his eyes. "Some evil thing has fallen upon us. I would give my life to help you if I could. But I am only good for hammering and smoothing metal. It is all I have ever known."

Vireon tightened his grip on the man's shoulders. "Think!" he said. "Any detail you might recall could be a clue as to who conjured this curse."

The blacksmith wept in his King's grasp, opening his mouth and closing it dumbly again, like a fish gasping for air. Vireon endured this for a moment, then stood and turned away.

"A lady ... " murmured the blacksmith. His choked voice was barely audible.

Vireon turned back to him. "Yes?"

"I heard ... just before I opened the door and saw ... the blood. I heard something like ... "

"What did you hear? Tell me!"

The blacksmith's swollen eyes turned to Vireon. "It was the sound of a lady's voice ... and she was laughing. I thought it came from inside the tavern ... but there was only death inside." Trevius stared into space, amazed at his own recollection. "Surely it must have fallen from some open window nearby ... but I was sure it came from within the tavern."

Vireon sighed. His big hand squeezed the man's shoulder. "I believe you," he said.

"What could it mean, Majesty?" asked Trevius. "All the ladies inside were ... were ... "

"Perhaps not," said Vireon. He ordered the blacksmith's chains removed, and the man returned to his smithy with a few new gold coins in his pocket.

Vireon had gone back to his throne. There he sat brooding for the rest of the day, while Ryvun and his legions secured the city with the support of the Ninety-Three Uduri.

Now, as Ryvun entered the palace once again, the white flame glimmering on his silvered corselet, he accepted a cup of wine from a servant. "How is the King?" he asked.

The servant shook his gray head. "Not good, Sir Ryvun. He's sat right there in the Great Chair all day, staring at his own thoughts. The only respite from his brooding was when the little one came to sit upon his knee. She sleeps in his arms now."

The servant also told him the Queen was in the high tower, though the City General already knew that. The spread of the white flame across the grounds had told him as much.

Vireon cradled the Princess Maelthyn in his lap. Her tiny head lay in the crook of his beefy arm. It was as if he held a sleeping babe, not a child of seven years. He stared at the great windows along the front wall where white flames dripped like a syrupy rain. About the throne brooded seven Uduri spearmaidens, as was customary, and at each of the room's twenty pillars stood one of Ryvun's Palatines, mailed in silvered bronze like himself. The crimson plumes atop their helmets seemed ludicrous in the oppressive mood of the hall.

There were two extra Uduri in the throne room now: Dahrima the Axe sat pensively on the dais steps before the King, and old Gallida the Eye lingered nearby, leaning on her ancient staff of black Uyga wood. Her long braids were gray, ringed with bands of green bronze. She was the eldest of all the surviving Uduri, and her age made her resemble a human woman in her seventies. Yet Gallida was several centuries old.

Ryvun approached the throne with a low bow and presented himself for report. Vireon watched the dancing flames and scarcely noticed the City General. Only when Ryvun addressed him directly did his reverie break. He turned his eyes toward Ryvun, the man who was his voice and his fist in the streets of the city. Something about Ryvun reminded him of Tadarus. Was it the cast of his face, or the bearing of his shoulders? Perhaps it was the single-mindedness with which Ryvun took his duties – more seriously even than his life. Next to Vireon, Alua, and the loyal Uduri, here was the being who held the most power in Udurum.

In the days of Vireon's ancestors, humans were not even permitted north of the mountains, let alone into the city or in command of its legions. Yet Ryvun Ctholl had earned his status. Men must be ruled by Men, or they will grow to resent their ruler. Vireon was little more than half-Man. Vod had been half-Man, half-Giant, so what did that make his sons? What did it make Maelthyn? Such thoughts swirled in Vireon's head like murky vapors as he watched the white flames dance. He was tired.

"Pardon me, Your Majesty," said Ryvun. "A word?"

The warm comfort of Maelthyn in Vireon's lap drew his attention before he responded to the City General. Alua was locked in the high tower consulting the Spirits, spinning her white flame in order to snare some truth. Would she find the same truth he expected? Would she see clearly the Curse of Fangodrel, and, if so, could she do anything to end it?

"I am listening," said Vireon, turning his eyes away from Maelthyn's face to Ryvun's own. "Speak."

"All that you commanded has been done," said Ryvun. "The cold blocks are full of prisoners, with special accommodation for those accused of sorcery. Interrogations will commence at any moment. The streets are restless, but all insurrections have been quelled. Yet when the dawn comes, the people will demand answers. And freedom."

Vireon looked about the hall at the blurred faces of his advisors, the chancellors, the servants waiting for his next order, then back to his daughter's sweet face. His greatsword leaned naked against the throne, close to his right arm.

I let them in. He heard Maelthyn say it again in the echo chamber of his mind. What had she meant by those words? She was only a frightened little girl. He did not tell Alua what Maelthyn had whispered to him when they found her among the dead Uduri.

They came for me. He could not let his daughter believe such a thing. He had urged her to silence. Alua had bathed and dressed her while attendants cleared the bedchamber of blood and bodies. The royal family spent the morning in the courtyard, surrounded by a hundred Palatines and twenty-six Uduri guards, who bore their grief in silence.

Whatever devils had crawled into Udurum had eaten the hearts and lives of six Giantesses in addition to a tavernful of humans. Perhaps the missing hearts were the keys to the mystery. But what could this consumption of living hearts portend? The question had plagued him all day. He had not the wisdom to answer it. He hoped Alua would find some supernatural guidance.

"The people will have to wait," said Vireon. "We will see what the night brings. These unseen devils may come calling again."

Ryvun bristled beneath his armor. "If we inform the populace of the *reason* for our drastic measures, it might provide them with more patience."

Dahrima the Axe stood now, golden braids clanking against her ebony corselet. The long-hafted weapon that inspired her nickname stood balanced on the marble floor at her feet. Her right hand lingered on its upraised pommel. At any moment she might lift that weapon to the defense of the crown. In the past two days Vireon had grown accustomed to her constant presence, and the Uduri had naturally accepted her as their captain.

"The King has invoked Uduri Law," said Dahrima. "He need give no justification for this, Legionnaire."

Ryvun raised his eyes to meet those of the Giantess. "I am not a legionnaire, Dahrima. I am the City General. Address me properly or do not speak in my presence."

Vireon saw Dahrima's fists tighten. She bore little love for the Men who helped secure the city. To her the Uduri were all the military might Udurum needed. When the Uduru were here, Vireon might have agreed that an armed force of Men was redundant. Now, though, it was primarily a City of Men, with the Uduri living in perpetual denial of the fact. If Vireon told them to drive all humans from the city tomorrow, they would do it without question. Their unflagging loyalty had been a source of great comfort to him over the past seven years. Yet now, seeing how mortal even these colossal warrior-women were, nothing seemed as certain as it had been a few days earlier.

"I hear wisdom in your words, Ryvun," said Vireon. "Yet I will not fill the streets with word of these blood-hungry spirits. People would panic, they would seek escape. Violence would be the only result. First we must know more about this elusive enemy."

"How fares the Queen in her . . . studies?" asked Ryvun.

Vireon stared again at the white flame dripping past the windows, blazing in the courtyards, dancing along the outer walls.

"We will know soon," he said. He turned back to Maelthyn in his arms.

They will never take you, he promised silently. *I will die first.*

"I see," said Ryvun. "So there is little to do but wait."

"So you see we are waiting," said Dahrima. She sat once more in her place at the foot of the dais. She turned her face from Ryvun and stared at the floor.

Gallida the Eye stepped toward the throne. Bone talismans and metal charms tinkled in her silver hair. She walked with the help of her staff, pressing its bronzed butt against the marble to support a weak leg. One of her eyes was larger than the other, and the Uduri said she could see beyond the living world with it. Gallida had the Sight, and Dahrima had brought her to the throne room at Vireon's command. When Vod had come to claim his crown decades ago, Gallida was the first to confirm the truth of his Uduru bloodline. She had seen the truth of his existence, for that was her gift.

So far this day the Eye had nothing to tell Vireon. Yet now she shuffled forward and peered directly at the sleeping Princess.

"Such a beautiful girl . . ." said Gallida. Vireon studied the wrinkled map of the Giantess's face. Once, long ago, she had been beautiful. Her eyes were not always so skewed, her flesh not so withered, her shoulders not so bent. He felt the great power of her stare, and he could tell that she still carried much strength in her great wiry arms. The seeress reached a gnarled finger out to caress Maelthyn's cheek. Quickly she withdrew the digit, as if she had touched a hot flame. She sucked in a breath quickly between yellowed teeth.

Vireon saw the shadow that fell upon her face as she stared at Maelthyn. A wholly different look than before – awe . . . confusion . . . fear?

"What is it, Old One?" asked Vireon.

Gallida backed away, but her milky eyes remained locked on Maelthyn. Her black-nailed finger still pointed at the girl. "Here lies your child," she told Vireon. "Yet it is not your child."

Vireon drew a deep breath. Gallida was known for speaking in riddles. Riddles that led eventually to Truth. Yet she was old and tired. Could her legendary Sight be trusted?

"Explain yourself," Vireon ordered. He wiped a loose strand of hair away from his daughter's closed eyes. "This is surely Maelthyn, Princess of Udurum."

"Yes," said Gallida, her eyes (big and small) never leaving the child. "And no."

Vireon caught the gazes of Dahrima and Ryvun, one displaying a keen interest, the other full of doubt.

"Something has . . . emerged . . . " said Gallida. "Some dark seed has taken root and grown here."

"Speak plainly!" Vireon demanded. Maelthyn shifted restlessly in his arms. He regretted his raised voice. He did not want to wake her. It had been a troubling day for them all, especially the little one.

Gallida tore her gaze away from the child and looked at the father. She leaned in close to the man-sized throne and breathed a sour wind into Vireon's face. Her voice was a ragged, terrified whisper: "Something hides itself within your daughter, Vireon Vodson."

Vireon gave no response. The Giantess pulled away. She whispered once more, "Something wicked . . . and *hungry*."

A simmering rage clouded Vireon's vision. He fought the urge to order Gallida the Eye thrown out of the palace. He gritted his teeth and looked upon Maelthyn's sweet face instead. Gallida wandered out of the throne room, silent as a brooding raven.

Vireon turned to Dahrima, who looked at him with concern. "What did she mean?" he asked.

Dahrima shook her head. "She is old, Majesty. She does not see clearly anymore. Her gift is lost." Vireon knew she was lying. The Uduri were terrible liars. Their eyes gave it away every time. She could not meet his gaze. Dahrima believed what Gallida had seen. But she would not let it affect her duties in any way.

"Shall I have her arrested, Lord?" asked Ryvun.

Dahrima glared at the City General. Her eyes spoke a challenge that her mouth dare not.

Vireon shook his head. "Let her be."

He recalled the blacksmith's confession. *A lady's laugh.* Thoughts clanged together in his thick skull like the ringing of iron shields. *Something hides within your daughter.*

Your children will be born into shadow.

Vireon's eyes welled. Hot tears ran, then cooled and dried upon his cheeks. Ryvun and Dahrima said nothing as they watched their King weep over the sleeping form of his daughter. What could they say to comfort him? What could any man – or Giant – say? That he was cursed?

This he already knew.

Alua's scream shattered the silence. It fell from the high tower as clearly as the peal of an iron bell. The white flames danced higher and flamed brighter, a diamond-flickering lattice across the entire palace and its grounds. Travelers must have seen that mountain of brilliance flickering far out along the Western Way, where they endured a night of mud and nervous bellies.

Maelthyn was the first to respond. Her blue eyes flew open and she leaped from her father's lap, running down the steps of the dais.

"Mother!" she cried. Vireon came down after her. He bent to catch her as she raced toward the sound of Alua's pain, but she was too fast for him. She had all of his inhuman speed and none of his bulk. All he could do was run after her. He took up his greatsword and did so. Palatines and Uduri came rushing after him. He raced along the central corridor to the wide stairs winding up into the King's Tower. Maelthyn ran ahead of him, her black hair bobbing up and down.

It reminded him briefly of the day, eight years past, when he had chased Alua through the northern snows. She had worn the form of the white fox, and he was her desperate hunter. The fox had avoided him for days, eventually revealing her true self. He never caught her, but later she rescued him from a prison of the blue-skinned Udvorg. So their love had been kindled in the frosty northern clime.

Now Maelthyn raced quicker than a fox up the stairs. Vireon

followed, taking two steps at a time. He half expected his daughter to suddenly become a leaping cat or flying bird, so great was her speed. Obviously she had inherited something of her parents' power.

Or had she?

Something hides within your daughter.

The doors of the royal bedchamber stood open, releasing a flood of white light. The two Uduri who guarded the doorway stood staring at the fierce glow, captivated by the spectacle of Alua's floating body. She hung suspended halfway between floor and ceiling, centered in a nimbus of rushing, blazing light. She was the nexus at the core of the web of white flame. The pure light of her sorcery radiated from eyes, mouth, fingers, and toes. The Queen of Udurum should be immune to all enemies here, at the heart of her seething magic. Yet she had screamed in agony.

Maelthyn and Vireon raced between the dumbfounded Uduri and stood beneath Alua's hovering figure. The trance had claimed her completely. She did not or could not acknowledge them. Could she see at all with those pale flames blasting from her eyes? The white magic washed over Vireon, prickling his skin, making his mane of hair dance to invisible winds. Maelthyn raised her little hands toward Alua. She cried out something, a word Vireon could not hear. The thunder of the white flames rushed to fill his ears, and the merciless light blinded him.

Alua turned her blazing face downward, and she screamed again. Now a fresh wave of white flame erupted, driving Vireon back toward the door. The guards rushing into the chamber fell back, along with the Uduri. Looking past his upraised forearm, Vireon saw the vague outlines of mother and daughter at the center of a swirling inferno. Maelthyn was rising, even as Alua descended to join her. Then his eyes were forced to close, or else be blinded forever.

He had seen this display of power once before, on the day Shar Dni fell to a Khyrein invasion. The day he'd killed his murderous brother and Alua had destroyed Ianthe the Claw. The Sorceress of Khyrei had tried to flee, but Alua's white flame caught her, immolated her, devoured her. There was nothing at all left of the wicked Empress when the light had faded. Alua's magic had burned her out of existence.

Now the blaze faded again, and Vireon dared to open his eyes. They stood on the floor now, mother and daughter, locked in an embrace. The white flames ran along their bodies, spilling like rainwater from their skins, sluicing across the floor, out the open windows, flashing across the city.

Slowly the flames faded to nothing. The glow outside the palace was once again that of moon and stars.

Alua embraced Maelthyn with a loving smile. Vireon raced forward to join them, but stopped when both their faces turned to stare at him. They smiled as one.

"The evil is gone, My King," Alua told him, stroking Maelthyn's hair. "I have cleansed it from the land."

Vireon blinked. Maelthyn looked up at him and smiled. Her mother's smile. They were so much alike, it still amazed him. He dropped the greatsword and wrapped them both in his arms.

"Don't fret, Father," said Maelthyn, taking his great hand between her two small ones. "Everything is as it should be." Her blue eyes bored into his. Her pupils were now of such a dark blue that they seemed nearly black.

Vireon nodded and laughed. He took her in his arms and lifted her up. Alua kissed his cheek. Her pale skin still gleamed with the glow of fading magic.

"You can let the fools in your dungeons go free now," said Alua. "They are all innocent."

"Tell me what happened," Vireon said.

"Later," said Alua, caressing his cheek. "I am weary. I must rest . . ."

"Of course."

Maelthyn would not leave her mother's side. She slid into the great bed with Alua. "Come," Alua beckoned him. Some instinct or restless itch dissuaded him.

"No," he said. "I will not sleep this night. Take your rest now. I will remain here, watching over you."

Vireon dismissed all but the two Uduri door guards, and soon mother and daughter lay asleep beneath the purple blankets. He sat near to the bed on a cushioned divan, watching the two of them. They breathed in a simultaneous rhythm. Each day Maelthyn grew more and more like her mother. Had Alua truly destroyed the heart-eating devils so easily? He could not be sure until he spoke with her more at length. Until that time he could only sit here, greatsword across his knees, and ensure that his wife and daughter slept undisturbed. He took a little mulled wine from a discreet servant, but did not remove his gaze from the royal bed.

Sir Ryvun approached him after a little while, bowing to ask, "Should I release the prisoners and open the gates, Majesty?"

Vireon watched little Maelthyn's chest rise and fall. The love he bore for her was so mighty, it could ultimately destroy him. This is what it meant to be a father. To open yourself to the risk of tragedy in order to receive the blessings of love.

"No," he told Ryvun. "Let it stand."

The City General marched off to his supper while Vireon sipped at his cup and watched his family sleep. Dahrima the Axe lingered outside the chamber door, conversing softly with her two sisters. Wrapped in the sound of their whispers, nestled in the flickering warmth of torches, Vireon felt his eyes grow heavy. He laid his head back against the divan.

In his dream he spoke with his dead father, as he had done on many occasions. Vod was an idol of stone, but his mouth and eyes moved as if they were living flesh. Vireon was a youth again, just old enough to learn the way of the sword. Father and son sat in a dark cavern somewhere far beneath the earth. Flames burned somewhere beyond the enclosing shadows, casting the dream in shades of orange and black.

I never wanted to be King, said Vod. His voice was grinding stone.

You were a Great King, said Vireon.

So say Men and Giants. But there are others. Those who walked this world before any of our kingdoms existed. A flow of blood and ages you cannot fathom. We are tiny things tossed on the ocean of time.

Why did you leave us? Vireon asked.

I loved you, said the stone Vod.

Why did you leave? he asked again.

I was mad, said Vod. *She drove me mad. You know this.*

Mother? Mother drove you mad?

The stone Vod frowned at him.

No, Son. It was the other one. The sorceress. The White Panther. Ianthe.

He started awake with a jerk that nearly toppled him from the couch. His sword fell clanging to the floor. The name in his mind had shocked him awake.

Maelthyn, too, was awake. She sat on the edge of the bed, staring at him. She blinked. "Did you have a nightmare?" she asked. Her voice was innocent, playful.

Vireon looked at his daughter. Alua lay still sleeping behind her. He rubbed his face with both hands.

Maelthyn stared at him with infinite patience.

The crackling of flames in a brazier filled the silence.

"What is your name?" he whispered.

Maelthyn smiled. "You already know."

She leaped for him, as she had leaped into his arms many times.

But this time she landed in his lap with her little fingers wrapped tight about his throat. She bared her teeth like a rabid dog. Her eyes were glistening black jewels.

The torches died in an instant, the burning braziers extinguishing themselves. A flood of darkness fell into the room through the open casements. Suddenly the tiny hands about his throat were great grasping claws pressing into his stone-hard flesh.

Shadows flowed across the floor where the white flame had earlier danced. They converged on Maelthyn as she crouched in Vireon's lap. She opened her tiny mouth impossibly wide. A black maw full of crooked fangs hung before his face. She roared at him, assaulting his ears. Alua slept an arm's length away.

It was not his daughter that squatted atop him. It was a black wolf, flapping leathery wings against its shoulders. Larger than a full-grown man now, it strangled him, seeking to drive the points of its talons through his bronze skin. In the corners of his eyes, similar beasts prowled about the room. Some walked on all fours, others upright like wolfish Men. Some sprouted extra arms from their sides, multiple claws for rending and tearing. A black Serpent flowed in through the window and wound itself about a pillar. Its head was a leering wolf skull with crimson eyes, staring at him with a bottomless appetite.

The wolf-beast atop him whispered in his ear.

Blood is power, Father. I want your blood.

The Heart is Emperor of the Blood.

Give me your heart . . .

The cold talons dug at his chest now, piercing his skin like no arrow or blade had ever done. This thing – Maelthyn? – wanted to open him up. To feast upon the very center of his being. He understood now. These shadow-things took power from the hearts they devoured. They took life from the slaughter.

Black shapes slithered and loped beyond the door of the

chamber, where the battle cries of Uduri rang out against the night. Soon other voices joined. The clash of *steel* and the tramping of boots. The ghosts were filling the palace, searching for blood and hearts.

They serve me, Father. They feed it all to me. All that blood. All that power.

I've waited so long for this.

Seven long years . . .

Vireon cried out, sinking his fingers into the dark substance of the wolf-beast on his chest. With a grunt, he hurled it across the room. Something hit the far wall. It was again the frail body of Maelthyn, with bloody little fingers. She wept, then laughed horribly. Once again Maelthyn pounced, this time crossing the entire length of the bed. Vireon bent to grasp the hilt of his fallen sword. She landed on his back, tearing and rending his stubborn flesh. She was a frightened little girl inside a ravenous wolf-shadow, a blood-hungry monstrosity.

The howls and screams of dying men filled his ears now. The hungry spirits were feasting. Alua slept through it all.

He wrenched himself backward, slamming the beast on his back against the wall. He heard a little girl's moan mingled with a beast's yelp. It sickened him. He leaped away and faced the swirling mass of shadow that had been Maelthyn. She stared up at him with a lupine face, fangs distorting her jaw, distended and horrible. Her eyes were the same: black jewels, though now they gleamed with malevolence. Her arms had grown longer than her body, the claws curling and twitching, dripping with her father's blood. A red tongue slid out from between her fangs to lick at the crimson droplets.

All at once it came to him: this was not his daughter. Whatever it was, it was not Maelthyn. There was no Maelthyn. Only this mockery of life, this dark seed waiting to bloom.

Something is hiding within your daughter. Something wicked.

Ianthe.

He said the name aloud as he stared over his glinting blue blade at the wolf-ghost.

She laughed. It was not the laughter of a child, but the malicious glee of a grown woman.

Shadows swirled behind Vireon, swarmed about his legs, over his shoulders, into his mouth. Ravenous maws gaped close to his flesh, while heavy chains seemed to wrap his limbs. He could no longer move. The sword in his fist was useless. The shadows held him steady, baring his chest for Maelthyn – *Ianthe!* – as she drew near.

She reached a single talon out to draw a red line across his chest, just above the heart.

Such power in the heart of a Giantborn, she said.

Power you never even knew.

The talon's tip punctured his skin with a popping sound and sank deep.

He would have screamed, but wriggling fingers of shadow choked him.

A flash of silver split the gloom. Dahrima's axe cleaved the dense shadow. Now the massing darkness split, dividing itself between Vireon and the Giantess. It coalesced about Dahrima's limbs and torso, digging fangs and talons into her flesh. The hungry ghosts sought both their hearts now. The axe blade sliced through the shadows restraining Vireon, but it could not harm them. Might as well fight water with a knife.

Dahrima would die for him, as would any of the Uduri. They would all die this night if he let this thing devour him.

Maelthyn clung to his chest and shoulder, her feet now claws wrapped about his thighs. She tore at his flesh, scoring and slashing his skin in the effort to reach inside his ribcage.

Vireon leaped across the chamber with the strength of an angry tiger, and all the shadows but Maelthyn lost their grip for a fleeting moment. The jump landed him atop the broad bed where Alua slumbered. Maelthyn's wolf jaws snapped at his face, slathering him in shadow filth.

The mass of shadows rushed forward to reclaim him as he raised the greatsword high. He plunged it into the snarling she-beast with all his might. The blade sank deep into the mattress, pinning the false Maelthyn beneath him. She wailed a cry of pain that combined a child's torment with a demon's lust. It broke his heart.

He wept as she writhed on the blade, the entire shadowy substance of her wolf-body flowing away from the metal like greasy pitch. The shadows enclosing his body faded into nothing, nightmares vaporized by a waking dreamer.

Maelthyn, only a little girl again, scurried across the bed to her mother. Alua woke immediately at her touch. Vireon pulled his blade free of the mattress, scattering a cloud of goose feathers across the sheets. The cobalt *steel* was soiled with black blood. Or whatever passed for blood among the ghost-wolves.

Alua stared at Vireon in utter horror as Maelthyn's tiny arms wrapped about her neck. They both looked at him now as if *he* were the monster. He stood over them, greatsword poised, panting and bleeding and ready to kill. In the eyes of Alua he saw only terror. She grasped Maelthyn closer to her. The child was bleeding red from a deep puncture wound at the center of her belly. The same wound gaped from her narrow back.

"Father wants to kill me!" she screeched.

Alua rolled from the bed with her daughter held close. Maelthyn buried her head in Alua's bosom, sobbing like an infant.

"Vireon! Get away! Stay away from us!" Alua shouted. Her eyes were fixed upon Vireon's bloody sword.

Behind him Dahrima lay panting and bleeding on the marble. The shadow-beasts had fled or gone into hiding beneath the palace stones. Now he knew who summoned them, and why. This creature was *not* his daughter.

"Give her to me," he said, reaching a bloody hand to his wife.

"No!" Alua bellowed, dashing away from him. "You're mad! Like your father!"

"Look!" he yelled at her. "See what this *thing* has brought upon us! This is not our daughter! It's not!"

Alua looked across the chamber at the dazed Dahrima. The Giantess rose slowly to her feet, searching for her fallen axe. If there were any signs of the shadow-beasts left, Alua surely did not see them.

"She is Ianthe," Vireon said. "She made you sleep. She has fooled us both since the day you burned away her body. This is not our child . . ."

Alua called for the guards, but none came. She moved toward the tall open window. Stars glittered in the black canopy of night. "Stay back," she said. "You're mad, Vireon. Maelthyn is your daughter — *our* daughter — you know this to be true! You love her as you love me! Lay down your sword. Don't do this thing."

Vireon shook his head. Sweat and blood flew from his locks.

"No, she has you in her spell. Give her to me. She is Ianthe."

"Ianthe is dead!"

Alua unleashed a wall of white flame. It rushed across Vireon, this time with terrible heat. He screamed and dropped the blade.

Through the brightness he saw the faces of mother and daughter looking at him. Maelthyn kept her arms firmly wrapped about her mother's neck. Alua said nothing as the white flames blew through her hair.

It was the false Maelthyn who spoke for both of them. "I don't need your blood after all, Father," she said. "I already have it."

The white flame swirled about the mother–daughter pair and Vireon squinted into the glare. "No!" he screamed. "Let her go!"

A sphere of white flame surrounded them both. Vireon knew what this meant.

The flaming sphere flashed out the tower window.

Vireon leaped empty-handed after it.

His arms penetrated the flames up to the elbows. His fingertips brushed Alua's heel as she rose higher into the night.

He fell then from the highest window in his colossal palace. Time ceased its flow. He watched the white flame race like a comet into the northern sky as he plummeted.

The courtyard trees rushed up to meet him like a forest of green spears. His view of the comet was lost behind the palace's outer wall when he fell past its rim. The tangled foliage accepted him as a pond accepts a heavy stone. Branches cracked and splintered.

He crashed to earth, steaming like a doomed meteor.

8

Bloodshadows

H er first sensation was the sound of rain pelting stone. A chorus of thunder moaned somewhere in the distance. The cool night wind caressed her face and arms. She opened her eyes to discover the apex of a vaulted ceiling. She lay on a soft bed, her body wrapped in dark silk with hems of black lace about the neck and sleeves. The flickering of a single flame cast dancing light across the walls. About the chamber seven leaf-shaped windows stood open to the storm, revealing only darkness and silvery rain.

She could not raise her heavy head from the pillow. Trying to do so only brought pain . . . a raw sensation of torn flesh beneath the line of her jaw. Her fingers twitched on the brocaded blanket, but her arms would not obey. The muscles in her legs flexed, but she could not move them. She lay helpless in the silver gloom as damp mists wafted in through the windows. She tried to cry out, but only produced a gurgling moan. A twinge of fire burned inside her gashed throat.

Something dark and glittering lurked in the far corner of the chamber. It moved slowly from an open window toward the bed. Her eyeballs shifted inside their sockets. The bed itself lay at the very center of the room, and she could not see the floor. Nor could she see the face of the dark figure that strode closer. Yet this she did not need to see. She knew it was her half-brother who stood over the bed now. She reached past his looming presence into the storm itself, called upon the lightning to strike this chamber, reduce it to rubble. Another knell of distant thunder was her only answer.

A low chuckle reached her ears as she fought to change her shape. As owl or eagle she would flee into the storm and take her chances. Yet her stubborn body lay where it was, heavy as lead and helpless as an infant. A pair of yellow eyes gleamed above her. A white smile framed by thin lips red as blood. His hair was long and black, combed smooth as the silken bedsheets, his robe a starry mantle of darkness set with constellations of tiny jewels.

"Sister, at last you awake." His voice was deep and calm. There was none of the wolf in it. He could obviously hold that side of himself completely at bay. A pale hand reached out to caress her cheek. His flesh was cold against hers. A rash rose across her skin. Her tongue, like her body, would not move. The predator's eyes stared into her own. "It pleases me greatly that you have come. You are most welcome here."

A coughing in her throat. "You wish to speak?" he asked, smiling. "Only promise that you will treat with me gently. I could not bear harsh words from you."

Suddenly her tongue broke free of its bondage. "Fangodrel—"

He cut her off with a raised finger. His nails were long and black. Talons.

"No," he said. "Never call me that again. That name was given to me by a false father. My name, as I have told you, is Gammir. If you wish to speak, you must remember this."

"Gammir." The word fell from her mouth like a profanity.

He nodded, stroking his pointed chin, where a narrow beard

was plaited with silver thread. He had removed the black crown, exposing his alabaster forehead.

"Yes." He grinned. "Now you have it."

"I knew it was you," she said.

He sat down on the bed beside her. She could move her mouth, but her body still lay immobile. The coppery smell of blood lingered about him. "Of course you did," he said. "You were always such a smart girl. You and your books . . . such a curious child. See where it has brought you?"

"You . . . you killed Tadarus," she said. "Why?" Tears might have welled in her eyes, but she did not even have his permission to weep. His mastery of her was total.

"Tadarus was a blustering fool," he said. "He always hated me because he sensed that I was different. I needed his blood to awaken my sorcery. The Blood of Vod is powerful. That same gifted blood fills your own veins."

"Will you . . . " she could not say it. She tried again. "Will you feed on me as well?"

How was he forbidding her magic? Even when Elhathym had turned her to stone, she had been able to reach out with her mind, to call upon an ally. Now her consciousness lay trapped within her mortal shell, and her mortal shell was trapped within this storm-racked tower.

He laughed. "I already have," he said. His fingers brushed the open wound in her throat. She bristled with agony. "And your blood is far sweeter than your poor brother's."

Now she understood. His fangs had opened her neck. He drank her blood. This was how he gained control of her entire body.

The Part is the Whole. While my blood is in his belly, he is the master of my physical form. What have I done?

"You begin to understand," he said. "You are mine, as long as I wish it. This mortal flesh of yours is only so much clay for me to mold. However, I enjoy its natural shape." He ran a hand along her arm. She gritted her teeth. "So I will be gentle with you."

"You rend my flesh, drink my blood – hold me prisoner – and call this 'gentle'?"

Gammir rose from the bed and turned to stare at the glimmering sheets of rain outside the windows. "Very well," he said. "You may rise."

A sudden warmth rushed into her arms and legs. She raised herself from the pillows, groaning at the pain of her neck wound. She lifted a hand to explore its severity. Gingerly she probed the split flesh. Upper and lower incisors had raked her throat to create parallel lacerations. The mark of a rabid hound. The twin gashes were puckered and swollen now. Bloodless. Were they healing already?

She moved her legs off the edge of the bed and sat leaning on her right elbow. A great weariness lay still upon her. How much of her blood had he drained so far?

The gown she wore was antique in style and craftsmanship, yet stunningly beautiful. Her feet were bare on the cold stone. She shivered in the damp air. Now she saw the source of the flame, a single brazier hanging from a rafter chain. Beyond the windows lay only rain and rushing stormclouds thick enough to blot out moon and stars. Somewhere far below the seven windows slept the black city. This chamber must sit high atop one of the palace's barbed towers.

Gammir turned from the window to face her. "You like the gown? It suits you."

She ignored this. "Fa— Gammir," she said. "Why not simply kill me? Do you keep me alive only for the pleasure of mocking me? Or would you make me your slave?"

"That is entirely up to you," he said. He stepped closer, black robe glistening. She flinched. "Tell me, has the Royal Court of

Yaskatha lost its appeal? Have you grown weary of that foolish boy who wed you?"

The face of D'zan sprang into her mind. It was not King D'zan with his crown and golden corselet. It was the D'zan she knew in the quiet hours, the tawny-haired lad that she fell in love with so many years ago. Where had that lad gone? Kinghood had devoured him.

"Your silence tells me everything I need to know," said Gammir. His eyes flashed golden. Thunder cracked the sky outside the tower. The storm renewed its fury, beating at the black stone walls. Across the chamber she spied a door of heavy wood bound with iron. The room's only exit. She might run, but he would not allow it. She might leap from one of the windows to either die or escape his control and become a bird of the night. This, too, he might prohibit.

"Your Lord Husband has disappointed you," said Gammir. "Love is not the grand spell you thought it to be. Now you see the truth of the world. Love, like all things, is merely an illusion. Did not Iardu teach you this?"

She dared a glance at his wolfen eyes. "Iardu taught me many things," she said. She tried again to send her mind forth into the storm. Gammir raised a hand to forbid it. Her thoughts quaked, rattling like frozen pebbles inside her skull.

"He taught you some truth, I see," said Gammir, smirking. He walked closer. "And many lies."

"What do you want with me?" she asked. Why had she come here? To find the truth of Gammir's existence. But had she been ready to kill him? Was that even within her power?

"I should ask you that same question," he said. "But I already know. You *came* to me, dear Sister. I did not summon you. Your false lover in the Kingdom of Orchards is not worthy of you. Meanwhile, Vireon dotes on that bitch Alua and has no time for you. You came to me because you need me."

"Why would I need you?"

"I am your family," he said. "Your eldest brother. The closest thing you have to a father."

"We share the same mother, that much is true. But you are not the Son of Vod."

"Of course not. I am so much more. I am the inheritor of this ancient empire. Khyrei belongs to me. My kingdom grows stronger than ever. You knew this ... just as you knew that I alone would truly understand you."

Sharadza blinked. "What do you mean?"

He leaped forward, faster than she could see, and grabbed her hands in his own. Cold.

"You still care for me," he said.

Sharadza had no words for that. She remembered days with Fangodrel in the gardens of Udurum. She was a tiny girl when he was in his teens. He would run and hide from her in the hedges, daring her to find him. She almost always did, for he would jump out and scare her, lifting her in his arms and spinning her madly. They rolled laughing through the leaves and moss. Yet when Tadarus and Vireon were about, Fangodrel hid his affection for her.

Later he was the cloistered poet, working on verses in self-imposed isolation. Once in a while his servant would bring Sharadza a ballad or ode he had written for her. He had never spoken publicly of these sentimental works. Perhaps he feared that showing love for his sister would be seen as weakness. Or his hatred for Vod's "true sons" had spoiled his love for her. Yet there had been good times between brother and sister.

Now this arcane being in the dark robes ... could it really be the same person who had run alongside her in the leafy courtyards of Udurum? Who had composed sad rhymes for her? Or had he changed so much through the arts of murder and blood magic that he could no longer be counted any relation to her?

"I fear you," she said. "I fear what you've done to Udurum . . . what you've done to Khyrei . . . to yourself . . . and what you will do to us all."

He smiled. "What I will do . . ."

He released her hands and turned to face the storm again.

"Even now my enemies plot against me," he said. "So I do what I must. I will destroy them. All of them. I will wade through a sea of blood and bones until I am master of this world. This is what conquerors do, Sharadza. It is why I was born. And reborn."

"You could *change*," she whispered. "Embrace the humanity you have cast aside. Remember the verses you wrote. Remember love . . . "

He laughed into the mist of rain. "You and I . . . and all those like us . . . we are far beyond *love* and *humanity*. Surely you know this. We are descendants of the Old Breed, who ruled the world before mankind was born. Power is our birthright."

"Ianthe has poisoned your mind," she said.

He turned to glare at her. His smile was close-mouthed, black eyes twinkling. Thunder boomed above the city. "Ianthe opened my mind," he said. "She bequeathed to me the full depth of my father's legacy. She taught me the Power of the Blood. The Strength of the Shadow. She will return again someday, and I will lay this world at her feet."

"You will fight a war against overwhelming forces," she said. "Udurum, Uurz, Yaskatha, even Mumbaza will rise against you. They rise even now."

"Ha! They squabble and bicker among themselves, unable to choose a single course of action. This is their weakness. There is no unity, no one to bring them all together against me. So I let them squabble while Khyrei grows stronger every day. And on that day when they finally march to meet me on the field of battle it will be too late. They will fall like ripe wheat before the scythe."

"There are . . . others," she said. "Sorcerers who will oppose you. You may rule a dark kingdom, but you rule it alone."

"You have no idea what is coming," he said. "The depth of your world is so very shallow. You see no farther than the deep waters that surround us. Yet there is so much more out there . . ." He looked into the roiling stormclouds as if viewing some glorious secret vision. There was something he was not telling her.

Gammir waved a hand and she stood. She walked to him. Once again she was helpless in his invisible grip. His will alone forced her feet to shuffle across the floor, forced her arms to wrap like pale vines around his neck. Beyond his lupine head she saw the city below: a concentric accumulation of fiery pinpoints and innumerable chimneys belching columns of soot into the rain. Beyond the bastions of the city's southern wall steamed the jungle, black as pitch beneath the moonless sky.

Sharadza shivered as a chilling fog drifted through the casements. His bony chest against her bosom offered no warmth. His skin was cold as the mist itself. Together they stared into the seething sheets of rain. She could not look away, even if she wanted to.

"You speak more truly than you know," he said. "I am lonely."

"Let me go," she asked.

Instead he turned to face her. Their faces lingered close in the manner of two lovers.

"You will be my Queen now," he said. His eyes were amber jewels, sparkling with hidden depths. "You have the blood, you have the beauty."

"I am your *sister*."

He breathed upon her cheek. The charnel odor of a beast's mouth, reeking of raw meat.

"*Half*-sister," he corrected her. "Vod was not my father."

"Even so," she said. "Shaira carried us both in her womb. We have her blood as well. The blood of Shar Dni."

He sneered at her. She could not turn her eyes away from his fangs. "Ah, what delicious blood the Sharrians had," he said. "I drained the entire royal family, you know. Well, most of them. This was before we left their city crumbling into ruins. I have savored a bit of that Sharrian flavor in your own blood this night."

She felt the onset of panic. Her mind shuddered between her temples. Her arms and legs trembled, but would not bend or meld or change as she willed them. He placed his chill lips upon hers. She endured the kiss because there was no other choice.

"No!" she screamed, pulling free of his arms. She realized that he must have allowed her this privilege. A brief illusion of freedom to sweeten her agony. "You are my brother and I am the wife of D'zan!"

"Listen to me!" he said. She sat upon the edge of the bed again, for she could do nothing else. "My mortal bones were charred and crushed beneath Vireon's boot. The body that Shaira birthed is long dead. What you see now, this flesh that I wear ... it is a sculpture of blood and shadows. No more related to you than the darkness outside this tower. As a mortal, I was your half-brother. But I am mortal no longer. I will show you ... teach you ... how to rid yourself of this weak body that hinders your true power. You will be reborn as I have been, a conquering spirit in a new housing. No one will be able to control your flesh then ... not even me. The death of this physical form," he jabbed a finger at her stomach, "will set you free. You have learned much these past years. You know I speak truth."

Sharadza considered D'zan, whose body she and Iardu had sculpted from hair, earth, and raw sorcery. She recalled her readings: *The Lifting of the Veil*, *The Gateway Beyond Flesh*, and the *Grimoire of Sanctorus*, all ancient texts that spoke of sorcerers using death as a doorway to ultimate power. She remembered Elhathym re-forming his body from smoke and shadow upon the Yaskathan throne, even after D'zan murdered him on the field of battle. Had Iardu himself shed his physical form ages ago? Perhaps this explained his fondness for taking so many different shapes. It seemed he had a new alias for every kingdom he traveled. She had first known him as Fellow the Storyteller, then as a grizzled crone who taught her the rudiments of sorcery in a musty cave. Her own form was fluid when she wished it, but she always knew who she was ... and what she was. Sharadza, daughter of Vod and Shaira, was her fulcrum, the one reality that she could not change ... the immovable pillar at the center of a mercurial universe.

Death itself was the passage through which she must pass if she were to embrace the fullness of her power. Yet she did not trust Gammir's knowledge of this process. It could easily be a trick to provide for her some fate worse than death.

"Will you ... kill me?" she asked.

Gammir chuckled, walking near to her again. "No," he said. "I will *free* you."

"What if ... what if I rise up more powerful than you? What if I destroy you?"

He reached for her cheek, but she grabbed his wrist. "You *love* me, Sharadza," he whispered. "I was once your brother ... now I will be your Emperor ... your lover ... your husband. You will not kill me because I have seen the depths of your love. It is why you came to me, why you are here right now."

"You are mad," she said, turning away from his eyes to stare at the flaming brazier.

"Love makes us all mad," he said. "This is a mad world."

"So I have no choice?" she asked. "You will force me to your side?"

Gammir shook his lean head. Thunder punctuated the movement. "No," he said. "I will simply free you of this mortal shell. Once I take the last of your blood you will enter the sleep that

Men call death. You see these runes?" He gestured to the circle of sigils and wards encircling the bed. She had not noticed it before now. The marks were intricate, swirling, graven into the basalt flagstones of the floor. "I have already prepared the way for your rebirth. Don't worry; I will help you. I will bring blood and shadows for you. The raw materials of your new existence."

He is going to do this, she realized. *There is no choice for me here.*

He wants my blood and he will have it. He has enslaved me as his own father enslaved my poor mother before I was born. But he will never have my love.

Now, in a flash, she saw the way out of his trap. A ray of light seeping into the dark prison where he had her chained. He would take her life, destroy her mortal body. She could not prevent that. Yet her own power could create a new shell for her living spirit, just as the Shaper and she had created one for D'zan.

In her new body she would be free of Gammir's power. Free to bring his black towers thundering down, free to end his realm of brutal slavery. To wipe him from the face of the earth. Let him think he is reinventing her. He would sow his own doom without even realizing it.

She knew now that this was the only way.

Eight years ago she had determined to learn sorcery against Iardu's warnings. She had opened many gateways to great and dreadful knowledge. Now it was time to continue that journey to its ultimate end. Time to embrace death, and so overcome it.

Let it come.

"Very well," she said. "What has this life to offer me but loneliness and sorrow?"

Gammir nodded, taking her hand in his. He bent to kiss her knuckles.

"My Queen," he said.

She lay back on the bed, exposing her neck for him. The twin lesions throbbed. Her pulse raced as Gammir bent his head. His ivory fangs elongated, his mouth opened obscenely wide. A red tongue licked at her wound as fangs sank deep. She grimaced as the terrible suction began.

She prayed without sound.

Father, give me strength.

Gammir did not drain her completely on that first night. Yet he drank enough to leave her weak and helpless on the grand bed. He even lay there with her until pink sunlight began to creep in through the casements. He arose, waking her from a dreamless slumber, and pulled thick tapestries down before each of the windows. The bulk of the storm had passed, but the light rain went on, a whisper against the tower walls. Gammir kissed her lips as she lay drowsy and pale. He slipped through the single door and was gone. She could not keep her eyes open.

The next night he came again to drink from her throat. He muttered sweet words and kind promises to her, as if she were truly his lover. Yet he did not touch her in any intimate way, save for the penetration of fangs and questing tongue. He drew the life from her slowly. She could not move at all now. She could barely think. Her thoughts were lost in a fog of confusion. His yellow eyes hung before her always.

On the third night he finished her. The shimmering of his black robe was the last thing she remembered before ultimate sleep fell upon her. She called D'zan's name a final time, a single tear escaping her left eye to run along her cheek.

Then darkness, deeper than any sea, older than any world.

She floated in the endless dark, a spark of sentience in a bottomless void. Only her memories of the Living World saved her from utter annihilation. That world was precious to her, with all its pain and suffering, all its glories and triumphs. Here there was only a Great Nothingness, but the world she had left was a feast of possibilities. Sunlight on her skin, wine on her tongue, the wind in her hair . . . these memories persisted. The smiling face of her mother, the salty breezes of the Cryptic Sea. The exhilaration of flight, the warmth of tender flesh against her own. D'zan . . . the boy she had loved, who had loved her. The pain of that love, and the sweetness of it. She clung to these memories as a drowning girl might cling to shards of flotsam.

All of these things – feelings, thoughts, sensations, concepts, words, birth, death, transformation, love, hate – only Patterns. In the World of Spirit there were no Patterns . . . which was itself a Pattern. The Living World, composed of earth, air, fire, and water, was an illusion, but so was the World of the Dead. She hung suspended between the two Great Lies now, a mote transversing two infinite Patterns composed of endless sub-Patterns, an endless succession of them. Yet there were no distinctions. *All Is One.*

She reached out, weaving patterns with the darkness, searching for the light that lay beyond. They were the same, Dark and Light, Being and Non-Being. The Will was the only constant. She willed herself toward the world she loved and entered its Pattern once more.

She had done this before, when Shaira forced her infant self out of the womb. A squealing, helpless thing, she had emerged. Now she emerged once more, drawn to that which awaited her. The circle of runes took precedence above all other Patterns. Like a whirlpool it pulled her toward its epicenter. She knew pain then, and joy, and a thousand other emotions at once. A grand and nameless euphoria.

She lay upon the bed at the center of the runes, a mass of congealing shadows. She could not yet see, but she sensed the presence of Gammir hovering nearby. She felt the ancient words he spoke. She was not manifesting here entirely of her own volition. He was drawing her from the void. It might have consumed her if he had not. Despite her consent, she had not been fully prepared for this resurrection. She fought his influence, writhing and squirming on the bedsheets.

A vision came: her mortal body, drained of life, withered and corpse-white. Soldiers in demonic masks carried it toward a blazing furnace. They cast her dead body into the flames, where it caught like dry kindling. The flames consumed flesh and bone.

The bed lay empty in the highest room of the tower. Empty but for the rushing shadows that filled the room and sank into the whirlpool of her emergence. They converged on the downy coverlets as Gammir sang his ancient incantation.

The vision passed and she opened her newly formed eyes. Gammir wailed and waved his jeweled fingers about the rune circle. Two female slaves sat naked on their knees, one at either side of the bed. She raised her head and saw the shadow-substance of her body bubbling and forming, warping and bending, flashing through myriad colors. Would she be reborn in some deformed, distended body?

She worked the Patterns to weave the rushing shadows into her former shape. She willed her new shell to resemble the body that was so healthy and alive before it was drained like a wineskin and devoured by flames.

Gammir approached the first of the slaves and raised a gleaming dagger. The slave looked at Sharadza writhing on the bed, shadow struggling to become flesh. The girl's eyes were dead, empty of hope. She neither wept nor begged as Gammir raised her chin and slid the dagger's edge across her throat. The pale flesh opened and red blood squirted forth. Instead of spilling across the girl's quivering breasts, it flowed *upward*, into the swirling mass of shadows. It joined the black mass and swirled downward, adding substance to Sharadza's new form.

No, she tried to scream. *You didn't tell me this . . .*

Her mouth was only a jagged whole in the oval of her half-formed head.

The slave girl dropped to the floor as the last of her lifeblood flowed into the black cloud and then sank into Sharadza. Now Gammir walked about the bed and opened the second slave's throat. The blood of the first victim had given Sharadza substance, and now she screamed from her properly formed mouth. But it was too late. The second blood offering joined with the first, swirling into her new physical presence. She soaked it up, drinking it in through her newly formed pores. It flooded into her mouth, down her throat, hot as fire.

"Yes!" breathed Gammir. "You are almost there. Take the final step. The power of blood and shadow is yours."

With a final thrust of willpower, Sharadza completed her new form. A perfect copy of the body she had abandoned to Gammir's bloodlust. She lay naked on the bed now, exposed to his hungry eyes in the most explicit way imaginable. She breathed deeply of the blood-scented air. It filled her new lungs and sent wellness coursing through her limbs.

She rose from the bed like a floating spirit, spreading her arms and glorying in the newness of her flesh. A pale Goddess, she hung above the dark Emperor. She gazed upon him and knew that her fresh eyes were the color of the dead slaves' blood. Her hair, black as shadow, flowed about her in dancing winds. Outside the windows a new storm raged. Lightning slashed the sky and the roaring of thunder shook the tower stones.

The power of that storm surged in her veins, and the lightning responded to her call. A blue-white thunderbolt shot in through the window and bathed her in its radiance. Its flame sank into her pale skin.

Gammir twisted and jerked, transfixed by the same bolt as it fed her.

"So beautiful!" he shouted through his pain.

The lightning had set the bed aflame. It burned now like a pyre for the two dead slaves. Ignoring the blaze, Sharadza called shadows in from the storm and wove them into a robe to clothe her new body. Her flesh and Gammir's steamed in the wake of the thunderbolt. Her feet touched down on the stone floor, but its coldness no longer bothered her. She was beyond such discomforts as coolness and heat now. She was reborn.

She stood tall before Gammir, unafraid and unhindered. He reached a hand timidly toward her. She took it in her own and he pulled her near. Their lips met in a lingering kiss. They were no longer brother and sister. Those were terms to describe bodies that had faded from the world. They were indomitable spirits now, masters of the material world and all its Patterns.

No.

She tasted the blood on his lips, bittersweet and delicious.

No, this is wrong.

"I thirst," she told him.

Gammir smiled and hissed through his fangs like a proud viper.

"My Queen," he said, "taste now the wine of your kingdom."

The heavy door opened and an armored sentinel hauled in a boy, quivering and weeping. Another slave. He could be no more than twelve. Young blood was sweet blood.

He lied to me. He's changed me . . .

She felt the beating pulse of the boy from across the room. Blood ran hot in his veins.

But I am not like him. I have free will now.

She leaped like a cat and took the boy in her arms as if to embrace him. Her head reared back and her fangs grew large.

No!

She sank them into the soft flesh of the boy's throat, drinking deep of ecstasy.

The wailing voice in the back of her head faded as she guzzled the slave's blood. Hot and vinegary on her tongue. Sweet and filling in the depths of her belly.

Gammir urged her on with obscene whispers, caressing her new skin, watching the boy twitch and die. She dropped the brittle carcass to the floor, wiped her red-smeared lips with the back of her hand.

"More." She demanded it.

He smiled and kissed her bloody mouth.

"As you wish."

Hand in hand they descended the steps of the black tower.

Thunder shook the world outside.

9

The Godstone

"Tell me," said Iardu. "What do you know of the world beyond your plantations?"

"Only what I've heard in stories." Tong chewed on a thick slice of roasted mushroom. Like flavorless bread it was, and he craved meat. Pork and fowl were staple foods for the hard-working slaves of Khyrei. He saw no signs of livestock in Sydathus, excepting the swarms of black beetles. Still, the fungus steak filled his belly and vanquished his sudden hunger.

"And what have you heard?" asked the wizard. His eyes blinked lavender, then emerald, then settled to mother-of-pearl-gray. The eyes of the White Serpent.

"That Khyrein ships rule the Golden Sea, all the way to the Jade Isles at the Edge of the World. That the Undying One destroyed the city of his northern enemies years ago, then arose from the ashes of Shar Dni. Many other things ... whispers ... legends ... *fears*."

Iardu shook his gray head and rubbed the smooth line of his jaw. Faceted stones of beryl and agate glittered on his fingers. "So you really know nothing at all," he sighed. "Of course you were not permitted knowledge that would not serve your bondage."

Tong drank from a stone crock full of icy fresh water. The Sydathians had assigned him a modest cave, its walls and floor green with a soft shaggy moss. White blossoms grew from the walls in places, exhaling a sweet aroma that mixed with the smoke of his dinner. The cave was more pleasant than any slave shack, and Tong was grateful for it. His new quarters lay at the base of the columnar city, which climbed toward the great cavern's apex. Scattered minerals in the rocky dome served as subterranean constellations, refracting the light from below in a hundred glittering hues.

Tong imagined the metropolis of honeycombed stone as a great and godly tree sprouting amid the vast grotto. Sydathus was a marvelous abode full of ancient mystery. The past few days had convinced him that these Sydathians were far more than blind monsters.

"Born into slavery you could know little of the lands beyond your own," Iardu said. "Realms where your people would not have to endure such suffering." The sorcerer smoked a thin pipe of white wood carved into the likeness of Mumbaza's Feathered Serpent. Tong had seen the beast stitched on the sails of trading vessels when he was a child. Mumbazan ships no longer visited Khyrei, although each year a few Mumbazan mariners were captured by the Khyrein navy. Those who survived battle on the open sea were executed in public spectacles, or were sent to work in the fields with the native slaves. Plantation life was short and brutal for such prisoners.

The deep purple smoke from Iardu's pipe wafted about his red robes. The azure flame on his chest continued to dance and flicker at the end of its silver chain. "Khyrei is the last of the great slave empires," he said. His face fell from handsome to grave. "It must be destroyed if it is to be saved. The time grows short. I should have seen to this long ago." His words sounded like an apology.

Tong swallowed the last bite of mushroom and studied the mage's face. Ageless, yes, but full of ancient sadness . . . regret . . . compassion? Iardu stared directly at him, and the insight was lost. His sorcerer's mask slipped back in place.

The warlock grinned. "You will need more than that longknife to take the black city."

"What do you have in mind?"

Iardu stood at the mouth of the little green cave and looked out at the greater cavern. A cluster of toadstools large as blood oaks bordered the deep fungal forest. Sydathians moved between the upright boles like white moths through orange twilight.

"Soon the Sydathians will go to their holy Godstone," Iardu said. "You must go with them."

"You want me to pray . . . to a rock?"

"Not a rock, a crystal. And no praying."

"Why must I do this? Slaves worship only the Earth God. No other Gods will bless us."

"One, you are no longer a slave," said Iardu. "Remember that. Two, you need an army."

"The eyeless ones?"

"They see more than you know. You said you wanted to free your people. This is the path you must walk in order to do that."

Tong wiped the grease from his knife, then slid it back into the scabbard hanging from his loincloth. Once again he pulled onto his feet the boots of an Onyx Guard. The boots he had killed for. They reminded him of the vengeance he had taken in Matay's name. It was enough for now. There would be more; he would be patient.

"Go to the Godstone," said Iardu.

There was no song or alarm raised to signal the beginning of the ritual. Gradually, one by one or in pairs, the Sydathians meandered

into the depths of the toadstool forest. An unspoken communication, or perhaps the imprint of habit, called them down from
their terraced caves and balconies by the thousands. Tong felt that
nameless urge himself. It was time for something vital, something
sacred. In Iardu's face he saw the calm wisdom of an elder, despite
the lack of wrinkles on the smooth brown skin. The warlock
placed a hand on Tong's shoulder and led him from the mouth of
the cave into the fungal gloom.

Purple undergrowth filled the avenues between the giant
mushroom boles. Mottled stalks, bulbs, and waving tendrils
glowed with a violet luminescence. Spores and dried fungus
patches crackled to powder beneath Tong's boots, while Iardu and
the Sydathians moved without any noise at all. The eyeless ones
filed deeper into the purple glades surrounding Tong and Iardu.
It was not Iardu's insistence that called Tong onward, but his own
need to know something mysterious and profound. Some ancient
secret lay buried here . . . some lost understanding. How did he
know this? Was the wizard putting things into his mind? No
matter. He was a free man now. He could make his own decisions.
Already he enjoyed the naked thrill of freedom. He followed the
pale beastlings into the heart of the earth not because he must, but
because he chose to do so.

At last a cave yawned black and misty in the glow of the lavender lichen. The Sydathians filed into the fissure with Tong and
Iardu walking quietly in their midst. The passage sloped down
and down, twisting and turning back upon itself innumerable
times. All in solid darkness, which the eyeless ones did not seem
to mind. The floor was smooth and well trodden, and the presence
of so many close forms around Tong held the primeval fear of
darkness at bay.

They came eventually to a great stairwell, curving deep into the
bowels of another massive grotto. A white mist crawled up the

steps, and a pale glow illuminated the stairs. As the Sydathians reached the last turn of the passage, the light grew stronger until it shone brighter than the fireglow of Sydathus proper. Now Tong and Iardu came into the new cavern's threshold, joining the multitude of Sydathians gathered about the source of the white light.

A single pillar of black rock hung from the domed vault. Instead of terminating in a pointed tip, the rocky spar supported a tremendous egg-shaped crystal. It glowed like a miniature moon hanging in the bowels of the earth.

The Godstone seethed with a steady light at the center of the eyeless horde. Those directly below the great crystal were nearly tall enough to touch its gleaming surface, if they had climbed upon the backs of their brothers. Many did just that, caressing the Godstone with reverence, and all in perfect silence. Here was the object of worship, but no sound of worshipping.

Tong stood still among the crowd, Iardu an arm's length away from him, as the last of the Sydathians filed in behind them. Then some voiceless signal, some mass will, gave the command to kneel, and the thousands kneeled as one below their hanging Godstone. Tong could no more resist this urge than a swimming man could deny the power of a great wave sweeping at him.

The Sydathians and the two Men kneeled together, and the deepest silence Tong had ever known pervaded the cavern. If they possessed eyes, the Sydathians would have been staring directly into the brilliant depths of the stone. The snouts of their horned heads focused on it. They no longer twitched and sniffed and moved their claws in arcane patterns. They had become still as stones, every one of them. Even the children.

"I don't understand," Tong whispered to Iardu.

"Clear your mind of all thoughts," Iardu breathed. "That is all you have to do."

Tong considered this. To clear his mind of everything would be to forget Matay and his unborn son. Could he do that? Even for a moment? Did he even want to? Matay's memory was all he had left. She had been the grace that gave his days purpose. Yet he had lost that grace.

He closed his eyes and turned his face up toward the Godstone. A faint image of it lingered on the inside of his eyelids. Then it faded, yet the darkness inside his head was not complete. Pinpoints of white light glimmered in his mind's eye, a raging river of light struggling to burst through hidden walls into his consciousness. Slowly the inner light ate away at the darkness behind his eyes, until the white light glowed inside his vision, blinding him even while his eyes were shut.

His thoughts were scattered, burning things when the inner light fell upon them. They dissolved like spices in boiling water. Was his mind boiling? Was this what Matay's sun looked like up close? He expected to be blind still when he opened his eyes. Then he forgot that he possessed eyes, and that he was human, and that he kneeled in a cavern leagues beneath the poison jungle with a multitude of inhuman brutes.

Then he no longer thought at all. He simply *was*.

Time was a lotus with ten thousand petals opening before him, spilling the breath of peace into his body. For the first time he realized the true depth of his newfound freedom. Here, in a mental space beyond the reach of all things, he existed in a time-less perfection. His body, his life, his slavery, all became less than dim memories. They called to him like voices across a great expanse of water. Half-heard ghost-selves wailing at him, remind-ing him, recalling him back to himself.

You are not a slave. You are a Man.

An eternal spirit wearing a disguise of flesh and bone.

Tong's eyes sprang open as twenty thousand Sydathians raised their heads. He sat in their midst beneath the glow of the Godstone.

Iardu rose to his feet nearby. Tong blinked and looked not at the wizard, but at the shuffling forms of the eyeless ones. They moved in complete peace, bathed in the deep calm brought by their ceremony.

Tong released a terrible pressure in his face and found himself smiling.

"What happened?" he asked.

"Quii," said Iardu. "The Sydathians' sacred meditation. The crystal enhances their empathic nature. It brings them together in a bonding of mind and spirit. It will do the same for you, if you allow it."

"It gave me peace."

Iardu smiled, his white teeth flashing in the Godstone's glow.

"It has given you more than that."

Sydathians swarmed about Tong now, reaching out their long fingers to caress his arms, chest, and back. The females hung on him like eager cats, licking at his arms and legs. This went on for some while, until they began to file up the great stair. The red-robed priests followed last of all. One of these holy luminaries approached Tong.

The Priest of Sydathus touched his cheek softly. Understanding sank into Tong's mind as if he had heard spoken words in his own language.

Son of the Black City.

The priest recognized him.

You will lead us forth. Some to death, some to honor. We have seen this.

The priest understood him.

Gladly will we pay this price to walk freely in the Land of the Sun.

The priest believed in him.

You will end our long isolation, Son of the Black City. We have seen this.

The Sydathian removed his hand from Tong's cheek and the

flash of understanding was gone. Tong stood dazed and full of awe. The red priest turned away to join his people as they ascended to their city cavern. Tong watched the last of them climb the stony stair, lingering beneath the brilliant Godstone. "You must come here with them every day for thirty days," Iardu said. "Then your understanding of the Sydathians will be strong. And you will know the power of Quii."

"Is it sorcery?" Tong asked. He followed Iardu up the great stairway.

"No," said Iardu. "It is only meditation. Bringing the true self into alignment with the Source of All Things. The fount of all peace, strength, and creation. You are blessed to experience this awakening, for most men spend their entire lives in ignorance."

Tong fingered the hilt of the knife at his waist. "If I do what you say . . . they will follow me . . . fight for me . . . die for me?"

In the gloom of the subterranean stair Iardu's eyes gleamed bright as torches, shifting from scarlet to saffron, from emerald to azure. "The Old One who touched you has already seen this. Their decision was made before you ever arrived."

"Why would these people spend their lives to save mine?" Tong asked.

Iardu explained as they trudged up the long stair. "Long ago the Sydathians ventured into the upper world. Having explored the vast expanse of their subterranean region, they wished to discover the world of sun and sky. It was a new frontier that excited the imaginations of an ancient folk. So they carried a great tribute of jewels to the Empress of Khyrei – yes, that same Claw who sits upon the throne today. She took the tribute and slaughtered the emissaries without mercy. Sometime later a second band of ambassadors approached the black city. They were tortured to death, their carcasses hung from the palace walls. Khyreins were taught to hate and fear Sydathians, even to hunt them in the red jungle. So the eyeless ones were driven back into their underground realm. Eventually the Khyreins forgot all about them. Ages passed.

"Yet the wisest priests of Sydathus spoke of a day when Sydathians and Men would walk together hand in hand beneath the sun. The surface world, once freed from the grip of tyrants, would open its wonders to those from below. The sun would no longer be a stranger to them. Certain of the Old Ones saw this vision in the depths of the Godstone.

"You heard the priest's words. You are the Son of the Black City. The time has come. You will give them the frontier they have so long been denied. The world of sun and sky."

Tong felt the pressure of forgotten history upon his shoulders. Could he be the man to liberate not one but *two* oppressed peoples? The idea seemed little more than some improbable legend told around the cookfires of slaves. Yet here he stood in the bowels of the earth with a shape-shifting wizard and a multitude of beastlings ready to storm the walls of Khyrei. His head swam, as if he stared down at the world from some great height and did not quite recognize what he saw there. The world was far greater and far more complex than he had ever imagined.

"What is this Godstone?" he asked.

Iardu shrugged. "What is the moon? Or the ocean? Or a mountain? These things exist because they are a part of the natural world. Since men do not understand the natural world, they fret and ponder the true nature of things. They fail to see the essential unity underlying all of existence. The Godstone is a reminder of that unity."

After the trek to and from the chamber of the Godstone a great weariness fell upon Tong. He stumbled back through the mushroom wood toward the glittering city-column. He sought only the soft bed of moss where he would lay himself down to sleep.

"Your wounds have healed, but your body is still weak," said Iardu. "You have not worked the fields in weeks. The daily journey to the Godstone will do you good in more ways than one."

Tong drank a bowl of water and fell asleep on the moss. He dreamed of faraway lands that he had never seen. Shining towers of alabaster and gold rose from walled cities on plain, coast, and cliff. They had names, these bastions of human civilization, yet he did not know them. Like a soaring hawk, his vision turned back to Khyrei. A blot of darkness where the crimson jungle met the Golden Sea. He looked upon the green fields where his people lived and worked, he floated low above the endless rows of grape, bean, wheat, and corn.

Slaves worked the fields with all the desperate intensity he remembered, but when he sank lower he saw they were not human. Thousands of horned Sydathians worked the harvest, filling baskets with green stalks, shucking corn, picking grapes. Demons in ebony masks whipped and smote them to greater efforts.

He woke from the dream parched and with aching muscles. A fresh draft of water brought him walking into the orange gloom of the cavern. The dancing firelight here never altered: there was no night or day, so there was no way to know how long he'd slept. Only the hunger in his belly told him it had been a long time.

Now came the time of the Godstone again. He felt it growing in his gut, even before the first of the Sydathians lined up and marched into the fungus woods. It had awakened him.

He almost took a step, but Iardu's voice halted him.

"Tong," said the wizard. He stood not far away, wrapped in a cloak of black feathers. "I must leave for a while. I will return soon. Remember the Godstone."

Tong raised his hand in a gesture of farewell. He did not look behind when the sound of beating wings filled the air then faded into silence. He walked toward the forest and the hidden fissure that led deep into the bowels of the earth. He walked lightly, feeling that he now lived truly in the realm of the Earth God. The entity his people venerated had saved him from the Deathlands long enough to allow him this gift. The secrets of the earth itself were opening to him. He did not fear the eyeless ones, or dread spending his time with them. He moved forward in sublime serenity with his thousands of new brothers and sisters.

The dream had opened a gate of wisdom in his heart. These Sydathians were as much his people as were the slaves toiling and dying in Khyrei, as were the citizens of all those cities the dream had shown him. He did not need to know their names, their customs, or their languages. He needed only to know of their presence.

By virtue of a common existence, all living things were of the same family, united behind the masks of shallow differences.

He smiled into the dark as he descended toward the chamber of the Godstone.

The Sydathians, grotesque and beautiful, crowded about him. *This Great Truth*, he mused. *I will carry it to the world above. These, my brothers, will help me spread it.*

By spear and blade and fang and claw, we will spread this wisdom. This freedom.

10

Emperor of Uurz

The Chamber of Orchids stood adjacent to the gardens of the eastern courtyard. Six pillars of lapis lazuli sparkled about a pool of turquoise water, replenished daily from the depths of the Sacred River. Servants heated the bath with hot stones baked in sacred fires. They seasoned the water with fragrant petals, costly oils, and secret spices known to invigorate the skin. The chamber was open only to the Queen and her immediate family; its attendants were seventeen lovely girls plucked from the corners of the known world.

Yaskathan maidens with golden curls, dusky daughters of Mumbaza, almond-eyed beauties from the Jade Isles, all handpicked to serve the Queen in her most intimate of rituals. When Talondra wedded Tyro she had insisted that a majority of Sharrians be assigned to the maintenance of her bath. As in nearly every instance, Tyro acceded to her wishes.

The twelve dark-haired Sharrian girls Talondra honored with this duty had lost their families to the Khyrein invaders eight years ago. She saved them all from a mean existence on the streets of Uurz. Talondra also made sure that any dark-eyed Khyrein girls were suitably discharged. Her hatred of the Pale Race was legendary in the green-gold city. No one in Uurz could deny her right to this prejudice; the Khyreins had destroyed her family and her nation. Here in the inner sanctum of her privacy she would allow none of that race. The rumors that she had put several Khyrein girls to death were true.

Early stars blinked to life beyond the lattice of orchid vines that served as the chamber's eastern wall. The evening sky glimmered violet above towers limned in twilight. The day's heat had worn away and a pleasant breeze entered the bath chamber through the nearby gardens. It rustled the white orchid blooms in such a way that they seemed a hundred bobbing heads emitting vanilla breath into the steam.

Talondra lay at ease, floating atop the hot water. Her black hair spread across its surface and mingled with the fragrant petals. Barefoot girls in brief togas came and went silently, replacing hot stones as needed and perfecting the blend of botanicals. She called them forth to scrub her body and hair with delicate soaps. When that was done, she lay back once more and admired the watery light playing across the polished ceiling. A hearth and twin torches glowed brightly beside the pool. The last rays of daylight were lost beyond the wall of orchids.

The eastern doors flew open to crash against the wall. Maidens yipped and scattered from Tyro's path as he stalked across the chamber, his long hair a disheveled sticky mess. Dripping scarlet smeared the golden lion's head on his breastplate; his face was hot with sweat and rage. The gilded bracers on his forearms were nicked and scarred, and a dozen minor lacerations scored his muscled arms like red welts. His sword was missing from its scabbard, but a silver dagger hung still at his broad belt.

"What have you done?" he seethed. He kneeled at the pool's edge, spilling dark drops of gore into the sweet water. His breathing was loud. His fists clenched and unclenched and clenched again. He supposed there was murder gleaming in his eyes. Yet there was no mirror in the Chamber of Orchids, so he could not see it for himself.

Let her see it. Let her know the depth of my anger.

She must have plotted this for months.

Talondra raised herself to a standing position in the middle of the waist-deep pool. She frowned at the bloody sight of him, but more at his tainting of the bathwater. She pulled her thick black tresses behind her head. Beads of water like tiny diamonds gleamed on her smooth brown skin, dripped from the buds of her breasts.

Even in the depths of his red fury he wanted her.

Conniving lioness bitch.

"Tell me!" he bellowed. "And who it was that helped you."

Talondra smiled fearlessly. "Calm yourself, My Lord," she said, making her way toward the far steps. Two trembling girls held up a white robe for her shoulders. "You look a fright."

"Do not play with me, woman," he said. "Time for your confession."

The robe hung loose about her slim figure now, and she did not bother to close it. He forced his eyes away from the brazen display of her womanhood as she turned to face him.

"Would you treat your wife as a common criminal?" she asked. "Interrogate me with whips and hot irons? A confession implies a crime committed. I have done a great service for you, Tyro. And for the realm."

He lunged forward and took her jaw between his bloodstained fingers and thumb. He pulled her face near to his own, and she resisted. His other hand grabbed her arm, tender as a twig in his grip. Her green eyes blazed at him. He gritted his teeth.

"I should kill you," he said.

"Then kill me," she whispered. Her eyes closed and she offered him her slim neck to break. "It is my honor to die by the hands of an Emperor."

He breathed hotly into her face. A lovely mask of flesh sculpted by the clever hands of the Gods themselves. He squeezed until she whimpered. He kissed her hard on the lips, then tore the robe from her body. A single hand pushed her splashing into the pool, and he tore off the buckles of his breastplate, removed the soiled tunic, the plaited bronze girdle and sandals. Then he slid into the bath and took her in his arms. Servant girls crouched behind the blue pillars as the Emperor and his Queen made love in the steaming water. Afterwards the couple lay side by side with their heads against the lip of the pool.

The blood and sweat and rage was gone from Tyro's body, but a red stain lay upon his conscience.

Talondra kissed his broad chest and lifted her eyes to regard his face.

"The Stormlands are yours now," she said. "No more Scholar King to stand in your way. No more fractured court. No more obstacles to our just war."

"He is my *brother*," said Tyro, as if she had never recognized this fact. "And she belonged to him. I think he even loved her." His eyes grew moist. Perhaps it was only the steam.

"She was a Yaskathan harlot," said Talondra. "There are twenty thousand more exactly like her."

"Who did it?" he asked.

She said nothing. He looked away toward the pale orchids.

"No, don't tell me. I don't want to know."

"As you wish." She kissed his lips.

"They found . . . her head . . . in the lower cellar . . . surrounded by the sigils of some obscure sorcery. Did it need to be so—"

"Killing Ramiyah would be pointless if it did not paint your brother as a mad practitioner of the dark arts. They will say, 'He sought to sacrifice his wife to demons so that he might rise above his brother and seize the Empire.' It was the only way to break this stalemate. In your iron heart you know this to be true. Now you must see it through."

"How can I?" he said. The lovemaking had washed away his fury. Only sorrow had replaced it. The sorrow of an Emperor, and he must wear it like a set of chains now. A far heavier burden than any jeweled crown. "How can I stand before the court – the entire city – and proclaim my brother a murderer, a sorcerer, and a madman? I know these are lies ... and worse than lies."

She placed a hand on his cheek and turned him toward her splendid eyes again. "Lies are only tools. Some say they are the most important tools a ruler can wield. More powerful than blade or spear, more deadly than venom. You need only learn how to wield a lie as you wield a sword ... to cut down your enemies without mercy."

"So must I cut down my own brother."

"For the good of the realm," she said. "And for the good of the *world* once Khyrei is no more. What stakes could be higher?"

He rose from the bath and accepted a robe from the attendants. Talondra followed him past the lattice of orchids to sit upon a divan overlooking the darkened gardens. The moon was a silver crescent hanging sharp as a dagger in the starry night. A cool wind blew across the courtyards, and distant melodies wafted from a band of strolling musicians. Drum, flute, and lyre blended into a song both melancholy and sweet. Tyro could not hear the lyrics, and the gentle strains brought him no peace.

"Where is he now?" asked Talondra.

Tyro stiffened, ran a hand through his wet hair. "Mendices came to the sparring field and told me of the murder. I took a squad from the field and entered the western wing. I heard Lyrilan screaming before I reached his apartments. The Green Lords set

their men before his door. The fools actually expected me to turn
away and ignore my brother's mad cries. Swords were drawn and
blood was spilled. Several men died on both sides. In the end it
was Undroth, my father's old friend, who halted the fight and
opened the sealed door . . . "

His words faded beneath the memory of Lyrilan's distorted face
stained with Ramiyah's blood, runneled with tears, his eyes
empty of all but pain. The girl's headless body lay on a red sheet
that had once been white. A pair of legionnaires restrained
Lyrilan, but not even old Volomses could calm him. They gave
him wine but he tossed the cup away. A physician came to
inspect the body, and he forced a noxious potion down Lyrilan's
throat. The Scholar King grew silent at last, mired in the depths
of his loss. Tyro went to him but could not dispel the emptiness
on his brother's face.

Gradually, details of the murder emerged. The dagger found
was Lyrilan's own; he was known to carry it on ceremonial occasions. On Tyro's orders and with the consent of Undroth, they
moved Lyrilan to a clean quiet chamber low in the Western Tower.
Eventually he slept, while Tyro led the investigation. He examined the soiled bedchamber with great care, knowing in the back
of his mind that it was all Talondra's doing. One of her agents had
done this, one of the many scions of shadow who moved through
the city unseen and unheard, dispatching death and vengeance at
her command. One of the silent killers she used as pawns to
pursue her private vendettas. Yet there would be nothing to link
her officially with the slaying. Instead, everything was arranged
to point directly at poor Lyrilan.

When the missing head was found, Tyro went below to see the
signs of sorcery for himself. Such a scene was not terribly difficult
to construct. The great library was full of books detailing the
marks of sorcery and witchcraft, most of which were meaningless,

harmless, or both. There were magicians in Uurz, and probably even a few true sorcerers, but they did not reside in the palace and they certainly did not get their powers from such antiquated tomes. Yet Talondra's agent had done well, both in assembling a convincing scene of demon worship, and in leaving barely enough droplets of blood along the corridors to lead directly into the cellar. The subterranean vault where Lyrilan had attempted his evil spell.

Tyro sensed the falseness of the scenario instantly. He knew his brother was incapable of such a heinous act. Yet he said nothing. Surely the failure of this blood sacrifice accounted for Lyrilan's sudden madness, Mendices posited. Surely no King would grieve so deeply and powerfully over a mere dead wife. No, Lyrilan *must* be a dabbler in the ancient and forbidden arts. An aspiring blood mage. So much evidence could not be discounted.

When news of this theory spread, only hours after the murder, a contingent of the Green Lords had decided to attempt a coup. Cohorts of green and gold forces clashed in the paved courtyard below the steps of the Great Hall. Most of the Green Lords took advantage of the chaos to flee the palace – and perhaps the city itself – but Undroth remained with Lyrilan in his sickness.

Tyro was not bound to join the fray. In fact, it was unheard of that a modern-day King should take up a sword to defend his own palace grounds. Yet the pain in his heart was easily smothered by the press of bodies, blades, and shields. He waded into the skirmish and killed seven men wearing green tabards. Three of these had been skilled swordsmen. One came close to piercing Tyro's eye with a quick blade before he died at the Sword King's feet.

The Gold Legionnaires, inspired by their King's savage presence, fought like tigers. As the sun sank beyond the golden towers, Uurzian hacked Uurzian to bits. Soon the men of the Green lost heart as they realized their lords, and their chosen

King, no longer stood behind them. Those who surrendered were cast into cells as traitors.

Later, when hot tempers cooled, Tyro would give them a chance to swear a fresh oath and repent their treason. With war looming on the horizon, every capable warrior would be of value. The rest of the Green Lords were already surrendering their forces to Tyro via proxies. They had no choice now but to accept him as their sole ruler.

Emperor at last.

There was only the matter of what to do with Lyrilan.

Tyro had marched livid and bloody from the courtyard littered with the bodies of his countrymen. So he had confronted Talondra, and as usual she soothed his boiling blood and reminded him of the essential nature of his royal duty.

Now he lay with her on the divan and wondered at the cold beauty of the stars.

Forgive me, Lyrilan.

"He gave me a book," Tyro told his wife. "All about Dairon. He chronicled our father's life one year at a time. I was . . . I was reading it." Tears welled in his eyes. He might never be able to finish reading those pages now. Every drop of ink would remind of him of the innocent blood shed in his name.

She wrapped her arms, then her long legs, about him. Like a mother she held his head to her bosom, making gentle sounds.

"Weep now, Emperor of Uurz," she whispered. "Mourn your brother's loss and know that you walk the righteous path."

"What can be righteous about what we have done?" he asked. "Or what I will now have to do?"

"Everything!" she said. "The Gods respect *strength*, Tyro. The blessings of Earth, Sea, Sky, and Sun will fall upon the second Emperor of the New Blood. The people will rejoice. An empire deserves an Emperor, and by these deeds, bitter though you find them, you have gained the great throne."

He drew in a deep breath, expanding his chest, and sighed. "I need wine."

She motioned the servants to bring refreshments.

"Lyrilan does not speak?" she asked. "Not even to defend himself?"

"Not this day," he said. "Perhaps never. This may have killed him as surely as a spear in the heart. We will see."

"If he does not speak, so much the better. He will not then deny the charges you lay upon him, or the sentence you prescribe. He is done."

He looked at her again, studying the contours of her perfect face: the proud nose, the sloping cheekbones, the high forehead. She had no brothers, at least none living. No family left at all. Could she understand his bond with his brother? Did it even matter, the bond itself or her understanding of it? He did not have the answer.

They shared a carafe of strong red vintage, she sipping and he guzzling. The heaviness in his breast was replaced by a numb warmth. Killing men was easy. War was easy. The ways of the sword were cleaner and simpler than the ways of politics. In war a man might spare his enemy and gain honor. In politics, honor was an illusion, like a morning mist taken on the shape of a forlorn ghost.

"The realm is yours." She toasted him with a raised goblet. "And we will have our war. Death to Khyrei."

Tyro nodded and drank. All he need do was condemn his brother. Turn his back on the person who loved him most in the world. Enforce a lie that was a weapon and use it to kill a King. Talondra had done the messy work for him. Now he must do the inevitable and learn to live with himself.

Yet there would be the glorious chaos of war to drown his remorse. Blood and smoke and death in which to lose the memory of this betrayal. In the smoking ruins of Khyrei he would find vindication. Or the Gods would punish him for this crime and he would die on the battlefield. Let them judge him as they saw fit. Such was the role of Gods. The role of an Emperor was to lead. The role of a warrior was to fight. Such were the ways of the world, and so would it ever be. Life was a battle and pain was the soul of it.

Tyro called for more wine and drank until he slept.

He welcomed the nightmares when they came.

Three days later an anxious gathering filled the Great Hall. Lords and ladies, courtesans, chamberlains, sages, priests, stewards, philosophers, constables, prefects, and generals, all dressed in their best silk and satin. From the vantage point of Tyro's throne, the crowd seemed sprinkled with the dust of precious gemstones. The Royal Legions no longer wore either gold or green, but had joined their colors once more: gilded bronze cuirass and helm, olive tabard and cloak, silver spears, and round shields bearing the Golden Sun of Uurz on a green field. Several of the former Green Lords were still missing, yet most had given up their cause. What hope did they have now that Lyrilan was lost to them?

The Scholar King's throne sat empty next to Tyro's own. Talondra stood close at his elbow. His heralds had done well in spreading word of Lyrilan's insane crime. They hardly needed to bother; such scandal and tragedy captured the fancy of every Uurzian. Even in the lowest of streets the common folk spoke of the Scholar King's madness. Vigils honoring the dead Queen Ramiyah sprang up across the city. Those citizens with keen memories compared Lyrilan to Fangodrel of Udurum, the Kinslayer who murdered his own brother to feed his blood-hungry magic. This act had led to his ultimate doom, just as it must for the Scholar King.

Talondra disguised the gleam of triumph swimming in her eyes, but Tyro saw it clearly. A silvery eel gliding in dark waters. Soon she would be the wife of an Emperor. She understood his pain, yet she did not feel it. He followed her example, dispelling emotions to the back of his mind. Today, this day of days, he wore the great crown, a thick loop of gold set with three egg-shaped emeralds above eyes and brow. Already he felt the weight of his impending reign on his head. A golden corselet and green kilt completed his royal attire. The greatsword hung at his side, and the emerald in its pommel matched perfectly the stones of his crown. He might have worn the cloak of emerald silk embroidered with a golden sun, but the day was already hot at mid-morning. He sweated uncomfortably beneath the waving fans of his attendants.

Lyrilan had spoken no words since the morning of his loss. He lingered silent and alone in his lofty chamber, accepting no company save that of Undroth. Tyro had gone to try and speak with his brother, but he could not bring himself to enter Lyrilan's presence. What could he say that would possibly matter? To apologize would only cement his guilt. Lyrilan might even talk him out of what he intended this day. Or he might never speak again. In order to have the strength for what he must do, Tyro chose not to face him at all. Let it be done, and let their lives move on as they must, in separate directions.

That which is painful is best done quickly. Now was the time.

The Sword King rose before the assembled masses. Outside, beyond the trees and hedges, past the outer wall of the palace, the roar of milling commoners was the booming of an ocean shore. Inside the Great Hall every voice fell to silence as Tyro stood. He gazed mournfully at his brother's vacant throne. The sour–sweet scent of blooming heartflower entered the hall, wafted through the high windows on an errant breeze.

"My brother's throne sits empty," Tyro said. His voice rang against the domed ceiling and echoed between glistening marble columns. "The Scholar King will not speak to me. He will not deny what you have heard and what members of this court have seen with their own eyes.

"As I love Lyrilan, I will speak on his behalf. I will speak of Lady Ramiyah, who lies now in the tomb of our ancestors. Faced with the reality of his bloody crime, my brother's mind and heart have deserted him. I know that he grieves for Ramiyah, even as I know he killed her. I know that he repents his pursuit of the dark arts. He is no sorcerer. I know that it was an evil voice in his ear, the tongue of a demon from some dark hell, that raised his hand against the woman he loved. So where Lyrilan will not repent for his crimes, where he will not ask for mercy, I do it for him."

The hall remained silent as his words faded. A lady wept softly somewhere amid the gaudy throng. Someone coughed.

"When power lies just within a man's grasp, yet just out of his reach ... this can bring a fever to the soul, a poisoning of the spirit. So Lyrilan thought to grasp what had eluded him while I yet lived. Every man here knows that my brother was a master of quill rather than blade. He had no hope of defeating me by traditional means. To raise his hand against me in violence would have brought him nothing. So he sought this blood sorcery to bring me low, but instead found his own demise.

"Ah ... my heart is riven. Would that Lyrilan had taken up a sword and found my bare breast. Such would have been a cleaner fate for us both. Yet he chose the way of the shadow, the coward's way. He placed his faith in powers that can never be trusted to guide the destiny of Men. And in that dark investiture, he failed. His demon did not come; his wife lies dead by his own hand, and his sanity hangs by a thread."

Tyro allowed another moment of calm to envelop the chamber. He glanced at Talondra in her sparkling gown of black and green. Her golden crown was a lesser version of his own.

Yes! Her eyes spoke to him. *The power is yours. Take it! Seize this golden moment!*

He turned back to the expectant court.

"The penalty for murdering a noble ... is death," Tyro said, struggling to keep his voice even. His stomach trembled, but he hoped the golden cuirass hid it well. "The penalty for treason is also death. And it is true that my noble father, Emperor Dairon the First, did put to death more than a few warlocks in his day. There is no place in Uurz for this obscene sorcery. Three times my brother has earned his death!"

Now the tears came and Tyro did not stop them. He paused and gathered his breath. Some in the crowd moved forward, moved by his display of grief. Many of those present had loved Lyrilan. Including Tyro.

Forgive me, Brother.

"Yet who but the Gods themselves has the authority to condemn a King to death? I ... I, who love my brother despite his madness and his treachery ... I will not consign him to die. I have not the h ..." He paused. "The heart for it."

Somewhere in the hall a woman cried out. The sounds of sobbing grew louder.

"So I declare on this day, before the High Court of Uurz, that my brother Lyrilan, Son of Dairon ... be exiled. The term of this banishment will be the remainder of his years. So do I give my poor brother life in place of death. Let him take what retainers he wishes to nurse his shattered mind back to health, and enough gold to secure a princely domain in some distant land. Let him walk no more in the City of Sacred Waters or in the Stormlands that serve it.

"Let this decree be inscribed in the Books of Law. Let it be set down in our histories."

The applause began as a smattering then grew to a wave of noise. Nodding heads and approving voices yammered to fill the upper air of the hall like hot smoke.

Tyro inhaled the perfumed sweat of his audience and prepared himself for the final stroke. The battle was almost won.

A raised hand silenced the crowd.

"I, Tyro, Son of Dairon, proclaim myself on this day sole Emperor of Uurz, Sovereign of the Stormlands, Lord of the Sacred River. Let all who are loyal kneel before me in the presence of the Gods. I go now to their house, to receive the holy blessings."

Every man and woman in the hall kneeled then, even the soldiers stationed against column and wall. The moment was pristine and as pure as a drop from the holy river. Even Talondra bowed her head in salute to her husband. Her Emperor. He took her hand and bade her stand. Now she spoke aloud, voice bright with victory.

"Hail the Emperor!"

"Hail the Emperor!" The crowd echoed her words, their common voice ringing from the windows into the courtyards. It reached the dusty streets where the masses waited to hear the news.

Soldiers lifted Tyro in his chair and carried him through the hall, out through the courtyard where the spilled blood and maimed bodies of the skirmish had been removed. They carried him into the teeming streets toward the Grand Temple. There he would take the Emperor's Oath and make his conquest complete.

He wept as if humbled. Uurz cheered and howled and praised his name.

"Look! The Emperor weeps for his poor brother!" someone yelled from a garden wall.

Mistaking the source of his sorrow, they only loved him more.

In their eyes he was the merciful brother, not the mad one.

All the way to the golden walls of the temple towers they shouted his name and proclaimed his worthiness. Talondra followed atop a palanquin of cushions and silks borne on the backs of brawny servants.

"Hail the Empress!" someone called.

Tyro lowered his face into his hands.

Forgive me, Father.

He vowed silently to finish reading Lyrilan's book. Perhaps one day he would see Lyrilan again and tell him how much the gift had meant to him. Or perhaps the Gods would intervene and smite him in the coming war. He might die before ever seeing his brother again. This was, in fact, the most likely outcome of today's events. The world was harsh and the ways of Men were cruel.

Either way, the path to glory lay open before him.

Emperor of Uurz. Conqueror of Khyrei.

All for the cost of a brother's love.

Eventually Lyrilan gave in to the demands of Undroth and took a little water.

A few bites of food. Tasteless. Like mud on the tongue.

He lay on the couch of his sumptuous prison chamber and twisted his hands together. Through the single window he watched western Uurz glimmering in the sunlight, a toy city of golden domes and spires. Somewhere below lay the gardens she had loved. He had waited too long. He should have given her children their first year together. His damn books took him away from her too many times. They even took him away from his throne when he had it.

He said nothing as Undroth explained to him the plot that had claimed Ramiyah's life. She had been used like a game piece, a speck of quartz to exploit and throw away. His brother was a murderer and a liar. Yet he could not believe Tyro did the murdering himself. Killing any woman was beneath the Sword King.

Yet it must have been done with Tyro's approval. How could it not be?

Talondra. She was the soul of it. Now Tyro called him a mad sorcerer, a fiend who would murder what he most loved in a quest for unholy power. Power! As if that had ever mattered to Lyrilan. The power of the written word was his only magic. Now words had failed him utterly. The book of Dairon's life was worthless in his brother's eyes.

". . . has declared himself Emperor and even now takes his oath in the Grand Temple." Undroth droned on in a soft but rugged voice while Lyrilan tugged at the frayed hem of his robe. They had dressed him in dark green, but it seemed the color of dried blood. He had refused to bathe since servants had scoured the blood from his senseless body three days ago. The smell of his own sour sweat reminded him of the reality that lay beneath the surface of all things. Underneath the stink of his living body lay a reeking, rotting corpse waiting to be born.

So does all the world seem now to rot and decay, he mused. But he did not speak such thoughts aloud, or write them down.

Worse than the pain of losing Ramiyah was the agony of guilt. He could have abdicated and given Tyro what he wanted. Yet Lyrilan had refused to give up a throne that he held less worthy than a roomful of parchment and ink. That stubborn refusal had led to his wife's death.

He contemplated leaping from the window. His prison chamber was still high enough in the western tower that the fall would certainly kill him. Whenever Undroth caught him staring at the window like that, the bearded lord placed himself between it and Lyrilan. Very patient, like a father, Undroth attended him always. Was there evil in him as well, lurking beneath the patient words and kindly visage of his uncle?

"Do you hear me, Majesty?" Undroth asked.

Lyrilan turned his eyes away from the mosaic stones of the ceiling. Old Volomses had entered the room unnoticed. He stood behind Undroth with a trio of shuffling attendants bearing coffers and scrolls. Lyrilan stared at them, the muscles in his face and jaw gone slack.

"You must leave the Stormlands," said Undroth. The words sank slowly into Lyrilan's consciousness, as if he lay underwater. "Your exile begins tomorrow. Volomses and I are going with you. I have a few loyal soldiers who will ride with us. We will see to your portage and your funds, but we must move quickly. Is there anything you desire to take with you?"

Lyrilan cast his gaze about the chamber. What mattered this opulent shell, this palace, this city, this Great Assemblage of Lies? The only thing he wanted in this place was Ramiyah. His eyes burned. On a table across the room lay a stack of six dusty tomes. *The Books of Imvek the Silent*. Somehow Volomses had managed to smuggle them in here during the investigation.

Lyrilan raised a bony arm and pointed to the books.

Sorcery. It lay on those pages.

For the first time since the murder, Lyrilan spoke. His voice was a hollow rasping sound. His index finger trembled.

"Bring those," he said.

Volomses bowed low and packed the six books into a small trunk.

Undroth and Volomses shared a hopeful look. They seemed to like the fact that he was now speaking after so much silence.

"Yaskatha," Lyrilan muttered.

"Pardon, Majesty?" said Undroth, drawing nearer to him.

"We will go . . . to Yaskatha."

"As you wish, My King," said Undroth.

King D'zan, a trusted friend, had once lost his throne. He would understand Lyrilan's plight. And there was Sharadza,

Daughter of Vod, who took D'zan as her husband. She was a well-known sorceress.

"Yaskatha," he said again, nodding only to himself.

The two lords did not hear him this time. There was too much scuffling and babbling in the room. The effort to pack a King's entire life into trunk, coffer, and bag had begun.

Lyrilan stared out the window at the jubilant crowds along the tiny streets. They shouted Tyro's name. Another mighty celebration had overtaken the City of Wine and Song. Such parades were not uncommon, but it was not often that the coronation of a new Emperor was their cause.

The green-gold city sighed and moaned beneath him like a great ignorant beast.

He contemplated once more the idea of throwing himself out the window. Letting his bones shatter on the white marble, his flesh burst like a dropped gourd, his blood fountain up to enlighten the festivities.

No. There were better things to do with flesh and blood.

"Yaskatha ..." he mumbled, sitting still amid the flurry of activity.

He breathed and blinked and nodded. He stared at the gray mineral of the floor.

He bit his lip until a drop of red fell from his chin.

"Yaskatha ..."

11

Mountain of Ghosts

The White Mountains did not exist on any map made by the hands of Men. Few, if any, had explored the colossal forest known as Uduria, the untamed realm known as the Giantlands. Fewer still survived the northward trek to view the frozen peaks hemming the northern lip of the continent. Here in the Icelands, on frosted plateau and glacial mountainsides, the blue-skinned Udvorg hunted the great moose and the shaggy mammoth.

King Angrid the Long-Arm was Lord of the Icelands and all the Giant clans north of Uduria. Twice Vireon had walked the eternal snows and entered the vast palace of ice and rock where the Ice King held his court. Yet now, standing once more in the shadow of the icebound peaks, he did not seek the Udvorg King or his counsel. He ran instead up the slopes of frozen hills into the face of a driving storm. He followed the spark of white flame that lingered deep in his heart.

Dahrima the Axe and twenty sisters of the Uduri trailed him, their purple cloaks and black armor sheathed in patches of blue-green ice and pristine frost. Neither Vireon nor his followers felt the bite of the cold, not in the way a human would suffer. They had run for days on end, stopping every third night to rest beneath a frozen moon. They ignored the signs of wild herds passing through the great forest, for this was no time to hunt simple meat. They hunted a Queen and a Princess, and for Vireon nothing else existed in this world. Least of all the driving snow, the smothering winds, or the whelming ice.

At first he went alone into the wild, following in the wake of the white flame. Only the fastest and hardiest Uduri ran after him, as he knew they would. Each day his long strides ate up the leagues of ground between the titanic trees, and each evening as he rested the Uduri caught up to him. After three such evenings he stopped ordering them to turn back. It was no use. Dahrima was as headstrong as any Uduru; her sister-cousins would follow her into death and beyond. So he brooded atop a moonlit boulder while they roasted a freshly killed elk to feed him. Otherwise he would not have eaten at all.

Alua was not herself . . . the child that was not a child had somehow conquered her mind. It must have been easy for the sorceress to twist a mother's love into doting slavery. It was Alua's magic that carried them into the northern sky, yet it was Maelthyn who demanded it. How could he have not seen it sooner? The long trance . . . Alua's crying out . . . her casual dismissal of the problem . . . her sudden sleep. Yet how could a father ever dare to think that his daughter was not his offspring at all, but a vessel for something ancient and wicked? Was there any of Maelthyn left in the tiny body he had cradled and protected for seven years? Or was there only Ianthe the Claw now? And, if so, what did that mean for his family?

For nine days Vireon ran north through the green forest, resting briefly at each sunset. On the ninth day the summer heat was lost beneath cold rains and a sea of rolling gray clouds. On the tenth morning a network of frozen hills arose from the forest proper, a jagged rolling escarpment that was the southernmost bulwark of the White Mountains. The Uduri stared at the sparkling range at sunrise after running all night, and they were breathless. None of them had come this far north, into the realm where their menfolk had gone to join the Ice King's court.

Despite the loss they had endured, the Uduri were grateful to Vireon. He had opened the way to the Icelands, where the pale Uduru could breed with blue-skinned Uduri of the Udvorg to produce the next generation of Giantkind. These Giantesses with their burning hearts were barren inside, like the iced-over waste-land that ringed the peaks. Their most selfless act was in letting their males go north, where they could find new wives and make families. The barren Ninety-Nine had stayed behind to serve Vireon and the City of Men and Giants.

Now they saw for the first time the sparkling realm that had stolen their husbands, brothers, and lovers. The lonesome vastness of it seemed to humble them. Some dropped to their knees in the snow and gave thanks to the nameless Gods.

Vireon climbed a tor and stared into the distance. He scanned the slopes of the white peaks from horizon to horizon as the sun mounted a blue and cloudless sky. The snowstorms had ceased for a while, yet he stood hip deep in the drifts. He heard the scram-bling and cursing of Dahrima as she climbed the slope after him. Always at his heels, that one. She, too, had known his father. Perhaps she saw Vod in Vireon's face when she looked at him. Whatever the reason for her loyalty, he was glad to have her com-pany, though he was loath to say it aloud. In the back of his mind, he wondered how much of himself Vod had shared with Dahrima in the days before he took Shaira's hand.

"Majesty," huffed Dahrima, pulling herself to the top of the hill. She towered over him and squinted at the panorama of wintery mountains. Her golden braids glimmered in the early sunlight Tiny showers of snow and ice fell from her broad back, where her great axe slept. The rest of the Uduri awaited him at the hill's base, catching their breaths and chewing on strips of dried elk flesh. Vireon shifted the scabbard strap that held his greatsword between his shoulder blades. After so many days running, he was beginning to feel the weight of the blade. The spear he carried helped him to navigate treacherous ground, but the sword was only baggage until he needed it. He chose not to think about exactly how he would use that blade, but deep in his heart he already knew.

"What lies beyond these mountains of ice?" asked Dahrima, her breath a white plume.

"A frozen sea," Vireon answered. He had seen that sea only on ancient maps in Udurum's library. Not even the Udvorg Ice Clans roamed that terrific expanse of frozen saltwater. It was the upper end of the world. Here, in these mountains, there was much life. Here the Udvorg made their ancestral home and enjoyed the wild game and isolation of a people at peace. The clans might fight among themselves at times, but the blue-skins had not known war since the Age of Serpents, when they had split with their Uduru cousins and sought the Icelands. Now the two strains of Giantkind were united once again. All save the childless Uduri.

"This devil we hunt," Dahrima said, her voice lowering. "It is the same one that killed my six cousins?"

"It is," said Vireon, his eyes caressing the great peaks. Some sign, anywhere, anything . . .

The mountains breathed cold winds down upon him, as if warning him to turn back.

"It has stolen the Queen," Dahrima said. "And the little one . . . "

Vireon nodded. How could he explain to Dahrima that the "devil" was a sorceress who should have died years ago? How could he make her understand that this murderous bloodthirsty thing did not kidnap his daughter, but simply *was* his daughter? Could that even be true? Was there any truth to Maelthyn at all, or had her existence been merely a disguise? A ruse meant only to provide rebirth for Ianthe. Alua had not burned her from the world as he had so long believed ... she had only incinerated Ianthe's physical form. Had Alua ever been truly pregnant? His eyes welled with salty tears and the wind quickly froze them into tiny icicles. He wiped them away with the back of his hand.

"We will follow you across this world if we must, and into the next one," Dahrima said. "But how do you know where to find them in all this wasteland?"

Vireon spat into the snow. "I know," he said. He slammed a fist against his black-mailed chest. "Here."

"This is blue-skin country," she said.

He nodded. "They know we have come," said Vireon. "They watch us even now. I've smelled them since we entered these frigid hills."

Dahrima looked about the snowy landscape with wary eyes. "Yet we do not see them."

"Soon," said Vireon, running down the hill and heading north. A new day of running had begun. "Soon you will ... " he yelled back at her. She and her sister-cousins followed.

The Udvorg met them at the bottom of a snow-choked ravine. Running was next to impossible here, so Vireon slowed his pace while the Uduri caught up to him. His first encounter with the Udvorg had been violent and poisoned by ignorance. He wondered if they would recognize his authority this time. He had left his gleaming crown in Udurum. Yet who else would travel this far into the Icelands with a band of fierce-eyed Uduri?

Several hunting parties had converged to meet him as one. Each of the thirty-two Udvorg stood as tall as the Uduri, a few even taller. Vireon waited between the two bands of Giants as they marched toward one another. The Udvorg wore beards matted with hoarfrost. The dyed pelts of gargantuan tigers and snow lions hung from their shoulders. Their hair, white as the snow itself, contrasted greatly with their skin, which was the color of the sky or a slightly more pale blue. They snuffled with flat noses and stared at the Uduri with eyes red as blood. They had obviously never seen or smelled anything like these pale females. Some grunted like bulls, ready to charge and force a mating. Others stood quietly behind the Leader of the Hunt, a brawny Giant with a chain of iron and icy jewels hanging about his tree-trunk neck. Their spears were longer and thicker than those of the Uduri, the keen heads forged of black iron. Each hunter carried at his waist an iron mace or hammer, as well as a skinning knife. Talismans of bone, bronze, and gold hung from ear, nostril, and earlobe. The Udvorg went barefoot in the deep snow.

If they stood here long enough, the snows would bury them all. How many frozen Giant corpses lay buried far beneath the drifts even now? The huntsman called to Vireon as a light snowfall began.

"Hail, King of the South!" bellowed the huntsman, raising his spear. His fellows stood cautiously behind him, more interested in the Uduri than the tiny King. The day was growing long, and deep shadows moved along the ravine. Soon it would lie in total darkness.

Vireon raised his own spear in a corresponding salute. Trudging forward, he stood within a bowshot of the blue-skins. The Uduri crept cautiously behind him, Dahrima nearly at his back. He could only imagine what went through their heads as they looked upon their ancient cousins and recognized the savage vitality their own tribe had lost centuries ago.

"They stink," Dahrima whispered. Vireon might have smiled, but he was in no mood.

"Say nothing," he told her.

The Udvorg huntsman called again in the language of his people, which, despite certain differences and strangeness of accent, was the same as that of the Uduru. "I am Thurguz of the Ivory Seekers," he announced. "We go to stalk the high plateau where the mammoth roams. Yet before I leave the realm of my King, here I see another King come walking."

"You know then who I am," Vireon yelled through the rising wind.

The Udvorg laughed. "Only the King of Udurum would travel with such a retinue. Who are these Uduri?"

The crimson pupils of the Udvorg studied the snow-frosted Uduri with evident lust. The Giantesses stared back at them, unspoken challenges flickering in their black eyes. Dahrima lifted the great axe from her back and stepped to Vireon's side.

"They are my personal guard," answered Vireon. "The Daughters of Udurum. The Ones Who Stayed."

Thurguz shared a few rough words with his hunters, then turned his eyes back to Vireon. "We shall accompany you to the Palace of the Ice King, where these Uduri may visit their male cousins."

"No," said Vireon. "We too hunt on this day."

Thurguz blinked and a shower of ice crystals fell from his jutting brow. "Surely there is much game in the southern forest. None but Udvorg may hunt the mammoth, or the moose, or the tiger. The White Mountains are closed to those not of our clan. Even to Kings."

Vireon drove the point of his walking spear into the frozen snow. "I care not for your game. I hunt for my missing child and wife."

The Udvorg stood silent, shifting from foot to foot and studying the Uduri with animal fascination.

Thurguz laughed again. "How could mother and child be so far from home? This land is death to those born in the south. Surely your hunt will find only corpses."

Vireon ignored the callous words.

"I seek a white flame," he said.

The Udvorg exchanged a series of grunts and suspicious glances.

"You have seen it," Vireon said.

Thurguz bent low and rested his weight on one knee. His craggy face loomed near to Vireon. Dahrima's eyes followed the Udvorg's movements with a burning intensity. She might kiss his frosty lips or slice off his head. Either was as likely. His voice was a coarse whisper cutting through the wind.

"There is a haunted mountain not far from here," he said. His breath was like winter itself, colder than the night. "We passed it on our last hunt and saw the blazing of restless spirits about its summit. They burned like white flames in the night. This place is called Kyorla, Mountain of Ghosts. Knowing of its nature, we left these ghosts to themselves as we always do. They are the lost souls of those who died on the ice."

"Will you show me this peak?" Vireon asked.

Thurguz ran a hand through his wild beard, pulling free the accumulated ice, frost, and snow. It rained down at Vireon's feet. The Udvorg's eyes turned to Dahrima. Her jaw was firmly set, her eyes unknowable.

"That depends," he said, smiling. His teeth were the light blue of a frozen pond. "If this one gives me a kiss . . . and promises to bring her sisters to my lord's palace when the hunt is done."

Dahrima spat at the Udvorg's feet. "Unwashed savage!" she said. "You ask favors beyond your station! We are warriors, not courtesans!"

Thurguz smiled again, threw his head back and laughed. "You

misunderstand me! We invite you as honored guests, not carnal conquests. We are the brothers of your ancestors! We lay our spears at your feet to show our respect." He tossed his black spear into the snow, and his thirty-one brothers followed his example. Dahrima glanced back at her sister-cousins. They spoke without words, sentiments moving from eye to eye. The blue-skinned Udvorg women had taken their males; perhaps some of the lonely Uduri would take Udvorg males as husbands. Vireon would release them from their oath of servitude if they so desired it. But their great pride would prohibit the asking of such a thing.

"To the second part of your bargain I agree," said Vireon. "The Uduri will come to Angrid's Hall before the next moon rises. As for your first request ... that is up to Dahrima."

The proud Giantess looked down at her King, and Vireon wondered how she would choose. He would not order her to debase herself, but he trusted her to support his quest. Alua and Maelthyn were the goal, and this was a small thing to ask. Yet the Uduri's innate sense of nobility was something no Man or Giant could outguess.

Dahrima sighed, dropped her axe into the ice, and approached Thurguz the Huntsman. The Udvorg's crimson eyes grew large as she grabbed his great head, knocking the horned helm from his brow. She planted her warm lips on his cold ones, and for a while only the wailing of the night wind was heard in the ravine. When she released him, Thurguz fell backwards into the snow. His fellows roared with mirth and shuffled forward as if they, too, would receive hot kisses.

Dahrima took up her axe and faced them. "The first to touch me loses his manhood, then his head." The Udvorg redoubled their laughter and ceased their clumsy advance. Thurguz pulled himself out of the snow and stood once more at his full height. He picked up his spear and let his gaze linger on Dahrima.

"I like this pale Uduri!" he shouted to his brothers. "Her kiss brings the heat of the sun to scorch my loins." More laughter ensued as the hunters regained their spears.

Vireon looked up at the crescent moon sliding from behind the heavy clouds.

"Come, King of the South," said Thurguz.

He followed the mass of Udvorg, and the Uduri followed him. They tramped up the far neck of the ravine and stood inside a ring of glacial mountainscapes. Thurguz pointed a meaty arm in the direction of the Mountain of Ghosts. East, toward the distant shore of the Far Sea. Yet this far north the sea was most likely frozen, making it part of that nameless ocean of ice that smothered the edge of the world.

The Udvorg fell into their accustomed hunters' jog, which was somewhat slower than the pace Vireon had set for the past ten days. The Uduri had no trouble keeping up with him. Now they filed along precarious mountain trails where the snows were not so deep. In this way, following trails only Udvorg could see or sense, they moved from slope to slope, on through the night.

Vireon saw the white flame well before they reached the side of the mountain. It danced and flashed like a pale aurora about the ice-clad summit. The white spark in his heart was kindled into a fresh blaze, almost hot enough to dispel the chill in his weary limbs. In the back of his mind he wondered if Ianthe were leading him to this place, and then he decided she must be. Unless it was Alua, calling to him from afar. Yet if she was in the grip of Maelthyn's spell – Ianthe's spell – how could she do so? No, it must be the sorceress who stole his daughter's body, urging him onward to his death. He might die here, but Ianthe would not escape a second time. He put all other thoughts out of his head as he climbed.

Vireon, thirty-two Udvorg, and twenty-one Uduri scaled the frozen slope, digging fingers and toes into solid ice, drawing themselves inexorably upward. The white flame was not constant. At times only darkness lay upon the mountain's crown, but always the burst of colorless light returned again. A beacon of death, his own or that of his enemy.

Now the earth shook and a vast portion of the mountainside fell away into darkness with a deafening roar. A rain of jagged icicles and avalanches of snow fell upon the climbers. One of the Udvorg lost his grip and fell howling into the lower dark. The winds blew fierce and terrible, driving sleet into their faces as they climbed onward. Vireon scrambled at their forefront, his urgent need driving him faster and faster up the peak. He might have told the Udvorg to stay below. They might even have listened, unlike the Uduri, who would not abandon him regardless of their fate. He supposed the blue-skins did not want to be outdone by the females, so they came along. Vireon was too set in maintaining his upward path to speak aloud of the matter.

All through the night they climbed, crossing sheer faces that no human could survive without the strength and fortitude of Giants invested in his body. The storm never ceased, and the ice at times froze over Vireon's mouth and nose. He paused regularly to crack it from his face in order to breathe. This was not an issue for the Udvorg; snow and ice were as balmy breezes to them. The Uduri climbed on, painfully yet silently.

Perhaps an hour remained before dawn when Vireon pulled himself onto a narrow tableland within three bowshots of the mountain's peak. The white flames danced above this great ledge clear and bright as lightning. Now he saw the source of it as he brought his legs up to kneel on the icy shelf. A tall crevice opened in the side of the mountain. A gout of white flame poured from it like a raging spirit, flying about and disappearing into the sky. Every few seconds another flash brought another flame spilling from the cave into the upper air.

Vireon walked toward the flashing cleft. The Giants scrabbled up behind him, finding their own room on the narrow plateau one at a time. Before Dahrima and Thurguz had finished their climb, Vireon stood halfway to the cave mouth. Perhaps Alua lay within, hurt or dying, sending her white flame out again and again as a message. Could Maelthyn be with her? Could she have driven Ianthe away from this forsaken place? He forced himself to remain calm as he pulled the greatsword from its scabbard on his back.

A frosted corpse lay half buried in the snow before the cave.

Vireon's heart shattered into icy shards.

Alua . . .

She lay with eyes open, staring at the cold stars. Her pupils gleamed with that same cold light, like iced gems. Her long blonde hair was mostly lost beneath the snow, and her ribcage was a jagged hole. An empty crevice yawned where her heart had once been. Blood had spilled and frozen into the ice about her, leaving two lines of red from the corners of her mouth to the back of her jawbone. An artificial smile; the death mask of a naked skull. There was little of beauty left in her vacant, blue face.

Vireon's breath came in difficult gasps now. He blinked at Alua's dead body, realizing what her missing heart meant. The Giants closed in behind him, wordless, spears pointed at the black crevice.

Another blast of white flame shot from the darkness. The naked figure of a full-grown woman stood limned in the glow of sorcery. A mane of snowy hair flew about her shoulders, dancing in the deathwinds. Her black diamond eyes glowed like twin stars. The light and its flame were Alua's own . . . but it was not Alua who stood in the cave's mouth. Nor was it his daughter. Not any longer.

"*Father* . . . " The word fell upon him like a physical blow, borne to his ears through the cutting wind. "I knew you would come. I've been waiting here for you."

The greatsword trembled in his hands. "Maelthyn?" he said, already knowing that name was forever dead.

She stepped forward and the white flames about her hands lit up her face. It was the face of Maelthyn, so like that of Alua. And yet it was not her face at all. Her hair had changed from black to bone-pale, and there was nothing of blue left in her ebony pupils. The last traces of Vireon's blood had been shed like a viper's skin. Where was the tiny body, the delicate limbs, the pretty face of his daughter?

Elements of Maelthyn lingered in the lovely face, distorted as it was by a cruel smile. A touch of Alua's chin . . . the cast of the nose . . . Yet the cheekbones were all wrong, and the black eyes nearly almondine.

Khyrein. She looked at him with Khyrein eyes.

"Is this all the Giants you could rouse for me?" she asked. Laughter lurked at the edge of her voice. "They must be a lazy bunch."

The Udvorg growled and the Uduri crouched as one into their killing stances. Yet Vireon stood motionless before the slayer of his wife and daughter.

Ianthe. He must not say the name aloud. Something inside him knew it would mean his doom. Yet it was her. The Claw of Khyrei.

Her smile was wicked and gleeful. The white flame surged and she became a great white panther tall as a warhorse. It bared yellow fangs longer than daggers and spoke to him in Maelthyn's voice. "You did not think your whore of a wife actually ended me?" The words fell impossibly from the panther's maw. "You knew all along that something was not as it should be. Tell me you never had the urge to smother the little brat while she slept. To slit her throat and be done with it."

Vireon tightened his knuckles about the grip of his sword. He took one step closer.

"No," the beast said, wistfully. "You were a kindly father, and I thank you for that." The panther glanced at the mutilated corpse of Alua. "And she was a dutiful mother. She brought me here to save me from *you*."

A tiny sound fell from Vireon's lips, almost a whimper.

"She was as ancient as I am," said Ianthe. "Yet still so ignorant. She thought to burn my life away, but that was only my physical shell. I planted my immortal essence inside her womb like a seed in fertile soil. All I needed was a new cradle of flesh for this world, and she birthed it for me without ever knowing the truth. For seven years I dreamed inside that tiny crucible . . . until I remembered who I was. Then the bloodshadows came to answer my call . . . feeding me with the hearts they stole . . . and I grew."

Vireon recalled the white panther soaring above the dying Shar Dni. The cries of panic and chaos, the bloody streets choked with bodies. He saw again Alua release the full power of her white flame and the panther dissolve like smoke in its blinding glow. Alua had fallen to earth, scarred but whole, and he had lifted her in his arms. The spirit of Ianthe had already infected Alua's body, though he would never know until it was far too late.

His daughter's entire existence was a lie.

"So nice to wear the flesh again," said the panther. Its black eyes flashed. "So many pleasures to indulge, so much blood to taste."

Vireon's eyes darted to the corpse of Alua and back to the great cat. A red tongue slithered out to lick its chops.

"Her heart was tender and delicious," said Ianthe. "And now her white flame is mine. Yet still I am hungry. Thank you for bringing these lovely Giants to me. Already I smell the power of their ancient blood."

The cry that escaped Vireon's lips was something between a growl and a bellow of agony. The blue blade of his sword swept across the panther's throat. The beast pulled back its head and avoided the weapon's bite. It reared above him on its hind claws as he brought the blade back in the opposite direction. A crimson weal appeared across the cat's wide chest, then forward claws and gnashing fangs fell upon him like a storm. Its weight seemed that of a mountain, and he fell beneath its bulk to the floor of the broad ledge.

Twelve great spears came flying. Each one sank deep into the beast's snowy flesh. Its wounds rained scarlet upon the snow. It caught Vireon's right arm between its jaws, but the fangs did not break his stony flesh. Its slicing claws tore his mail shirt to shreds. His left hand grabbed a fistful of its underbelly fur, and he heaved it back toward the cave. Spear hafts splintered and cracked as it rolled across the ice and came up on all fours. The seeping wounds did not faze it.

The swipe of a great claw caught the side of Vireon's head, and he tumbled toward the lip of the plateau. He would have fallen into the great chasm below, had he not driven the sword's point into the ice like a climbing spike.

Uduri and Udvorg circled the raging beast, some jabbing with spears, others swinging iron maces or axes. The panther moved faster than the wind itself. Its long claws found throats and eyes, puncturing both. Udvorg hunters screamed, and their violet blood stained the snow. The weight of the beast's front and back legs shattered more spears, snapping their shafts like twigs. Bronze spearheads went flying and Giants toppled bleeding.

Vireon climbed to his feet, barely noticing the lacerations on his arm where the fangs had finally broken through his skin. The panther vomited a gout of white flames now, and the blue-skins burned, wailing. Some of them fell, or leaped, from the ledge, hurtling into the glacial dark, smoldering until they hit the snows far below.

Dahrima cleaved the beast with her axe, opening its flesh in three places. Her sisters fought with sword and spear, though the beast was too fast for most of them. It swirled, a whirlwind of claw and fang, knocking Giants back, wounding, killing, or casting them from the mountain.

Vireon charged through the great legs of the Giants and found an opening. He drove the point of his blade deep into the panther's heaving side. Already it bled from a score of wounds, yet it did not slow or howl with pain. Unlike a real panther, it did not growl or roar. It only breathed another flood of white flame, catching Vireon in the blaze.

He lost his grip on the sword as the full force of Alua's stolen power fell upon him. Never before had he felt the sensation of *burning*. It was a new agony for one immune to the earth's natural heat and cold. He stumbled back, howling, and his stubborn flesh steamed.

The panther grabbed an Uduri's head in its fangs and crushed the skull to pulp. Dahrima screamed as the first of her sisters died. The beast lapped at the hot blood spilling from the headless body, and Vireon watched its score of wounds closing and steaming with white flame. How could he kill this abomination?

He took up a fallen Giant's spear and charged forward again, his skin red and blistered. Again she caught him in the sweep of a mighty claw and sent him flying. He crashed into the hulking body of an Udvorg, solid as a marble wall. Regaining his senses, he saw that it was Thurguz.

"Up, King of the South!" howled the Giant, raising his bloody mace. "We kill or we die!"

Thurguz leaped into the fray, where Dahrima and the others suffered beneath a new blast of flames from between the beast's jaws. The Uduri howled their pain across the mountaintops, a sound that would chill the bones of the Gods if they bothered to listen. Several Giants of both tribes died in that single moment,

flesh turned to ash over blackened bones. Death played no
favorites.

Thurguz slammed the panther to the earth with his great mace.
Now it was a panther no longer, but a young woman once again.
Naked and savage. The distorted face of Alua gleamed, the last
remnants of Maelthyn's smile lingering there. Her dark eyes
flashed and the Udvorg huntsman fell strangely still. Vireon
leaped forward but it was too late. Ianthe wrapped her lithe arms
and legs about Thurguz, digging fangs into his neck. She ripped
through the solid flesh as if it were straw, drinking deep of his
cold, indigo blood.

The blue-skin hunters rushed forward again. She whirled the
Udvorg body around to shield her as she feasted. Three spears and
a sword blade plunged into Thurguz's gut and chest. His allies
had not been quick enough to turn their attacks.

Vireon watched the life go out of the huntsman's ruby eyes
while the battle paused, the Giants and Giantesses horrified by
their own error. Now the huntsman's body fell forward on its face.
The snow-maned woman crouched on his back, dripping purple
blood from her narrow chin.

Vireon lunged for her, but the force of her scream held him at
bay. A winter storm poured from Ianthe's gore-smeared mouth.
The shrill wailing of a cyclone rose from her throat into the sky,
and the mountain itself trembled beneath her. Great sheets of
ice broke off from surrounding peaks and tumbled into the
darkness.

Then the peak of Kyorla, Mountain of Ghosts, shattered into
a storm of frozen splinters.

Vireon and the Giants fell, many pierced by lances of ice, others
tumbling amid the great boulders of frosted stone. Vireon reached
out and grasped the lip of the ledge with the fingers of his right
hand. The wind tore at his blistered skin and the screeching cry

of the sorceress shivered the world. He dangled above the roaring abyss.

As the last of the Giantesses sailed past him and was lost in the chasm below, his only thought was to hold on. She could not escape him a second time. Her crime was too great. The Bitch of Khyrei must die this day, on this crumbling mountain. A howling void yawned below him, eager to swallow his tiny form.

Now she stood on the flattened summit of the mountain, atop a pile of bloodied ice and torn bodies. At the bottom of that frozen cairn lay the remains of Alua, unless the demon winds had already scattered them to nothing. At last the screaming stopped and the white flame raged about Ianthe's lean body like a torrent. She was laughing, awash in the glory of her new power, stolen from the heart of Alua and the blood of Uduri and Udvorg alike.

She did not look at the dangling Vireon. Her flaming eyes stared southward.

In the ecstasy of her seething sorcery she ignored him. She was bloated on the blood of Giants, and she must have thought him fallen, dead, or lost with the rest of them. Now was his chance. He strove to bring his left arm up to join his right one, grasping a narrow spar of ice at the terminus of the ledge. He sank powerful fingers into that ice and pulled himself upward. He would lunge at her from below, and once he got his fingers around her neck let her burn and bite him. He would not let go until she was dead. Even his own death would not prevent this.

It was not the strength of his limbs that betrayed him. It was the ice that crumbled beneath his double grip. He clutched only a meaningless chunk of it now, and he fell into utter blackness.

For the second time he fell watching a pale comet speed away into the sky.

Khyrei. The name lingered in his mind as he plummeted into the chasm, a far greater fall than that from his tower.

The white flame soared across the southern sky, and he knew exactly where it would alight. Ianthe was going home.

He would have shouted a promise to pursue and destroy her once and for all, but the sudden impact of his body carried him deep into a vast bank of frozen snow, and on through the layer of ice beneath it. He knew only darkness then, and all thoughts faded as rushing snow filled his mouth and throat.

How does one measure time when trapped in the jaws of death?

How long he lay sleeping under the ice he could not guess.

The first inkling of his own continued existence was a burst of sunlight on his face. Deep cracking sounds filled the cocoon of ice and snow in which he lay. Something had broken through above him, admitting the sun's golden rays. He blinked into the brilliance. The shaggy head of an Udvorg looked down at him, then called out to his fellows. They tore the compacted snow and ice away from him and lifted him from the hole.

The day was painfully bright. The flesh of his arms, chest, neck, and face was red, and he bled from a score of wounds. He was unaccustomed to feeling such discomfort. Yet when he focused on his suffering, it gave him a kind of reckless strength. He stood by himself on the surface of the frozen snow.

The surviving Udvorg had been digging out their fellows all day. Nine Uduri lay senseless but alive on the bright snow. They had also been dragged from icy graves. Seventeen Udvorg had survived the collapse of the mountain peak. Hot tears brimmed in Vireon's eyes and ran across his burning cheeks.

Dahrima . . .

Her name was a sudden flame bursting to life in his breast.

She lay among her sister-cousins, weaponless, her armor battered and torn, dried blood crusted or frozen along her limbs. She, like him, had been burned. Yet she lived. Even now she groaned and lifted her head from the snow. The Udvorg milled about them, sniffing the snow for other survivors they might dig free. They found none. The White Mountains stood high and imperious about them in all directions. The peak directly above was broken Kyorla, standing like a crownless king among his glittering brothers.

Vireon stood near to Dahrima as she raised herself into a sitting position. She moaned and cracked her back with a stretch of her torso. She blinked into the sunlight. Her gaze fell across her sleeping sister-cousins.

"How many?" she asked.

"All but nine," he answered. "I am sorry."

She ignored the apology.

"And the panther bitch?"

"Gone," he said. "To Khyrei."

"Then we march . . ." She paused to spit a mouthful of blood from her torn lip.

"Yes," said Vireon. "We march. But remember our bargain with the Udvorg."

"Must we go with them?" she asked.

"I would go regardless," he said. "To see the Ice King. To win all his forces for the Long March."

"Majesty?"

"War," he said. "War on Khyrei."

Dahrima stood and dusted the frost from her limbs.

"You will join with the Sword King of Uurz?"

Vireon nodded, focusing on his pain. His reminder. His touchstone.

"I will bring the wrath of Giantkind down upon her head," he said. "I will crush her black city into dust. I should have done it long ago."

Dahrima's voice sank to a whisper. She touched her King's

shoulder tenderly. Her lips came close to his ear. "What of the little one? And the poor Queen?"

Dead, he wanted to say. *Both are dead.*

One never had a chance to live at all.

Instead he said nothing, but only sat down in the snow and wept.

12

The Red Wine of Khyrei

Sunlight became an unpleasant memory. Sharadza slept by day in the tower of her rebirth, its windows shuttered behind tapestries of black wool. Each evening the moon called her forth, the invisible weight of it hanging above the city. Wisps of silver moonlight crept across the onyx stones of the palace. She met Gammir in a sunken courtyard beneath the diamond stars. In that place a wild grove of the jungle had been re-created for the Emperor's pleasure. The gnarled, crimson trees twisted their branches into the night like grasping claws. Leaves the color of ancient wine fell upon the cobblestones and faded to the pallor of dead flesh. This was the Red Garden. Here the deadliest of Khyrei's flora grew from roots watered with the blood of young slaves.

Among those sharp-edged leaves grew the ruby blossoms of the bloodflower. Sharadza walked with him in the grove of poisonous foliage and watched his long pale fingers pick the choicest blossoms. She carried a wicker basket into which he tossed the scarlet petals. They sat on a garden divan carved into the likeness of a winged Serpent with a pair of great bloodstones for eyes. A slave girl brought Gammir's long pipe of silver and pearl; Sharadza watched as he stuffed the red petals into the bowl of the pipe and lit it with a burning taper. So it went every night.

She had learned to enjoy the acrid yet sweet smoke of the bloodflower. It elevated her perceptions, showing her the sea of blood constantly moving and flowing about the city. With the dun smoke creeping from between her lips, she saw the red glow of that blood, singing and surging in the body of every slave and soldier, every courtier and courtesan, every peasant and noble. Any of them might offer her a meal to thrill and amaze her newborn senses.

The first few times the hunger came she fell immediately upon some hapless slave and drained him dry. Gammir watched laughing from the dark divan. In time he taught her not to rush the feeding. He showed her how to savor the hunger, to enjoy the onset of the Great Thirst . . . to take her time in choosing whose sacred fluid would fill her belly.

It was a lesson she had taken to heart.

Each night, after sharing the bloodflower, they rose above the city as leather-winged shadows. She soared with him about the forest of ships' masts in the harbor, the black and red reavers that made Khyrei the terror of the Golden Sea. Swarms of sailors crawled like ants across the decks and wharves. They winged above the peaks of noble estates where the upper class of Khyrei conducted their feasts. Along a thousand streets and alleys they fluttered and careened, sending wary nightwalkers running for the comfort of hearth and home. They fed on the blood of wayward harlots and drunkards, leaving bodies drained and withered in the filth behind squalid taverns. In the palace victims were carefully chosen and prepared for them; in the streets they were predators snatching easy prey for the savage pleasure of it.

South toward the jungle they flew. Sharadza looked upon thousands of slaves gathered about tiny huts among the vast and bountiful fields. Companies of Onyx Guards on charcoal steeds kept order in this second city lying outside the high walls. Hearthfires gleamed in the shadow of the great wilderness. On they flew, diving into the deep shadows of the jungle itself, where the moonlight could never reach. He showed her terrible things that lurked in the red gloom, told her the secrets of the venomous herbs and insects that made it their home. At times these night flights even took them far out over the Golden Sea, where the waves danced madly and the bloated moon reigned supreme. There she discovered the origin of that sea's name by the yellow glitter of moonglow across the main.

How many lives did she take, living in this way? She soon lost count.

They were only slaves anyway. Most of them.

Only humans.

How many times did she lie with Gammir, lost in the pleasure of his dark embrace?

Why put a number to it?

His touch thrilled her like no mortal man ever had.

There was only one.

Gammir was her Lord, her Prince, her Emperor, her Lover.

For his part, Gammir had little to do with the daily business of the city. The Council of Lords, an assembly of the heads of noble houses, ran the mundane affairs of Khyrei. They reported to the Emperor every seven days. When their decisions displeased him, Gammir corrected them with torture and death. Fear of these two penalties made them strive most heartily to meet his every desire, even when it cost the lives of their wives or children. And there was always the threat of having one's noble status revoked. Being cast into instant slavery was far worse than death for the highborn citizens of the black city. So, as Gammir shared with her, the city practically ran itself. His empire consisted of the Golden Sea, the city, and the southern jungles. His ships held the sea, fear held the city, and the deadly jungle took care of itself.

The Great Thirst was her constant motivator. She craved blood as a drunkard craves wine. Yet at times a single ray of light speared through the blood and shadow in her mind, and it troubled her. Like a needle slipped into her skull just behind the eyes. It danced and gleamed like a white flame, but she ignored it until the pain grew too great to bear. Then she fed, and the warm blood smothered the light, bringing comfort and strength.

Gammir spent much of the time alone in his high tower. He would not allow her to set foot there, not since the first night she had arrived and felt his velvet embrace. She had no doubt that he wove some great spell at the top of the barbed spire. She heard his voice ringing from the upper windows, a strange language that she could not understand. Flashes of emerald, azure, and violet burst from the tower windows when he worked his hidden sorcery. He mentioned it to her only in vague whispers and riddles.

"You are my Princess now, Sharadza," he told her. "In time you will know all ... "

She might have invaded his sanctuary and demanded a part in his machinations, but the Great Thirst always came upon her when she dared to set foot on the lowest of his stairs. Instead of walking up the stairwell and joining the sorcery he worked, she found herself flying from the courtyard again, seeking more of the Red Wine of Khyrei. A vintage that could only be found in the hearts and veins of the city's living populace.

Tonight was no different. Except that she had chosen to walk the city. Draped in a cloak and hood of sable fabric, she passed among the lanterns, gates, and walls of her dark kingdom. Most of those who roamed the streets after sunset were laborers, citizens who made their living by the sweat of their brows. They shuffled hurriedly through the gloom, keeping one eye on the shadows at their backs and carrying unknown burdens in sack and keg.

The youths of noble houses cavorted well into the night on the Street of Eighty-One Delights. They poured from the noble quarter in garish silks and gaudy capes, seeking bottles of drink and illicit substances to drown their ennui. They were a handsome lot, if completely foolish: pale of skin, dark of hair and eye, heedless of good taste, and arrogant as Princes. Their highborn women were the most ostentatious, traveling by slave-borne palanquins draped in silks and tinkling baubles. Their enormous headdresses reminded Sharadza of spiderwebs, intricate nets of agate and jade. She had seen less flamboyant gowns worn by Queens, though she could not remember where.

No Khyrein saw her as she passed among them, for such was her will. Yet men shuddered and women gasped as she walked near. They lingered on street corners and jousted drunkenly, made love sloppily in the nearest of alleyways, and finally staggered into the shelter of a drinking house where their status would be recognized. The proprietors of such establishments had little choice but to treat these young nobles like Kings and Queens.

All of these young fools pretending to be royalty. Pretending to be Gammir, their omnipotent Emperor, the Undying Lord who had eluded death.

Something deep within her suggested that she share their rollicking company, but the Great Thirst called her back into the night. She passed a couple fornicating beneath the awning of a sidestreet merchant shop, then took the thoroughfare leading to the Southern Gate, which closed every night just after sunset.

Keep walking. Walk through those gates and never come back to this place. Fly!

She hissed and a gray-eyed cat leaped from a heap of garbage, terrified by her passing.

The city was a pulsing living organism spreading all around her, and she was the black-tongued wolf set to rend and devour it. Her nails grew into claws and the fangs in her jaw crept out between her lips. She stood at the corner of two main streets, insubstantial as a fog.

Silently ravenous.

A troop of masked sentinels marched along the way, members of the Onyx Guard returning from a day among the fields. What must the hearty blood of the plantation slaves taste like? Perhaps among those who knew neither leisure nor luxury, she would find a stronger drink. She had grown accustomed to the thin blood of the city slaves. Occasionally, she and Gammir chose a victim from one of the noble houses. The blood of nobles was richer, darker, more flavorful. Every few generations an unlucky noble house was cast into slavery to invigorate the breeding pool of the workforce. To strengthen the blood of the slaves.

"If we drank only noble blood," Gammir jested, "there would be no city left to rule."

A likely bit of prey walked among the night vapors spilling from sewer and hearth. A young girl, low-bred, wrapped in a tattered shawl. She carried a bundle in her arms. An infant.

Shardaza did not care if she was a whore or a good wife. She cared only for the pulsing red within. The newborn life was too insignificant, so she brushed it aside with one long arm. The baby, wrapped in thick swaddling, fell onto the muddy stones with a muffled cry. Its mother stared into Sharadza's commanding eyes. Sharadza saw herself reflected in the girls' pupils. Pale oval of a face, ivory fangs between ruby lips. The young mother would have screamed, but Sharadza gripped her by the throat, turning her head to expose the throbbing neck vein.

No. Not again . . .

Her fangs sank deep into the soft throat. The warm essence of eternity spilled across her lips, caressed her tongue, and slid down the gully of her throat. The glimmer of light in her skull faded once more, and she quivered with ecstasy. The baby lay between them, wailing for a meal that would never come. Perhaps in any other city, someone would have run to answer the cries of a desperate child. But this was Khyrei. All children knew suffering here; age was no bar to tragedy. The night did not belong to the people of the city. It belonged to the Emperor and his pets.

Is that all I am now? His pet?

She drank deeply, taking every last drop of red from the young mother. Finally she picked up the emaciated body and tossed it into the trash of the alley. It weighed no more than an empty wine sack.

A pair of glinting eyes drew her attention. A black hound watched her from the shadows at the back of the alley. She hissed at it, spewing tiny drops of red across the pavement, but it did not run. It only slunk back into the shadows. Still she felt its eyes upon her.

In the euphoric depths of her satiety, she forgot the fallen child completely. It squalled a forlorn little song as she rose like a great bat into the sky.

She flapped her black wings and sped toward the palace.

Tonight he sat in the Great Hall on his throne of onyx and cloudy crystal. Seven advisors stood about him in a half-circle, bowing as they took in his soft words. Each wore the tall hat of a functionary, ludicrous blends of fabric and silver thread hung with talismans of bone and jewel. Their robes were white and each wore a sash of a certain color: green for agriculture, yellow for city works, black for military, silver for palace functionaries. Among the seven stood three generals: the Sea Lords Hinjutu and Muiduk, and the land-bound Warlord Kuchai. Each of the three wore a curved scimitar in a jeweled scabbard. About the pillars of the hall stood a dozen spearmen, Onyx Guards with faces inscrutable behind their fanged masks. The flames of hanging braziers bathed their black armor in bloody hues.

Sharadza entered the hall in her black gown. The satin rustled like the sound of folding wings, and Gammir raised his narrow head to smile at her. A wave of his hand dismissed the advisors. They dare not spare her a glance as she approached the throne. She sank to her knees on the topmost step of the royal dais and laid her head against his knee, wrapping an arm about his calf.

"My wandering Princess," he cooed, running fingers through her thick curls. "How was your hunt this evening?"

"Fruitful," she breathed.

He cradled her chin and turned her face to him. His beautiful eyes gleamed blacker than night itself. "Yet you seem despondent."

"My Lord keeps secrets," she said.

He grinned, then lowered his lips to hers. "No longer," he said. "The time has come." He rose from the throne and led her by the hand toward the stairwell of the high tower. Whenever his flesh met her skin, she trembled, not with fear, but with a fearsome desire. His was the power to kindle her lust even with a glance. He was her Lord. Her Master.

He is your brother!

He was the Emperor of Khyrei. She belonged to him, as did everything else beneath the stars. Now he led her up the winding stairs to induct her into the inner mysteries of his house. Soon he would raise her from Princess to Queen by taking her hand in marriage. He had promised it. She longed for that day. Oh, the blood that would spill to commemorate their joy . . .

Anathema! Death is preferable.

At the top of the stairs he opened the iron door and escorted her inside. Here was the highest chamber of the great tower, a domed hall filled with shelves, books, vials, tables, and a thousand thousand cryptic things for which she had no name. The four windows stood open to the flaring stars, and in the very center of the room two circles of runes had been carved into the floorstones by acid or chisel. The smell of rotting paper, ancient dust, and dried bones met her nose. Weightless globes of living fire hung about the chamber, shedding ruddy light across Gammir's sanctum. Grinning skulls leered at her from the shelves between jars of fleshy curiosities.

He drew her by the hand again, leading her to the spot where a yellowed map hung on the wall. It showed the known world, all the Great Cities drawn as towered icons by some skilled hand. Since the map was old, proud Shar Dni still stood on the northern edge of the Golden Sea. The real city had been a haunted ruin for eight years now. She studied the tiny cityscapes of Khyrei, Yaskatha, Uurz, Mumbaza, and the vague representation of Udurum, which had remained a half-legend until some thirty years ago, when Vod united Giants and Man.

"What do you see?" Gammir asked.

"Your map is outdated," she told him.

"To be sure," he rejoined, staring at the faded ink. "I keep Shar Dni alive on this parchment to remind me of my first great conquest."

You died there and were reborn in shadow.

"Why do you show me this?" she asked.

"What do you see?"

She paused and scanned the ancient map. The Southern Isles were a string of pearl-sized land masses. To the far right, the Jade Isles appeared as a larger version of those same islands. The north end of the map was empty, as no explorers knew what lay beyond the Icelands. Still, this was a fair representation. How little it had changed since the map's rendering. Only one city gone forever.

"The world," she said. "I see the world."

"Aaaahh," sighed Gammir. "You only think you see the world. But you do not see it. Not *all* of it."

She turned from the parchment to search his dark eyes.

He lifted a small stone from a nearby table littered with scrolls and quills. A perfect sphere of black marble. He held it up before her eyes.

"Do you see the stone?" he asked.

"Yes."

"How much of it?"

She blinked. "All of it. In your hand."

He smiled. "No, you only see the side of the stone that is facing your eyes. What is it you cannot see?"

"The other half of the stone," she replied.

"Exactly." He kissed her lips. A sensation of death and rebirth at once flowed from her mouth along every limb of her body. She moaned, drew a breath sharply, then regained her focus.

"When you look at this map," said Gammir, "you see only *half* of what we call the world."

"Do you mean—"

"Yes," he interrupted. "Our true world is like this stone. Not defined by four rugged edges spilling into the void. But round . . . a sphere. With *two sides*, Sharadza."

He laid the stone down next to a shriveled human hand and pulled her across the room to a tall oval mirror against the wall. At its apex a snarling demon's face was carved into the molding with a murky topaz locked in its jaws. It reminded her of the masks the Onyx Guard wore over their human faces. The rest of the mirror's base was a conglomeration of minutely carved devils, gargoyles, and vipers, twisting themselves in an orgiastic loop that encircled the misted glass.

I know this mirror . . .

"Look now into the Glass of Eternity," said Gammir. He waved a hand and the cloudy mirror filled with colors. She winced at the glow of sunlight from the mirror's surface. A bright scene of midday filled the glass, as if she were looking out a window. Yet outside the actual windows of the tower Khyrei seethed and smoked beneath the dark embrace of night.

She pulled away. "What is this?"

"Look . . . " he whispered, and she found that she could not turn away from the glass. A vision swam inside the mirror, and she marveled at its clarity.

A palace of white stone, large enough to swallow the one in which she stood. A great face, the face of a handsome warrior, dominated the upper half of the structure. No, it was the face of a God, it must be. This was no palace, but a temple. The greatest and most magnificent temple she had ever seen. Yet the towers that rose from its lower walls and the gilded domes set with patterns of gleaming jewels spoke of a King's House. About the monolithic temple-palace with its sublime face of stone there stood orchards and gardens greater and thicker than even those of Uurz, whose gardens were the stuff of legend. About these gardens lay a massive white wall, and outside the wall a vast city built of that same pale stone.

The azure sky gleamed bright and familiar, yet the city was unknown to her. The pathways of its streets, the curious forms of its domes and ziggurats, the placement of its mighty stones, the ambition of its great porticoes and arches . . . all of these were alien. Beautiful. Exotic of make and mold, and carved with symbols she could not identify. A river bright as silver coiled through the city and emptied itself in the green sea beyond. Throngs of people filled the streets in foreign garb, a riotous blend of colors, styles, and forms that left her head spinning. Hairless mammoths lumbered among the crowds bearing pagodas, their tusks sheathed in ornate silver. Guardsmen roamed the city's bridges on the backs of two-legged Serpents the size of horses.

Now a great shadow fell over her viewpoint and she saw the first of the ships. A wide-bodied galleon sailed into view above the city like a gargantuan eagle. It flew a purple sail from its main mast and one more from each of its sides, like a bird's wings. The foreign crewmen shuffled about the deck, securing bales and ropes. Yet the sea lay a quarter-league below. The ships were flying miracles. Now she saw more of them, docking at the balconies of high towers, or sinking low to the harbor for gentle landings in the water of the great bay. Cohorts of armored warriors walked their decks.

The people themselves were not all that different from those she might recognize. Outside the walls of alabaster stone, hordes of slaves worked the well-ordered plantations. The teeming crowds of the city had keen eyes like those of Khyreins or Jade Islanders, but their skin was primarily a golden brown, like wheat loaves baked to perfection. Yet there were clusters of pale and dark-skinned folk everywhere as well. She saw warriors in white turbans and silken pantaloons; horsemen draped in silver mail and *steel*; maidens chattering in carriages pulled by striped desert horses; commoners shuffling through the dust delivering wares, building structures, or sitting at ease in public gardens.

The wealth on display was incredible. Yet nowhere did she see signs of mirth, or even a smile. Their faces were tightly drawn, as if some invisible weight lay upon each and every man's shoulders. The richest of the women wore veils to hide their sad faces. Even the children milling among the crowds were grim and dedicated to whatever tasks they had been set. No music, no play, no foolishness. None of these things were allowed in this strange empire.

"What . . . what is this?" she asked.

"The other side of the world," Gammir answered.

The mirror's shifting vantage point showed again the temple-palace and its godly face of brilliant stone. Gammir whispered in her ear, as if he muttered something profane.

"Look upon the face of Zyung the Conqueror," he said. "Zyung the God-King. This is the seat of his power, the center of his empire. On the other side of our world he rules all. The Kings of every kingdom bow to his shadow."

Sharadza had no words for this revelation. To all the sages and priests and Kings, the map on Gammir's wall was the world in its entirety. At last it came to her that this vision in the mirror was *real*, the hidden side of reality that none save Gammir had seen before now.

Now the mirror's viewpoint dropped beyond the great city to the purple plains beyond. From the city's outer wall, stretching across the tableland to the foothills of a misty mountain range, there camped a vast army. Hundreds of thousands of tents and cookfires; great phalanxes of armored men marching in drill formations; the airy pavilions of generals and Kings; a sea of baroque spears and flapping banners grown like wheat across the flatland.

This was the Great Army of Zyung, and the sheer size of it took her breath away. Now she saw ancient and terrible things, winged lizards with beaks like amber blades. Entire flocks of them soared above the great host. Some of these beasts lay at ease amid the ocean of tents, chewing on the flesh of burned offerings. It seemed that she gazed on some ancient empire out of dim legend. For a moment she doubted the truth of Gammir's words.

"Does all this . . . does it really exist?" she asked.

He laughed. "Now you know the truth of the world, Sweet One. Zyung is of the Old Breed. While our civilizations rose from barbarism and built the Great Cities, Zyung was conquering all the lands on the far side of the world. Do you understand? One single all-encompassing empire bearing his name. He even cast

down their Gods. Now they worship only Zyung. Only a master
of the Old Breed could achieve such greatness. Impressive, is it
not?"

She stared again at the inhumanly perfect face of white stone.
If it were to fall from the heights of the temple-palace, thousands
would die beneath its weight. It seemed inconceivable. Yet here
it was. She knew now that Gammir did not lie. Not about this,
his great secret.

The mirror faded to cloudy gray once more, and she turned to
face him.

"Why did you show me this?"

"So you will know what is to come," said Gammir. "I have
treated with the God-King himself. He intends to expand his
empire until it encompasses the entire world. Both sides of the
stone. This means our own world must fall to the one he has built.
It has been his goal for untold ages." He took up the black sphere
again, squeezed it in his fist. "His power is unimaginable."

Sharadza's eyelids fluttered. "Your words bring me fear."

Madness! All of this is madness.

Gammir chuckled at her mock naivety. "My little Princess, do
you not see? When Zyung and his numberless legions come to
claim our world, he will have one ally – *only one* – to aid him in
this conquest."

"You," she said.

He smiled and struck a kingly pose. "I will continue to rule
Khyrei in his name, while the rest of the Great Cities crumble and
burn and die. Zyung will build new ones in their place. Such a
great and fine slaughter it will be. All my enemies and their kingdoms will fall, and the spires of Khyrei will stand above them all."

"My Lord . . . " she breathed. "You would . . . serve . . . such a
being?"

"For a while, yes," Gammir said. "Long enough to see Yaskatha and Uurz and Mumbaza and Udurum wiped from the earth." He turned away from her and walked to the center of a circle of runes. His eyes caressed the worn floor there, as if it held all the secrets of the cosmos.

"Then ... when *she* returns ... we will take the God-King's power." He looked at her with a new kind of lust blazing in his lupine eyes. "And the world will be ours."

He took her body there in the center of the rune circle, as if the carnal act could summon his missing Empress. His fangs raked across her neck as his fingers explored her body. She was, as always, helpless beneath his touch.

Drops of her own blood spilled across the black flagstones. He left them there to dry among the runes, so their power might kindle a spell he long wished to cast.

Thirteen bloody nights later, the high tower seethed brightly enough to blot out the moon. On the darkened streets hunting her prey, Sharadza looked up to watch a blazing comet fall out of the sky. The summit of Gammir's barbed spire burst into flames. No, the flames poured from its four windows, white and fierce as the naked sun. She turned away to spare her eyes.

Something dark and heavy fell within her chest as the white light faded. A thicker darkness replaced the shattered gloom of evening. Doors slammed and dogs howled. Somewhere a stabbed man's death cry rang across the night.

She finished sucking out the life of a brawny blacksmith and left his drained body lying across his anvil. She flew as if summoned to the palace and up the winding stairs. No longer was Gammir's sanctuary off limits to her. She was his Princess.

His slave. Only his slave.

Flinging open the iron door, she rushed into the high chamber. Gammir kneeled inside the circle of runes, his arms wrapped about the waist of an imperious figure. His smile was a mask of total bliss, and Sharadza knew he would never love anyone the way he loved this woman with the steaming pale skin and black diamond eyes. She stared at Sharadza now, her mane of white hair wild as a northern blizzard. Entirely naked, she radiated power. Her fingers, tipped with feline claws, stroked Gammir's face. When she spoke her ivory fangs sparkled. The last of the white flame dripped like water from the pink tips of her breasts.

"I knew you would return," Gammir moaned, his cheek pressed against her pale thigh. "I knew it . . . "

The tall woman held Sharadza's gaze. She could not look away, even if she chose to.

Gammir turned his eyes upon Sharadza and grinned. She expected him to offer her neck to this fanged Goddess. Sharadza would gladly lie down and offer up her hot blood if asked. But the decision was not hers to make. She belonged to Gammir, as Gammir belonged to this other.

He reached a hand out to her, and Sharadza moved across the chamber to take it. She kneeled now at the edge of the rune circle. The sigils throbbed with a scarlet light, overpowering the last of the white flame's glow.

"Grandmother," said Gammir. "Meet your new daughter . . . my Sweet Princess . . . my gift to you."

The pale Empress smiled. She kissed Gammir's lips and took Sharadza's hand from him.

"My Favored Son has been lonely," she said. "This one has the Blood of Vod in her."

"Not anymore," said Gammir. "She is reborn to us in blood and shadow."

The Empress raised one of her thin eyebrows.

Her loveliness was blinding, like the sun at midday.

Sorceress!

She killed Father! She killed . . .

Ianthe kissed her and gave her hand back to Gammir.

"My children," said the sorceress. "You make me so very proud."

She smiled, and Sharadza's heart leaped. Nothing could be a more worthwhile endeavor than to please this Queen of Queens. This Empress of Immortality.

The Claw.

"It seems a Royal Wedding is in order," said Ianthe. She pulled Gammir and Sharadza close, her long fingers cradling their chins.

Sharadza's cheek burned against the cool skin of her thigh.

"But first," said the Empress, "let us drink deep the Red Wine of Khyrei."

13

Masters and Slaves

In a tangle of red foliage Tong crouched amid a band of twenty silent Sydathians. Their pink snouts sniffed at the evening air while he scanned the broad fields beyond the jungle's edge. A collection of irrigated plantations lay between the wilderness and the black wall of the city. As the sun lowered itself in the west, thousands of slaves walked the dirt roads between the great crop squares. They carried bushels of beans, corn, lemons, and grapes on their heads; others hauled great sheaves of wheat on two-wheeled carts.

The Onyx Guard rode sable horses among the workers, a constant reminder of the Emperor's power over those who dwelled in the fields. Each plantation was supervised by an Overseer who barked orders and consigned the day's pickings to the beds of wagons bound for the Southern Gate. The occasional crack of whips in the distance made Tong's shoulders jump reflexively.

A long line of carts, wagons, and bent-backed slaves filed onto the gate road. Spiked towers stood on either side of the portal, built from the same volcanic stone as the city wall. Sentinels with pennoned spears paced from station to station along the great ramparts. The bulk of the Onyx Guard filed into the city through

the crowded gate, where busy taverns and cheap wine would fill
their off-duty hours.

In the fields after sundown the Overseers and their personal
squads retired to comfortable plantation estates. Crowds of slaves
finished their day's work and trudged back to their rows of ragged
shacks. Women started the evening cookfires and prepared their
allotted portions of pork, fowl, or beef. Usually there were surplus
vegetables for these simple families, the lowest class of Khyrein
society. Underfed slaves were useless, and the Overseers ensured
that those who worked would eat. Yet in lean times slaves were
the first to starve, and they were driven by scourge and club to
work until they died. Those too old or sick to be productive were
taken from the fields and never seen again. There was no doubt
what happened to such slaves: they lay numberless in unmarked
graveyards hemming the fertile fields.

A league from the city wall the River Tah completed its long
winding journey from the volcanoes of the southern jungles,
losing itself at last in the Golden Sea. Bands of women and young
girls carried water gourds and buckets to the river and back to the
huts. The river's dark water was the only source of drink for the
clustered slave communities. No fishing was allowed in the river
due to the venomous predators and vipers that lurked there. How
many times had Tong seen a girl-child dying from the bite of a
river beast, skin purpling as the poison rushed toward her heart?
He had lost count.

The Sydathians ringing Tong sat still as stones. For hours he
had watched his nation of slaves complete their daily chores.
Patience was the first of his weapons. Surprise was another.
Darkness crept at last from the red jungle shadows, spreading
across the fields to engulf the black city. The dusky towers of the
Emperor's palace snared the sun's dying light, burning red and
gold above the hidden streets.

Tong could not see the great harbor on the city's northern side, but a few ships' masts were visible beyond the reedy estuary, dark galleons bearing the Khyrein banner. Perhaps those ships would return with foreign slaves to break and put to work in these fields. Such captives never lived long: deprivation and exhaustion stole their lives if the brutality of the Overseers failed to do so. If slaves were no better than loyal hounds, then foreign slaves were the most hated of the breed.

As the ships grew tiny against the darkening horizon, Tong made a silent vow. By the time the sea reavers returned to Khyrei, there would be no more slavery here.

Now the Southern Gate rumbled shut for the night. The wall would not open again until the light of dawn touched its parapets. For a few hours all the plantations would be sealed off from the majority of the Onyx Guards. Only the Overseers and their squads of estate guards ruled the fields now. An army of slaves slipped into their nightly respite from constant toil.

Tong wondered exactly where Matay's body was buried. The graveyards of slaves were mass affairs, rough holes filled with the bones of those who died that week, piled upon those who had died the previous week. He put it from his mind. Matay was in the Deathlands, where none of the blood and fire that was to come would harm her. She would be proud of him for what he was about to do. He had to believe it so.

Vengeance was one thing, but freedom was far more precious. He would see his people free, or he would die in the attempt. A worthy death was preferable to a wasted life. As the rim of the sun disappeared, Khyrei became a mass of glimmering amber lights beside the moonlit river.

The smell of roasting meat drifted across the fields from the nearest slave huts. The Sydathians inhaled and licked their lips with prehensile tongues. He understood their fascination. He understood far more of their world than he had thought possible. Weeks of shared meditation before the Godstone had guided his mind and theirs to a common destination. The creatures had no spoken language other than their curious singing ability, yet Tong comprehended now most of their arm and claw gestures, as well as the quirks of arm and leg and snout that held specific meanings.

The eyeless ones used thought and emotion to communicate the same way Men used words. After living among them he had come to share their thoughts and emotions, as they had begun to share his own. They understood that Tong's people suffered in bondage. They would follow him into blood and fire in the cause of freedom. They were his brothers, these voiceless beasts from below the world. Tonight began their holy crusade.

Tong climbed high into the branches of a tree to get a better view of the dark fields. The eyeless ones followed, and soon they all squatted among a welter of branches. He pointed toward the nearest houses of the Overseers, stone-built manors encircled by low walls of rock and gates of barred iron. Each house hosted a squad of at least fifty Onyx Guards, half of whom were on night duty at any given time. Across the maze of plantations he estimated at least a hundred such manor houses.

A hundred well-guarded Overseers. Tonight they all must die. The Sydathians must cleanse these fields. Only then could his people rise up and take what they deserved. The road to freedom ran though a forest of death, beyond a roaring sea of blood and fire.

Tong closed his eyes and reached out to his horned brothers.

All those who wear the mask must die.

The eyeless ones nodded and snuffled among their branches.

All those who carry the whip must die.

They waved claws and arms in the signs of agreement.

All those who carry the sword must die.

The Sydathians shuffled anxiously. They knew these things already. They had seen a vision of all this terrain, this darkling city and its vast fields, in the mind of their newest brother. Tong shared their eagerness. They shared his anger, his need for vengeance, his lust for liberation. They longed to see the rebirth he had promised them, to be a central part of it. A reborn Khyrei that would welcome Sydathians inside its gates. They had dwelled in the dark long enough – they knew all the subterranean secrets the underworld could teach.

Tong was their key to the world of sun and sky. A whole new existence in a realm they hardly knew. They sought a remedy to the long-borne loneliness of their race, and an end to ancestral isolation. They craved a place among Men, the fresh liberty of the upper world. Theirs would be a kinship born in this struggle for freedom.

He sent ten of them back into the jungle, there to reconnoiter with the others who had climbed out of deep Sydathus at daybreak. Six thousand strong they lurked in the deep jungle. Now let them come forth.

The night grew blacker; the day's heat faded beneath the rapid chill of evening. In the bunched huts slaves finished their modest meals and fell into slumber, or sat about dwindling fires telling tales of ancient days. Inside any one of the manor houses an Overseer might be entertaining guests from the city, or enjoying the charms of a young slave who had caught his eye. Others would be lost in bowls of wine or lying helpless in their soft beds. Let them dream. They would awake in the Deathlands, where the Gods dispensed punishment, dividing the just from the wicked and casting the latter into the Outer Darkness forever.

A raven flapped out of the darkness and perched in the tree next to Tong. It spoke with Iardu's voice.

"What I feared is true," said the bird. "The Claw has returned. Seven nights ago."

"What does this mean for us?" asked Tong.

The bird ruffled its black feathers. "Her power is great," he said. "And she will certainly take a hand in the city's defense."

"What of the girl?"

"She is still there . . . a slave to shadow . . . a drinker of blood."

"Will you kill her?"

"Not if I can free her of Gammir's trap. She could be of great aid to us."

Tong nodded. The jungle rustled behind him. "They come."

The raven turned its ebony eyes at him and blinked.

"Will you not reconsider?" Tong asked. "Stand with us tonight?"

The raven shook its head. "I must seek the girl."

"Is she your daughter?"

The raven did not answer. Instead it spread its wings and flew back toward the steaming city.

Tong climbed to the ground and watched the jungle come alive with pale, emerging forms.

Come, my Brothers!

They responded to his unspoken call. He ran into the fields, followed by a loping horde of Sydathians. They rushed soundless and without light across row after row of leaf, stem, and stalk. The first of the manor house gates loomed before Tong now. To his east and west throngs of Sydathians moved toward similar structures. The Overseers did not even lock the gates of their outer walls. How could they expect to be assaulted here in the very center of their power? Tong's heart raced as he pulled the long sabre from its sheath. The knife was gripped in his other fist, point downward for quick stabbing. His eyeless brothers needed no weapons. Their claws and fangs were far more deadly than his two lengths of Khyrein *steel*.

Tonight is for you, Matay. And for our son.

The Sydathians outpaced him with their apish running gait. The first one to reach the manor house crashed through the front door as if it were a paper screen. A second later three more hurdled through the low windows of murky glass. When Tong entered the doorway, the blood had already begun to fly. The eyeless ones tore apart a roomful of off-duty guardsmen before they could even draw blades to defend themselves. They had been dining with the Overseer. Tong was not sure which one was master of the house, but it did not matter. All were guilty. All would die. Fresh crimson splattered across the feasting table.

"What is happening here?" a wide-eyed soldier yelled. Without their monstrous masks, they were little more than frightened boys. Tong answered with his sabre, skewering him cleanly through the heart. He died before his body hit the lush carpet. Now the entire house was in an uproar, men shouting for blades and armor and horses. The Sydathians poured in through doors and windows like a white flood, a tide of surging destruction. The masked sentinels rushed forward to die two by two, their swords and spears unbloodied as they fell. The Sydathians were too fast for the men's blades, probably even too fast for speeding arrows. Time would tell.

The first manor house fell easily. Tong killed four panicked guardsmen with sabre and knife. He grabbed a brand from the hearthfire and set the house aflame as he fled with his leaping brothers. A small corral of perhaps fifteen horses stood behind the manor. Tong kicked down the gate and let the beasts run free. They galloped into the fields in all directions, fleeing the conflagration. Yet one of them lingered in the pen as if it were afraid of liberty. Tong approached the stallion, stroked its nose, combed its black mane with his fingers. It was a young horse. In his boyhood he had dreamed of riding such a fine creature; but only the Onyx Guard was permitted to ride south of the city wall.

The Sydathians rushed onward, striking down any man who fled, converging on the next manor house. The same scene played out across the length and breadth of the plantations as the eyeless ones invaded the sanctuaries of the Overseers. They ran on all fours, bounding white spiderlings. Slaves came rushing from the field ghettoes to cheer and weep in the face of the destruction. The Sydathians did not touch Tong's people. They recognized the slave folk as brothers and sisters. They sought the tender, fleshy faces behind the metal masks. They tore apart the bones and sinew of their enemies with a ruthless ease.

Tong, inspired by the madness of the moment, leaped atop the timid horse's back. It responded to him instinctually, like one of the Sydathians would. An understanding beyond the use of words. There was no saddle; it had likely burned with the house. The horse whinnied when he pulled at its mane. He grasped its back between his muscled legs, and it raced toward the next plantation. Tong found himself smiling, caressed by the cool night winds. His dripping sabre gleamed bright as silver in the glow of burning manor houses.

He held the blade high and rode like a mad specter through the hordes of rushing Sydathians. They swarmed the estates of the Overseers, pulling the wicked lords from their houses and feeding the earth with their blood. More structures went up in flames as the eyeless ones tore flaming logs from stone-built hearths.

The wails of slaves and fleeing guardsmen filled the night. The sounds of slaughter would soon reach the city walls. Tong rejoiced as he cut down armored men who ran like frightened boys from his army of monsters. As far as he could see across the fields, manor houses burned and leaping shadows hurled themselves ever closer to the great sealed gate of the city.

How many men he killed from the back of the horse, he could not say. Either he trampled their bones into the dust when the stallion overtook them, or his blade hacked off their heads and arms as he passed. They must have thought him a demon, slaying in the company of demons, wreaking the vengeance of some dreadful God. A God of slaves come to liberate his people.

A patina of shining blood covered his body by the time the stallion ceased its headlong flight. The chaos of slaughter churned about Tong like a storm. He eyed the watchtowers of the black wall, where sentinel fires grew brighter and the horns of alarum pierced the night with urgent wails. Now the city's defenders knew that its fields were under attack. Now the battle would truly begin.

Brothers!

Dropping from the horse, he rubbed its charcoal neck in admiration. He called to him a throng of his eyeless brothers. Thousands more stalked the fields, chasing down and ending the lives of anyone who was not a slave.

Stay near to me, Tong signaled with mind and hands. *I must speak with my people.*

With a band of the beastlings at his back, Tong led his stolen horse toward a group of shacks deep in the midst of the fields. The slaves regarded him with suspicion, naked fear gleaming in their eyes. Mothers grasped children to their bosoms, while fathers and their half-grown sons brandished clubs and stones. Before this moment none of the inhuman invaders had paid them any attention. All across the plantations, slaves watched their masters torn to bits while they stood unmolested, shocked into silence by the strangeness of their liberators, who neither spoke nor looked at them. How could they look? They had no eyes with which to see. Now Tong brought a pack of them like friendly hounds to sniff at the huddled families.

"Friends!" shouted Tong. "Cousins and Brothers! People of Khyrei! You are no longer slaves. Tonight your bondage ends! I am one of you – Tong, Son of Thago and Omita. My uncles are Soth, Dorno, and Phialmos." He gestured to the white forms crouching about him. "These ... are my brothers from the red jungle. They have looked upon our slavery and seen the wrongness of it. They have pledged to aid us. Throw off your chains and join me in freedom! Death to the Overseers!"

The congregated slave families muttered nervously and stared at the horned Sydathians. The cries of dead and dying men filled the air, the smoke of burning manor houses. The smells of burning flesh and wood mingled into an unpleasant reek. The forward slaves passed Tong's words to their fellows at the back of the crowd.

"The people of Khyrei are no longer slaves!" Tong bellowed. "Let us fight! Let us storm the black walls and tear down the stones of our oppressors. Let us be free! Death to the Emperor!" He raised the sabre to sparkle in the glow of moon and flames. Thickening blood dripped into his hair like a slow rain. He mounted the horse again and renewed his call. "Death to Gammir!"

A single voice echoed his cry. A young slave stepped forward, a boy of no more than seventeen years. He raised a clenched fist, and Tong beckoned him forward. He gave the boy his soiled knife. "What is your name?"

"Tolgur," said the youth. His face was round and bloodshot.

"Tolgur fights for freedom!" yelled Tong. "Who fights with us?"

"Death to the Overseers!" yelled another slave.

"Death to the Emperor!" cried another.

"Freedom!" Crazed voices rose into the night. A song of hope and rage that became a ceaseless roar.

Tong galloped toward another group of milling slaves, the Sydathians striding after him. He replayed this scene a dozen times. By the time he finished uniting his people, the city's southern wall was lined with archers. Every manor house had burned to the ground or was still burning. Between city and jungle a hundred great fires danced like wild Giants. Flames had spread into the fields themselves. Entire tracts of crops blazed like massive bonfires. It must have been quite a sight from atop the city walls.

Now the Sydathians gathered at the center of the fields, aligning themselves along the Southern Gate road. At least a thousand able-bodied slaves joined them, picking up the swords and spears and shields of their slain oppressors. Their numbers grew to at least two thousand by the time Tong rode his mount along the unpaved road. He smiled at the irony of the simple math taught to slaves for the counting of bales and bushels of produce; now that same skill served him well in counting the number of soldiers in his army of freedom fighters. No wonder the Overseers limited the education of their slaves to serve practical purposes, yet such precautions gained them little in the end. Knowledge was power, and like water it flowed where it wished and could not easily be stopped.

Few Sydathians, if any, had died in the taking of the fields. By midnight the eyeless ones stood six thousand strong about a core group of three thousand slaves armed with whatever weapons they could find or make from farming tools. Tong sat at the heart of the throng on his tall horse, to which he had given the name Liberty. Other slaves had stolen mounts as well, some with less than satisfactory results, yet some could ride reasonably well. They had worked and lived with these horses their whole lives. A few had learned to ride secretly for years, hiding such activity from the Overseers.

A rain of black arrows fell like stormclouds from the city walls. A legion of archers fired into shadow and the trickery of firelight, but their keen darts fell so thickly that it made little difference.

Raven-feathered shafts pierced human and Sydathian flesh as one. Men screamed and scattered. The eyeless ones bore their pain in silence. It would take a score of arrows to kill a single one of them, unlike a human, who could easily die from a single poisoned barb.

A second volley launched as Tong shouted orders: "To the trees! Seek shelter in the jungle!" He whirled his steed around and galloped southward. Slaves would not go deep into that wilderness, but they held no fear of its nearby shallow glades. He rode hard toward the distant line of forest, outpacing even the Sydathians. The runners left dead men lying behind them, twisted bodies rife with feathered shafts. The wounded stumbled along with the help of friends and cousins. Another volley blotted the stars and fell into the fleeing horde.

Envenomed arrowheads killed at least a hundred men before the slaves made it out of bow range. The Sydathians plucked shafts from their dense bodies as if they were no more than bothersome insects. The slaves and their liberators raced into the shadows of the jungle trees. Most of their women and children had already fled there to escape the flames and slaughter.

By the light of crude torches and the shouts of their fellows, they assembled into a single mass. The youngest and strongest among them came forth to smile at Tong and clasp his hand and call him cousin. Whether they shared a common bloodline or not, all these slaves were cousins of circumstance, united by generations of bondage. No more would that be the case. They would die or be free this night.

Tong climbed atop a stone monolith draped in hanging moss. Moonlight glared across his blood-slick skin. From the ancient rock, he spoke again to his people. Sydathians lingered in a great ring about the gathering of slaves.

"Soon they will open the Southern Gate!" Tong shouted. All ears turned to hear him, even those of children whose faces were stained with tears and mud. "Soon they will come for us. They think us weak and afraid. Yet we must fear them no longer, for we have the strength of our Sydathian brothers!" He waved his arms to acknowledge the pale lurking forms that surrounded the glade. "Do not fear them. They will harm only those who enslaved us. The Earth God has sent them to foster our freedom."

He paused for a moment to let his words sink in. The slaves stared at him, ragged and bleeding, and not one of them questioned his leadership.

"Soon they will come for us," he said. "But it is too late. We are already free!"

Most of the pale slaves cheered, while others wept. Already the fighting had claimed too many lives. Men died so their families would be free to fight on.

"Cast aside the fear that lives in you heart. You are the true People of Khyrei!" Tong told them. "This is *our* land. How long have we worked it, coaxed life from it, bled for it, been buried in it? Khyrei is ours! Let us take it!"

"Death to the Emperor!" someone cried out.

"He will come!" said Tong, and the anxious voices quieted. "Gammir the Undying . . . the Reborn . . . the Drinker of Blood. I say let him come!"

Tong raised his arms toward the high trees, and the former slaves gasped as they looked skyward. A woman cried out. A little boy laughed.

Silence fell upon the glade. In the high branches of the jungle canopy, silent as moss on twigs, another ten thousand Sydathians waited with clever claws and zealous snouts. The eyeless ones sat thick as leaves among the trees. A second, far larger force had joined the six thousand who had taken the fields. Here was an army that could and would take the whole city; the true heart of the Sydathians' might had been held in reserve.

Now the slaves saw the depth of Tong's ambition, and they cheered his name.

He was the Hope-Bringer, the Brother of Beasts, the Onyx-Killer.

The light of their gnarled torches glinted in his eyes as he spoke.

The Sydathians did not speak his language, but they understood his every word. They felt the fear and desperation of these people turn to wonder and delight. They knew what lay at stake here. Tong had shown them all in his mind.

Let the Emperor and his bitch come and try to stop them.

"Let the Emperor come forth!" he bellowed. "Let Gammir know the taste of our vengeance instead of our blood!"

The slaves cheered him on.

None saw the Southern Gate open, or the armored legions that rode into the burning fields.

As always, she awoke to hunger.

The Great Thirst coiled like a viper in her belly.

She arose from the wide bed and stretched her limbs, then stepped beyond the circle of runes that enclosed it. Soon a body slave would enter and pull back the black drapes that hid the daylight while she had slept. She might feed upon the servant if she wished, but she preferred to hunt her prey. Some instinctual urge deep inside her demanded it. Besides, if she drained her body slave, who would pull back her drapes each evening and tend to the mass of night-blooming flowers that decorated her chamber? After slaking her thirst on the streets of the city below, she would rejoin her Master and Mistress. The plans for a lavish wedding had begun.

As she called forth the substance of shadow to weave herself a dark gown, a rustling at the window drew her eye. Hers was the topmost chamber of the western spire, so it must be some bird or bat flown into the billowing drapes. A spark of annoyance fueled her hunger. She bounded across the room and pulled back the curtain. There on the casement perched a solemn raven, wings glossy with twilight. The last of the sun's ruby glow lingered on the horizon. The raven stared at her with eyes even darker than her own.

She grabbed it in her clawed hand and stuffed it into her mouth. The bird was no substitute for human blood, but it made a fine appetizer. Black feathers fell about her feet as the creature writhed between her fangs. The bird was now a poisonous viper, shifting and slithering in her jaws, tail and neck hanging level with her waist. She spat it upon the flagstones, wiping at her mouth. Not a drop of blood lined her lips; she had not broken the viper's scaly skin.

She crouched and hissed at the reptile, but now it was the black hound she had seen weeks ago, staring at her from the shadows of an alley. Once again she stood transfixed by its mysterious eyes.

"Sharadaza." It spoke her name in a voice that rang familiar.

Iardu!

Now the sorcerer stood in his manly form between her and the open window. He held a crooked staff of umber wood. His eyes were chromatic stars.

"Listen to me," he said. "This is not you. You are the Daughter of Vod, not a slave. Remember this!" His eyes sparkled with forgotten colors.

"All Is One," she said. "There can be no distinctions."

Iardu smiled. His teeth gleamed white in the gloom. "You at least remember the principles I taught you. It is true . . . the only distinctions are the ones you choose for yourself. However, in the form you now wear, you let Gammir choose for you. The time has come to reclaim yourself."

Yes! Let the nightmare end . . .

Her right hand lashed out, claws slicing across his chest. The blue flame burning there was cold, and its power drove back her talons. She would feed *now*. There was no need to roam the streets tonight. This fool would do just fine.

She pounced like a jungle tiger, and black wings spread from her back. Iardu staggered back as the weight of her fell upon him. Her fangs snapped at his face. He held the staff against her throat, keeping her mouth away from his neck. Her red tongue lolled as her skull elongated to wolfish proportions.

The blue flame on his chest flared again, blasting forth to engulf her body. She leaped away from him, chilled by the cold fire. He waved the staff and she fell to the floor, twitching and mewling. He mumbled ancient words and her form shifted once again. Now she lay as herself on the floor, the gown of shadow tattered and singed. Iardu's hand waved above her and black chains grew from the stone floor to encircle her. She stared up at the wizard, gnashing her sharp teeth. The thirst raged in her belly, burned on her brow like a fever.

Kill me, Shaper.

Death is preferable to this.

He stood over her and looked into her eyes. "Calm," he whispered. His hand touched her brow gently. She struggled against the mystic chains but could not move. "I am speaking to the one inside this shell of shadow. I know you can hear me, Sharadza . . ."

Yes . . .

Iardu sighed. "Once again you leap before you look. You should never have come to this place. Your half-brother has stolen your old life and built a new one for you. His blood magic has infected your physical self. The longer you live this way, the more permanent it becomes. There is a way to restore you. Yet it carries its own price."

I don't deserve it. I am worse than a murderer.

Kill me now, if you can.

"No," Iardu said. Her body craved release, violence, rent flesh. Hot sweet blood. Yet her spirit cried out in anguish. She had betrayed everything she believed. Stolen the lives of men, women, children. Gammir had made her like him. He had won.

"Killing you now would only allow him to bring you back as his slave again," said Iardu. "Unless . . . unless you bring yourself back. Cancel his influence with the purity of your intentions. I can help you do this, if you let me."

I deserve death . . .

"I am afraid you have forfeited that privilege," he said. "You have only two choices here: remain the plaything of these dark forces, or cast this untrue life aside and rebuild your own. You are still a sorceress, as years ago you wished to be. Now you know the depth of this path, and something of its nature. Make your choice."

I want my old life back.

Somewhere far beyond the window, orange flames lit the night. Great fires burned beyond the southern wall.

"That you may never have," said Iardu. "But I can give you this."

He raised the umber staff. Its lower end was pointed, whittled to sharpness. He held it above her chained body like a spear. Three times he sang a strange refrain, then plunged the weapon into her ribcage. The wood steamed as its point punctured her heart. A spray of red blood, none of it her own, sprinkled a row of potted flowers and the wall behind them.

She squirmed and struggled against the confining chains as the wood burst into flames. Iardu continued his low song. The staff flared and melted like wax, sinking into her body. Soon it was gone and so were the magical chains that held her. She lay still now, eyes open and staring at nothing. The gown of shadow ran from her corpse like polluted water, and her pale flesh melted like the staff had done. Now she lay fleshless, a pitiful skeleton, until that too dissolved. It became a mound of gray dust along the floor.

An unspeakable lightness filled her conscious mind, and she realized with a flash that she was no longer linked to shadow flesh or dusted bones. The Great Thirst was gone, only a terrible memory ringing like an echo.

Iardu's thick fingers enclosed her. She was a sphere of dancing light caught in his palm. If she had lungs, she would have sighed with the greatest relief she had ever known.

"Our time grows short," said Iardu, his eyes flashing as he studied the scene beyond the window. He brought the globe of light to his face, and Sharadza looked into the glowing orbs of his prismatic eyes.

"You have made the journey that all sorcerers eventually make," Iardu said, "trading your mortal body for one of your own making . . . the product of your sorcery. I tried to spare you this, but Gammir has left us no choice. When the body born of woman has been shed, the sorcerer must rebirth himself, creating a new shell for his lifeforce to inhabit. In your case, Gammir has interfered with this process. Now your immortal essence, your undying spirit, is tied to the very stones of this chamber where your new body manifested. See the runes about your bed? They are Sigils of Rebirth, the nexus of your power on this layer of reality. These inscribed stones are as much a part of you now as were the bones of your earthly body. If you manifest here again, creating another new shell from blood and shadow, you will be again as you were . . . a mindless predator addicted to the blood of the living. Gammir's slave."

No! It cannot happen again. Anything would be better.

Iardu scanned the walls and floor of the chamber. "Yes, these blocks of basalt are forever linked to you now. Yet I sense that you would rather face annihilation than be reborn as a fiend of Khyrei again and again without end."

Yes. Annihilation is what I deserve.

"This rune circle is the seat of your power, Sharadza. Now and forever. The only way to escape the curse of this place is to move the stones themselves. This can be done once only, and my options for aiding you are limited. If you wish it, I can transport them to a place of safety and peace."

I beg you, Iardu. Do this for me.

If you will not destroy me once and for all . . . then do this thing.

Iardu nodded.

Even now she felt the pull of the rune circle, a strange gravity drawing her essence closer to itself. Iardu carried her to the ring, but did not step inside. He waved a hand and the bed with its pile of pillows and silks slid across the chamber to block the doorway. The Circle of Rebirth lay empty before him now, a yawning whirlpool threatening to draw her into itself forever.

The sorcerer raised his arms. The light of her immortal soul blazed, a sphere of sunlight captured in his hand. He sang an ancient incantation and the black tower began to tremble. Shadows were snuffed out by the glow of his luminescent eyes. Gradually the chamber grew brilliant with white light flowing from nowhere. As if the very air itself had caught aflame, the great glow drowned all sensation. Iardu's voice rose louder, mixing with the rumble as mortared stone tore itself apart.

Sharadza would have screamed then if she possessed a mouth. Since she did not, she merely endured the terrible pain of his spell. His own bellow of agony came unexpectedly.

The tower erupted in a globe of swirling flame.

Black stones rained upon the city like burning coals.

At the heart of the rushing mob, Tong ran alongside his freed companions. About them ran fifteen thousand Sydathians. They spewed from the wall of jungle as the legions of Onyx Guards

from the Southern Gate rode in formation across the ruined farm-
land. Nine thousand devil-masked horsemen bearing lance, shield,
and sword met the beastlings at the center of the smoking fields.
Walls of roaring flame lined the gate road on either side. There
would be no fleeing this battle.

Fight or burn.

Tong and his people chose to fight. The Sydathians raced ahead
in their hound-like fashion, falling upon the legionnaires with
silent fury. They plucked the lead cavalrymen of the host from
their saddles like slaves picking fruit. Most of the killing would
be done by the talons and fangs of the eyeless ones. Taking the
fields had been easy, but the original advantage of surprise was
now gone. Tong's crude legion of three thousand slaves with stolen
blades was the beating heart of the invasion force. Yet the eyeless
ones were their true weapons. He watched the Onyx Guardsmen
die beneath the furious speed and flailing arms of Sydathians, and
he thanked the Earth God they were his allies.

A great band of women, children, and elders took their shelter
beyond the treeline, guarded by a thousand horned beastlings.
They would be safe there until the fighting was done and the city
liberated. Until every last Onyx Guardsman was put to death or
lay helpless in chains. The city's general had underestimated the
full strength of the rebellion, just as Tong had intended. The black
legions were greatly outnumbered by the Sydathians, each of
whom possessed the strength of ten men. The carnage in the fields
was only a prelude. The true slaughter had only begun.

Sydathians and legionnaires clashed between walls of leaping
fire. Tong wished he still rode on the back of Liberty, but the
slaves could not convince their stolen mounts to enter the blazing
fields. Even the calvary horses, trained to endure the chaos of
battle, were skittish and frightened beneath the Onyx Guard, who
whipped their flanks to drive them forward. Many of the armored

ones abandoned their mounts for the steady feel of dirt beneath their heels. They drove forward on foot, only to die under a mass of leaping Sydathians.

Tong made his way through the ranks of warriors and beast-lings, striving always to reach the southern wall. He came face to face with a dismounted captain as the warrior pulled his greatsword from the body of a dead Sydathian. His thrust had impaled it through the chest, and it died like a withering insect in the blood-soaked mud.

Tong's sabre collided with the captain's blade as he raised it.

Through the eyeholes of his fanged mask, the captain's eyes were slits of darkness. His heavy blade moved quickly, battering away at Tong's limited defenses. The escaped slave was no trained swordsman; yet the captain was exactly that. As the tip of the broad blade slashed a red line across his chest, Tong realized that this warrior would soon take his life. It was only a matter of sec-onds until his weary arm could no longer stop the greatsword's arcing blade.

The press of soldiers and beastlings about them was tight. There was no disengagement possible. Tong raised the sabre again, his right arm gone numb as it absorbed the shock of the greatsword's latest blow. A few more strokes and the blade would either slip into his bowels or take off his head. Tong sweated and screamed and beat his own blade uselessly against the captain's armor. He chipped black lacquer from the bronze, but drew no blood.

The greatsword flashed sideways, and the sabre's narrow blade broke in two. The useless hilt fell from Tong's fingers.

The captain raised his blade again for a death blow that never fell. A pair of long white claws grabbed him from behind and tore the helmeted head from his shoulders. A gout of crimson rose up like a fountain, raining down upon Tong's head and shoulders. He laughed at the death that had almost claimed him, gave a wordless thanks to the Sydathian brother who saved him, and took up the fallen greatsword as his own. He hoped it would serve him better than it had the headless captain.

So went the battle. Tong had learned to hold back and let the Sydathians do their grisly work. They did it easily and very few of them perished. Yet those slaves who rushed into battle with the trained soldiers fell quickly. Tong barked orders and curtailed the bloodlust of his freed brothers, while the eyeless ones tore the black legions apart. They reminded him of slaves scything down rows of ripe wheat. In less than an hour it was done.

Tong stood amid his fellows waving bloody blades at the stars, their faces red in the glow of untamed flames. The Sydathians did not cheer, they only convened once more in a great circle about Tong and his people. The eyeless ones did not celebrate victory, for they were not human and had no appetite for the butchery that came so easily to them. The Sydathians gathered up the bodies of their fallen; less than fifty of the beastlings had fallen to the war skills of the Onyx Guards. Yet they had slaughtered three entire legions of armored Khyreins.

How many more legions lay hidden beyond those black walls? Even as he shouted victory, Tong feared to see the great gate open and spill forth a fresh host. He knew only what all Khyreins did: that a great number of troops had been sent west recently to fortify the Border Legions at the edge of the Great Marshland. Rumors of war with Yaskatha and Uurz had been growing for years. While Matay had still lived, she and he had stopped their work briefly to watch the long lines of warriors filing into the jungle, following a hidden road toward the distant swamps. Yet Tong was sure the city retained a few legions for its own defense.

Despite a deep cut on his forearm that bled profusely, the lad

Tolgur had thus far survived. He stood near to Tong, leaning on a bloody spear. He was the first to raise his hand and point toward the black wall. Between the twin gate towers, bathed in the glow of the burning fields, there stood two winged figures. The flesh of each one burned white, even in the glow of orange night, and living shadows swirled about their bodies. Their wings were pointed, featherless things, folding upon their backs and rustling. At first Tong thought them two great pale bats. Then he saw the bright crowns gleaming on the brow of each figure.

Emperor Gammir had come forth to view the rebellion. His pale Empress stood near to him, raising lithe arms, shedding white flames from her eyes. Gammir the Reborn had returned from death only seven years ago, and Iardu said the Empress Ianthe had returned now as well. They were immortal beings, and their power was not confined or limited by death. Every man knew these things.

As he watched the darkness swirl about the bright couple, Tong knew that Ianthe herself had come to crush his people. Could even the Sydathians stand against her power?

The Empress sang a screeching song, and men grabbed their ears in pain. The Sydathians sniffed the acrid air, sensing the presence of something they did not recognize. Yet they knew enough to fear it. Tong felt their fear as surely as he heard the hellsong of the sorceress.

The flaming plantations were snuffed out in an instant. A pall of smoke hung between the fields and the distant stars. The moon was lost behind dark, roiling vapors. Now these vapors shifted and flowed and joined with the shadows rising from the bloodstained earth. Shadows tore themselves from the stony substance of the black city's walls and strode like Giants into the ashen fields. Winged shadows arose like great bats from the battlements where faceless guardsmen watched in awe. Serpents of living, seething darkness slithered from the river depths, gliding toward the Sydathian horde and its core of desperate slaves.

The host of crawling shadows fell upon the eyeless ones, thicker than black smoke. It rushed forward like a river of pitch to drown the army of pale beastlings. Some of the shadow horde resembled cobras, bats, wolves, Serpents, or deformed Giants; others shambled forward with no certain forms, conglomerations of talon, tentacle, beak, fang, and claw.

Tong's forces had stood in the bloody glow of victory moments earlier, but now his brothers cringed before a tide of rushing darkness. In seconds it would smother them all, tear the lives from their bodies, and feed on the mangled debris of their souls.

He squeezed the grip of the greatsword with both hands and prepared to die.

I tried, Matay. Now at last I come to be with you.

Angry thunder split the night. An orb of fire akin to the sun itself erupted over the black city. Beyond the wall of rushing, creeping shadows, Tong saw a tower of the Great Palace disappear in a blast of churning brilliance. Rays from the miniature sun flashed in every direction, piercing the horde of shadows. A great cry rose into the night, the wailing of ten thousand damned souls in agony. The looming shadows burned away like wisps of fog in the glow of a sudden dawn.

A storm of basalt shards showered down upon the city. A few of the flying fragments toppled guards from the city walls or shattered the watchtowers between battlements.

Bathed in the radiance of dispelled horror and reborn hope, Tong smiled.

Iardu.

Atop the great gate, Emperor and Empress turned their heads to stare at their fractured palace, where the westernmost tower was no more.

"*Forward, Brothers*!" Tong cried, lifting up the greatsword once again. "Make for the gate! Our moment is now!"

Sydathians and slaves rushed forward in a great wave. The eyeless ones dug their talons into cracks between the stones of the great wall, climbing like a swarm of pale spiders toward the battlements.

14

Two Old Friends

The capital of Yaskatha sat proud and gleaming on the edge of a turquoise sea. Its lean spires shone silver against the blue heavens, and its flapping crimson banners bore the Sword and Tree sigil of King D'zan's house. The Royal Palace stood atop a hill at the center of the city, surrounded by vineyards and orchards ripe with pomegranates, peaches, mangoes, plums, and other bounties of nature. The city streets were arranged in a series of concentric avenues and spacious colonnades. Public gardens grew thick with homeflower, jasmine, coconut, and starblossom. Sun-browned folk with golden hair filled the seaside marketplace, filing in from the green pastures east of the city.

Below the polished ramparts, marble wharves swarmed with activity. Hundreds of trading vessels unloaded spices, silk, and exotic wines. At either end of the crescent bay, three hundred tall war galleons sat poised for sailing, the famous Yaskathan fleet, second only to Mumbaza's in size and grandeur. The King's banner flew from every gilded prow, and the sails bore greater versions of the Sword and Tree.

Lyrilan stood in the bow of the *Sunrider* with Volomses and watched the gaudy sails of foreign traders flow in and out of the port. After thirty-three days at sea it would be good to feel solid ground beneath his feet again. The voyage had been an easy one, despite several summer storms. No pirates or sea monsters to endure. He had survived the sinking of *Dairon's Spear* eight years ago thanks to dumb luck and the valor of Vireon Vodson. No far-seeing necromancer was striving to sink his vessel this time, which was fortunate because the *Sunrider* carried no heroes today. In addition to the busy crewmen, there was only Lyrilan, Undroth, Volomses, and the dozen legionnaires who had accompanied them from Uurz.

Lyrilan breathed deep the salty air, laced as it was with the aroma of foreign spices and peeled fruits. The warm scents of Yaskatha, where he hoped to find sanctuary.

The trip from Uurz to Murala remained a dull blur in his memory. His mind had still been fragmented during that leg of the journey, sodden with the terrible weight of guilt. Undroth had hired a carriage and four strong stallions for Lyrilan's exodus. Volomses had ridden beside him on the thick cushions of the coach's interior. Undroth and his loyalists rode escort on mailed horses. In order to avoid the mass of crowds and the acrimony of those who might waylay or harass the banished Scholar King, the carriage had left the city well before dawn.

Only a few wandering drunks and a squad of gate guards witnessed Lyrilan's departure. None of them had fair words for Lyrilan or his retainers. Any such sentiments might see a man jailed or killed now that the Sword King was Emperor. Lyrilan curled himself upon the carriage's couch and slept, waking only at the prompting of Volomses to eat dried fruit and drink a bit of stale wine. Ramiyah's kisses still burned on his tongue, and he tasted nothing else.

Two heavy chests rattling on the floor of the carriage contained all that was left of his royal status. The first one held the *Books of*

Imvek the Silent, along with a few fresh quills and rolls of good parchment. The second chest held a fortune in tourmalines, topazes, opals, emeralds, garnets, and other precious stones. Undroth had chosen well the most valuable items from Lyrilan's personal treasury. Although he was no longer King, he would still live like a monarch wherever he decided to go.

One piece of jewelry stayed gripped in his hands for that ride, and Undroth could not remove it with soft words or prying fingers. Ramiyah's necklace of pearls was set with a single great ruby; it was all he had to remind him of her. He moved the pearls tenderly through his fingers, kissed the bright ruby, and at times he even spoke to it. He offered to the stone the apologies that he would never be able to bestow upon his wife. Volomses indulged him, though often Undroth would peer in through the carriage window, braided beard heavy with the dust of the road, and wipe his sweaty face in consternation.

Lyrilan spoke very little as the carriage pulled them along the Western Road, past villages destroyed by the long drought. Undroth gave out bits of copper and bronze to appease the crowds of beggars, but he did not stop the little caravan often. Lyrilan peered out the window at the brown and yellow fields that were once verdant and prosperous. They passed by like sad dreams sweltering in the heat of day. It seemed the Stormlands were dying.

Tyro had won the Empire, but it would crumble beneath him. His war would sap the land of its strongest and heartiest men, and the drought would continue to drain the land of everything else. Eventually this realm would all be desert once again, as it was in Dairon's day. The Desert of Many Thunders would return. All those who survived would have to leave the Stormlands or move to Uurz itself, where overcrowding and starvation had already taken hold of the poorest quarters. These were the problems Tyro and his advisors ignored as they planned for the red game of war. Madness.

Lyrilan wondered if his own miserable condition was simply part of the madness that infected his homeland. Perhaps a Great Dying had come to the realm, and there would be no escape from it. No escape except, perhaps, for that of an exiled King. He laughed that day in the carriage, imagining himself the last survivor of the dead and decaying Stormlands, yet unable to ever set foot there again. Tyro and his descendants would soon rule a kingdom of dust and bones.

Dreams of Ramiyah tormented him during those nights on the seaward highway. When there was no inn, or when he wished to keep their presence hidden, Undroth made camp in the dry grasses far off the main road. There Lyrilan's retinue slumbered beneath the stars, and all the men heard his moaning as he attempted to sleep. He clung to Ramiyah's necklace and whispered to it when he awoke in the dark, then fell back into dreaming her murder over and over again. He remembered few of these nightmares, but in some of them Tyro executed him before the assembled crowds of Uurz, shearing off his head with a double-bladed axe. From these dreams he awoke calm and full of disappointment. For an instant he thought himself mercifully freed from the burden of living. Volomses ignored his perpetual heavy sighs, enduring them like a patient physician. He prepared boiled herbs and mulled wine to ease Lyrilan's pain.

The carriage and its guardians crossed a stone bridge spanning the Western Flow, where a few tiny fishing villages still clung to life. Fishermen pulled catfish from sluggish waters. Not enough to trade for any kind of profit, but nearly enough to feed themselves and their meager families. The river flowed brown and low from its source high in the Grim Mountains. In better days there would be riverboats gliding to and from Murala, trading the river's bounty for the sea's riches. Not so in these troubled times.

Six days on the road brought the Scholar King's company to the coast, where the hearth smokes of Murala rose to join the flat gray sky. Beyond the unwalled town's squat towers and peaked roofs lay the blue face of the Cryptic Sea. Ocean breezes carried the scents of brine and roasting fowl along the narrow avenues. Swanships from Mumbaza sat in the harbor alongside slim traders from Tadarum and a few Yaskathan galleys with billowing triple sails. Here the cliffs of the coastline sank low so that the town itself sat directly above the bay with several muddy roads leading directly to the wharves.

Murala itself was as unremarkable as ever, excepting its colorful blend of peoples and the enticing nature of its tavern girls. Harlots did a brisk trade with the endless parade of seadogs and soldiers passing through the port. Here the drought had less effect on the populace, for the storms of the sea often fell to land. The wells were full, as were the pockets of traders and fishermen. In another twenty years, Murala might grow as large as Uurz itself. In that same time, the City of Sacred Waters might have dwindled to a pile of sacred ruins.

The sight of the open sea was good for Lyrilan. As the land fell away, so too did the weight that he had borne all the way from Uurz. He stepped from the carriage's open door and blinked at the sinking sun, letting the immensity of the ocean view wash over him. He ran then into the bustling streets, past the calls of leering strumpets, ignoring the cries of fish vendors, canvas makers, and tanners hawking leather goods.

Undroth sent three men after him, but they ran slower than Lyrilan due to the weight of mail hauberks and longblades. By the time they caught up to him he was already wading into the white surf, giving himself to the roaring waves that battered against the sand. He might have run on into the deep sea and drowned himself like poor, mad Vod had done decades ago, but one of the soldiers caught him by the shoulders and dragged him back to the beach. He later learned that the man's name was Haruud, and thanked him for the favor with a jewel from his travel chest. Yet, that day, he only wept and sat mute upon the beach, watching the waves roll in and out. Undroth let him sit there for hours, until the sun went down. Volomses then persuaded him to seek rest at a local inn.

"We have secured southward passage, Majesty," the sage told him. "The *Sunrider* sets sail for Yaskatha tomorrow, after a successful trading venture in Tadarum."

"Yaskatha." Lyrilan repeated the name. It held a fresh meaning for him that night. The spell of the ocean had cleared his head of cobwebs. His heart was still heavy, and the betrayal of his brother was unforgivable. Yet he breathed more easily, and he ate a solid meal of roasted lamb and boiled lobster. Volomses and Undroth took heart from his renewed appetite.

In the morning they boarded the *Sunrider* and Lyrilan greeted its captain in the formal manner. The brawny trader bowed low before him, vowing to give safe passage under penalty of his own life. The mariner knew, as most Yaskathans did, that Lyrilan was a close friend of his own King. He introduced himself as Captain S'dyr. His ship's hold was loaded with ingots of ore and raw *steel* from New Udurum, both acquired at Tadarum. Also among his cargo was a selection of expensive Uurzian wines taken on at Murala. The captain offered his private cabin to Lyrilan, although Volomses quartered there as well. The sage made himself at home on a pallet of blankets near to the bed where Lyrilan would sleep.

As the ship cast off and Murala diminished in its wake, Lyrilan stood at the railing with Ramiyah's necklace, studying the waves and the purple horizon. He prayed to the Gods of Sea, Sun, Earth, and Sky, but not for the blessings of a safe voyage. He prayed for Ramiyah. They had only let him see her tomb once before he fled the city. He had set a bouquet of fresh roses next to the mausoleum door, then guards had escorted him back to his room. That had been his last day in Uurz.

He ran through a litany of prayers for the dead while stray memories rose like bubbles to the surface of his mind. The day of his marriage, a glorious ceremony of gold and green splendor. Before that, the first time he lay with her in a Yaskathan garden outside D'zan's palace . . . the same citadel in which he now sought refuge. Ramiyah's arrival in Uurz and the foolish way she substituted Yaskathan etiquette for Uurzian protocol, gifting baskets of ripe fruit to the lords and ladies of the court, as if she were a fawning tributary instead of a King's wife. He had shielded her from the laughter and pointed remarks of the courtiers who found her rustic ways amusing. She had a giving heart, Ramiyah. Always looking for some way to help with the duties of the realm. Perhaps in two years' time she had grown bored with the idle life of a northern Queen. He had no doubt she would have made a fine vizier or diplomat.

It was the warmth of her broad smile that had first drawn his eyes across a hedge purpled with blossoms; that smile won the hearts of every man that met its radiance. He recalled the evening he had proposed to her on the beach below the southern capital. She wept when he asked her to be his Queen; he thought for a moment that she would deny him. Yet they were only tears of joy. She said, "Yes," and they stood cheek to cheek while the surf pounded at their feet. The ocean was an abyss of watery stars ruled by the moon's silver reflection.

Only once had she lost her gentle temper with him. He was assembling notes and journals for *The Life of Dairon* when she came into his study. One look at her sweet face gone to gray and he knew the pain in her heart. She had endured his isolation and lack of attention while he wrote the previous book – the writing of it had consumed half of their first year of marriage. But this second volume seemed beyond her patience.

"It is time you produced an heir, Scholar King," she scolded him. "These books that you are so fond of writing ... they will not rule your kingdom when you are gone. Nor will they warm your bed at night!" She turned to storm out of the room, but he caught her by the shoulders.

"I do not blame you for asking this of me," he said. "I love you more than any book or jewel or kingdom." She would not meet his eyes as he explained the importance of Dairon's biography, how it might create understanding for Tyro and himself. How it would set the tone for the next fifty years of Kingship in Uurz. Not only would it be a testament to his father's wisdom, it would bond the Twin Kings together as only a father's love could do. "My father gave me a throne," he told her. "The least I can give to him is this one last tribute. One more year is all I need to complete what will be my greatest work." He begged her to understand.

"You are my King," she said at last. "And my Lord. I will do as you command."

He grimaced. "I do not *command* you, Ramiyah. I only ask you to believe in me."

She met his eyes again. He stared into the deep blue of her pupils, the color of love itself.

"One more year," he said. He kissed her forehead, wrapped her hands in his own. "I promise. Then we will have a dozen children if you wish it."

She laughed unwillingly and smacked his hand from hers. "You make a fool of me!" But he was winning her over. He grabbed her about the waist and she wiggled away from him. He strove to kiss her lips but she was too quick. She bounded to the door and raised a hand to stay him.

"You ask me to wait, so I will," she said. "So too must *you* wait, Scholar King."

He tried to sweep her into his arms, but again she evaded his grasp.

"Ah-ah," she said, peering from behind a pillar of glossy stone. "Perhaps if I deny you certain . . . *pleasures* . . . your year will shrink to a few months . . . or days." She smiled in mock wickedness.

He poured wine into crystal cups, but when he turned around she had slipped from the chamber. He dispelled the desire in his loins by drinking deeply of the vintage, and it took him nine days to get her back into his bed. There were many nights when he worked alone until dawn, yet when he came seeking comfort in her arms, she never again denied him. At this point she might have refused the arts of the palace midwives, who taught northern women how to stave off pregnancy with herbs and ancient remedies. She might have fooled him, taken his seed sooner than he had wished. Ultimately, it was a woman's decision whether or not to use such arts. Even in the absence of them, it still took years for some women to conceive.

Yet Ramiyah kept her faith and her word: she had waited for him to finish the book. She waited too long, and it was all his fault. Now she would never know the joy of a son, a daughter, or a family. Now she waited only in the realm of the Gods, some mysterious netherworld where only the dead might go. He did not believe the priests of the Grand Temple, who pontificated that loved ones are united in the realms beyond death. Those were only words to comfort simple-minded mourners. If he killed himself to join Ramiyah, he would likely find only oblivion. Not even the greatest of philosophers could prove otherwise. And he had read them all.

His prayers complete, he kissed the ruby heart of the necklace one last time. Then he cast it far into the churning waters with all his might. *Let this precious bauble sink and be lost to Men, as Ramiyah has been lost to the world. Let it linger in the sands of the seabed until the day her death is avenged by my own hand. Let it rejoin the deep earth as an offering to Sea and Sky.*

Only Volomses saw him cast the priceless memento into the sea, but the wise sage said nothing about it.

Lyrilan spent the first day's voyage on the deck, lost amid the cries and shuffling of busy sailors. Undroth came to stand near him, and the two of them enjoyed the rolling freedom of the sea. The old warrior did not say much, and Lyrilan was glad of it. Undroth had given up everything he had ever worked for . . . as had the twelve men under his command. It was a gift Lyrilan could never repay. A silent understanding passed between deposed King and devoted subject.

Tucked away in the captain's cabin after sundown, Lyrilan opened the first of the traveling chests. *The First Book of Imvek* lay dusty and faded beneath his fingertips. He called for a cup of wine, which Volomses hurried to find for him, and began to read. In fact he read more than he slept during that first week at sea, until the weariness of travel and grief finally caught up to him. He studied the esoteric theories and obscure philosophies that lay behind much of sorcery and its demands. He read the exploits of Imvek, the wayward Prince who had left his imperial home in Uurz to search for ancient knowledge. He had found it in the ruined temples of the Southern Isles.

Unlike Lyrilan's predicament, Imvek's exile from the green-gold city was voluntary. Yet soon Lyrilan found himself identifying with the shrewd Prince. Among the tribes of idol-worshipping islanders Imvek discovered the gateway to a lost cache of treasure, the scroll chambers of a kingdom long dead. He spent years studying the lost language of the scrolls, learning from them the precepts of magic, defying the curses that accompanied such knowledge.

At the first volume's conclusion, Imvek returned to the islanders and gifted them with jewels pried from the depths of the ruins. He worked small miracles for the tribes, improving their crops, ridding them of the amphibious raiders who came out of the deep sea to plunder the islands. The King of the Southern Isles was a warrior known as Caramong the Great. His grandson would one day unite the islands to wage a war against Yaskatha and its allies. Yet Caramong himself was not as ambitious as his heirs would be. He loved Imvek and wanted to keep him as a bondsman. Yet, seeing how determined the Prince was to regain his homeland, he relented and gave only one condition for Imvek's safe return to Uurz.

"You have raided the tombs of our ancestors," declared Caramong from the steps of his great pyramid temple. "You have learned the secret of powers long forgotten by my people. Our stone Gods do not wish this knowledge spread to our enemies. Therefore, if you leave us, your tongue must stay here, so that you may speak to no one of the great wisdom you carry."

For months Imvek lingered, weighing the choice of a simple life among the islanders against a return to the power and prestige of Uurz. He longed to taste the Sacred Waters again, to feel the hot breath of the Desert of Many Thunders on his skin, to see the girl he had left behind and vowed to wed one day. He was the eldest son of his father, so he must return to take the throne. Otherwise there would be civil war and riots when the Emperor died.

The Prince of Uurz wrote at length about the irony of his situation. The islanders had lost the art of written language, so their King did not understand that Imvek – even tongueless – could still communicate his arcane discoveries by means of ink and parchment. For a whole year he brooded on Caramong's decree, until finally he accepted it.

The feathered volcano priests drugged him so that he would not feel pain. Then their High Priest cut out his tongue with a knife of steaming obsidian. As soon as he recovered from the mutilation, he bade farewell to the Island King. On his journey back to Uurz, he began writing the first of his six volumes, and that is how the book concluded.

Discussing the book's contents with Volomses, Lyrilan found his voice again. He spoke of the sacred power of blood and its relationship to true sorcery. The sage listened with careful intent. Together they recalled the names of the philosophers of old who had confirmed and hinted at the dark truths in Imvek's work. Ultimately, the Silent One had outsmarted the Island King because knowledge of the islanders' forgotten magic was passed on to Uurzians in his books. Yet, in another tragic irony, that hard-won knowledge had lain forgotten and disused for centuries.

Until now.

While the first of the summer storms rocked the ship, Lyrilan read his way through Imvek's second volume. This took far longer as the text evolved from narrative to a succession of formulas, recipes, and rituals. At times the book veered off into myth and legend, transcribing the tales of ancient beings and primeval realms whose origins and endings must be understood to provide context for conjurations. By the time Lyrilan finished the second book, the ship had been at sea for seventeen days. He stopped his reading there, turning instead to his quill and parchment. He assembled notes to reconfigure the book's various truths, translating them in his own way for greater understanding. He scribbled complex formulae and strung together the syllables of enigmatic tongues.

Volomses had given up the duties of a sage for those of a body servant. He supervised Lyrilan's food, drink, clothing, and various needs without a word of protest. Lyrilan vowed to find a good position for the old man somewhere in D'zan's archives. The libraries of Yaskatha were nearly as extensive as those of Uurz. He was sure the southern sages could use someone of Volomses' wisdom and character. For now, he was glad of the old man's fatherly attention.

These men that followed him into exile were his true brothers. Tyro was his flesh and blood no longer. In full sight of the Gods and the moonlit sea, he vowed to repay the cruelties Tyro had bestowed upon him.

The second storm of the voyage took the lives of two men. Waves carried them overboard, and the ship was battered until Lyrilan believed that all aboard would soon perish. Drenched and desperate, he made his way across the pitching deck to his cabin, stopping only to retrieve a large unbroken mollusk from a covered barrel. Inside the tiny room, tilting and swaying in wretched motion, Volomses lay on the floor and moaned in his own sickness.

Lyrilan opened Imvek's second book and lit a tallow candle.

He drew the princely dagger from his side and cut a shallow gash in the palm of his left hand. He spilled this blood upon the shell of the mollusk, where it mingled with traceries of clinging seaweed. Then he sang an incantation from the book, holding the candle's flame above the bloodied clam. The ship lurched, and he accidentally singed the hem of his robe with the candle.

Again he sang the incantation and more of his blood dripped to cover the mollusk. The candle gleamed in his unsteady hand. It was the sun, and the mollusk was the earth. His blood was the sea in which the mollusk had been birthed, and from which it had been torn by the hands of men.

He flung open the cabin door and braved the tempest once again. Stumbling through the wind and rain to stand at the ship's rail, he dropped the mollusk into the angry sea, mouthing a final refrain. He returned to the cabin, where he made sure to keep the candle burning. Slowly the storm lost its fury. The rain fell slow and steady now, but the winds had died away. The surging waves fell back into their depths. Eventually even the rain stopped, and the early moon emerged from a mountainous pile of black clouds.

Volomses laughed, regaining his feet and his stomach.

"Majesty!" the sage breathed. "You may have saved all our lives."

"Or it may have been a coincidence," said Lyrilan. "All storms must die eventually."

The sage frowned at him. Lyrilan's heart fluttered. He recalled a secret that the tongueless Imvek had also known. A nameless understanding of the world's hidden workings. One of many such secrets . . .

Volomses said nothing else, and the rest of the journey passed without storms. On the twenty-fifth day the *Sunrider* passed within view of the white cliffs of Mumbaza. The City of the Feathered Serpent flew the image of its legendary guardian on every banner, from low-lying wharves to cliff-top metropolis. Domes and towers gleamed white as pearls, with shades of crimson, blue, and silver dancing in the sunlight upon its smooth stones.

Lyrilan could see little of the city from so far out, but the wharves at the foot of the great cliffs were full of ships from every nation except Khyrei. The Mumbazan navy, matchless in all the world, comprised hundreds of white galleons built in the likeness of swan and seabird. They gleamed bright as dreams upon the dark waters. On the western horizon stood a misty island where even more Mumbuzan swanships were known to be stationed. Lyrilan could barely see its dim outline across the purple main.

The *Sunrider* was halted by a swanship so Captain S'dyr could display his merchant papers.

"We might stop here, Majesty," suggested Undroth, staring at the white cliffs. The old campaigner had exchanged his bronze corselet for a loose robe of green and gold silk. The longblade that never left his sight hung now upon his back like a lonely wing. "We'll find respite from these waves, along with fresh food . . . and that famous Mumbazan wine."

"No," said Lyrilan, gazing beyond the cliffs at the pearly towers. "Eight more days brings us to Yaskatha. I know that D'zan will aid me. The same cannot be said of Undutu – the Lord of Mumbaza will remain aloof. Who can say where he sides with Tyro's war? No, I'll endure the discomfort of sea travel a few more days for the luxuries to be found in Yaskatha."

"A wise choice, My Lord," said Volomses. "After all, it was your father who provided young D'zan refuge when the Usurper stole his throne. He cannot now refuse you sanctuary under such considerations."

"He will not refuse," said Lyrilan. "He is my friend."

The sage nodded, and Undroth let his men know there would be no shore leave on that day.

The Third Book of Imvek was far more dense and less comprehensible than the second. Lyrilan had barely cracked the first chapter's secrets when the call came from the upper deck. He set the tome aside and went up to stand on the prow. Bright Yaskatha came into view across the sun-speckled waves.

Volomses and Undroth stood beside him as the ship glided into the great port. Sails of every color and make passed them by on either side. At the docks a cohort of D'zan's elite guard awaited them; word of a lord's arrival had been sent from Murala by a trained Yaskathan bird. The Yaskathan soldiers stood at attention in silver mail and crimson tabard, pennoned spears glinting like the ocean.

"King D'zan sends an honor guard to receive you," said Undroth. "This is a good sign."

Undroth and his men unloaded their fifteen Uurzian mounts from the hold, saddling the horses and dressing them in jeweled caparisons packed for this moment. The time for keeping a low profile was done. Now the folk of Yaskatha and their King must know that a Lord of Uurz rode among them. Undroth settled with the captain, and Lyrilan's band of exiles rode their steeds down the plank onto level ground. There the captain of the escort greeted them with official words and bows. Lyrilan stared at the bright city and its soaring palace.

They rode through the Seaward Gate into the bustling streets. Half of the mounted escort went before them, while the other half trailed close behind, riding beneath the Sword and Tree banner. Undroth flew a lesser banner, the Golden Sun of Uurz, from the seat of his own steed.

The citizens of Yaskatha were a plain but happy lot. Their tan skins and gleaming hair fascinated the quiet Lyrilan. Now the crowds of merchants, laborers, harvesters, and nobles divided in the path of the Uurzians. He admired the fine horses that thrived here; every Yaskathan learned to ride at an early age. Oxen and horned goats pulled wagons and carts through the lanes. Public wells stood open in carefully tended grottoes thick with leaf and blossom. The music of minstrels and poets fell from the windows of taverns and alehouses. Children ran in laughing gangs about the streets, flitting between column and arch, trying to catch a glimpse of the Scholar King as he passed.

Many streets were lined with trees whose green foliage neither turned nor fell. There was no winter in this part of the world, or at least nothing compared to the winters of Uurz and Udurum. Here there was only the Hot Season and the Rainy Season. The heat was mitigated by the breezes of the ocean; Lyrilan found it far more pleasant than parched Uurz. Aqueducts carried fresh water throughout the city, and public baths were not uncommon.

The Uurzians and their escort passed through a noisy bazaar where every manner of bright bird, sturdy horse, and fresh-caught fish was on display. In the chaos of shouting commerce Lyrilan and his train were practically ignored. The green hill of the palace lay directly ahead. The riders wound unhurriedly up a spiral hill-path, passing beneath the boughs of a hundred orchards before they reached the outer gates of the palace.

The aroma of the blossoming orchards was overpowering. It filled Lyrilan's nostrils with delight and made his head spin. Birdsong wafted from the high branches of trees. He wished Ramiyah could have seen once more the beauty of her homeland before she died. His eyes welled; he fought against the tears.

The time for weeping was done.

He turned his burning gaze back to the silver gates as they swung open.

D'zan received him with opulence and ceremony. The great hall of his palace was lined with courtiers and courtesans, a multitude of bejeweled individuals in all the garish colors one expected from southern nobility. A cohort of soldiers stood at attention about the hall, where musicians, dancers, and jugglers awaited a chance to display their skills. A great table sat before the high throne, and servants rushed to cover it with steaming meats, golden breads, heaping platters of grapes, and diced fruits. The fine goblets and platters along the board shone like some lost treasure hoard unearthed for public display.

The walls to east and west were open colonnades coiled with hanging grape vines and blossoms. The sea air found its own course through the great hall, making the flames of braziers and torches dance as if to invisible melodies.

The King of Yaskatha left his throne to meet Lyrilan at the entrance of the hall, a sign of the great warmth shared between them. D'zan looked much the same as he had four years ago. A few new lines on his boyish face spoke of worry. But when he smiled his teeth flashed in the sun. He wore his hair longer now, a blond mane falling past his shoulders. The crown on his brow was jeweled platinum, and his golden armlets were set with fine diamonds. He took Lyrilan in a laughing embrace.

"Lyrilan, Son of Dairon!" D'zan squeezed him fiercely. By the power of those limbs, Lyrilan knew that his friend had not abandoned the sword. D'zan had the arms of a warrior now, and it was Tyro who had set him on that path eight years ago. "You look healthy! Come and see the banquet I've set for your company." The King of Yaskatha turned to shake the hand of Undroth, bowed low to Volomses, and saluted the twelve Uurzian soldiers as one.

All the eyes of the Yaskathan court fell upon the Uurzians as they gathered about the table, the faint stink of fishy brine lingering on their cloaks and boots. The musicians struck up a lively tune on fife, lyre, pipe, and drum. Dancers in colored veils whirled between the great table and the two lesser ones set in either wing of the hall. D'zan's golden throne glimmered upon a dais before the great Sword and Tree banner, alongside a lesser chair meant for his Queen. Lyrilan had caught word of Sharadza's leaving, and of D'zan taking a second wife already with child. He admired the tall beauty at the head of the table who rose to take the King's hand. This must be Sharadza's rival, or her replacement.

"Sit!" called D'zan. "My table is yours, Lyrilan. Eat and drink and wash the weight of the sea from your backs. Later we will speak of weighty matters, but now we celebrate the reunion of old friends." He paused as his lady stood and beamed a smile at his guests. "Cymetha, Second Wife of the Throne, I present to you Lyrilan, Scholar King of Uurz. Cymetha bears my first child, whom the Sea Priests tell me will be a strong boy."

"Congratulations, Great King," said Lyrilan. He noticed now

the round belly of Cymetha, heretofore hidden behind her gown of spun gold and indigo. "I am honored to be received in your gracious manner, as I am undeserving of such splendor."

"You always were too modest," said D'zan, taking his seat next to Cymetha. The Uurzians followed his lead, placing themselves about the table nearest to the monarch. The remaining seats soon filled with advisors, generals, and courtiers.

Lyrilan found it easy to ignore them all. He sat at the corner, nearest of all to D'zan save Cymetha. Volomses and Undroth sat at his left elbow. The music swelled, and the smells of braised meats made his stomach growl. Along the table sat a feast to sing about in legends, a board fit for heroes. A servant poured dark wine into his goblet.

D'zan lifted his own chalice and toasted the new arrivals. "To Friendship! A power greater than all save Love itself."

The tables were full now, and all those present drank to the King's words. The wine was sharp, yet sweet and potent. Lyrilan's head swam.

"Eat! Drink! Your presence does my house honor," called D'zan. "You have many admirers among this court. Most of my courtiers have read *The Perilous Quest*." He said nothing of Ramiyah or her death. The last time Lyrilan had come here, he left with her by his side. D'zan must have known she was dead, yet he would not burden his friend with questions, or magnify Lyrilan's sorrow with pity.

Lyrilan avoided giving a response by stuffing his mouth full of roast pork. A floodgate of hunger opened, and he dined like a warrior fresh from the battlefield. He ate until his stomach felt as full and round as Cymetha's. The Yaskathans engaged in polite conversation, at times prodding Undroth and Volomses to join in their dialogues. Yet D'zan was kind enough to let Lyrilan fill his belly before drawing him into deep conversation.

After the feast the two Kings retired to a private terrace overlooking the western half of the city, where the harbor played host to a forest of varicolored sails. Volomses and Undroth were assigned to quarters in the palace proper, and Lyrilan had charged them to stow his possessions and secure the rooms. His discussion with D'zan could wait no longer.

They sat in deep chairs, staring past a viny balustrade at the Cryptic Sea. The last rays of sunlight burned crimson on the far horizon. It reminded Lyrilan of Ramiyah's blood spattered across white sheets. He put the image from his mind as an attendant filled the Kings' cups and left them to their peace. A guard in silver mail and crimson cape stood near the terrace's edge.

"Ah, my friend, it is good to see you again," said D'zan, surveying his crowded harbor.

"It has been too long," said Lyrilan. "Dare I ask about Sharadza?"

D'zan frowned and sighed. "Sharadza comes and goes as she pleases. Much like the wind." A faraway look came across his face. This was obviously a subject upon which he did not intend to dwell for long.

Lyrilan let silence overtake them both. Then he asked: "So you know everything?"

D'zan looked at him. "Only that your brother denounced you, accused you of murdering your wife, and banished you for life."

Lyrilan laughed without humor. "Then you know *almost* everything."

"Pigeons," said D'zan. "The only birds privileged to serve Kings and wise enough to do it well." His eyes were deep green, the same color they had been ever since he defeated Elhathym the Usurper and took back his kingdom. Some sorcery unleashed by the Tyrant had resulted in the change of eye color, but D'zan never spoke to anyone about it. Perhaps the truth of it was best left unsaid, since everything else about D'zan seemed unchanged by his struggle.

The Yaskathan King placed a hand on Lyrilan's shoulder. "I grieve for Ramiyah . . ."

"Then you do not believe . . ." Lyrilan could not finish the question.

"Believe what? Tyro's lies about you meddling with sorcery?" D'zan exhaled. "I know you, Lyrilan. How could I believe such nonsense?"

A pang of guilt writhed in Lyrilan's stomach. He nodded.

He told D'zan of the book he had written to chronicle Dairon's life, how he had gifted it to his brother, and how it had made no difference at all. He spoke of Ramiyah, how deeply he had loved her, and his hopes for a child, a decision he had made far too late. He spoke of Tyro's wicked wife, Talondra, and the schemes of Mendices. He spoke of treachery, lies, and the lust for power. He might never have spoken with such candor and rarely so vividly, but the Yaskathan wine had loosened his tongue. D'zan listened as attentively as a patient priest.

"These political games are the most deadly of all," D'zan mused. "I feared this would happen when Dairon appointed you the Twin Kings of Uurz."

"I am a man without a home," said Lyrilan. He accepted that fact for the first time even as he said it aloud.

"No, Brother," said D'zan. "As long as I am King here, you will always have a home."

Lyrilan grinned, something he owed entirely to the wine. "You have my gratitude . . . *Brother*."

"Is this some jest of the Four Gods?" said D'zan. "You stand now in the straits where I stood eight years ago."

"Then you know what lies in my heart," said Lyrilan.

D'zan breathed deeply of the cool evening air. "I know you dream of revenge. Of taking back your title and your throne. What else would a King dream but these things?"

"It is . . . " said Lyrilan, "a heavy weight to bear."

"Then let me lighten your burden a bit," said D'zan. "I have struck a bargain with your brother."

Lyrilan stood and grabbed the banister, his fists crushing the green leaves that sprouted there. "You will join his mad war?"

D'zan stood beside him. "'All war is madness.'" He quoted Therokles the Sharrian, one of Lyrilan's favorite philosophers. "Yes, I've agreed to join Tyro ... as have the Kings of Mumbaza and Udurum. There is even talk of some Giant-King from the Frozen North, a fierce ally of Vireon's. The time has come for Khyrei to pay for its many crimes."

Lyrilan slumped back into his chair. Somewhere below, in the gardens lined with fountains and statues, a minstrel strummed upon a lyre and sang a song of lost beauty.

"You, who claim friendship with me, have allied with my sworn enemy."

"With your *brother*," D'zan corrected him. "Remember that, Lyrilan, no matter what has happened. You and Tyro share the same blood. Dairon's blood."

"No longer," said Lyrilan, turning away. He watched the moon-light sparkling on the dark ocean. "*You* are more my brother than him who betrayed me. You resisted this war of vengeance for many years – why give in now? Is it the voices of your royal peers that sway you? Do you forget the suffering that war brings? You are well read, wise in learning. You know this path is treacherous, built on the suffering of men, women, and children."

"Listen to me," said D'zan. "I know you speak from a wounded heart. I know you believe in peace, as I do. I also believe that you would have me change course now simply to thwart your brother. But you have not heard the core of my reason.

"You ask why I join this Alliance of Five Nations, why I am willing to send my navy against the black reavers of Khyrei. Why

I am willing to suffer. My covenant with Tyro was sealed by his agreement to specific terms. First, he has recanted your lifetime exile. He allows your return to the Stormlands after a period of five years. Second, you shall be restored the title Prince of Uurz. Third, you will rule as Lord of Murala for the rest of your days, and may return to visit the City of Sacred Waters as often as you like."

Lyrilan sat speechless on the terrace. The wind ruffled the tapestries at his back.

"You would do this . . . for me?" he asked. "You would condemn hundreds, likely thousands, of your people to death . . . simply to restore a portion of my lost dignity?"

"And to destroy Khyrei once and for all," said D'zan.

Lyrilan stared into his friend's emerald eyes. They seemed colder now. Less human.

"How could you make such an accord?"

"How could I not?" asked D'zan.

"I . . . I don't know what to say," Lyrilan whispered.

"Then say nothing. Only drink more of this wine with me." D'zan reached for the flask and refilled their cups himself. "Even now the northern Kings march toward the Eastern Marshes, where Khyrei's Border Legions no doubt stand ready to meet them."

"Will you march, then?" asked Lyrilan. A strange mixture of drunkenness, remorse, and gratitude swelled in his chest.

"No, I will *sail*," said D'zan. "Yaskatha and Mumbaza will join our navies and enter the Golden Sea. Our combined forces will assault the black city from the east, while the legions of Tyro and Vireon converge upon it from the west. Vireon has stirred the Ice Giants to wrath. They march alongside the Men of Udurum. The Giants are finally on our side. Khyrei is doomed."

Lyrilan sighed. Nothing was ever so simple. "There is nothing

I can do to change your mind about this? To keep Yaskatha from the conflict?"

"Nothing," said D'zan. "And if you did, you would be stuck here in Yaskatha for the rest of your life. I know my hospitality is rich, yet I wager you would like to go home someday, eh?"

Lyrilan considered the question. *Five years*. Would it be long enough? D'zan's work on his behalf would bring him close to Tyro. Far easier to find vengeance when you are close to your enemy.

"Yes," he said, distantly. *Home*. The word rang like thunder between his ears.

"Look on the brighter side of the coin," said D'zan. The King of Yaskatha leaned in close and lowered his voice. His sea-green eyes stared deep into Lyrilan's own. "In the red fury of war, Tyro might easily fall. And if such a tragedy was to occur . . . it would put you back on the throne of Uurz."

Lyrilan rubbed his eyes. The world was moving on, as it always did, regardless of what he wished. It was so much easier to chronicle the events of history than to live them. Simple scribes need not fret over the matters that troubled Kings.

Kings could not be scribes.

Five years.

Or sooner, if Tyro died on the battlefield.

"When do you sail?" he asked.

"In seven days," said D'zan, "when Undutu's Swan Fleet reaches my shores. We'll have a force the likes of which the world has never seen. Sail with me, Lyrilan!"

Lyrilan shook his head. His black curls were unkempt and wild from days of sea winds. "As you say, I am no warrior," he said. "I grow too old for such adventures." He was only thirty, the same age as Tyro. But D'zan said nothing of this; he knew the twins were not of one make.

"Very well," said D'zan, shrugging his broad shoulders. "You will find the Royal Library at your disposal, as well as the libraries of the temples. And there are plenty of hot-blooded women here in the palace eager to soothe the pain of your loss. I trust you will keep busy while I am gone."

"Oh, yes," said Lyrilan. His thoughts turned to the candle and the mollusk.

The blood.

Five years to plan my vengeance.

"To friendship," he said, echoing D'zan's words from earlier in the evening. He raised his cup and stared at the dark ocean as if toasting its deep mystery. He swallowed the last gulp of wine as D'zan did the same.

The King of Yaskatha refilled both chalices and made his own toast.

"To friendship, war, and the deaths of our enemies."

They drank deeply of the ancient vintage.

15

Stairway to Glory

When the Giants returned to Uurz, they brought with them an end to the long drought. Sages and drunkards alike praised the name of Vireon Vodson. As his father's sorcery had shattered the Desert of Many Thunders and birthed the Stormlands, so did Vireon's power bring the thunderstorms rushing back to the City of Sacred Waters.

Vireon had no conscious designs on the weather, yet Men and Giants had long told him that Vod's sorcery was his birthright. Certainly his sister had displayed a command of such magic, and now Vireon considered the possibility that he too might possess hidden reserves of power. His great strength, speed, and durability were already legend, so if Men chose to call him sorcerer then he no longer cared to deny it. Yet none accused him of this to his face.

The Giants came in a great marching horde, flattening the fields of brown grass as they filed out of the Grim Mountains through Vod's Passage. The cold air flew before them as if to announce their coming. The Men of Lakehold first saw Vireon's advance, and they shuddered behind the walls of their tiny fortress. Behind the King of Udurum on his great black charger came a personal guard of forty Uduri spearmaidens, followed by two legions of Men on horseback and seven more legions on foot.

After the Men of Udurum came the sight which struck fear into the hearts of the most grizzled warriors: a legion of blue-skinned Ice Giants numbering three thousand strong, fronted by the hulking form of King Angrid the Long-Arm. At the Ice King's side walked a single Uduri, a blue-skinned shamaness bearing a staff topped with living blue fire. This was Varda the Keen Eyes, a guardian of the blue flame which did not singe wood or give warmth. All of them, Giants and Men alike, marched or rode beneath the Hammer and Fist banner of New Udurum.

The mountain waterfall that fed the Uduru River had diminished to a trickle, as had the young river itself. The army of Men and Giants had followed the river's sluggish course from the mouth of the pass to Lakehold, leaving a swathe of trampled grass along its western bank. When Vireon approached the village and its modest fortress, he looked upon the low waters of the dying lake. A cold wind rushed before him and rattled the stones of the keep.

By the time the Giant-Kings spoke with the Lord of Lakehold and assured him of their armies' peaceful passing, a gentle rain had begun to fall. The fortress gates opened and a mass of citizens, formerly terrified of being crushed to death or eaten by Giants, rushed into the village streets in a state of madcap jubilation. They danced in the rain, cheering and laughing; they filled buckets and hats and bowls with it. Some took off their clothes and bathed naked in the rainfall. The ranks of Udvorg, camping within full view of the village, chuckled at the antics of the tiny rain-loving folk. Still, no villager would approach the blue-skinned warriors, even when the sound of jovial laughter mingled with the low thunder above the lake. The Men of Udurum set up tent and pavilion outside the village, preparing for a warm yet sodden night. The blue-skins set up no tents; they were heedless of the elements. While Men huddled about their tent fires and struggled to keep their polished metal dry, the Udvorg slept beneath a blanket of roiling sky.

The forces of the north rested for a single night outside Lakehold. From his own tent a sleepless Vireon watched the lake waters rise all night long. He had heard many tales of the long drought and its pain. If his coming improved the lives of the Stormlanders, so be it. He was his father's son.

The northerners resumed their southward march under a gray dawn, leaving behind them a raging storm. A night rider had been dispatched from the fortress to carry word of Vireon's coming to the newly ordained Emperor of Uurz. The hoofprints of his galloping steed were still embedded between the endless stalks of tall grass. Soon they were obliterated by the slogging feet and hooves of Men, Udvorg, and Uduru.

The blue-skins did not grumble much, but it was plain to see they missed their frozen lands. They had left behind all heavy furs, save for loincloths, kilts, and woolly tunics. Most retained their mammoth-hide boots, although some had chosen to walk barefoot through these foreign lands. The icicles had long ago melted from their white beards and hair. At night they built no normal fires, but gathered about several blue bonfires set by the staff of Varda. They basked in the waves of cold emanating from these azure blazes as surely as Men relaxed in the warmth of their cookfires. The Icelands Giants were hardy and adaptable; Vireon learned this quickly. The lack of cold air was uncomfortable for them, but not debilitating. In fact, they seemed to miss the frigid air less and less the farther south they marched. They were born from the ancient stones of the earth, which weathered heat and cold with equal strength.

Among the blue-skins was a cohort of bronze-skinned Uduru,

about half the total number of those who had gone north eight years ago to start families with blue-skin wives. After so many seasons living among their cousins, these black-haired Giants were fully accepted among the Udvorg tribes. Vireon's uncle, Fangodrim the Gray, stood among the council of chieftains left in charge of the Ice Clans by Angrid, just as Vireon had left Ryvun Ctholl in command of Udurum's affairs. Ryvun retained a guard of over fifty Uduri to watch his back and help keep order in the City of Men and Giants. Ryvun would serve faithfully, and the loyal Uduri would ensure that he kept the city secure. Who would dare attack Udurum, even with its monarch abroad? The city's only known enemy lay south in distant Khyrei.

Storms rolled ahead of the northern armies, as if to announce the coming of Vireon and Angrid. When Vireon rode within sight of the walls of Uurz, the sky was its own leaden empire casting thunderbolts and sheets of cool rain upon the thirsty earth. He had passed dead farms, one after another, victims of the drought and heat. Peasants came out of their withered fields to bow and worship the Giants as they passed, and the Udvorg found this another hilarious sight. Men, to them, were little more than creatures of legend. They expected violence and savagery, but found instead only spectacle and gratitude.

Behind the city's massive granite walls the populace rejoiced, yet they grew restless at the approach of the Giant host. Over thirty years ago a lesser host of Giants came and conquered Uurz in a matter of days. Yet the Emperor Tyro rode from the main gate in a white chariot followed by a legion of mounted cavalry. Citizens and guardsmen lined the outer ramparts, trying to catch a glimpse of this meeting of Kings.

Tyro received Vireon on the brown plain before the high gate, while the welcome rain fell upon soldiers and monarchs alike. Tyro bowed and took Vireon's forearm against his own in the traditional

Uurzian handshake. Then he bowed before the Udvorg King, gifting him doubly with a cask of aged wine and a strongbox brimming with frosty diamonds. These formalities concluded, Vireon rode into the green-gold city to spend a night at the palace with Dahrima and Angrid at either side. The host of Men and Giants pitched their encampment in the fields outside the gates of Uurz, leaving only the northern and western roads clear of their tents and pickets.

Dahrima had been Vireon's first choice to rule Udurum while he was away, but she had refused. In fact, ever since the deaths of his wife and daughter she would not leave his side. He soon grew tired of trying to rid himself of her constant company. Every King must have a personal guard, he reckoned, so why not this faithful Uduri? He had grown accustomed to her handsome face and the glittering gold of her braided hair. She spoke little, and when she did there was wisdom in her words. So she walked on his left as he rode next to Tyro's chariot, and the people of Uurz gathered along the muddy avenues, the rainslick tops of walls and roofs, and the burnished platforms of temples. They cheered the rain and the Giant-Kings as one.

Vireon knew not if they loved him merely for the storms, or simply because he was the son of the legendary Vod. He shifted the weight of the greatsword across his back as he rode, a *steely* reminder of his purpose. He kept a solemn face as the procession entered palace grounds, and thunder rolled above the city's golden spires.

Tyro's best artisans had built a great chair for the King of the Icelands. Angrid and Vireon sat with the Sword King about a table piled heavy with whole roasted pigs, fowl, and oxen. The best of his wines had been hauled from the cellars. Since this was a war council, Tyro had banished the bulk of his court from the

Feasting Hall. Twenty legionnaires bearing golden shields stood between the columns, and Generals Mendices, Aeldryn, and Rolfus sat at table with the monarchs. Dahrima stood, leaning against a fat marble pillar behind Vireon's sculpted chair. Servants offered her wine, but she would take only water.

"Your coming is the greatest honor of my life thus far," Tyro told his guests. He wore his lion's head corselet of gold with a necklace of blood-bright rubies to rival the green jewel of his crown. "Uurz welcomes you as brothers, allies, and liberators. Together we shall bring an end to this long-standing Khyrein oppression of land and sea. Never has the world seen such a force gathered as ours. Let us raise our cups and toast the Alliance of Five Nations."

Vireon and Angrid followed Tyro's gesture.

"Both D'zan and Undutu have joined our cause?" asked Vireon.

Tyro's handsome face beamed. "How could they refuse? What we are doing will change the entire known world for the better. We are about to make history."

"What plans have you drawn?" asked Vireon.

Tyro related the pincer movement his generals had decided upon: the fleets of Yaskatha and Mumbaza would swing around the southern edge of the continent, striking at Khyrei from south and east, while the three armies of the north approached from the west by braving the Eastern Marshes.

"Already I have sent forth work crews," Tyro said, "to carve a great stairway in the face of the Earth-Wall, so that both Giants and Men may climb easily into the forests of the High Realms. This shall be done along the great cliff a hundred and fifty leagues inland, so avoiding word of its construction reaching Allundra. The seaport still endures occasional trade with the Khyreins, mostly out of necessity."

A low peal of thunder resounded above the palace walls as the rain continued. Vireon sipped at the wine but had little appetite for meat or bread. Angrid, however, tore into the meat with gusto. The Udvorg were accustomed to eating their meat raw, since their blue flame did not blacken or scorch. Yet the Long-Arm seemed to relish the taste of cooked flesh, if the grease on his mighty beard were any indication.

"The Southern Kings have long refrained from such enterprise as this," said Vireon. "How did you finally win their allegiance?"

Tyro frowned. "D'zan's affection for my poor brother made him amenable to certain agreements. His kingdom lies closest to Khyrei, so he could not hold out forever in the face of its menace. Undutu pledged his own navy as soon as he heard that D'zan had committed the Yaskathan fleet. I believe the King on the Cliffs feared to miss such a historic conflict. This is Undutu's chance to win renown and rid himself of the title of Boy-King once and for all. At the age of nineteen he is more than ready to spill the blood of enemies ... and his mother no longer controls his fate. Of course, a few treasure casks delivered to his door helped to sway his mind."

"I know none of these strange names," said Angrid, chomping the bones of his meal into powdery grit between his molars. "Yet show to me the face of our enemy, and I will crush it beneath my heel."

Tyro grinned at the blue-skinned Ice King. "Lord of the Icelands, your presence brings honor to both our races. Yet your people have known only the northern climes for all of history. Why do you now decide to join our noble crusade?"

"Blood," answered Angrid. His scarlet eyes turned to Vireon across the table. "The Son of Vod is blood of my blood, as are all of the Uduru. Vireon it was who brought the pale-skins to our lands, where they give our women strong and healthy babes. Vireon it was who united our long-divided peoples. Vireon's enemies are my enemies. We Giants are carved from the stone of a single mountain. We are *Uduraal*."

"I know this word," said Tyro. "You are *family*. The oldest bonds are the strongest bonds." He raised his cup again and made another toast, this time to the holiness of family bonds. His face grew grave, and he spoke to Vireon in a voice laden with sorrow. "I mourn for the loss of your wife and child. Long have I suspected the continued existence of the Claw. Now that it is a proven fact, there can be no other course but to root her out and destroy her once and for all. Along with her fiendish son . . . or grandson . . . or whatever this Gammir might be."

"We will bring justice to a land that knows only blood and terror," said Vireon. "My father cast the Palace of Khyrei into ruins when he was young. His mistake was in allowing the Claw to rebuild it and maintain her power. He should have razed the entire city and made the world safer for his descendants. Vod did many great things, but the one feat he left undone his son will do for him. The fact that all nations stand united on this course only proves its worth."

"Indeed," said Tyro. "I've prepared twenty legions of strong Uurzian soldiers. Sixty thousand well-trained warriors. Add to that the legions of Men and Giants you bring southward, and we stand a hundred thousand strong. And the might of Giants cannot be measured as that of Men, so our true strength is far greater than our numbers. In the might of Giantkind lies the true greatness of our force, and with the world's two greatest navies at our side, we cannot fail."

"Have you any word of my sister?" Vireon asked. He had received no message or news of Sharadza in months. There would be sorcery in Khyrei, and she would be an asset if he could bring her to the field. Or perhaps she decided to sail with D'zan.

Tyro sighed and called for a servant to refill Vireon's cup. "Has

no one told you?" Vireon stared at him. "It seems Sharadza has left
D'zan. He has taken a second wife, who now carries his child.
They say Sharadza fled into the night, perhaps on some errand of
sorcery. Yet no one really knows the truth of it. I would like nothing better than to see your sister among our company. Perhaps she
will join the crusade as it moves south."

Vireon grimaced. The news did not sit well with him.

"When the slaying is done," he said, "I will speak with D'zan."

The armies of three kingdoms moved south and west across the
rainswept plain. A train of ten thousand civilians followed the
triple host: armorers, bowyers, fletchers, blacksmiths, weaponers,
cooks, wagoneers, squires, minstrels, harlots, and shepherds driving flocks of goats, sheep, and cattle. Some foraging would be
done in the High Realms, but even then the supply train was
needed to ensure enough food for the host. And wherever soldiers
made their way, women of opportunity were never far behind.
Poets and musicians strove to set the unfolding history into verse,
while earning small fortunes in the process.

The Men of Uurz had not marched to war in fifty years, when
an earlier generation of warriors had joined King Trimesqua's
host in the War of the Southern Isles. As the green-gold legions
departed with the northern host, the city broke into furious celebration. The rebirth of their dying land lent it a special fervor. The
voices of those who still spoke out against the war were ignored or
silenced in the teeming streets. The return of storms to the
Stormlands was a sign from the Sky God that the new Emperor's
cause was righteous. Vireon cared little for such sentiment, but if
it served his ends, let the Uurzians enjoy their own fancies. Let
them believe it was Tyro who commanded the triple host; without
his northern allies he would never dare this great march.

Every village along the way offered food and comfort to the

armies, and at night the great camp seemed a small city all its own. The Giants dined on roasted steer and drank barrels full of Uurzian ale. Like their King, the blue-skins were fast acquiring a taste for cooked meat. By day the host moved in three long files stretching parallel across the Stormlands: Udurum legions, Giants, and Uurzian legions.

The three Kings traveled together at the head of the vanguard, where Dahrima insisted on pacing alongside Vireon's steed. She seemed as tireless as Vireon himself, and if he had five thousand like her at his back he might leave the main host and run all day and all night to reach the black city sooner. However, this war must be fought by both races, so he must travel at the speed of Men. The great legs of the Giants ate up the leagues and, unlike Men, they did not complain of sore feet and fatigue after a long day of marching. They were the Stoneborn, and they knew little pain in this life. On the third day's march Vireon sighted the peninsula of the highlands, that section of the Great Earth-Wall known as the Promontory. The Giants would have rushed forward and climbed the great cliff right there if Vireon had given the word. Instead, Tyro turned the entire host directly east, where his work crews had gone weeks earlier. The triple host marched now with the Stormlands on their left and the rugged Earth-Wall to their right, its heights lost among the leaden stormclouds. After five more days of gentle rain and kind winds, the host came upon the site of the Great Stair.

Tyro praised his architects and builders as he surveyed this new Wonder of the World. Where the Earth-Wall turned its course from southeast to northeast, the engineers of Uurz had done exactly as they were bidden. A massive set of stairs was freshly carved into the bare brown rock, leading all the way up through the clouds to the wild forests of the high plateau. Each stair was carved low enough for Men and horses, yet wide and broad enough for Giants. The Great Stair ran more than a league from start to finish, ascending west to east along the cliffside. A gigantic network of wooden scaffolding was still in place as the last of the Stair's detail work was completed. The sculptors would have to cease their ornamental work to let the triple host pass upward, and by Tyro's order they were glad to rest. It would take weeks' or months' more work before the rough-hewn staircase was complete with columns, fringework, insignia, and other aesthetic considerations. Vireon was concerned only with its functionality.

It was the stairway to glory, and the northern Kings would be the first to climb it.

Seeing this evidence of what a determined force of Men could achieve, the Giants were greatly impressed.

"This Earth-Wall is like a mountain turned on its side," Angrid told Tyro. "Yet the Men of Uurz have mastered it. There is more strength in your race than our legends tell." The Ice King stroked his cloud-pale beard and admired the sculpted face of the continent-spanning cliff.

Tyro stared at his great construction and swelled with pride. "The Great Stair is but one of our many accomplishments. Did you happen to notice the city we built a few leagues back?" Angrid laughed at the jest; Men and Giants both took heart from the booming sound.

"Let us camp below the Wall tonight," said Vireon. "We will climb the narrow way in daylight."

"My exact thought," said Tyro. "Tomorrow these tall ones will see the High Realm for the first time. I wonder how it will compare with the forests of Uduria?"

"I have seen both," said Vireon. "There is no comparison."

Tyro grinned and called for the setting up of his nightly pavilion.

"I do not like our position here," Dahrima muttered to Vireon. "We are prone to ambush from the land above." She gripped her great axe as if she expected an army of foes to fall from the murky sky.

Vireon slid down from his saddle. He looked up at the clouds hovering at the lip of the wall. "Up there are nothing but wild animals, ancient trees, and a pile of forgotten ruins. And there are working men at the top of this stair who would raise the alarm if any foe did appear in the night. Rest easy, Uduri."

Again the great camp sank its roots into Stormlands soil. The rain fell sporadically all night. The Men of Uurz did not mind marching in mud, so glad were they to see and taste the blessed rains. Cookfires sprang up like a constellation of stars along the base of the cliff.

Dahrima slept on the bare ground, curled up with her axe before the entrance to Vireon's tent. He thought of inviting her inside, but she might interpret his invitation wrongly. If he were tall as a Giant, perhaps he would lie with her beneath the warm furs. It might ease the pain of losing Alua. Yet he was mostly glad that her size kept them from sharing a bed; he had no wish to dishonor his wife's memory. There was no replacing Alua, but how long must he wait until he might take another Queen? If he must wait until his heart no longer ached, he might wait forever. He forced lingering thoughts of Maelthyn from his mind and fell into a troubled sleep. He awoke before dawn to drink mulled wine and walk about the sodden camp as it stirred to life.

In the overcast morning, as ten thousand night-fires were snuffed out, soldiers accoutered themselves with sword, spear, shield, and hauberk, while the squires of cavalrymen strapped their masters into corselets of lacquered bronze. The Giants awoke ready to march, tossing mace, axe, or spear over their shoulders and yawning into the ashen sky. They milled about, throwing stones at wild birds, and traded stories, while the ranks of Men slowly prepared themselves for the ascent.

The three Kings went first up the Great Stair, Vireon and Tyro on horseback, Angrid afoot with Dahrima close behind him. They stopped only once, at the midpoint of the great steps, to look back upon the Stormlands and the great host spread across the plain. Only then did Vireon realize the true scale of the triple host. It set his blood to racing in his veins, and he thanked the Four Gods for gifting him with such an assembly of warriors.

All of this for you, Alua.

And for little Maelthyn, if she ever truly existed.

At the top of the Earth-Wall Vireon gazed southward at a second wall of towering, green-leafed trees. The ancient forest spanned the great cliff from horizon to horizon, hemming the southern world as far as the eye could see. It stretched all the way to Yaskatha and the remote shore of the Cryptic Sea. A kingdom of green shadows thrived beneath a cerulean sky laced with strings of pearly cloud. Looking back, the plains of the Stormlands lay hidden beneath an endless panorama of thunderheads.

There would be no storm magic up here where the legacy of Vod's magic did not reach. Yet the upper land was green and fertile, as it had been for thousands of years. The forests of the High Realms grew wild, tangled, untamed, and nearly impenetrable. There were no great Uygas here to dwarf the Udvorg and make them feel small, for this was not the Giantlands. The most ancient of the High Realms trees rose barely three times taller than the Giants, as Giants stood three times taller than the average Man.

"My foresters have gone ahead to mark our trail," said Tyro from the back of his mailed stallion. "We must rely on the Udvorg to flatten and widen our trail as we go. Based on our travel speed from Uurz to the Earth-Wall, we should see a week of rough passage before we reach the lowland marshes. There our hardships will begin."

Vireon agreed. Twice now he had stood atop the great cliff and

looked upon the seething cloud-roof of the Stormlands. Distant
thunders rose dimly to his ears. Somewhere behind him, and farther west toward the Promontory, lay the ruins of Omu the Jade
City. There the young Alua had ruled a kingdom of Men ages ago.
The spirits of her people still haunted the deep groves of this
place. Ancient superstitions, fierce predators, and dense foliage
accounted for the lack of settlements here. Yet hunters from every
realm came to the High Realms to stalk the game of this forest.
Many were the bands of intrepid Uurzians or Yaskathans who
never returned to tell their tales of the haunted wood. Knowing
the secret of the shunned place, Vireon was no longer suspicious
of its nature. The high forest reminded him of Alua: beautiful and
full of mysteries. He wiped his welling eyes and called for the
swelling lines atop the cliff to reposition themselves. A vanguard
of Giants must go first now into the green shadows.

Lord Mendices and a retinue of fifty Uurzians rode ahead with
a company of a hundred axe-bearing Udvorg. They followed the
trail signs left by Tyro's foresters, while the Giants cut down trees
and stamped the undergrowth flat for the triple host's passage.

The smell of earth and moss lay thick upon the air, mingling
with the aromas of Giant sweat and the pleasant tang of splintered
wood. Birdsongs rattled among the endless canopy of leaf and
branch, overpowered now and then by the sound of a falling tree
or an Udvorg's rumbling laughter. Foxes, squirrels, hares, and tiny
monkeys came running through the underbrush in terror, fleeing
the northern titans. Vireon spied a black leopard leaping from
branch to branch. The hunter inside him wanted to leap from his
horse and give chase. But his true prey lay in the black heart of
Khyrei, and he would not lose sight of it.

So the host passed through the length of the high forest, the
Giants cutting, chopping, and stamping a crude highway into existence. Mendices suggested burning large swathes of undergrowth,

but Vireon rejected the idea. Tyro agreed with Vireon. A smoke trail might be seen for hundreds of leagues, and the mariners of Allundra might easily carry word of the triple host's passing to Khyrei. Perhaps they already knew. Perhaps Gammir and Ianthe had already fortified their swampland border with enough legions to oppose the great northern host. Yet there was no way to be sure, and stealth must be maintained for as long as possible.

The host marched for seven days and spent seven nights camped amid the wilderness. Each evening the trailblazers cleared land for tents and horses and camp followers. Some Men and Giants went on brief hunts while the sun lingered low in the sky. The Men returned with the fat carcasses of pheasants and bright-feathered peacocks. One of Tyro's best archers brought down a horned stag with a pelt white as snow. This was acclaimed as an omen of coming victory by all the Men of Uurz; such pale beasts were unheard of in the Stormlands. Word of this good omen soon spread to the Giants, who also believed it.

The Giant huntsmen fared poorly in this Men's wood, for the tramping of their great feet set wild creatures running before them and gave warning to the armies of birds filling the branches. Still, a few of them managed to snare wolves or bears, which the Men would not deign to eat. To the hungry Udvorg it was fresh meat and nothing to pass up. They stitched new cloaks from the hides of these upland creatures. After a single Udvorg ate monkey flesh and became violently ill, they quickly learned to leave the skittish tree dwellers alone. The furry ones were too much like Men in appearance and facial expression, or so Angrid decreed. They must carry the souls of dead men in their tiny bodies, and so were poison to Giants, who had not eaten manflesh in several millennia.

The host crossed three raging rivers and spent a night on the shore of a hidden lake where Men pulled fish large as hounds from the water. There was feasting and drinking aplenty, and the barrels of ale and wine were nearly all gone when the host's vanguard reached the sinking land. There the great forest plateau sloped gradually downward. Clusters of trees grew thinner with each passing league, until the vast swamp lay spread before them like a sea of steaming mud.

"The Eastern Marshes," announced Tyro from the back of his warhorse. "Beyond lies the red jungle of Khyrei. Here our course must turn straight into the east. Passage will be slow and difficult. The vipers and venomous toads gather thick as flies here, and tales of the swamp's great lizards cannot be ignored."

"Aye, Lord," said Mendices. His golden helm lay in the crook of his arm. "Poets say the marshes are haunted by the restless ghosts of a race that died ages ago. A people that were not quite Men . . ."

Vireon stared across the wetlands from the back of his own steed. An endless expanse of black mud, dead trees, strangling vines, and green meres of unknown depth. There was no solid path through the place, and a Man might easily drown in seconds if he dared to pass this way alone. He wondered at the host's best course of action.

Angrid called forth Varda the Keen Eyes. The blue Giantess came forward in the company of two Udvorg brothers. The tip of her staff blazed like an azure torch. She wore a cloak of black wolf's fur. Three bronze rings bright as gold hung from each of her ears, and a single ring depended from her shapely nose. The scars along her comely face were purposeful, indicative of her rank among those who wielded the cold flame. While most Udvorg hair was the color of snow, Varda's was as black as Vireon's own mane. A telltale sign of the common origins shared by all Giants.

Angrid spoke with the shamaness, and Varda turned again and again to survey the midday gloom of the swamp. Winged worms flitted among the rotting glades like bats, and Men traded guesses as to their nature. Vireon heard the first instances of grumbling among the hosts of Uurz and Udurum. No man wished to tramp through this chaos of filth and venom. Yet every warrior would take that awful journey. Men knew that glory and victory lay at the end of this long march. They believed in the might of their Kings and the righteousness of their crusade. And they had the Udvorg on their side.

Men and Giants transferred bale, keg, and crate to their backs, for no wagon or cart would travel through the mire. A great portion of the camp followers formed a makeshift settlement on the near side of the swamplands to await the triple host's return. Yet the soldiers and their Kings must forge ahead with diminished resources. Vireon decided that Giants must again go first, not only to test the depth of the swamp, but also to confront any great beasts that might arise from it.

Varda walked to the head of the vanguard, her shaggy boots sinking ankle-deep in the muck. She raised the blazing staff above her head and sang in an ancient tongue. Vireon saw the three thousand Udvorg kneeling as one, as if the shamaness conducted some holy ceremony. Among their number, only the proud Ice King stood unbowed as Varda worked her spell.

The heat of the sun fell away from the swamp, and the brightness of the blue flame increased. A sphere of indigo fire floated from the staff like a bubble rising in water, hovering for a moment above the marshland. Varda continued her chant as the globe grew brighter than the sun itself, bathing the world in shades of sapphire and azure. The cobalt sphere radiated a terrible cold as the true sun radiates heat. Men shivered while Giants sighed with pleasure. Vireon himself could feel the intensity of the cold, a sensation he was not normally privy to.

Now Varda lowered her staff and the sphere of blue flame sank into the ground of the marsh. A sudden crackling filled the air as the muddy domain began to change. The mud froze as if caught in the grip of winter, and the scum-laden pools of water turned to solid ice. Men pulled their cloaks tight about their shoulders and marveled at the white fog of their breaths, while the Udvorg rose up, shedding cloaks and mail shirts to better enjoy the chill. They laughed and stalked into the frozen wasteland. One of them struck a tree with the butt of his spear; the icy wood cracked and splintered into a thousand gleaming fragments.

"By the Four Gods," said Tyro to his Giant peers. "It appears this crossing may be less grueling than expected."

The icy expanse reached nearly a league in all directions. Yet the air had grown warm again. Already the slick surface of the frozen mire was beginning to melt in the sun's warm glow. They must travel quickly across this hardened land.

Varda the Keen Eyes bowed to the three Kings and resumed her frosty silence.

Word traveled backward along the lines and soon the march resumed.

In the day's third hour, the first of the great lizards arose from the muck. Varda stood at the head of the columns, singing her flamesong for the second time in order to extend the icy path. From the yet-unfrozen ground rose a scaled behemoth, dripping mud and water from its spiny back and blunt snout. Even on all fours it stood half the height of an Udvorg. Its loose flesh was olive-green and mottled gray, draped in the scum of its habitat. Since it had only four legs it was not therefore a true Serpent, nor did it breathe fire as did those creatures of legend. Yet its toothy mouth split the circumference of its head. The yellow fangs within were as long as Uurzian swords, and far thicker. Despite its great size it lunged swift as the wind across the frozen marsh.

Before word of the monster had reached the center ranks, an Udvorg died in its jaws, spine chomped in half, severed head rolling like a pebble. The Giants near enough to witness the attack leaped forward with spear and axe, eager to test their mettle against such a beast. Here was game worthy of Giantkind. Here was a thing out of legend, whose speckled flesh might feed the entire Udvorg legion.

Vireon held his horse back and called for Dahrima to stay with him, as twenty Udvorg encircled the behemoth. Tyro watched the battle with a fascination bordering on gleefulness. Vireon drew his greatsword but remained calm on his steed. If there were more lizards such as this, the going here would be slow. Still, he admired the vicious nature of the Udvorg as they harried the monster with pole and blade. They danced about its snapping head and thrust spears into its hide. Others braved its claws to deliver crushing blows with axe and mace.

By the time the great lizard was dead, lying on its back with a dozen Udvorg spears sprouting from its pale underbelly, Varda had finished her new spell. Once again the swamp lay frozen before the host. The ice near the slain beast was smeared with its black blood. One of the Udvorg claimed the lizard's head; he would hollow out the skull and wear it as a helmet. The rest of the beast's killers sliced off hocks of its dense flesh to fill their packs. Some dug their stony teeth into the raw red meat instantly, praising its wild flavor. They buried their fallen comrade quickly in the solid mire, marking the grave with a horned helm. Soon the triple host was again underway.

The iced landscape drove vipers and toads into their lairs or killed them outright. The carcasses of black-and-crimson reptiles and bloated amphibians littered the frozen mud. By the time the last members of the host crossed the frozen landscape, it was trampled into oozing mud and broken clumps of melting ice. Vireon and Tyro led their legions of Men forward with Varda, Angrid, and a small company of Udvorg on either side, while the bulk of the Giants came last across the marsh, traversing the half-frozen mire with far less difficulty than the feet of Men or the hooves of horses. Vireon's captains kept the legions marching at top speed.

Night overtook the hurried host, and weariness claimed Varda shortly after sundown. The triple host would have to spend a night in the swamp, which would be long thawed by morning. Clouds of stinging insects rose up from their temporary hibernation and harassed the flesh of Men and horses, though their bites could not penetrate the skins of Vireon and the Giants. Soldiers chose carefully the ground on which they erected tents; some chose to sleep on logs or narrow spars of dry earth. The majority would awake to find their blankets sunk into the soft earth, but companions would help dig them free. Despite the cold, the Kings allowed no fires to be lit, for the smoke and light might give away their presence to the Border Legions stationed directly ahead, untold leagues farther on, where the ground rose up to support the crimson jungle.

Varda shared the tent of the Ice King, while Vireon and Tyro kept their own pavilions. This time Vireon insisted Dahrima sleep inside. She curled up on the muddy rugs his attendants had spread to create a makeshift floor. The three armies passed an uncomfortable night lying on half-frozen ground and gnawing strips of dried meat rations. There was no singing or merriment this night, for the minstrels, harlots, and poets had been left behind at the edge of the marshes, and neither Man nor Giant held the mood for festivity.

Cries in the night woke Vireon more than once. Men slept uneasily in this place, haunted by the alleged ghosts that lurked here, or perhaps by their own superstitious minds. In the darkest part of the night, another great lizard wandered into the camp. It

devoured two Uurzians and four horses before the Giants rose up
to slay it. There was little sleeping among the ranks after that
battle. Each of the three Kings doubled the watch under his command, but no more attacks came that night.

In the morning the camp rose early, eager to leave the horrid
landscape behind. Vireon blinked away the remnants of nightmares. He had dreamed that Alua and Maelthyn were lost in the
treacherous marshland. All night long as he slept he chased them
and called out their names, and so awoke frustrated and unrested.
This only angered him, and he pushed the troops to assemble
themselves at a record pace. They must leave this place behind
before its abstract terrors became real enough to do lasting harm.
The loss of a few Men and Giants to the swamp was regrettable,
but acceptable. All warriors knew the risk of a campaign. Yet the
bulk of the triple host must remain intact when the three Kings
reached the far side of the marshes.

They traveled fifteen leagues the next day, each one frozen by
Varda's magic, and the Giants slew two more hungry lizards. The
Udvorg now professed great satisfaction with the raw flesh of these
creatures. They had learned how to tip the beasts over to expose
their vulnerable undersides. They offered cuts of bloody lizard
flesh to their human allies, but the Men had not yet grown desperate enough to dine on such grisly fare. The Udvorg found great
humor in the sensitivity of Men's bellies. Angrid agreed with
Vireon that, while the mammoth lizards dwelled in the swamp,
the beasts must hunt for prey in the red jungle. There was no suitable game for creatures of such great size in the marshes. None but
the host passing through it now.

In the fading light of early evening, Vireon first glimpsed the
red jungle rising from the mists. Mighty trees, many of them tall
as northern Uygas, gleamed scarlet and ruby, changing to shades
of burgundy and carmine as the shadows of night crept eastward.

The darkness beneath their tangled limbs was thicker than the swamp mud. If there were eyes staring upon them from the jungle depths, Vireon could not tell.

Only a few final leagues of marshland lay between the vanguard and the blood-colored jungle when Varda the Keen Eyes spotted the first of the watchtowers. The edge of the jungle marked Khyrei's true border. Officially Ianthe's empire included the swamps, but no Emperor of the black city was foolish enough to try and fortify the sunken land. Instead, a network of towers stood along the line of demarcation between swamp and jungle.

The towers were built of black basalt, like the city that gave them birth, and their summits were barbed with upturned spikes thick as ships' masts. They rose from the jungle's edge, spaced about five leagues apart, forming a north-to-south boundary. The line of fortified spires was known to extend into the southern reaches of the swampland, all the way to the Cryptic Sea. There was nothing to do but confront the Border Legions here, where they might still salvage an element of surprise.

"How many Men do you think are garrisoned inside one of those towers?" Tyro asked Vireon.

"At least a hundred," Vireon guessed.

"Pardon me, Lords," said Mendices, who rode near to Tyro. "My sources say a thousand men can live comfortably within these lean citadels, double that if pressed. Their size cannot easily be appreciated from this distance."

"And if these towers stretch all the way to the southern shore as you say, how many must there be? How many legions control this border?"

"Rumors of war have been flying for years now," said Tyro. "I suspect the Khyreins have boosted their defenses along this line. We must send scouts ahead to give us numbers and suggest formations."

"Good," said Vireon. "Send Men. Giants are too noisy."

"Agreed," said the Sword King. Tyro set Mendices the task of assembling a covert force of Uurzians to explore the jungle's edge and survey its black towers. The band of scouts ran into the darkness with only the sounds of sucking mud to mark their passage.

With the last two leagues of swamp ahead of them, the host stopped to rest by the light of a full moon. The Kings saw flames dancing in the upper windows of the nearest watchtower. Standing on the shoulders of a Giant, Vireon saw three such towers, including one directly ahead of the triple host. The second and third towers rose to the north and south of their path. He saw fires dancing amid the jungle trees too, sign of additional troops encamped outside the strongholds. The Kings allowed no encampment this close to their enemy. Not until they discovered exactly what lay before them. They might have no choice but to rush forward and wage a nocturnal battle. If they did choose to stay in the marshes until dawn, it would be another night without fire or warm food. A restless mood fell across the waiting host.

The time for the spilling of Men's blood was almost upon them.

Not long after the company of scouts departed, the wailing of horses drew Vireon's attention. Men rushed from the lines, bellowing warnings of black tentacles or colossal vipers risen from the muck. Six riderless horses fell or were pulled into deep pools of marshwater. Vireon went prowling about the edge of the camp with Dahrima at his back. Men and Giants watched as the black waters of a great mere rippled.

"There!" a soldier shouted, pointing with the head of his spear. A dark tendril shot up from the muck and extended itself toward him. Soldiers poked at it with spears. They leaped back into the midst of their fellows, trying to avoid the grasp of the slippery thing. Vireon bounded forward as the appendage wrapped itself around a spearman's torso and lifted him from the ground.

"My Lord!" The helpless warrior screamed, arms pinned to his sides, eyes pleading at Vireon. "Help me!"

Vireon's greatsword flashed in the moonlight. The warrior fell into the mud, half the severed tentacle still wrapped about his waist, twitching and oozing a noxious ichor. The dripping stump withdrew into the waters. Soldiers pulled their brother free and sliced the tendril into quivering bits, which they kicked back into the fetid water.

Another shout rang out in another part of the camp, and Men screamed in alarm. Vireon looked above their heads where another tentacle, greater in size than the first, rose from the muck to linger eyeless and pointed. It struck like a viper, pulling warriors into the air, then directly into the dark waters of the lakelet. They would soon drown if they were not immediately devoured by whatever beast lurked below the swamp's surface.

Vireon raced through the ranks of startled men, and now cries of surprise and horror came from all sides. Oily black tentacles burst from the newly thawed muck to strike at Man, Giant, and horse alike. Sprays of blood filled the air as the tendrils crushed flesh and bone to ghastly pulp.

Men ran to avoid the arc of Vireon's blade as he slashed at the darting coils. It seemed the earth itself sprouted clammy members to steal the lives that dared its cursed ground.

"They're everywhere!" someone yelled.

"Gods preserve us!" rang from another place in the panicked ranks.

"Ghurvald! It's taken Ghurvald!" cried a stricken Uurzian. Chaos replaced the orderly nature of the lines, and their formations fell to pieces.

The black tendrils rose up everywhere, dripping with silt and tangled roots. The northerners sliced and hacked at them, but there was no end to their number. The marshy ground trembled beneath Vireon's feet as he shouted orders and severed another serpentine limb.

A great moan rose like thunder from the marsh, and the world turned upside down.

A colossal thing of mud and tremulous flesh rose up beneath the triple host, trailing slime and mire from its shambolic bulk. It stood tall and broad as a craggy hill, stinking of ancient filth, a forest of tendrils striking out to entrap its victims. Men, horses, and even Giants toppled sideways and fell from its quivering back as the impossible mass boiled up from below, scattering lives and loamy boulders by the score. Its tentacles grabbed most of those who fell from the rising heap, squeezing and ripping and dousing the host below with hot blood.

It had no definite form, this mad creature from beneath the swamp. Its blistered, warty flesh was rife with fanged mouths, a hundred gnashing, mewling, vomiting maws. Tentacles deposited the choicest bits of Men and horses into these champing orifices, and sometimes whole Men died between the rows of jagged fangs. A chorus of wailing voices fell from its unknown summit, the tremulous cries of tortured animals or Men.

Giants strode forth to battle the Swamp God and they, too, were caught in its *steely* grip. Axes and spears sank into pustulant flesh with little effect. Vireon lay in the mud for a second where the beast's uprising had tossed him, and he realized the entirety of the scene.

This nameless obscenity was the true guardian of the Khyrein border. It was no coincidence that it slumbered so close to the line of watchtowers. The creature writhed and shivered across the marsh, the height of its shapeless body dwarfing even the tallest Giant, its numberless tentacles faster and deadlier than vipers. It loomed large enough to blot out stars and moon.

Somewhere along the western edge of the triple host, someone screamed a fresh warning between the blasts of an Uurzian war horn.

"Khyreins! Border Legions!"

Another note from the horn tore through the night. Vireon struggled to his feet and tore at the dragging tentacles about his waist and limbs. One of the fanged maws loomed above him, gnashing rows of uneven teeth and spewing filth. It yawned wider than the mouths of the great lizards, mindlessly eager.

"The Khyreins! They come!"

Men and Giants wailed and fought and died while the horn bellowed its warning.

Vireon understood now, but it was too late.

There was never any chance of surprising them here.

They were waiting for us.

Waiting to unleash this abomination.

A blue flame flickered somewhere in the howling darkness.

16

Shards of Dawn

An abiding tranquility replaced the fading thunder. A universe of brilliant flame died away, replaced by warm golden sunlight. Green leaves rustled on the rim of awareness. Vision was a blurred and shifting thing at first, but sound came more easily into focus. The songs of gulls mingled with the trilling of island birds. The sighing of gentle winds rustled the tops of trees. From somewhere beyond the whispering foliage came the rhythmic pounding of surf against sand.

Smells came next, the scents of fresh loam, summer grass, tree bark, honeysuckle . . . then jasmine and the ripe flesh of hanging fruits.

Vines coiled together beneath a roof of twining leaves. A pair of red plums dropped from a low tree branch. Bits of stone buried in the brown loam shifted toward the surface and joined with the mass of busy foliage. Plant, fruit, and stone merged in a two-legged, two-armed pattern.

A body of living vegetation lay in the dappled shade of the green lawn, soaking in the raw powers of sun, wind, and sky.

I live.

She pulled her leafy limbs together, sent the stone flowing like water through the center of them. The fallen plums turned to glinting emeralds, then opened as a pair of sea-green eyes. The immense power of the earth seethed like an ocean; she floated on the skin of its roiling surface. It flowed into her from the roots and leaves of the curling vines. She wrapped more of the ropy plants about the skeleton that had been the naked stones. Blossoms of darkest purple crept forward to encircle her skull, becoming at once her flesh and the locks of her hair.

Elemental energies converged like stormwinds, and Sharadza wove them together like filaments of silk or wool. Now she stood, flexing vegetable legs and raising her leafy arms toward the sun. The final movement of the song her mind sang with the melodious earth brought a transformation from fibrous green to brown and supple skin.

She stood tall and whole in the body she remembered, and she called forth a second skin of leaf and vine, which became a gown of green fabric laced with a neck design of purple blossoms.

I live, and I breathe.

And I do not thirst.

How long has it been?

A familiar voice interrupted her thoughts.

"How do you feel?" Iardu asked.

The wizard stood not far away, beneath the branches of a pomegranate tree. His red-orange robe refracted the sunlight even more than the jeweled rings upon his fingers. His mother-of-pearl eyes narrowed at her without their usual chromatic sparkle. He looked unspoiled yet weary. He rubbed his small silver beard as he looked her over.

Sharadza inhaled, welcoming the sweet garden air into her lungs. Tears smelling of plum streamed from her new eyes. "Alive," she whispered. "I scarcely believe it. After what happened . . . after what I had become . . ."

"A lie," said Iardu, stepping close enough to touch her shoulder. "Your half-brother twisted your natural pattern, adding his own foul ingredients. I've removed them as best I can. But see here the stones that were the floor of the tower chamber where he kept you."

Sharadza scanned the grassy earth about her bare feet. She stood at the center of a loop of rectangular stones. They were scattered in an uneven circle about the garden, blocks of dark basalt, each one as large as her head. On the exposed surface of each stone sat either an engraved rune, or a portion of a bisected rune. Her gaze followed the line of stones, taking in the intricacies of the sigils. This was the rune circle Gammir had carved all about her bed, where he had stolen and sculpted her first resurrection. Iardu had plucked these stones from the crumbling floor of the tower as his sorcery destroyed it.

"These stones are forever linked to your immortal essence," said the sorcerer. "I am sorry this has been done to you. Yet your free will has been returned, the curse of the shadow lifted; these runestones are the nexus of your new existence. You have passed through the Gates of Death twice now. This second rebirth marks the beginning of your enlightenment. You no longer wear the chains of the body your mother birthed. You have birthed yourself this time, without interference. I merely brought your spirit essence here, along with the stones that imprisoned it."

"What is this place?" she asked. Now she looked beyond the mortared walls that enclosed the garden. Three towers of pale stone rose outside the tree-lined enclosure, turrets and eaves decorated by spirals of precious gemstones. She recognized neither the architecture nor the landscape.

"This is my garden," said Iardu, opening his arms. "I've brought you to my island. My home."

"Of course." She knew this already, somehow. It would be some while before she could catalog and recognize all the things she now knew. A deep well of secrets yawned in the back of her mind.

"You will be safe here, far beyond the reach of your half-brother and his shadowlings. Whenever you shed this body, through violence or any other means, your spirit will return here to be reborn at the center of these stones." Iardu's ageless face darkened. "It was either this fate, or the one Gammir had in store for you. An eternity of slavery and bloodlust."

Sharadza wrapped her new arms about Iardu. "Thank you," she said. "I will never be able to repay what you've done for me. It was like a nightmare ... I knew that what I did was not of my own intention, but I could not ... I could not ... " She lost her voice as the memory of hot, sticky blood in her throat returned. She saw for a moment the face of a boy she had killed and fed upon, then the faces of a harlot, a tradesman, a father, a cobbler. More. Ranks of nameless slaves without name or number bleeding and dying at her knees.

The red, lingering kisses of Gammir ...

The breath rushed from her lungs and she fell at Iardu's feet. Her stomach roiled and would have emptied itself if it had contained anything at all. Yet this new body had eaten nothing but sunlight so far. She retched and heaved, drooling spittle into the grass. She wept.

Iardu bent down to wrap his arms about her.

"It's all right," he told her. His hands were gentle on her shoulders, warm against her back. "It's all right."

"No!" She pulled away, rubbing at her tears. She stared into his kindly face. "You don't know the things ... the things I've done. The *killing* ... feeding on innocence like some wicked beast! He *used* me, Iardu. He made me do *terrible* things. I'll never forget them. And I'll never be able to forgive myself." She shuddered as she wept, cupping her face in her hands. Her skin smelled of ripe leaves.

Iardu stood in silence while the waters of sorrow drained out of her. A bottomless reservoir of shame, guilt, remorse, and, beneath it all, an impotent anger. How could she? She should have killed herself rather than endure the filth of that dark existence. She did not deserve this liberation ... this enlightenment of which he spoke.

"I should have ..." she stammered. "I should have ..."

"You should have never gone to see him," Iardu said. "Yet you did. What happened was not your fault. We cannot change the past, Sharadza, but we can learn to live with it. You may think what Gammir has done has destroyed you. But hear me when I say this: it has only made you stronger."

"I'm a *murderer*!" she shouted at him. "A thousand times over! And worse!"

"*You are a sorceress!*" He shouted back, startling her with his vehemence. "I tried to sway you from this path many years ago, but you were determined to walk in your father's shoes. So you have. Tragedy and sorcery are no strangers. You are the daughter of Vod. You will endure. You must!"

She shook her head and stared about the garden. Between the slim fruit trees a shallow pool glimmered. Swift shapes glided in the crystalline water. A trio of brightly plumed birds flew down from the branches to drink from it.

"How can I live on, knowing the horror of what I've done?" she asked. She sounded like a child seeking advice from her father.

"If you have done ill," said Iardu, "then overcome it by doing the opposite. Balance the scales of your heart. This is the beginning of your journey, not the end. You carry the greatness of the Old Breed inside you. Do not let the darkness that enslaved you destroy what you truly are. You are Vod's daughter. You will *endure*."

She walked to the pool and watched the fat fish moving

through the water. Their scales flashed gold and white, crimson and silver. The birds flew back into their trees, squawking and singing. A mass of white blossoms grew about the pool's edge. Luminous dragonflies buzzed between the petals.

Suddenly she realized that someone watched her from between the trees. She raised her head, Iardu's voice still ringing in her ears, and met the face of her silent observer. The face was that of a lovely woman with tawny skin; her eyes were a mix of ebony and sparkling amber. A necklace of opals and amethysts hung below her slim neck, and below that swelled the broad chest of a golden beast. The watcher's body was that of a lion standing tall as a pony, complete with black claws and a swishing tufted tail. Tiny wings with white feathers grew from between her leonine shoulder blades; they were far too small to carry her majestic bulk, yet they unfolded and spread themselves wide as her human face smiled at Sharadza. Behind her ruby lips gleamed a set of lion's fangs, but there was no threat in their display.

"Greetings," said the creature.

Sharadza had no words to respond. Iardu spoke instead.

"This is Eyeni," said the mage. He spared a loving smile for the creature. "She watches over my home when I am away."

Sharadza bowed in wordless greeting. She was still not in command of herself.

The lioness nodded its woman-like head. "I recognize your sorrow," she said. "Know that in this place all wounds can be healed. Trust in the wisdom of the Shaper."

"Thank you," Sharadza croaked. She felt foolish and weak.

Can I truly live with these memories?

Eyeni paced around the pool and approached Iardu.

"How fares the island?" asked the sorcerer. He rubbed a hand over Eyeni's glossy coat. She purred for a moment as a true lioness might, then answered him.

"All is well, Father. Will you stay for a while?"

Iardu shook his head. "I cannot. Already I have lingered too long. A battle rages on the shore of the Golden Sea, and the fate of nations spins like a tossed coin."

He looked toward Sharadza where she sat on the grass near the pool. Tiny green monkeys with curious man-like faces scrambled through the treetops now, staring down at her and darting away like phantoms. They made no sound at all.

"This is Sharadza, Queen of Yaskatha," Iardu told the lioness. "Prepare a chamber for her. Something with a nice sea view, and not too far from the garden. She will stay here as long as she wishes."

"No." Sharadza raised her eyes from the sunbright water. "You're going back to face Gammir and Ianthe. So am I." She stood and breathed in the garden air, the tears drying now upon her cheeks.

Iardu shook his head. "Have you learned nothing?" he asked. "You rush blindly into danger like a farm boy eager for a sword fight. Elhathym imprisoned you in stone. And now Gammir—"

"I broke out of that stone prison," she reminded him, "and pulled you out of the empty void, as I recall."

Iardu sighed.

"You said I must earn redemption for the things he made me do," she said. "My redemption starts *now*."

"You do not understand," said Iardu. "There is far more at stake. The slaves of Khyrei are rebelling. The black city lies under siege. The future of Khyrei and all kingdoms will be defined by what happens next. And there is yet more . . . much more that I have not told you."

"Zyung," she said. Gammir had shown her the other side of the world in his enchanted glass. The monolithic empire of the one called the God-King. "I know what he is. I have seen his forces. And I know that he comes soon."

Iardu's eyes flickered like twin prisms. "How?"

"Gammir has allied himself with Zyung. He told me his plan to serve the Conqueror and one day replace him. Now Ianthe stands at his side again. You cannot go alone."

Iardu's shoulders tensed. He paced across the green lawn and rubbed his chin, lost in thought.

"You didn't know about Gammir's alliance until this moment," she said. She could almost read his mind. "You fostered this rebellion. You're trying to liberate Khyrei before the invasion comes."

"Yes, child," he said, staring at the pathway of green marble that wound through the garden. "Time is short. Zyung is eager to take this half of the world."

"*Your* half," said Sharadza. He looked at her, but his ageless expression was unreadable.

"You need to rest," he told her, pleading now. "You have suffered much and require time to heal."

"Only by returning to Khyrei and facing Gammir will I find any kind of peace," she said. She walked to him. Eyeni lay upon the grass where the sunlight bathed her glossy pelt. The tiny white wings lay folded on her back. Her clever eyes followed their faces, as a child watches its parents engaged in an argument.

Iardu sighed and threw up his hands. "You would walk through flames to take a swim," he said.

"What else will Gammir do?" she said. "Kill me?"

Iardu's brow lowered, casting a shadow over his gleaming eyes. "Oh, there are far worse fates than death for those like us." And she knew he had accepted her insistence.

"Sorcerers," she said.

"As good a word as any," he replied. "We must go now."

"Shall we fly?"

Iardu shook his head. The blue flame on his chest leaped and writhed. "There is no time. Even as eagles the flight would take too long. The slaves of Khyrei need help immediately." He paced to a clear section of the marble path and motioned for her to join him.

"To bring you and your runestones here, I opened a dangerous gateway," he said. "A realm of living fire that lies between our own world and many others. It was the only way to transfer ourselves and the stones at once. The light and flame that slipped through this gate destroyed Gammir's tower; it burned away his army of wraiths and bloodshadows. I will need to open it again, so that we can slip through that fiery dimension and step out once more into Khyrei. It will not be without pain."

"I am ready." Pain. How could simple physical pain ever scare her after the horrors she had endured? She would never fear pain again. Flesh and bones were ephemeral, a suit of clothing to be worn or shed at will.

She no longer wielded power. She *was* power.

How she longed to unleash it upon the heads of Gammir and Ianthe.

"Farewell, Father," said Eyeni, raising her head from her paws.

"Farewell for now, Eyeni," said Iardu. "See that Sharadza's quarters are established for our return."

"It shall be done." The lioness loped through the garden toward the trio of pale towers.

Sharadza kissed Iardu's cheek. Then she stood back and spoke to him with her eyes.

Take me to Khyrei.

Iardu raised his arms and sang the ancient worldsong of light and flame.

When the great gate swung open, three thousand slaves and ten thousand Sydathians flooded into the streets of the black city. The fields outside blazed, but the streets were mazes of gloom pierced only by the glow of hanging lanterns. The Sydathian van-guard, five thousand strong, had swarmed the southern wall in a matter of moments, casting down the torn bodies of Onyx Guards and hapless archers. There would be no more arrows rain-ing down on the Free Men of Khyrei. Once over the wall, the eyeless ones had no trouble forcing the Southern Gate open to admit the rebellion.

Tong lost sight of the Emperor and Empress. They had fled the wall when the eyeless ones began to climb it. No doubt they were investigating the fiery destruction of the palace's westernmost tower. Tong knew it was Iardu's work, a false sun to burn away the armies of shadow. He blessed the wizard under his breath as he rushed into the gloomy streets.

Earlier he had wondered how many legions still dwelled within the city, since the bulk of them were sent to secure the western border. He still had no answer to this question. His heart sank as a fresh legion of black-masked soldiers charged through the main street toward the ruptured gateway. The Onyx Guardsmen sprinted behind a shield wall brimming with pikes.

The pikemen would have killed hundreds of slaves in the first moments of the battle, except that they could not reach them. Sydathians ran along the horizontal shafts of their spears, bounded past their lacquered shields, and found tender flesh with their razory claws. Tong's sightless brothers would kill every armored man in the city, but they shared his understanding of mercy for women and children. His bond with them was beyond even his own comprehension, but he felt the city give way beneath the press of pale bodies, felt the warm blood gushing between talons and fangs that were not his own.

The screams of dying men rose to join those atop the wall, where the sentinel towers were forsaken and already full of bodies. Across the roofs of warehouses, granaries, and manor houses Tong saw the barbed spires of the great palace. Never had they loomed so close or so high. He had never been inside the city before this night. A labyrinth of streets and plazas lay between his army and the Emperor's house.

"Find all slaves!" he yelled to his human brothers. "Free them all! Let them join us!"

This became his mission as the Sydathians rushed through the streets, slaughtering the black legion. Tong, Tolgur, and a hundred other men bearing stolen sabres and spears rushed from house to house spreading the word that freedom had come to Khyrei. Women clutched their babies and shied away from their windows and doors; their husbands and sons came forward to take up the bloodstained pikes and blades of their oppressors. Within every manor house and squalid tenement the rebels awoke, and the numbers of Tong's slave army grew.

Another legion came marching from the city's eastern quarter to engage the Sydathians. By then it was too late: Sydathians far outnumbered Men as the city fell into chaos. Someone set a fire, intentionally or accidentally, and now the city's buildings burned like its fields. Some of the masked ones made the mistake of surrendering to the enraged mob. They were stripped of their fanged masks, then their armor and clothing, followed by tongues, eyes, and finally their lives. Tong could not speak out against this cruelty, and if he did no one would listen. His people had suffered so long that he expected such brutality. He expected more dead slaves as well, but the Sydathians protected the freed men who were brave or foolhardy enough to engage Onyx Guards in combat. As a loyal hound fights for his master, so did the eyeless ones protect the marauding slaves. Still, a few slaves were cut down before their Sydathian wards could intervene. Yet in most instances the eyeless ones ended such uneven fights with the swipe of a single claw.

A man who was slave to a merchant lord of the city came forward. Tolgur brought him to Tong because he claimed to know the city streets well. His ragged nightshirt was smeared with blood and he clutched a spear in trembling fists. His name was Odumi, and a mad joy blazed in his dark eyes.

"Can you lead us to the palace?" Tong asked. He pointed at the black spires.

"Yes!" answered Odumi. "I hear the Empress has returned. Let us welcome her with blood and fire!"

"We have pikes for both of their heads!" cried Tolgur. The lad raised a spear and howled with the throng.

Tong led the bulk of the freed men through the streets with Odumi at their head. What would he do when he reached the palace? He must face Gammir the Undying and Ianthe the Claw. Was Iardu done with aiding him? It did not matter. This rebellion could only end with a free city. Tong would die for the cause if he must. His would be a worthy death.

They ran through shadowed streets and smoke-filled avenues where the flames had not yet reached. Sydathians leaped in their midst. Any guardsmen who showed themselves were quickly speared to death or torn apart. In this way the mob came through the maze of walls, doors, and arches into a great plaza. Stained blocks of stone at the far end of the square were set with iron rings with chains attached. He wondered which of his ancestors had stood upon those blocks and been sold into the fields.

No man, woman, or child would ever stand there in chains again.

Beyond the open mall the ebony palace loomed nearer. Yet Tong could not see all of the structure due to the massive statue standing at the head of the slaving square. Carved from gleaming onyx, it stood taller than a sentinel tower, draped in the semblance of a sable robe that mimicked the starry sky. His jaw dropped as he gazed upon it. It wore a face of cruelty and wickedness, with eyes of solid ruby set below a seven-pointed crown. One clawed hand hefted a mighty spear, while the other held aloft a globe of murky crystal. The army of slaves stood in awe of the construct, having never seen anything of its proportions. The blind Sydathians largely ignored it, rushing up the broad steps to fill the plaza with their sniffing, bounding bodies.

In that instant of wonder which seemed to last hours, a great rumbling shook the flagstones. Nearby garden walls collapsed, and several of the plaza's columns fell over and splintered into rubble. A great moaning came from the sandaled feet of the statue, each one large enough to contain a granary if it were hollow. A wave of fear passed across the slaves then, and Tong felt it like a poison shot into his veins by some hidden dart. The Sydathians felt it too, and they grew still in the grip of the trembling earth.

The mighty statue lowered its head, ruby eyes glowing brighter than blood.

Some men went mad and fled shrieking from the plaza. Tong stood transfixed by the impossible vision. The colossal figure of stone and jewel raised one of its legs with a horrible sound of grinding stone. Baring its black fangs, it stamped down upon a mass of scrambling Sydathians. Dozens of eyeless ones were smashed to a greasy pulp of blood and bones. Others climbed the gargantuan legs trying to dig claws into its stony flesh. The gigantic effigy quivered and tossed them like vermin across the city.

Again its great foot rose and descended, flattening more Sydathians, shedding more from its living stone legs. The scene reminded Tong of the day he had trod upon an anthill in the fields. The insects had swarmed up his leg while he struck at them with palm and sandal. He had escaped the angry ants' fury only by running to leap in the River Tah. He did not think the great statue would head for the river. It would stomp here until every last slave and Sydathian was dead.

This must be the work of the Emperor's sorcery. Kill Gammir and the monstrosity would also die. But how to kill a sorcerer? And how to find him? The jewel eyes of the statue sparkled with a fresh blaze of light, and Tong realized that sunrise had broken over the Golden Sea. The night of blood and fire was over, but the battle for Khyrei was only beginning.

The statue bellowed a hateful word and tossed the crystal globe into the midst of the crowded plaza. The sphere exploded like glass, showering Sydathians and slaves with razor shards. Tong felt that brittle rain and sheltered his head with his arms. When it was done a host of bleeding lacerations covered his skin, and that of the men about him. Those closest to the sphere's point of impact had been cut to shreds. The minced bodies of Men and Sydathians were mingled in a ghastly pile.

Still a throng of eyeless ones tried to climb the hem of the statue's glimmering robe, and still it swatted and stamped them into oblivion. The beastlings might slay every guardsman in the city, but they could not harm the Emperor's terrible likeness.

Tong's blood dripped on the flagstones, and he considered for the first time that his rebellion and his death might change nothing. This was still Gammir's city. The morning sky was obscured by black smoke. The dawn of freedom looked nothing like Tong had imagined it.

The Emperor's statue raised its great spear. It might easily strike down one of the palace spires with that colossal weapon if it chose to do so. Tong shouted to his fellows; they ran for their lives toward the nearby palace while the eyeless ones fought and died for them. Any second now the head of that great spear would strike the earth and the city would quake again, its very walls collapsing like mounds of sand. The stones of the crumbling city would crush the rebellion as quickly as the foot of the titan crushed Sydathians. Gammir would destroy his own city rather than see it freed from his grasp.

Tong heard the crashing of a thunderbolt. Above the looming palace another false sun erupted, exactly like the one that had vanquished a horde of shadows.

This time its flames blossomed directly above the barbed crown of the central tower. The Emperor's Tower.

Iardu!

Golden rays shot across the city, bright spears piercing a canopy of oily smoke. The freed men rushed toward the palace gate, which stood closed to them as had the city gates. The statue of Gammir brought its terrible spear down in the midst of the Sydathians. The resulting earthquake scattered the eyeless ones like pitched pebbles. The city shook, and structures near the plaza fell into shards, claiming more lives.

Thousands of Sydathians rushed to replace their dead brothers, spilling toward the palace in a white wave as the second false sun faded from the sky. Two massive golden eagles soared above the spires now. Tong lost sight of them as his rebels reached the palace gate, which the Onyx Guards had already deserted. The freed men banged on its surface with the butts of spears and axes, hammered at it with jagged stones.

Sydathians climbed up and over the gate, claiming it as they had claimed the city wall, and with far less resistance. The masked ones would no longer fight these blind killers of men. They served out of fear, not loyalty, and their fear of the Sydathians outweighed their fear of Gammir or Ianthe on this fateful morning.

An arc of flame swept past the palace ramparts. One of the golden eagles sped toward the statue of Gammir as it thundered across the plaza, pulping the bones of Sydathians beneath its feet, punishing the earth with strikes of its godly spear. As eyeless ones flooded over the palace gate, Tong looked back at the plaza. Gammir's statue turned its ruby eyes toward the burning eagle. The bird fell like a comet against his black crown with a fresh burst of flame. The great spear splintered and crumbled, showering black dust across the plaza and nearby rooftops.

For one brief second a golden aura limned the mighty idol, and it seemed carved of precious metal instead of sable stone. It groaned and belched thunder, then collapsed into an immense heap of smoking ash. Its great ruby eyes fell steaming through the dusty vapors to crash somewhere on the far side of the plaza.

The screams of slaves drew Tong's attention back to the palace gate. A terrible brightness stung his eyes from above. A white panther tall as a stallion stood upon the arch above the gate, breathing a gout of pale flames across the Sydathians. Their bodies withered and fell from the wall like charred sides of beef, crashing and steaming at the feet of the rebels.

The panther roared a deafening challenge. It vomited a fresh blast of white flames, burning the last of the climbing ones from the gate.

Ianthe the Claw had come to defend her citadel.

Tong stared into the beast's open maw, past the ivory fangs, into the dark void from which the white flames would pour again any second.

This is how his rebellion would end.

Scoured from the earth by Ianthe's flaming ire.

A piercing screech penetrated his deafness, as the second golden eagle burst from rising smoke and struck the panther with tremendous force. Its flaming wings spread wide over the mighty cat as talons and beak dug into feline flesh. The panther threw its head back in agony, and white flames spurted skyward. Eagle and panther clashed atop the wall as a fresh wave of Sydathians climbed the gate. There was no stopping these eyeless warriors who feared neither flame nor death.

An oversized jungle bat flapped now about the barbed tower at the center of the black palace. The first golden eagle raced from its victory in the slaving plaza, trailing a line of golden flames. When these two beings collided above the city, a third sunburst split the leaden sky. A mass of whirling orange flames obscured their aerial duel.

Atop the palace gate, the white panther caught its avian foe's wing in powerful jaws and twisted back. Now the burning eagle was Iardu in his gleaming orange robe. The beast held his right arm clamped between its fangs. Its black diamond eyes blazed with triumph.

Panther and sorcerer fell backwards into the courtyard beyond the gate. Chromatic light erupted, glinting on the skins of the Sydathians surmounting the gate.

Thunder and lightning flared beyond the black iron portals. Tong stood ready with sabre and knife. Any moment his eyeless brothers would fling open the gate. His freed men waited, eager to storm the halls of luxury and privilege. Eager to bring the empire of Gammir and Ianthe crashing down.

"Open the gate!" Tolgur shouted, but he need not have bothered.

The gates swung open at the hands of the eyeless ones. A courtyard of grand garden walks, sparkling fountains, and fruiting arbors now stood ablaze with flames of a dozen colors. The charred skeletons of Sydathians lay strewn among the fires. Beyond the burning trees and terraced hedges stood the palace proper; yet between its portico and the stumbling slaves stood a pale Giantess with clawed hands and raging eyes.

Leathery black pinions twitched upon her back, where the bones of her spine protruded like a row of thorns. She clutched

Iardu's limp form by the silvery hair of his head, her fangs sunk deep into his neck. She suckled at his opened throat, guzzling vital fluid. The sorcerer's robe was torn to shreds, and his frail body hung in bloody tatters, white bones protruding from ruptured flesh. The blue flame no longer danced on his chest. A dark stain had replaced it.

Ianthe raised her white-maned head, spilling crimson from lips and chin. Iardu's lifeblood sparkled on her throat and breasts. Her eyes, shards of onyx gleaming with dark splendor, turned to the mob of Men and Sydathians.

Tong stood foremost in their midst, the Prince of Slaves come to meet his mistress. Her gaze fell upon him, as if he alone had burst through her gate.

She dropped Iardu's lifeless body to the ground, where it lay twisted and ragged.

"Come here, slave," she purred. "Feed me . . ."

17

Vod's Blood

Tyro ran from the shadow of the leviathan as it broke the surface of the marsh. His broadsword slashed at greedy tendrils again and again. They shot forward quick as arrows, wrapping about arm, leg, and waist. The monster had already claimed his stallion, tearing it to pieces beneath him.

Men and mounts were snatched into the shuddering darkness, where uncounted mouths devoured them. Three times the oily arms lifted Tyro like a squirming rat, and three times he hacked his way free, plunging into brackish waters.

There was no name for the terror that guarded this swamp. Nothing like it in the legends of Uurz. A living mountain of flesh born of nightmares and madness. And still it keened, a screeching, wailing incantation that might have been some dead language spilling from the mouths of rotted corpses. The sound came from somewhere above, not from the many gnashing mouths that puckered and snapped across its bulk.

Tyro's heart pounded beneath his golden breastplate, and the filth of the swamp stained every bit of his body. He strove onward through the muck, his boots heavy as iron. His feet made wet sucking noises when he raised them from the mud. He considered abandoning his bronze shield to make himself lighter; a warning in his gut made him keep it.

The next pair of tendrils took him by the legs, lifting him so that he hung upside down. The broadsword slipped from his slimy fingers. He watched it fall blade first into a mound of upturned silt.

He bellowed an animal cry.

I will not die here.

He took the round shield in both hands and drove its sharp edge into the tentacles gripping his legs. The fishy skin split and oozed a dark pus; a dozen more times he brought the shield's edge down upon the coils, while Uurzians hacked and shrieked and died about him. The war songs of giants filled the night, and then the blast of a war horn. At last his shield broke through the coiled flesh, and he fell once more into the muck.

Raising his sodden head, he recognized the long note that rang through the night. It was the horn of Cerrois, one of the scouts sent to spy on the barbed watchtowers.

"Khyreins!"

Climbing free of the fen waters, he scrambled across the uneven terrain and found his sword. He sprinted toward a plot of high ground as the horn sounded yet again. Men's voices shouted with fresh urgency. Warriors fled in both directions now, toward and away from the hungry leviathan. All sense of order among the ranks was lost.

"The Khyreins! They come!"

Instead of a battle plan, there was only chaos and terror. A cluster of blue-skinned Giants stood at the base of the leviathan now, making short work of its tentacles with axe, greatsword, and mace. This was a beast meant for the mighty Udvorg, not for the small arms and tiny blades of Men.

Vireon fought among the Giants, sinking his blade deep into

a fanged mouth. A normal man's arm would have been chewed off in an instant, but Vireon's skin was harder than any bronze corselet. He carried the Blood of Vod in his veins, all the strength and power of Giants in the body of a Man. Tyro envied the Vodson his durable nature. Vireon did not even carry a shield into battle.

Let him lead this rear assault. Let the Giants find a way to bring down the leviathan. "Forward!" shouted Tyro. "Take the towers! No quarter for the Sons of Khyrei!"

A band of determined Uurzians rushed westward with their Emperor. Directly ahead, black figures raced from the treeline brandishing pikes and sabres: the front line of the Border Legions. A volley of arrows flew from the jungle like a swarm of buzzing insects.

"Shields!" Tyro shouted. All those who still had such protection fell to their knees in the mire, raising their metal to take the brunt of the falling shafts. Men bellowed as the keen darts found their way to flesh between the grooves of armor and over the lips of shields.

"Advance! Advance!" He did not stop to see how many warriors followed him, or how many lingered still in the grip of the leviathan. No doubt hundreds had already died, and the slaughter that was now beginning would not end soon. The first wave of masked and armored Khyreins now stood in a patient wedge formation, letting the northerners weary themselves by trudging through the bog. A second line lingered among the roots of the great trees, ranks of archers loosing another volley.

Again Tyro's troops kneeled beneath raised shields. Sinking into the earth provided some defense for their lower bodies, and most of the shafts were thwarted. Tyro was the first one up and running again, and the soldiers took heart from his courage. They followed him, screaming rage and bloodlust at their faceless enemies.

Now even greater shadows emerged from the treeline, slinking into the marsh like Serpents. Tyro recognized them immediately as swamp lizards, at least a score of them. They scurried past the waiting Khyreins, who divided to let the beasts pass. On the back of each darting reptile sat a harnessed figure in black armor. The riders carried long lances, weapons designed for skewering enemies from the backs of their speeding mounts.

The great lizards moved faster than horses, splashing through the muck on webbed feet. The reptile riders were the first to meet the onrushing Uurzians; brave warriors died squirming on the ends of the long lances. Tyro sidestepped a killing thrust from a lancer whose scaly mount bore down upon him. Toothy jaws snapped at his head beneath its winged helm. He hammered its blunt snout with his shield.

These were the creatures that could bite Giants in half. Yet the enemy could not have many of them. Most likely they were a special detail meant for patrolling the swamps. His hopes sank when another score of lizard lancers glided into the fen from the treeline.

If he found a way to kill these beasts, the Uurzians could penetrate the jungle and take the nearest tower. Open a gateway to the red jungle and its black city. If he did not find a way, his righteous war would end tonight in this bloody quagmire. The Giants were too busy battling the leviathan; they could offer no help.

No, only a Man could do this thing.

Only an Emperor.

The masked rider thrust at him once more from atop the beast. Tyro's sword knocked the lance aside. He leaped forward, aiming to reach the lancer with the point of his weapon, but exposed himself instead to the jaws of the reptile. It clamped down on his arm as he shoved the shield lengthwise into its maw. The edges of the shield sank into the lizard's black gums, keeping its fangs away from his flesh. The shield quickly bent double under the power of that tremendous bite. Tyro pulled his arm free as the beast crushed the bronze disk between its jaws.

The reptile spat out his ruined shield as the lancer reached too late to unsheathe a sabre. Tyro launched himself forward and upward, clutching the saddle harness with his shield hand. He thrust the point of his broadsword at the rider's throat. It sank deep into the exposed flesh below the visor.

Tyro climbed up the side of the bucking lizard as it writhed, trying to bite him off its own back. He took hold of the lance and kicked the dying rider from the saddle. Sitting unharnessed in the seat, gripping its leather with all the might of his beefy legs, he raised the lance high and plunged it into the back of the lizard's wedge-shaped skull. The beast squawked and convulsed, whipping its tail hard enough to tumble Tyro into the mud.

He landed on his knees, and as the beast ran forward with the lance protruding from its tiny brain, he sank the length of his *steel* into its sagging white belly. Its own speed did the job for him. A mass of shiny entrails poured out of the creature, and it fell snout first into the mire.

Tyro climbed to stand upon the dead reptile's back and shouted orders. Wild cries praised his kill, spreading word of it through the ranks. The Men of Uurz admired his savagery; they mobbed the lizards and their riders, opening the beasts' bellies even as they died beneath fang, claw, and lance.

Glancing back at the battle of Giants and Swamp God, Tyro's heart sank. The bodies of Udvorg lay torn and shattered about the massive creature, mingled with the viscera and pulped bodies of Men. Varda the Keen Eyes stood behind a ring of Udvorg swordsmen, casting blue flames that froze grasping tentacles and shattered them to bits. Giants died screaming in the grip of the horrid mouths spread across the demon's bulk like palpitating sores. Tentacles wrapped Giants from head to feet whenever they could, jamming them into the fanged maws. It seemed the leviathan itself bore no wounds at all; for every tendril that axe or blade cut away, another one sprouted from the main bulk to replace it. The cries of dying Giants mingled with the growling war songs of their brothers.

Vireon climbed the monster's side using the stubs of severed tentacles. He stood atop the hill of dark flesh with a pack of desperate Udvorg, hacking at the beast, searching for a vulnerable spot. Tyro lost sight of him. The beast sent more appendages coiling about the Giants upon its summit.

The Men of Uurz and Udurum both realized that this contest of titans was not their fight. They had taken Tyro's lead and slogged forward to meet the advancing Khyreins, a horde of stained metal and terrified faces skirting the leviathan's bulk to north and south. The oncoming legions stayed just out of reach of the tentacles, thanks to the quick blades of the Udvorg.

Lord Mendices was back there somewhere, commanding the legions to press forward and confront their true enemies. Tyro thanked the Four Gods for Mendices' shrewdness in the face of carnage. The old veteran had endured great slaughters in his time.

Now the mobbing Uurzians finished the last of the great lizards, dragging the riders from their backs to die beneath a flurry of sharp blades. "Onward!" Tyro shouted as the forward ranks swelled. If the Giants had not been there to take the brunt of the Swamp God's attack, they never would have made it this far. Yet the line of jungle and its precious solid ground loomed close now, and Tyro's berserk cohort would be the first to take it.

He scanned the ground for a fallen shield, yet his eyes were drawn back to Vireon. Whipping tendrils lifted the King of Udurum into the moonlight above the leviathan. Tyro watched the greatsword fly from Vireon's hands, and the Vodson screamed as he was stuffed whole into a grinding craw. Swallowed like all those before him.

Angrid the Long-Arm bellowed Vireon's name. The Ice King hacked at the quivering mass with his great war axe, but Vireon was already lost in the creature's deep gullet. The Giants fought more fiercely than ever, with cries of "Vireon! Vireon!" on their foaming lips.

Tyro had no time to mourn. He turned to the treeline and joined the mass of legionnaires. Now at last the Khyrein line rushed forward into the muddy shallows of the fen, eager to spill foreign blood. The first one to reach Tyro struck with a flashing sabre, nearly opening his throat. A shallow cut on his neck leaked hot blood across his corselet. Any deeper and he would have died in an instant. He had been careless, his mind occupied by Vireon's tragic demise. No more.

His blade sang forward but the Khyrein's shield turned it. The two blades met now with a spark. Tyro stared past the narrow slits of the fanged mask into the desperate eyes of his foe. He shouted a curse and rammed his left fist into the side of the black helmet. This threw the Khyrein off balance, and Tyro's blade swung upward, biting deep into the man's arm. The sabre fell and the warrior howled in pain. In the next second Tyro's sword stabbed through his eye-slit and out the back of his skull.

Tyro took up the black shield with its painted crimson crown. He plunged into the mass of Khyreins filing out of the jungle. Impossible to say how many legions were stationed here, yet in the wake of the sprung trap he knew these towers had been fortified in expectation of the triple host's coming. The numbers of Khyrein soldiers soon matched those of the northerners, and the battle at the edge of the swamp began in earnest. There would be no more advance until thousands of black-masked soldiers lay dead.

A timeless blur of *steel*, bronze, blood, and bone drowned his thoughts beneath a red haze. He was a deadly wind, blowing fierce through the bodies of his enemies. A creature of instinct, a killer set loose to rend and slay. Gashes on his arms and legs spouted blood across the greaves of his armor, and somewhere in the madness his gilded helm was knocked from his head. Crimson flowed into his eyes as he shook his tangled mane.

Somewhere in the midst of the mêlée Tyro found a massive log and sprang atop it for a better view of the field. Instantly a mass of Uurzians surrounded him. "Defend the Emperor! Save the Sword King!" The early rays of sunlight glittered on the bloody gold of his corselet and bracers.

To one side the Khyreins filled the deep jungle glades, whole legions waiting for the order to enter the fray. Masked generals watched from the backs of stationary lizards. On the other side, the heaving bulk of the leviathan steamed in the sunlight as the swarming Giants carved tirelessly and futilely at its flesh.

Tyro saw Angrid lifted in a profusion of grasping tentacles, just as Vireon had been torn from the leviathan's back. A blue flame engulfed the Ice King, paled by the light of the morning sun, and he burst free of the brittle flesh. Varda grabbed him by the shoulder and rushed him away from the beast as a new mass of tendrils swept toward them both.

A fresh wave of Khyreins poured from the jungle.

There is no end to them.

Tyro tried to catch his breath.

Talondra. His mind's eye traveled across leagues of trampled earth in an instant, down into the green bosom of the Stormlands, to settle on a vision of his wife. He recalled her eyes, a deeper blue than the Udvorg witch's flame; he remembered the heat of her body against his own. His hand lay upon her smooth belly the day before he departed Uurz. She whispered a sweet secret in his ear. She carried now his first child.

A sudden darkness fell upon him in the glow of bloodstained
morning.

He would never see her again.

Never know the face of his son.

Men died by the score and he stood frozen in the grip of this
realization. In the back of his mind, Lyrilan's voice pleaded with
him. *Don't do this! All war is failure!* His brother would never
understand the realities of empire. The necessity of slaughters like
this one. The need to face death and spit in its eye.

As the spears of Khyreins surrounded him on all sides and the
soldiers protecting him were cut down, he lost all of these
thoughts. He was no weak-kneed scholar, no cowardly wailer. He
was the Son of Dairon. The Emperor of Uuz.

My son will know that I was a warrior.

He will read it in the scrolls of history.

This is how a warrior dies.

Howling and weeping, he raised his blade and leaped into a
thicket of gleaming spears.

Climbing atop the mountainous bulk of the Swamp God, Vireon
joined a cadre of Udvorg hammering and slashing at the beast's
slimy flesh. Only here, at the summit of its massive bloat, could
he see the source of the terrible chorus that rang through the
night. Seven swollen heads, each one tall as a Giant, grown in a
tight ring at the center of the throbbing fleshmount. Tufts of hair
grew from the desiccated skulls, little more than clumps of swamp
weed and tangled moss, but they were much like the heads of dead
Men or Giants.

Seven pairs of great blind eyes gleamed night-black and without
pupils. Mouths hung slack and dribbling with noxious secre-
tions, the teeth rotted to sharp stubs dark as charcoal. The flesh of
each head was dark brown, splotched with green and gray lesions

dripping pus. They were the heads of forlorn lepers, singing an ancient song of power. Serpentine tongues red as blood quivered inside their jaws, and the eyes rolled mindlessly. Yet they sang as one, an endless chorus of malformed syllables in a language that must have died long ago. The corruption of ages hung about the monstrosity, nowhere more evident than in these decayed yet living skulls.

Tentacles wound up from below, snatching Giants off the creature's peak before any reached the ring of heads with mace or sword. Vireon leaped between the Udvorg, slicing at greedy coils, making his way closer to the ring of heads. The mystery of this beast lay within that ring. Perhaps therein lay the secret to killing it.

Leaping over a Giant whose battle axe dug deep into the scabrous flesh, he vaulted from the Udvorg's shoulders and through the narrow space between two of the heads. He tumbled through scum and clinging vines toward the center of the ring.

Now the seven pairs of dead eyes fell directly upon him. It seemed they were not blind at all; or they saw with some deep sight born of nightmare and sorcery. Gripping his blade in both fists, he stared at the circle of leprous faces, caught at the midpoint of their sonorous wailing. It deafened him.

He shouted against the violence of their song, defying it with his own war cry, and rushed toward one of the idiot faces. He would slice all seven of those skulls from their perches one by one. Yet the strange song changed its pitch, and now the seven heads spoke to him as one. It was not his own language, yet he understood it. Their great spell did not cease, the terrible wailing continued to rise and fall, yet in some way they also *spoke* beneath the resounding chant. Stilled by words that hit him like iron hammers, Vireon could not bring his sword down upon the nearest of the twisted faces.

"*You are not the King of Storms*," said the seven as one. Their mouthings reverberated between his ears, death cries torn from a deep catacomb.

He could not reply. His throat was an empty well.

"*Long have we waited . . .*" said the seven-who-were-one. "*Since the White Panther plucked us from the smoking ruins of Omu and set us here to guard her border. She said the King of Storms would come to free us one day. We hoped that you were him . . . yet you are only a Man. Like we used to be.*"

I am Vireon! he wanted to shout. The seven did not permit it. In silence, he struggled against the invisible chains weighing down his limbs. He refused to let go of the sword's grip, though it had grown heavy as a palace gate.

"*Where is the King of Storms?*" demanded the seven.

Dead! Long dead!

He did not need to speak the words. They – *it* – understood. There were no more Giants atop the summit now. All had been cast down or devoured. Only Vireon remained on high, caught in the spell of the seven heads. A spider trapped in a web of sorcery. It was Vod the seven heads had expected, not him. Vod the Bringer of Storms, Breaker of the Desert, Slayer of Omagh. His father.

"*Noooooooo!*" The great heads wailed. They rolled and convulsed atop fat necks. "*There is no end to our suffering then. All hope of warm death and sweet oblivion is gone . . . dead like the King of Storms. So we must continue to serve Her. We, who were once the Lords of Omu, omnipotent in our glory. We were living Men – Kings! First she took our kingdom, then our souls. Our separate flesh she made as one with the soul of the swamp. Until the King of Storms comes to deliver us, she said. O, faint hope of a distant Age! Yet it was only another of her lies.*"

I am Vireon! Vod of the Storms was my father! Still he could not move or speak. The sounds from below, Men and Giants dying, mingled with the horrid screech of the Swamp God's song. It spoke one last time to him in seven cadaverous voices.

"You are not the King of Storms."

It heaved a ragged sigh that rose into an awful howl.

A greasy tendril thick as his waist slithered about Vireon. It yanked him from the ring of heads with terrible force, and his blade went flying from numb fingers. Blackness engulfed him as the tendril stuffed him into a gnashing lower maw, a tidbit of raw meat to feed its bottomless hunger.

The stink of the Swamp God's gullet was intolerable. Fresh blood and ancient filth. He sank through a narrow gorge lined with jagged fangs. The pulsing walls of flesh squeezed and clenched, trying to burst his stony skin. Since it could not break his flesh, it merely swallowed him deeper. He fought to breathe and got only a mouthful of noxious slime. He vomited and grabbed at the slippery chute, sinking his fingers deep into the raw flesh. The danger here was not in being gnashed to ribbons, but in suffocating from lack of air.

The beast pulled him deep into its bowels, some insistent tongue or tendril wrapped about his legs. He lost his handhold on the fleshy walls, nails leaving deep gashes as he descended toward the center of the leviathan's mass. He kicked and tore and strove to burst through the inner flesh, but it was too thick and too spongy. He was a fly trapped in amber, a solitary mote striving to tear its way out of a living mountain. His heart pounded and he tried again to breathe, unsuccessfully. Then he plummeted, drawing air for a half-second as he fell through steaming vapors into a dark and cavernous space. He splashed into a bubbling reservoir of noxious fluid that was certainly not water. Water would not burn his thick flesh in such a way. He swam mightily upward, pausing only to snap the tendril that gripped his ankles.

He broke the surface but could see nothing in the putrid darkness. Bones drifted against him in the caustic slime, the remains of recent victims. His skin sizzled. Soon his bones would join these others, burned away by this liquid fire. He screamed, and his voice echoed through the fleshy cavity. The belly of the beast.

Splashes sounded the arrival of more Giant victims, already dead by the time their bodies reached this nether region. The Giants possessed great strength and endurance, but they lacked the density of Vireon's compact body. Fate had distilled his gigantic strength into a human figure, making him quicker and more resilient than a true Giant. Yet even the best qualities of Man and Uduru combined would not be enough to survive this.

"I am the Son of Vod!" he cried into the sloshing dark.

A tremulous groan shook the immense gut, and the fiery fluid dissolved his skin slowly but surely. He swam about blindly searching for a handhold, something, anything to pull himself out of the corrosive lake. There was nothing.

He floundered, choking on the creature's bile. Like swallowing the flaming oil of an upturned brazier. He wailed in pain, vomited again, and wondered how long his sturdy skin would last.

I am the Son of Vod.

His potent blood runs in my veins.

I brought the storms back to the Stormlands.

"Father!" he cried. "Father!"

I am the Son of Vod, who was both Man and Giant.

I have his blood. The blood of a sorcerer.

His burning skin shuddered, his eyes closed against the gloom. He screamed again, not in words, but with the guttural sound of a lost soul lingering on the edge of annihilation. Something long buried awoke inside him. A shock of fresh pain, unlike any other, erupted from his heart, spreading through his arms and legs. The pain of the monster's gastric acid was less than nothing compared

to the rending, stretching agony he now endured. His only awareness was of the scream itself, rising like the squeal of a war horn
inside the cavernous gut.

He screamed, and the screaming *changed* him.

His chest swelled, and his shoulders. His legs grew like mighty
oaks, lifting him above the lake of death. Inside his expanding
skin, bones cracked and popped, lengthened and swelled. His
corselet, belt, and sandals split apart, abandoned by his burgeon-
ing mass. He grew tall as an Uduru, muscles flexing with
unnatural torment. The echoes of his own howl came back to him,
and he continued to rise. He raised his hands and found the roof
of the bowel cavern. Still he grew, until his arms burst through
that stubborn flesh like battering rams. He bent forward, dou-
bling over, and his back met the ruptured roof of the cavern now,
splitting it wide open.

A vision came to him as his body swelled and grew beyond all
proportion: his father, beardless and young, standing tall as a
mountain, locked in the grip of another leviathan, this one a great
Serpent. No, the Father of Serpents, Omagh himself, whom Vod
had killed and so changed the world.

Vireon watched the battle in the mirror of his mind as his
mounting bulk shattered gristle, sinew, and nameless flesh, growing to match the size of the enveloping leviathan. Young Vod
lopped off dozens of the Serpent-Father's clawed legs with each
swipe of his great axe, then wrestled the legless behemoth to the
ground. Mountains shivered and the sky burst into a hurricane as
Vod tore the Serpent's head from its vast body. Here was the beast
that had cast Old Udurum into ruin and wallowed like a pig in
its smoking debris. And here was the Man-Giant who grew to the
size of a God and ended Omagh's ancient life.

Here was Vod the Giant-King.

My father.

My blood.

My inheritance.

Vireon's fists burst into fresh air. Naked sunlight fell upon his gasping face. Still he grew, and his massive head followed his fists. His shoulders and torso came next, like a brutal infant tearing itself free of a mad womb. The leviathan's countless tentacles quivered in the spasms of its destruction. The Giants below howled Vireon's name as he burst through the summit of this hill of rancid flesh. The morning sun stung eyes and glittered upon the slime drenching his raw skin, red as that of a sunburned child. He lifted a great foot from the dying guts of the Swamp God and stomped down upon the seven bloated heads. They cracked like eggshells beneath his foot. The world shook beneath him. Again he stomped upon the putrescent hill of flesh, driving a legion of howling Udvorg away from the monster's death throes.

Colossal and steaming, Vireon gazed across a carpet of crimson wilderness at the western horizon. He glimpsed a range of steaming volcanoes along the southern edge of the continent. He might even see the black spires of Khyrei if he stared hard enough into the northeast, but matters unfolding at his colossal feet demanded attention.

Far below his sopping head the quagmire seethed with armored Men rushing to kill each other. The black legions flowed from the jungle like a river of darkness, blending with the triple host in a swirling dance of death. A sea of tiny faces gazed up at Vireon, straining against the sun's glare to admire the whole of his mountainous form.

These tiny Men and Giants.

They needed him.

He stomped the last of the leviathan's bulk into a dark jelly, then raised his voice in a shout that sundered the heavens. A clap of earsplitting thunder shook the marshland. A vast wall of stormclouds sparkled with looming thunderbolts, and sheets of cold rain fell across the clashing legions. Men and Giants cheered as one about his heels.

"Vireon! Vireon, Son of Vod!"

He reached a massive hand down toward the swamp's edge and scooped up a hundred Khyrein soldiers. They wailed and pleaded in his fist, some leaping to their deaths to avoid his cruel fingers. His fist tightened, crushing bronze, bone, and flesh into a red paste. It dripped like red clay from between his fingers. Again he bent forward, this time both hands capturing mobs of masked ones and a trio of great lizards. The scaly behemoths were less than flies to him. They died as easily as the shrieking Men.

Now the main force of Giants rushed forth to join the legions of Men. The tide turned quickly from despair to mad triumph. Vireon watched as the Udvorg rushed the red jungle, flattening trees and Khyreins alike. Their greatswords and axes drank deeply of southern blood.

The Khyrein lines broke and the northerners chased them through the jungle. Vireon saw clearly now the twenty black towers marking the border between marsh and jungle. He raised his great knee and took a single step. His bare foot fell upon the nearest tower like a toppled mountain. The edifice crumbled beneath his tread, a toy house built by tiny, soulless children.

After this symbolic destruction, the battle became a rout. Khyreins fled for the relative safety of the towers to north and south. Few of them made it as the northern legions pressed deeper into the wilderness.

A yawning weariness overcame Vireon. As the raging storm washed the slime and blood from his skin, he began to diminish. Lightning flared above a thousand scenes of slaughter, as Men and Giants avenged their fallen brothers. The dying screams of Khyreins were drowned beneath the noise of the tempest.

Soon Vireon stood no taller than his Udvorg cousins in the ruined swamp, surrounded by the twisted and torn remains of northmen, horses, and Giants. He fell to his knees in the blood-shot mire and fought the desire to lie down and sleep amid the ruined bodies. Instead, he raised his head toward the jungle and forced himself to walk forward.

The marshes had been crossed. The way to the black city had been opened.

The Blood of Vod had been tested and found worthy.

In the pouring rain he donned the clothing and armor of a Giant he found headless in the muck. He picked up a fallen greatsword. Through the driving storm, the songs of clashing metal and yowling Giants lingered in his ears. The cool rain soothed his chapped flesh.

A cadre of northern legions was already heading north toward a second watchtower. He wondered who it was that led them. Tyro? Angrid? Dahrima? What had become of his faithful Uduri and her sisters? He last saw her slicing tentacles among the ranks of Udvorg. Could her bones be among those he found inside the leviathan's belly?

Across the littered field he saw a figure rising from the muck. A Giantess. He ran toward her. A lean face framed by tousled black hair turned to look upon him. Varda raised her black staff and clasped her bleeding forehead. He offered his arm, helped her to stand. She pulled away from him, then grimaced with pain. Her scarlet eyes scanned his Udvorg-sized body. She had no words to account for his new stature, or the miracle of sorcery he had performed. Crystal tears flowed along her cold cheeks.

"Where is Angrid?" he asked.

Her blue face twisted into a mask of anger. "You dare to ask me this? You who convinced him to leave the ice and fight in your mad crusade? You who are neither Man nor Giant?"

He glared at her, trying to understand the words. His head swam, but he refused to fall.

"Where is Angrid?" he asked again, louder. Thunder punctuated his question.

"Dead!" screamed the shamaness. "Torn apart! *Devoured!*" Her ruby eyes flared with rage and heartbreak.

Vireon blinked. Rain ran along the blade of his sword, dripping like translucent blood from its tip. What was she saying?

"You saved us!" Varda screamed. "Why could you not save *him*?"

Vireon stammered; the proper words eluded him. "I . . . I . . ." His body diminished yet again, until he stood at his normal human height. Varda towered over him now, her eyes burning redder than the poison jungle. She turned away and stalked toward the demolished tower, where Men were setting up a defensible camp. A blue flame sprang up once more to dance at the head of her staff.

Vireon raised a hand to call her back, but the cry never left his lips.

He fell back into the mire, and his boiling thoughts sank into darkness.

18

The Vital Tongues

The libraries of Yaskatha were sumptuous and extensive, yet Lyrilan spent none of his time exploring them. Instead he stayed cloistered in his borrowed palace chamber with its terrace overlooking the Cryptic Sea. D'zan had set sail nine days ago, his golden galleons joining with the white swanships of Mumbaza.

Lyrilan took little food or wine, despite the protests of Volomses, who left his studies in the halls of parchment and scroll twice a day to visit. The old sage seemed to enjoy his new life in the southern capital; as a scholar of the north he commanded a certain respect in Yaskatha, and the women of the court found him endearing. Undroth, too, seemed less the eternal general and more like a retired lord. He spent most his time with discreet courtesans or exploring the royal vineyards. At times he drank with the veterans of the palace guard, reliving old glories.

Lyrilan took no woman to his bed and spared no time to get acquainted with his new neighbors. Word about the palace, relayed to him by Volomses, was that grief had made him a recluse. He did not care what the powdered and pampered folk of D'zan's realm believed.

Last night, by the soft light of thirteen candles, he had finished

The Third Book of Imvek. The secrets unfolding in his brain had followed him into a restless sleep. He dreamed the abstractions, the metaphysical propositions, the songs in ancient tongues. He walked the winding streets of empires long forgotten, dead cities scattered across the world like patches of moss obscured by smothering wilderness. He spoke with the savants of races who carved mountains into colossal cities long before mankind was a dream in the eye of its mysterious creators. He saw the Gods themselves in his dreams, lurking like shadows about the fires of primeval humanity. The worst of his nightmares brought him face to face with the deepest truths of Imvek's discoveries.

All these years Lyrilan had thought he understood the world and its history. What was any world but a complex collection of historical ages? Even as a boy he knew all the Ages of Man, from the Time of Serpents to the Sundering of Tribes, to the Founding of the Realms, to the Age of Heroes, the Plague Age and the Age of Discovery. A succession of wars and catastrophes and legends that comprised the whole of antiquity.

Yet it was all but the slightest glimpse of a world ancient beyond belief, where civilizations rose and fell and rose again; an endless cycle of rebirth, ruination, and reinvention. How many lost races had walked the surface of the earth and molded it to fit their needs? He could never know. Yet now he knew the names of at least a few.

Imvek's odyssey into the Southern Isles had brought him to the Lost Cities of K'Timba, whose mighty stones lay scattered across the islands beneath millennia of jungle growth. There he had discovered the bones of a capital that must have rivaled great Uurz in its day. The remains of mummies and the mosaics of ancient tomb walls spoke of a society where prehuman beings gathered to ponder obscure philosophies of space, time, and existence.

Imvek had learned the lost language of the Yl'ktri, whose

words were primal glyphs of power. Using those very words he had called up the ghosts of the creatures who inscribed them on tablets of antediluvian stone. From such phantoms he learned the subtle cadences of the Yl'ktri speech. Theirs was a language that manipulated the elements as a man's hammer hewed stone or wood. This was well before the wayward Prince gave up his tongue to carry his stolen knowledge home to Uurz.

Imvek's account also told of how he summoned a spirit whose race once roamed the starfields, spreading conscious thought like seeds across the universe. He learned the true shape of the living worlds, and the shapes earth held before Man existed. From the ancestors of the finny Sea Folk he learned the mysteries of the ocean depths. In visions he toured the palace of a winged people who dwelled among the clouds when earth's land masses were not yet formed. His research penetrated all the way to the earliest instance of life itself, when the secrets he learned became too great. He refused to set any more of his primordial visions on parchment.

Still, he had learned enough to fill six volumes with prehistoric wisdom. These books, one by one, pulled back the curtain of modern supremacy to reveal the wonders of bygone epochs. Throughout the untold eons lurked the presence of colossal beings who were not Gods, for they were greater and far deadlier than any God could be.

Imvek posited that these Walkers from Beyond were the original architects of earthly life, though he found no proof of this blasphemous claim. If the Gods had created Man, as their priests claimed, then why have the Celestials forgotten and ignored their creations for so long? Lyrilan found Imvek's unanswerable question to be the strongest proof of his theory.

Chief among the third book's revelations were the existence not only of the Yl'ktri language, but of an entire set of tongues that served as the basis for all spoken communication. These the author dubbed the Vital Tongues. The power of these languages was the power of sorcery. Yet their true authority lay not in the vocalization, the sounds made by lip, tongue, and tooth. The entities who invented these languages possessed very different physical forms to humans. To speak the Vital Tongues aloud as they had been in the earth's early ages was impossible for a human. No, the true power of these primal languages was the conscious meaning and intent behind the words, whether they were written or spoken.

As the greatness of a man lies in his heart, not in the might of his limbs, so did command of the Vital Tongues lie within the *mind* that conceived and expressed their meaning. The vigor of these languages was triggered by the power of living blood, the liquid foundation of all life.

Knowing all these things, Imvek no longer needed a human voice to command the languages of power. Therefore, he sacrificed his tongue willingly to an ignorant barbarian King in order to escape with the untold treasure of his discoveries. By losing one simple tongue, he gained several that were far more potent.

Sitting among the silken hangings and sculpted stone of D'zan's house, Lyrilan felt the great weight of the past lying upon the world like an unseen burden. It lay upon him, upon his traitorous brother, and all Kings and Queens and warriors and maidens; on all the children of the earth. He realized after reading that third volume his own insignificance in the face of the vast cosmos and its infinite wonders.

Then it came to him that the Vital Tongues, the prehuman songs of power, were his key to lifting that weight and remolding the world to suit his needs.

He had learned the power of living blood to invoke the influence of the Vital Tongues. Phrases and formulae lay scrawled across the volume's latter pages. Secrets torn from empires fallen to dust. How much more of the forgotten languages might he learn in the fourth, fifth, and sixth books? Yet before he continued his journey through the realm of Imvek's sorcerous knowledge, he longed to try another incantation, to feel the syllables of a Vital Tongue spilling from his own lips, miracles sprouting from the forest of his willpower. Like Imvek, he need not speak the Tongues aloud, but the act of speech provided a focus for him, like a school-boy reciting ciphers.

While the shroud of night lay deep and still about the palace, he assembled certain ingredients: a stone bowl, a dagger, the petals of a night-blooming flower, a bit of ground bone from the pork shank he failed to eat for dinner, and wine of an ancient vintage. This took some doing, but he bribed the custodian of the wine cellars with a splendid tourmaline from his coffer of Uurzian jewels. He combined these ingredients in the wide bowl, which he carried to the terrace. Midnight breezes played with the strands of his long hair. The Cryptic Sea glittered in the moonlight as if littered with floating diamonds. He breathed deep of the salty air.

He held the dagger's blade over a burning brazier until it glowed a bright crimson, then slid it across his palm. The shallow cut he had inflicted upon himself during the sea voyage had already healed. He sliced a parallel groove alongside it, and squeezed his fist over the copper bowl until twenty-one red drops joined the contents there. Then, holding his bloody hand toward the sky, he began the song he had chosen from Imvek's third volume.

A vision of Ramiyah lay in his mind, conjured only by his imagination. This was soul magic, the calling of a spirit from the Realm of the Dead. Imvek had learned much of his greater magic in this way, prying secrets from the specters of antiquity. Yet it was not esoteric knowledge Lyrilan sought this night.

The wind picked up and great waves slammed against the shore below the palace. The ships and boats anchored in the harbor bobbed and shifted with the uncommon turbulence of the bay waters. A great wind moaned through the orchards, and lightning turned the black sky to cobalt blue over the distant face of the sea. The candles in his room went out at once, followed by the hanging braziers. Lyrilan stood with darkness at his back and moonlight on his face, speaking sounds from beyond time and space.

"*Ramiyah . . .*"

He mixed her name into the incantation. Behind his closed eyes she smiled and danced and lay with him in a heated embrace. The sweet smell of her skin, peaches and rosemary, filled his nostrils. Or it could be that he imagined them. Perhaps it did not matter which was true.

A fog rolled up from the sea to hide the vineyards along the hillside. White vapors crept toward the palace as Lyrilan continued the ancient song. His heart beat faster, and he wanted to cry out, to laugh or weep, or hurl himself from the terrace onto the marble walks of the courtyard. A wisp of vapor coiled about the railing of the terrace and then curled about his legs.

He kept his eyes firmly shut while the clammy vapor caressed his face, shedding coolness and damp sea air.

"*Ramiyah . . .*" He called her name again.

How long he stood chanting over the bowl he could not guess.

Now his eyes opened and she stood before him in a gown of wispy vapors. Her golden hair shined to rival the moonglow, and her soft blue eyes regarded him with an infinite sadness. He gasped and his bloody fingers trembled. The spell had worked.

Lyrilan, she breathed and he fell to his knees.

"O, sweet Wife," he said, tears flowing freely now. They crossed his lips hot and salty. "Our love cannot be hindered by the shackles of Life and Death. To see you again . . . to hear your voice . . . it brings me such pleasure."

Ramiyah's ghost shivered about the edges, and she shook her blonde head.

There was no smile on her lovely face. Her gaze was as blank as a marble effigy.

Why have you done this?

Lyrilan blinked and reached out to her. His dripping hand passed through her body. She was insubstantial like the sea fog, perhaps made of it.

"Because I love you . . . I miss you . . . " he said. "I wanted to tell you . . . I'm so sorry . . . "

I am dead, Lyrilan. What can your sorrow mean to me?

Lyrilan sighed. "I will make them pay for taking you from me. You and our son. This I swear to you."

Our son was never born, said the wraith.

"An even greater crime to avenge. Come wrap your arms about me," he begged. "Pretend just for a little while . . . that we both still live and love."

Once more the apparition shook her misty head.

You still live. The Dead cannot love the Living. It is not permitted.

"Permitted? By whom? Who denies what I ask this night? I have sung the language of the Yl'ktri, a Vital Tongue. Come and embrace me!"

No, said the ghost. She turned away from him, facing instead the dark truth of the sea. *Leave me be, Lyrilan. Let me rest. You should not have done this thing.*

"I don't understand," he cried. "Why not?"

Because it is wrong. In your living heart you already know this.

"I do not care!" he said. "We were robbed, everything taken from us. This small token of sorcery brings us together again, even if only for one more night of bliss. Love me, Wife, as you did before."

Before I died? No. It is not permitted.

"I will decide what is permitted," said Lyrilan. "If you ever loved me, girl, turn and face me now."

She turned, her yellow locks tossed in a sudden updraft. Her face was a mask of white bone, staring at him with sockets stark and empty. She wore the naked grin common to all skulls.

Lyrilan fell back and howled at the phantom. The ghost raised its hands toward him as the golden hair fell from its nude skull. It floated closer to him, as if it would indeed take him in its vaporous arms. He writhed back across the carpeted terrace, pressed his back against the cold wall, and covered his face with his arms. His sliced palm was still bleeding. It dripped across his shuddering face.

The Dead cannot love the Living, whispered the skull. *Send me back to my rest.*

"Go!" Lyrilan shouted, waving his bloody hand in the face of the corpse. Yet it was already gone.

He lay weeping like a lost child on the terrace when Volomses found him. The sage helped Lyrilan to his feet and walked him to the cool comfort of his bed. He shut the burgundy curtains of the terrace.

Dawn was on its way, bringing the inevitability of a mortal existence to light once more. Lyrilan did not want it. Life was a worthless thing without love. And if love did not exist beyond the walls of Death, how much power could it truly possess? He pulled at his sweaty locks of hair and kicked the sheets from his bed. Volomses sat near the bed and soothed him with the patient tones of a worried grandfather.

After a while Lyrilan lay calm in the quietude of despair. The soul-deep wound given him by Tyro had been reopened. Was that unkind specter truly the spirit of Ramiyah, or only a figment of his tortured imagination? Impossible to say.

Volomses gave him mulled wine. He drank it sitting up in the bed, knees drawn up to his chest. The sage went to the terrace, took the stone bowl and poured its contents into the lower gardens. With soap and water he wiped the terrace free of blood and all other signs of conjury. Finally, he wiped the blood from Lyrilan's face, arms, and hand, stitching up the deep cut and wrapping it with a white bandage.

"Majesty," said the sage, "you really must avoid cutting yourself in such a way. Nothing good can come of it."

Lyrilan almost told the sage what he had learned from Imvek's books. The most powerful blood used in the working of sorcery was always that of the sorcerer himself. Besides, spilling the blood of others held no appeal for him. Only the blood of those touched with greatness would outshine that of a sorcerer. That would be a blood worth harvesting. Until he found such blood he must rely on the red potency of his own veins. He said nothing of this to Volomses.

Instead he called for the curtains to be lifted so the sunrays could find their way into his chamber. Volomses saw this as a good sign. He smiled and left the chamber on an errand to secure breakfast for the both of them. Lyrilan bolted the door behind the sage.

From the second of his traveling chests he lifted *The Fourth Book of Imvek the Silent*.

When Volomses returned with a platter of fruits and cheeses, Lyrilan denied him entry.

"Go away," he ordered through the door.

The wound beneath his bandaged palm throbbed. It mirrored the constant pain in his heart. He had grown used to it, and no longer paid it any mind.

He sat in the center of the ruffled bed with the book propped on his folded legs.

He opened the first of its musty pages and began to read.

Ramiyah's fleshless face lingered in his memory like an unheeded warning.

19

King of the Black City

Sharadza fell sideways into a cosmos of living flame. As Iardu had promised, the pain of the transition was immense. Her newly reborn body blazed, and she fought the urge toward annihilation, wearing a coat of golden fire that scorched every inch of her body. It would not destroy her unless she lingered too long here in the heart of the blazing agony.

Good, Iardu whispered in her mind. *Harness the flame! Wear it as your armor against the shadow. Fight the pain. Keep your center . . .*

She was blind in the seething torrent of heat and light, but she heard his voice clearly now, singing another ancient song. Again she fell sideways, and he thought-spoke to her once more as they dropped free of the flames into the heart of Khyrei's black city.

Gammir wears the body of his effigy. Destroy it and you will lure him from his high tower. Leave Ianthe to me . . .

She had no chance to respond or argue, as she followed the Shaper through the breach, back into her own world. For an instant they hung suspended within a corona of leaping amber fire. Iardu took the form of a great eagle, weaving the flames about himself. She joined him in this way, winging about the black spires. The city shuddered in chaos underneath the roiling smoke.

Thunder roared from the plaza of the slave market. She sped toward the great idol as it stomped the pale beasts swarming about its feet.

She was a creature of flame more than flesh or feathers. This was no ordinary fire trailing like vapor from her flapping pinions. It was the living flame of a world where darkness and shadow did not exist. She cast a bolt of it at the statue's great spear. The monolithic weapon fell to dust. The massive head of Gammir's effigy turned to regard her with its ruby eyes brimming with undisguised hatred. She sensed the spirit of her half-brother inside the colossus, yet his true body lay within the high tower. She spewed golden flame across the statue and circled about as it burned to ashes and rained down upon the fractured city. She lost sight of the great twin rubies as they fell, but noted that they alone did not burn.

Soaring toward the palace she felt Gammir's presence inside the barbed tower. In the shape of a great jungle bat he burst forth to meet her. The sound of his furious screeching was lost beneath an explosion of prismatic flames from the palace courtyard. She had no time to glance down and view Iardu's progress before she and Gammir collided like two renegade meteors. Black claws reached for her heart as they spun for a timeless moment, falling like the statue's ruby eyes toward the blazing gardens.

Wrapping her arms about the wolf-bat as it sank claws deep into her breast, she sang Iardu's song and forced open the Gate of Living Flame. The last of the golden flame about her avian body linked her to the burning realm. Sparks leaped from her eyes, encircling Gammir and herself. She burned away the substance of her own dimension, opening a passage back to the source of the living flame. She prepared herself for pain as the flaming cosmos engulfed her once again.

Gammir's screams were the high-pitched wails of a wounded

beast. A creature forged from shadow and blood, he could not long stand immersion in this endless conflagration. The flames ate away his black wings, and his body reverted to its pale human form, writhing and gnashing against the terrible trap into which she had lured him. His alabaster skin burned away, and the pink flesh beneath curled like burning paper, leaving only a chattering skeleton.

His white bones blackened as she watched, wrapping a fresh gown of flames about her body. She gritted her teeth and harnessed the pain. She could not stay here long either, but she could master the flames long enough to annihilate him.

As the last of Gammir's skinless face melted away, she grabbed his whirling skull. The burning void yawned toward infinity in every direction.

I pity you.

She plunged her thoughts like daggers into what was left of Gammir's fading mind.

You who once were a Man. Now I understand how you could fall so low.

She enslaved you . . . just as you enslaved me.

But I forgive you, Brother.

While I cannot free you from her bondage, I can keep you here long enough to end you.

Gammir's bones burned into ash, as his effigy had done in the other world. Yet in this molten place even the ashes were scorched into nothingness.

A bodiless voice came to her as the last dancing motes of Gammir disintegrated.

Sweet Sister . . . there can be no end.

You have only set me free.

She willed herself back into the living world, armored once more in a sheath of golden flame. The chaos of Khyrei writhed below her, and she floated among the tips of the black spires, watching slaves and apelings flood into the blazing courtyard. As Iardu had mentioned, this was nothing less than a full-scale revolution. An invasion of inhuman liberators and a rampaging mob of slaves rising up to cut their cruel masters' throats.

In the midst of the burning gardens stood Ianthe the Claw, tall as an Uduri. A twisted and bloodless corpse lay at her feet. An army of rebels poured through her gate.

The Empress waved a taloned hand, and the horde of slaves fell at once to their knees. They dropped their stolen weapons to the ground and wept in her flamelit shadow. They begged forgiveness for their sin of insurrection. Even the pack of eyeless apes bent low, groveling in a ring about the sorceress instead of leaping up to tear her apart.

Among all the mutineers flooding her courtyard, only one slave stood tall and defiant while his brothers bowed and scraped and cried. A lanky Khyrein, his exposed body a mass of scars and dripping wounds, his only garment a dirty loincloth. He clutched a bloody sabre in one fist, a knife in the other, black eyes smoldering. What could such simple weapons do against the Claw of Khyrei? Such singular bravery.

Outside the ruptured palace gate, thousands of horned apelings converged on the royal grounds. They dragged down squads of armored soldiers and tore them apart like hounds mauling panicked pheasants.

Sharadza took all of this in as she floated near to the barbed tower, shedding yellow flames from her skin. As the last of the pain drifted from her like pale smoke, she hovered lower above the blazing gardens. Now she saw clearly the body Ianthe had cast aside.

The drained and mutilated carcass of Iardu.

No! It cannot end this way . . .

Ianthe held the single unbowed slave by his neck, lifting him from the flagstones.

Sharadza dropped like a fiery stone hurled from the heavens.

Ianthe's dark and glittering eyes pierced him as surely as her black talons. Tong stood breathless in the glow of licking flames. Both his blades fell from numb fingers, clattering against stone. The freed men at his back, the proud Sydathians who had climbed over the wall and flung open the gate . . . everyone but Tong himself . . . fell to the flagstones and wept like shamed children.

I will not bow to you. Not any longer.

She stalked toward him, forgetting the corpse of Iardu.

Even if you feast on my blood, I will die standing.

I defy you with my last breath.

The Empress seemed to understand. Her claw wrapped about his throat, lifting him to her Giantess eye level. His arms hung dead at his sides, useless hocks of meat and bone. Hot urine spilled down his legs, dripping from the soles of his feet.

"You are the source of this sad drama," said Ianthe. Her sensuous mouth was large enough to bite off his head if she desired it. "You have a touch of greatness about you. Your blood must be delicious." She opened wide that mouth, displaying the fangs of a panther. Tong closed his eyes, ready to accept the final agony of those fangs sinking deep into his neck.

Instead a blast of scorching heat erupted between them. Her fingers loosened; he fell across the prone bodies of his fellow slaves.

A second Giantess stood now in the courtyard, this one wrapped in flaming armor. Her hair was dark as midnight, dancing in the updrafts of superheated air.

Tong glanced about at the simpering slaves. They had been so eager for blood and freedom only moments earlier. This was the power of Ianthe's reign, the strength of her dark glory, that Men could not defy her openly. He might have hated his fellows for abandoning their righteous fury, but he was not able. All of them had risked what little they had; all had been ready to die in the name of liberty. What chance had they in the face of such sorcery?

Now, without Iardu's magic, what chance did this burning Giantess have against the Claw? Tong lay numb and helpless amid the weeping slaves, trying to force his leaden arms toward the fallen sabre.

The Giantess struck out with a bolt of brilliant flame. Ianthe cast it aside with the back of a single claw. The pale skin of her hand sizzled, and black wings twitched on either side of her bristly spine. Her claw lashed out at the flaming armor, extinguishing it with a cloak of instant shadow. The fire wielder stumbled back as Ianthe sent both claws slamming into her chest. Now Tong saw that it was no true Giantess who defended the slaves, but a young woman no older than himself. The power of Ianthe's double blow sent her flying across the courtyard. The girl crashed into a mass of blazing foliage.

The Empress turned her blood-smeared face back to Tong. Still he could not move, or even hope to stand. His rebellion ended here and now. In utter failure. Iardu had led him to this, and even the great sorcerer lacked the strength to end the Claw's rule. How many times over the centuries had other slaves, hopeful and desperate, staged such an uprising, only to be smashed by Ianthe's boundless power?

It does not matter. I die as a free man, not a slave.

So do we all die.

Matay . . . at last I come to you.

Ianthe reached a claw toward him, smiling with keen bloodlust.

She paused, the tips of her black talons gleaming before his eyes. She pulled back, her head bobbing weirdly to the side. She curled her claws into fists. She stood shivering before the mass of cowed slaves and the cringing eyeless ones. A fresh pack of Sydathians had climbed the palace wall, sitting like gargoyles above the smoking courtyard. In other corners of the city they still ravaged the places where guardsmen strove in vain to stop their advance. The cries of dying men rang above the flames as Tong watched Ianthe perform an impossible dance of agony.

Her black eyes bulged, and her torso twisted like a slithering viper. Bones snapped inside her pristine skin. A curious bulge emerged from her smooth forehead. She vomited black blood and thrust her head forward like a lizard, jaws snapping.

A *finger* extended from the white plane above her eyes. Four more bulging lumps appeared about the first. She cried out in some forgotten language.

Four fingers and a thumb grew from the forehead of the Empress. An entire hand sprouted now from her chest, emerging between her gory breasts. She whirled and fell to the flagstones, her flesh coiling and swelling. The hands became entire arms, thin and wiry. Male arms. A third leg grew from her abdomen, bare toes wriggling, then another grew beside it. A Man's legs. Four-legged and four-armed now, she bellowed and thrashed. Tong's stomach turned as he watched the contortions of her massive body.

Her ribcage swelled now, straining against her skin. Her thick white mane of hair turned to pale gray. One of the new arms sank back into her breast. It re-emerged with her beating heart held in its hand, squeezing red fluid like juice wrung from a lemon. It dropped the heart onto the filthy flagstones, and Ianthe's face wriggled near to it. Yet it was no longer her face. The eyes flickered red, purple, emerald, silver. The fangs fell one by one from her mouth like a codger's rotted teeth.

Now she was two beings at once. A second familiar face stared from the side of her skull. She leaped upright on all four legs, two white and two golden brown. One of the brown legs rose, then came down hard to squash the fallen heart like a bloated plum. A final scream poured from her toothless maw. The spasms ended, but her body continued to shift and flow like a waxen candle, burning itself into a new form.

Tong found his deadened limbs alive once more. He struggled to his feet, picked up his sword. The slaves about him awoke from their dark dream of obedience and humiliation. Meeting his defiant eyes, they took up their fallen weapons. The Sydathians too rose up from their submissive postures, sniffing at the being who slowly emerged from the flowing flesh of the sorceress. Tong already knew the face and the name it bore.

"Iardu!" he called out. The twisting, bulging head turned toward him and solidified at last into the face of the Shaper. Tong's heart soared. The wizard had not failed his people.

Now the sorcerer stood naked and tall as a Giant; there was no longer any trace of Ianthe but the greasy smear of pulp that had been her black heart.

Iardu's name was echoed by someone else. The black-haired girl who had defied Ianthe walked out from a welter of flaming trees, apparently unharmed. No longer wrapped in a sheath of flames but a simple gown of golden silk, she rushed forward to embrace Iardu. A silvery beard sprouted in an instant from his chin. Once again the Shaper stood ageless and brimming with power. Tong felt it cascading from his new-made body like heat from the dancing flames.

As they stood with arms wrapped about each other, Giant and Giantess diminished until they were only Man and Woman, each no taller than the slaves. Tong and his fellow freed men stared, speechless in the grip of awe. Here was a spectacle of the greatest sorcery, the likes of which most Men would never see in their entire lives. Here stood a pair of living miracles.

"Iardu! Iardu!"

Tong lifted his blade high and joined the voices of liberated slaves praising the sorcerer's name. Iardu waved a hand and conjured a flash of light. Now he stood again draped in an orange robe, a blue flame burning at the end of his silver neck chain.

"Tong of Khyrei," said the Shaper, "meet Sharadza, Queen of Yaskatha."

Tong bowed to her in the highest display of respect possible. Those behind him dropped to one knee. Here was a new God and Goddess they would venerate for generations. He faced Iardu as the ashy courtyard grew ever more crowded with rushing slaves and Sydathians. The mass of former slaves was invading the palace proper now, while the broad gardens lay in charred heaps and piles of dying embers. The battle was over. Now came the time of plunder, a necessary prelude to the time of renewal.

"I had thought you dead," he told the Shaper, "and all of us freed men and Sydathians to die with you."

Iardu grinned.

"What happened?" asked Sharadza. She, too, stood in awe of Iardu's rebirth.

Iardu glanced at the pitiful pile of bones and torn flesh that was his previous body.

"She wanted my blood," said the sorcerer. "My essence. So I let her take it. She should have known that her spirit could not contain my own." He watched the fingers of his new hands stretch and bend before his spectral eyes. "No one ever told her to be mindful of what she ate."

Tong laughed despite himself. This brought mirth to Sharadza's lips as well. Iardu's former flesh became a mound of white sand, already scattering beneath a gust of hot wind.

"Tong. What now?" asked a freed man. "Are the blood drinkers gone? Is the palace truly ours?"

"I will answer that," said Iardu. "The Empire of the South has fallen at last. Within this palace lies the crown of Khyrei. Find it now, and set it upon Tong's head. Will you have him as your King?"

The crowd of soot-faced survivors shouted and milled about Tong. They cried his name aloud, as they had cried Iardu's. The Sydathians danced and capered like children among the jubilant throngs.

"Hail Tong, King of New Khyrei!" shouted Iardu. This title caught the crowd's fancy, and it traveled quickly into the teeming streets. Men bellowed it among the rubble of the slave plaza and carried it down to the fleet of warships moored at the docks.

Tong stood quiet in the wash of their adulation. For the first time he realized that Iardu had used him as a pawn in some larger game. What the stakes of that great gamble might be, he could not guess. He did not know if he was truly worthy of Kinghood, although there would be no denying his people their choice. They rushed forward to sack the palace and find him a crown.

Iardu and Sharadza looked not at the King of Slaves, but at the high tower.

"There," said the Shaper. "One last errand for us, my dear."

Sorcerer and sorceress rose on currents of drifting smoke, shifting once more into a pair of golden eagles. They no longer shed flames from their bright feathers, yet the city itself writhed with flames. The smell of burning flesh mingled now with that of charred orchards and fields.

The twin eagles disappeared through the highest window of the barbed tower. Moments later one last dazzling eruption incinerated the upper half of the spire, leaving only a jagged, steaming scarp of stone.

Tong joined the mass of rushing Men and Sydathians as they poured into the black palace. No longer were these lofty halls sacrosanct, or safe from the vengeance of a long-denied people.

"Tong the King!" they cried, slapping his back and shoulders. "Tong the Liberator! Tong the Avenger!" They lifted him on their shoulders and carried him through opulent corridors.

They should be calling the name of Iardu and praising the Sydathians. How many thousands of the eyeless ones had died in the assault? How many valiant slaves had given their lives as well? He had not done this thing alone. He was only the face of it.

When they found the jeweled crown of seven points and placed it on his head, he neither smiled nor wept. He stood upon the elevated dais among the glassy columns of the throne room, still dressed in soiled rags. He remained wordless and full of doubt. Yet when he raised the blood-smeared sabre, an imperfect symbol of their vicious deliverance, Khyrein voices rose to rattle the black stones of the city.

Inside the barbed tower's uppermost chamber Sharadza and Iardu stood before the two circles of runes. There was no activity there now, no shadowstuff flowing across the floor to congeal in the midst of the looping sigils. Yet she knew such a thing would happen eventually. Here was the nexus of power for both Emperor and Empress. The true seat of their power, and the secret of their iron-handed rule.

"We must abolish these circles," Sharadza said. "And the stones of this entire chamber." She looked about at the implements of sorcery, recognizing the Glass of Eternity. It stood, identical to the mirror used by Elhathym in Yaskatha. The one she and Iardu had shattered after casting the necromancer into a trackless void. Its cloudy surface glimmered with no distinct reflection.

"Yes," Iardu said. "Though I fear it may already be too late." He glanced at the leaden glass and raised a hand. The mirror shattered into a million fragments, leaving its grotesque frame oddly empty.

"Shall we burn it?" she asked.

He nodded. "Fire is cleansing. I will do it. You must go south into the red jungle. You will find a great host of Men and Giants marching toward this city. Your brother Vireon marches at their head. Tell him what we have done here. Tell him the old Khyrei is no more: it has been freed from the grasp of Ianthe and Gammir." He turned and put his hands gently on her shoulders. "Make him *understand*, Sharadza. Khyrei is no longer the enemy of every other nation. Tell him to come in peace and meet the King of New Khyrei."

She blinked. Vireon in the jungle? The Giants marching to war? It was all so unexpected, yet she knew better than to doubt Iardu's words. Then it came to her in a flash of insight.

"You set all of this in motion, didn't you?" she asked.

"Speak with Vireon. Convince him that the war he seeks is not with the black city."

"You're bringing all the nations together here to fight the hordes of Zyung."

His chromatic eyes blazed. "You have always been a clever pupil. Perhaps too clever. Now, go!"

She faced the southern window. Portions of the blackened fields still blazed; the purple glow of morning was fouled by the reek of smoke and blood. Beyond the flaming landscape stood the vast crimson wilderness.

"I begin to understand the true reason you are called Shaper," she said.

He sang the ancient song.

Once more an eagle, she glided from the window.

Behind her the pinnacle of the high tower thundered and was no more.

20

On the Hidden Road

It was not the heat of the midday sun that woke him, but the stench of blood, feces, and rotten vegetation wafting from the mangled marshland. Weariness hung like an iron chain about his body, the invisible weight of it pressing him against the earth. He forced himself into a sitting position, grimacing at the ache of limbs and joints.

His skin was raw. Resting his elbows on his upraised knees, he saw that his color was no longer a sun-kissed bronze, but a ruddy copper. He looked like a creature born of the red jungle. His body ached, but his head was clear. This clarity filled him with a deep calm as he peered about the makeshift camp.

Dahrima stood leaning against the crimson bole of a jungle tree, a spear nestled between her folded arms. Her dark eyes were on him, but she did not trouble him with words. White bandages wrapped portions of both her arms and left thigh. Her corselet of black bronze showed the dents and scars of recent battle, and the mud on her boots was murky with congealed blood. The shadow of fatigue dulled the brightness of her face, yet her braided hair gleamed like red gold. On crude pallets beneath a canopy of low-hanging vines, the band of surviving

Uduri lay at rest, camped in a ring about Vireon while he slumbered.

A few other spearmaidens turned their faces toward him, watching as he forced himself to stand on wobbly legs. He put a hand against the tree until the jungle stopped spinning about his head. Beyond lay a rugged trail torn, stamped, and smashed into the jungle by Giants. The wide swathe of upturned soil and felled trees ran along a shallow hillside and disappeared into the steaming marsh. A flock of vultures picked at the carcasses and entrails littering the wetlands. Piles of Khyrein bodies bulged from the fen waters, dead black beetles in crumpled armor. The stubs of broken spears stood thick as weeds among the carnage.

The basalt fragments of the tower his mountainous foot had crushed lay a bowshot away. The muddy Giant-trail ran toward a massive campsite of felled trees stretching eastward into the jungle. Tents had been set up on the leveled ground for the care of wounded and dying men. Their moans floated to Vireon's ears on a warm breeze.

In a broad circle surrounding the tents of the wounded sat several legions of Udurumites and Uurzians, mostly cavalrymen tending to their horses. Their ranks seemed far thinner than before the swamp crossing. Vireon counted the green-gold banners of two full Uurzian legions, and a single Udurum legion milling beneath the Hammer and Fist standard.

He stood naked but for a loincloth someone had wrapped about his waist. His Giant-blade had been cleaned and polished to a cold blue shine. Dahrima, no doubt. It stood propped against the tree next to his pallet of sweat-stained blankets, its ornate scabbard missing. He coughed, spewing mucous and mud from the back of his throat onto the ground, then raised his eyes toward the roof of bloodshot foliage. From north and south came the deep cries of Giants, the clashing of metal and stone.

Dahrima brought him a skinful of fresh water. He took it and drained half its contents, wiped his parched lips with the back of his hand. "Tyro?" he asked.

"The Sword King lives." She nodded toward the crude northern trail. "Quite the warrior, that one. He took several legions and a cohort of Udvorg to bring down the watchtower between here and the coast. The one called Mendices took another force south to assault the nearest tower in that direction. The gate to Khyrei has been opened."

Vireon grunted, rubbing the back of his neck. Someone had tended him, wiped the filth from his body, carried him here, and provided his rude clothing. He looked up into Dahrima's tired face. She wore a look he had never seen before. Concern? Disbelief? Some other mysterious emotion that only a woman could put a name to?

"Men leading Giants," he said. "It seems unreal."

"They lead in *your* name," said Dahrima. "Othgar the Strong heads the northern contingent, Korek the Mace heads the southern."

Vireon nodded. "What are our numbers?"

"We lost twelve sisters." A cold blade in his heart. How many more of Dahrima's sisters would die because of their faith in him? "Nearly five hundred Udvorg and six brave Uduru are also dead."

Gods of Earth and Sky! So many deaths. And they had not even reached the black city.

"And the Men?"

She turned to stare at the collection of tents. Vireon saw a blue flame moving about the pavilions of the wounded. "Both armies lost a full legion to the swamp. A third of the horses are gone as well. Taken by the monster you killed. Yet the Border Legions of Khyrei are broken. Once the Swamp God died, victory was no great feat."

Vireon rolled the numbers through his mind, breathing deeply of the dank air. So many lost. But still the triple host stood strong and victorious.

"That blue-skin witch has some skill at healing," said Dahrima. She offered him a strip of dried beef. He waved it away. The memory of his torment inside the Swamp God's belly drove away all hunger. "That cold flame of hers restores the Udvorgs' strength instantly. I have never seen the like. Yet she will not use it on Men. Them she tends with herb and leaf. A fever has begun to spread among the legions. Varda says the filth of the swamp has poisoned their wounds."

Vireon asked for wine. When she returned with a skinful of some Uurzian vintage, he asked the question he had been dreading. "Any sign of Angrid?"

Dahrima shook her head. "Only his crown of black iron."

"Where is it?"

She motioned toward the blue flame dancing between the tents. "The witch keeps it. I believe she intends to make it yours. Now that you have proven yourself a true Giant."

Vireon swallowed wine and stretched his arms. Already the pain of his burned skin was lessening. He hoped Tyro and Mendices did not stray far in their campaign to take the nearest watchtowers. The legions there had likely fled in the face of defeat. The triple host would have to leave the wounded here at the edge of the jungle. The northern forces must move forward as soon as possible. Days of marching through the deadly jungle lay ahead of them.

"Any sign of a road in there?" he asked, pointing to the deep glades.

"Not much of one," Dahrima answered. "Little more than an overgrown footpath."

"It will serve," he said. "And be widened by our passage."

Varda walked toward him from the mass of Men and tents. She carried something in her free hand, a glimmering loop of metal. Angrid's crown.

He met her scarlet eyes as she came near. Her stature dwarfed his natural size, as did that of all Giants. His head barely reached the height of her waist. She sank to one knee before him, bringing their heads to a level. Her black hair was tousled and wild, full of briars, mud, and dust. Yet she carried a savage dignity. The azure flame quivered atop her staff.

She laid the crown at his feet and bowed her head. Vireon could not help but stare at it. A massive coronet of iron set with three great sapphires bright as the cold flame itself. At this size, he might only wear it as a belt.

A band of blue-skins came from the edges of the camp to stand about the scene. They followed Varda's lead, kneeling before the Son of Vod. The worn faces of twenty-eight Uduri turned toward him as well. Beyond the ring of Giant and Giantess, Men in pocked armor stared through the red gloom.

"Angrid is dead," said Varda. "His three heirs are only boys, and they are far from us. His crown falls to you, Vireon Vodson. Vireon the Slayer. Vireon the Man-Giant."

Vireon stared at the crown, then at the blue faces and white manes of the Giants.

"I already have a crown," he said. "It waits for me behind the gates of Udurum."

"We have seen your power, Great One," said Varda, her voice loud enough that all could hear her plainly. "You grew as your father did . . . tall enough to trample mountains . . . tall enough to reforge the world and release its deep waters . . . tall enough to crush the Swamp God and save us all. You are both Man and Giant. The Lord of Hosts. A Worthy King of All Giantkind. Only take this crown, and let it be so."

Vireon shook his head. The power of his father had finally leaped into his heart. At last he understood the awe and worship that Men and Giants held for Vod. "The crown should go to Angrid's blood. His eldest son when he comes of age."

"That will be another hundred years," said Varda. She lowered her voice for Vireon's sake. "Until then we need a King. Can you deny it? I have already told the Udvorg you would lead them in Angrid's stead. If I did not make this choice for you, we might abandon this war of yours and march back to our frosty climes. I will not have Angrid's death rendered meaningless. He died for your cause . . . your vengeance. Wear the crown, Vireon."

Vireon lifted the heavy loop of metal and held it in his hands, studying the intricate grooves of its ancient design. A ring of tiny runes was etched about the outer edge. The sapphires were each large enough to ransom a kingdom. He had never seen jewels that could rival them. Taking this crown would make him lord of two kingdoms. He considered the responsibility of such a thing, and he realized that Varda spoke truth. There was no real choice here. He could not afford to lose the Ice Giants as he had lost their ruler. Not with Khyrei and Ianthe so close.

He closed his eyes and willed himself larger. Fresh agony spread throughout his limbs, although this time he was prepared for it. As his flesh and bones expanded, he stifled the cry of pain that he desperately wanted to unleash. Then it was over, and he stood the full height of an Uduru. The Giants caught their breaths, and now even the Uduri kneeled in a show of amazed fealty.

Slowly but surely he lifted the iron crown — not so heavy now — to his head and placed it securely about his shaggy skull.

The Giants cheered his name. "Vireon! King of Giants! Lord of the Giantlands! Vireon!"

He endured it for a while, then waved them into silence. He bade them stand up, and now he stood in their midst as one of their own. He met Dahrima's eyes briefly and was surprised to see tears brimming there. They did not fall, only lingered above her cheeks like pools of silver light.

"I take this crown to honor the memory of Angrid the Long-Arm," he told them. "Until the day his eldest son comes to claim it along with his icy throne. Today, we march onward to finish what Angrid began. We march to end the tyranny of Khyrei. To bring down the walls of the black city!"

The cheers of Men joined those of the Giants. Vireon let it wash over him like a warm rain. Cherry-hued palm leaves fell from the branches, and flocks of bright birds fled the trees about the camp. He did not want to rule the blue-skins, but he had come all this way, dragging them along, to find justice for Alua and Maelthyn.

Justice or vengeance. Which was the truth? He would have to decide that later. There was no turning back now. No restoring the lives of the Men and Giants who had perished in the swamp. War was a decision that, once made, could never be reversed. Even if he refused the crown and lost the Udvorg, he would still march onward with the Men and the remaining Uduri. Knowing this, he could not afford to lose the might of the Ice Giants; that would only mean greater numbers of dead Men ahead. He must be their King. "Send riders to gather the cohorts of Tyro and Mendices," he ordered. He lifted the Giant-blade, light as a dagger in his behemoth hand. "We march to Khyrei before the sun dies."

Giants and Men scuffled to do his bidding, and to spread the word of the new Giant-King. The legend of Vireon the Slayer would only continue to grow. They had seen the breadth of his inherited sorcery. They knew what he was capable of, and it filled their hearts with confidence.

He turned to Dahrima. "A tunic, breastplate, and sandals," he said. "And I'll have a haunch of that beef now."

"As you wish, Majesty," she answered.

He sat himself upon one of the great stones from the smashed tower, drinking wine and chewing dried meat.

In his mind's eye the black gates of Khyrei stood already before him. All the deaths, the terror of the marshlands, he had expected these. Yet still he had not been prepared.

All these Men and Giants, dead because of me.

He drained the wineskin.

More would die gladly, screaming his name.

For the first time, he felt the true power of Kinghood.

It rivaled the power of the sorcery simmering in his veins.

Thank you, Father.

May the Gods forgive me.

Tyro rode at the head of a cavalry legion winding out of the northern jungle. His gray stallion was draped in a chain-mail caparison. Dark stains lay upon the silvery links, and the bearing of the Men who rode with him spoke of victory. They tossed laughter among themselves along with waterskins. Pale Khyrein heads hung by the hair from the pommels of saddles, although Tyro himself carried no such trophies. Shorn of their devilish masks the Khyrein faces were sad and wide-eyed, the faces of confused boys.

Tyro slid from the saddle and walked across the encampment to the great slab of basalt where Vireon sat brooding. His wineskin was empty, and he had called for another. Dahrima had gone to scrounge for the last of the Uurzian vintage. Vireon watched the King of Uurz approach in silence, admiring his outward display of strength. The rigors of combat and lack of sleep had lined the Sword King's face with wrinkles.

Tyro doffed his winged helm and unclasped his green cloak. He wore a fresh corselet, lacquered green with a golden sun spreading its rays across his chest. In the wake of the Uurzian cavalry marched the cohort of Udvorg. It was obvious they had done the bulk of the tower-toppling. They too held bundles of Khyrein heads as prizes, but these hung from their belts like clusters of pallid grapes. Their snowy manes were wild above faces of scowling indigo, red eyes deepened to maroon by the jungle gloom.

"King Vireon!" Tyro greeted him with a raised palm. The Emperor of Uurz stood barely a third of Vireon's size now. "You bear a new stature and a new crown this day. I salute your unmatched greatness. Our campaign is not without losses, but it goes well. The tower between this glade and the northern coast is fallen."

Tyro's brawny arms and legs were wrapped in bandages, stained maroon by the slow seeping of his blood. Beneath the lower lip of his gilded corselet showed the hem of more bandages, likewise reddened by the stress of riding. Vireon marveled at the man's endurance. He should be lying in one of the tents with Varda tending his wounds, yet he had led the northern sortie in Vireon's stead. Beads of sweat dropped from his forehead and chin. Signs of fever, or simply the signs of heat and fatigue? Vireon could not tell, so solid was the Uurzian's demeanor. Tyro slipped off the belt supporting his broadsword and laid it against the block of basalt.

"It gladdens me to see you hearty and whole," said Vireon. "The Udvorg have named me their King in the wake of Angrid's fall."

"So I hear," said Tyro, stripping off his breastplate. More leaking bandages. The worst of them was a growing blot of crimson above his right hip. He grimaced at the pain of removing the corselet, making sure that none but Vireon saw his face. "Your Uduri have found our route to the black city. Mendices will return before sunset with the rest of our legions. We may rest here tonight and march at dawn. We are close, Brother. So close!"

"No," said Vireon. "We march tonight. If we wait until dawn the city may be warned by those who have escaped the towers. Already we risk that chance."

Tyro accepted a cup of wine from an Uurzian captain. He poured the drink into his mouth and stared at the Giant-King. The sounds of jungle birds rattled among the treetops. Tyro mopped his face and brow with a wet cloth. At last he nodded.

"You speak wisdom," Tyro said. "We'll leave the wounded here then, with a cohort of horsemen to guard them. Can you spare a few Giants for this purpose?"

Vireon looked toward the tents. Hundreds of Men lay suffering beneath the flimsy canvas structures. There would be jungle cats, vipers, and possibly outlying squads of Khyreins. "Thirty Udvorg will stand with your horsemen."

"Very well," said Tyro. With a slight groan he settled himself on a smaller piece of stone and took a deep breath. "They can begin the process of burying the slain."

Vireon nodded.

"How long do you intend to maintain this . . . bulk?" asked Tyro.

"I am their King," Vireon said. "It is fitting."

Tyro smiled and drained his cup. A warrior came forward with a poultice and rolls of linen. He began removing the bindings from Tyro's wounds one at a time, cleaning the raw flesh and replacing the bandages with new ones. The gash in Tyro's side was crudely stitched together. He would bear a mighty scar there for the rest of his days.

"Sleep now if you can," Vireon said. "I see the weariness in your face. But we must move into the jungle. Soon."

Tyro agreed. He walked toward the sea of tents, taking pains to hide his limp. The sound of breaking trees filled the glade. The Udvorg were expanding their camp yet again. Tyro halted and turned back to Vireon. "We found fresh meat and produce in the northern tower. Along with wine and medicines. We secured it all before the Giants demolished the structure. They would conquer the world for you if you asked them." He turned and disappeared among the tents.

Vireon stared into the depths of the red jungle.

"Khyrei will be enough."

The poison jungle enclosed them in its endless corridors of leaf, root, stem, and fern. Vireon was glad to leave the stink of the marsh and its rotting dead behind him. The jungle was full of perils: every berry, blossom, or sprout that grew here would bring a quick death. The host would find no easy game to hunt in the sweltering wilderness. Quickly passing through was the northern Kings' best chance of limiting fever and death among the Men.

Mendices had returned to camp shortly after Tyro, announcing a similar victory in the south. Vireon gave him two hours to rest, then called for the breaking of camp and resumption of the march. The hawk-nosed Warlord of Uurz had survived thus far without a single wound. Here was a man skilled at letting others do the fighting for him. Unlike Tyro, Mendices had held back and directed his ranks from a vantage point of security. How he had managed this even in the depths of the Swamp God's terrain, Vireon had no idea. He would not underestimate the war skill of Tyro's general. Even the Udvorg now spoke of him with respect.

With only an hour of daylight remaining, the triple host entered the deep jungle. Vireon took his man-sized form again and rode alongside Tyro on a sable charger. The crown of iron and sapphire shrank to fit his head, along with his new tunic and sandals. The Giant-blade in its new scabbard on his back did not change its size; his strength as a human was still that of an Uduru. Like his father, he was now both Giant and Man. What that would ultimately mean, he could only guess. His skin had already healed to its customary shade of bronze. A corselet of boiled leather, black with golden trim, held the clasps of his purple cloak at the shoulders.

The Uduri formed an unofficial vanguard, scouting ahead and clearing the overgrown road. Even a Giant could not run full speed through the dense undergrowth without falling face first into a thicket, a ravine, or patch of stubborn mire. The hidden road was an ancient one, likely cut from the jungle fresh every few months for the passage of Khyrein troops or supply trains. Yet the forest crept quickly back to reclaim the ground every time. The Uduri were skilled trackers and hunters: they followed the road with little difficulty, carving it free of encroaching vegetation with axe and sword.

Behind the two mounted Kings came Varda and a cohort of Udvorg calling themselves the King's Guard. Where they had served Angrid, they now served Vireon. When more than half their number had died along with the blue-skin King, other Udvorg stepped forth to fill the ranks, anxious to serve their new monarch. Vireon reckoned they had never seen such power as he wielded against the leviathan. This was true of himself as well, though none would believe it if he told them so. He kept his wonder at his newfound powers to himself, bearing the gift of his father as he bore the crown of the Icelands. Both were only tools. Weapons he must carry to win this war.

Hordes of carmine bats flitted between the massive trees. The roars of tigers filled distant glades, yet none of the great cats was foolish enough to approach the host. Behind the first cohort of Udvorg came the legions of Udurum marching shoulder to shoulder with the Uurzians. Despite their losses and the cloud of weariness that hung about them, morale was high. All of these Men and Giants had witnessed a miracle tall enough to shake the foundations of the world. Was this how Men had regarded Vod in the glory of his youth? Did they expect Vireon now to follow Vod's course, to reshape the landscape of nations? Perhaps he was already engaged in such a bold venture. He chose not to think of destiny and fate and the future, but to concentrate on the bloody road before him.

At the rear of the host came a second cohort of Udvorg, with the few surviving Uduru mixed among them. Here Mendices rode with his honor guard. If any Khyrein forces were to approach them from behind, however unlikely this was, Vireon trusted that Mendices would be up to the challenge.

The jungle might be a wonderland painted in a thousand shades of magenta, were it not for the poisonous nature of its flora and the unknown menace of its fauna. As night spread its wings over the vanguard, shades of glimmering scarlet turned to deepest black, and the jungle lost its eerie color. The host proceeded by torchlight. In the grip of constant shadow, Vireon found it easy to imagine himself traveling the road of some northern forest, albeit in a time of great heat. The muggy air had cooled only slightly with the falling of night.

Midway through the night march Tyro wavered in his saddle like a drunken man. Vireon called for a brief respite. Men lay down upon the rough road and slept for perhaps an hour, while the Giants traded war stories and swapped kegs of wine from the downed watchtowers. Varda went among them scattering the coolness of the blue flame. It revived the Udvorg far more than a full night's sleep would have done for the Men.

Vireon discussed siege plans with Mendices while Tyro lay slumbering by the side of the road, a guard of twelve Uurzians stationed about his pallet. Varda examined his wounds while he slept, calling for a new set of bandages. She prepared a fresh poultice for the worst of his lacerations. When she was finished, she breathed on the blue flame and it flashed in Tyro's face, waking him as surely as a toss of cold water.

The triple host marched on through the night, surrounded by the curious and indecipherable sounds of the dark jungle. A viper crawled across the road and bit the leg of a horse, which had to be put down. The archers among the Men began a grim game then, watching with nocked arrows for any sign of viper or crawling vermin. Before dawn broke over the scarlet canopy, seventeen such reptiles had been skewered by feathered shafts, along with nine venomous toads. Hundreds of soldiers stumbled in the grip of fever now. It spread slowly through the ranks, but the host moved onward. The heat of day returned swiftly, and the jungle came alive in a thousand shades of red.

In the hour after dawn, with the jungle stretching away in all directions, the Uduri came back from their scouting with three Khyrein captives. The warriors spoke only Khyrein, and there were few interpreters among the triple host. The northmen had not come south to speak, but only to slay. Yet Vireon could tell from the motions of the Khyreins' hands and faces that they had fled the black city in the wake of something terrible. Tyro questioned them for a while, but could gain nothing of any use. He ordered them put to death, since the traveling host could not spare resources to escort prisoners.

In the second hour after dawn, Dahrima reported to Vireon that other Khyreins were fleeing southward. Some of these groups were as large as military cohorts, but they marched in fear, fleeing into the mazy deeps of the jungle when they saw the Uduri. Vireon ordered one of his warriors to climb a lofty tree – the highest here grew three times the height of Giants – and the scout reported seeing the Golden Sea on the distant horizon. A pall of black smoke hung between it and the jungle's edge. The climber felt sure the black city must have lain within his sight, if only smoke was not obscuring the vista. Another day, perhaps a day and a half, and the triple host would reach its destination.

Vireon was ready to call another respite when the crimson canopy split beneath the wings of a golden eagle. It flapped down to perch in the road within a knife's throw of Vireon's horse. The great bird seemed unnatural both to the climate and the color of the jungle. It stood tall as a man, proud beak and black eyes focusing on the Giant-King. Vireon called the host to a halt. Tyro, who had ridden in silence, raised his head to stare at the eagle. About the two Kings rang the sounds of swords being drawn from their scabbards.

A flash of light blinded the vanguard for a moment. When Vireon's vision cleared seconds later, a Giantess with a familiar face stood where the eagle had been. Her long black hair stirred in a wind that he could not feel. Green eyes flashed against the copper gloom.

"Sharadza . . ." He called out the name of his sister with sudden certainty. There was no doubting that face or those eyes, though he had never seen her standing at the height of an Uduri before now. This double height must be the mark of their inheritance. She also shared Vod's gift. He could not help but smile at the sight of her.

"Vireon." She beamed, and bowed to one knee. "Greetings King of Udurum." She said it proudly, and he knew she rejoiced to see him. How many years had it been? He had thought her safely nestled in the bosom of D'zan's palace in Yaskatha. Obviously, there were many things about his sister that he had yet to learn. She was no longer a girl, but a grown woman.

Far more than that. A sorceress.

"And King of the Icelands," added Varda from somewhere behind him. "Lord of the Giantlands."

Vireon leaped off his horse and rushed to wrap Sharadza in his arms. A sudden burst of emotion brought tears to his eyes as he grew to match her Uduri tallness. The pain of it was barely noticeable this time. She laughed and squeezed him desperately. He pulled back to look at her. She wore only a gown of golden silk.

It matched the feathers she had worn as an eagle, and her feet were bare. Her body seethed with a great heat, as if she were the antithesis of Varda's blue flame.

"You've grown taller," he said, grinning.

"And you!" she replied.

Again they embraced, and Vireon felt the host milling and clanking with restless activity behind him. He turned round and called for a fresh respite. Men dismounted and found their places to rest. Tyro stayed alert upon his gray stallion, his eyes focused on the Giant brother and sister.

"Why are you here in this forsaken place?" Vireon asked. "You should be in Yaskatha."

She frowned, then smiled. "I come from the liberation of Khyrei. We have much to discuss."

He waved Tyro forward. The three of them, along with Dahrima and Varda, sat in a circle upon a square of muddy blankets. Sharadza told them of the great rebellion, the burning of the fields, the taking of the city, and the crowning of a humble slave as the King of New Khyrei. She spoke of Iardu, and the eyeless Sydathians that poured out of the jungle to foster the liberation of an oppressed people. Finally, she spoke of Gammir, who had been their brother Fangodrel in another life. Gammir, whose head Vireon had removed eight years ago. Yet he had lived again in a new body formed of blood and shadows.

"I have burned his life away," she said. "He will trouble us no more."

"What of Ianthe?" Vireon asked. His heart pounded.

Poor little Maelthyn.

"She drank the blood of Iardu," said Sharadza, "and it destroyed her. She, too, is no more."

Vireon stood and paced about the road. An abiding emptiness yawned in his stomach. His fingers and toes felt numb. His own sister had stolen his vengeance. Somewhere among the ranks a Giant's voice bellowed a hunting song.

Tyro stared at Sharadza in disbelief. "Surely this is some trick," he said. "How do we know you are truly Vireon's sister, not some minion of the Claw? You might tell us anything."

"Have you not seen the black smokes rising in the north?" she asked.

Tyro had no answer.

"And the refugees fleeing south," said Dahrima. "Yes, we have seen them."

"I speak only truth," said Sharadza. "Khyrei has fallen. Tong the Liberator now wears the crown. It happened only last night. The black city is no longer in the hands of Gammir and Ianthe. The last of the Slaving Empires is broken. There is only the black city and a multitude of freed slaves. *They* will decide what happens next."

"No," said Tyro, rising painfully to his feet. "We have come to storm the black city and storm it we will. What should we do — turn round and march home? Dishonor our fallen comrades with cowardice? No, our crusade must continue. We will show this Slave King mercy, but his city must fall before Uurz and Udurum, not before an army of beasts and slaves."

"There is more," Sharadza said. Her emerald eyes turned to Vireon. "Iardu sends me with a message for you and your host. You come to fight a war, and war you shall have. But Khyrei is not your enemy. Not anymore. The true enemy comes from across the Golden Sea. From the other side of the world."

Tyro tossed his wineskin to the ground. "What nonsense!" He turned as if to plead with Vireon. "What enemy could be greater than Khyrei the Wicked? *The other side of the world?*" He turned back to Sharadza. "You speak in riddles, woman. Stand aside and let us pass or be trampled 'neath our hooves."

Vireon's hand reached out to grab Tyro's shoulder. "You speak to my sister and the Queen of Yaskatha. Be mindful of your tongue."

Tyro stared at him in disbelief. "Surely you don't believe this mummery? Not *you*, Vireon. Can you not see a snare when it is set at your very feet?"

"Follow me to the black city," said Sharadza. "See for yourself. Speak with Iardu and let him show you what the future holds. Your enemy comes from beyond the sea, not from the black city."

Tyro turned his angry face to her again. "I will hear no wizard's words! We've come south to *slay* two wizards, not to fall for their tricks." A feverish heat burned in the Sword King's face. Vireon saw this, even if Tyro himself did not. For all his courage, all his might in battle, he was still only a Man, with a Man's weaknesses.

"We will hear Iardu," Vireon said. If Ianthe were dead already, what else could he do? And yet ... she had been dead before. Hiding in the womb of Alua ... waiting to be reborn. Perhaps vengeance was beyond his reach. Perhaps justice had already been delivered by Iardu, Sharadza, and a horde of eyeless monsters. The tale seemed incredible, yet this was surely Sharadza, and she surely would not lie to her brother.

Tyro scowled at Vireon. "You may hear the sorcerer, but I will not."

"You will," said Vireon, glowering at him.

A moment of awkward silence hung between the two Kings.

"*You* are not the Emperor of Uurz," Tyro whispered. Beads of sweat glistened on his red face.

"No," said Vireon. "I am the Lord of the Giantlands. If you were not my friend and ally, I might slay you this moment and take your legions for my own."

Tyro's hand hovered above the pommel of his broadsword. His nostrils flared and his dark eyes smoldered.

"You would not dare," he said, voice ringing with a stubborn defiance.

"Come and hear Iardu's words," said Vireon. "Then make your decision."

Tyro folded his bandaged arms and gritted his teeth. He stared into the tangle of vines beneath the great red trees. "It seems I have little choice." He wiped at the sweat streaming from his brow.

Sharadza smiled, raising her voice to dispel the tension.

"A Council of Kings, then," she said.

Tyro stalked away to find Mendices. Vireon watched his green cloak flapping among the restive Men and Giants.

"What is this new enemy?" he asked.

Sharadza looked at him. She had his mother's eyes and kindly face. He loved her. Had he ever told her so? Suddenly he missed Tadarus, his dead brother. He longed for the sweet faces of Alua and Maelthyn.

The world was filled with death, an endless ocean of it. Tiny islands of joy floated on that sea of woe. He stood on such an island at this very moment, knowing the dark waters would soon rush in to drown him once again.

"Zyung," she said, and would say no more until they reached the gates of the black city.

21

A Council of Kings

Two hundred sable warships with prows like horned devils lay at anchor in the Khyrein bay. Galley slaves had set fire to the five ships nearest the wharves after breaking the chains of their rowing benches and rushing the decks. The burning hulks sank slowly into the turquoise water, sending plumes of black vapor to join the great pall hanging between city and sun. The bodies of strangled Onxy Guards floated like driftwood or sank to watery graves. A crowd of slaves milled about the docks, liberating trade goods from the vessels.

Along the seaward horizon more smoke rose into the cerulean sky. A forest of white and crimson sails stretched as far as the eye could see. The navies of Mumbaza and Yaskatha had arrived with deadly force, sinking nineteen outward-bound Khyrein reavers since sunrise. No more of the black ships would flee the liberated harbor to face the jaws of the double fleet.

Tyro sat uncomfortably on the back of his mailed charger and scanned the ocean vista. According to figures presented by Mendices, this accounted for more than half the entire Khyrein fleet. At least a hundred more reavers plied the waters between the mainland and the Jade Isles, or roamed the high sea in search of traders to board and plunder.

Had revolution in the black city not occurred when it did, these two hundred rammers in the bay would be sailing now to engage the armadas of D'zan and Undutu. As it was, the sea battles were already done. The outlying ships had been overwhelmed by numbers far superior to their own. The double fleet sailed closer to the shore, skirting the smoking debris.

Tyro's eyes could not see all the ships approaching in a double wedge formation, but he counted at least three hundred of D'zan's golden triremes and four hundred of Undutu's glistening swan-ships. *Gods of Sea and Sky, what a battle it would have been!* Enough to turn the Golden Sea crimson. But the two Southern Kings, like Tyro, had been robbed of the chance to wage a full-scale war.

Instead of storming the city, the northerners must make peace with a ragged army of slaves. If not for the eyeless apelings moving through the cluttered streets, sniffing like half-wild hounds, these ignorant rebels could never have succeeded in throwing off the yoke of servitude. If not for the intervention of Iardu the Shaper and Sharadza Vodsdaughter, who was apparently the wizard's apprentice – or lover – *none* of this would have turned out the way it did. There would have been a river of blood spilled here, and the glorious legend of Khyrei's fall at the hands of Uurz would have ensued.

Tyro's wounds itched beneath his many bandages. The heat of the delta was oppressive, so much so that he doffed his war helm and golden corselet. What need of these things when there would be no more battle? For a moment he considered commandeering one of D'zan's ships and taking to the open sea in search of any absent Khyrein vessels. Now the bulk of fighting would be out on the Golden Sea, where crews of black-masked raiders had yet to recognize the end of the empire they served. Some would return and perish in a mad attempt to drive off the invading fleets. Others would roam the waves for decades, mercenaries and pirates without King or country. Still others would desert their broken fleet and find new lives in the Island Kingdoms.

So many Khyreins would escape paying for their crimes. It galled him.

The great slave auction plaza had become a stage for public executions. Onyx Guards, stripped of arms and armor, were chained there awaiting the mercy of the Slave King. Already Tyro had seen the masked heads of Khyrein soldiers impaled on the tips of pikes lining the market square and decorating every street corner. In death the oppressors were allowed to keep their faces hidden, a final and most brutal irony.

The flames in city and field had begun to die away, but the sickly-sweet odor of charred flesh had replaced the reek of tarry smoke. Tyro's gut churned; sweat poured from his brow and limbs, staining his green tunic with perspiration. His right palm moved anxiously over the jeweled pommel of the broadsword at his side.

Mendices sat beside him on a chestnut stallion. The Warlord still wore his breastplate, although even he had removed the visored helm to mop his face with a towel. He spoke little as they waited, but his eyes said that he shared Tyro's disappointment. Iardu had stolen their victory and given the city over to its slaves. There would be no spoils of war here, no songs of Uurzian triumph. In negotiating with this Slave King he might secure some reparations for the cost of the venture, but it would pale in comparison to the utter conquest he had intended. Vireon had proven his greatness yet again, and Tyro could do nothing but accept his demands. They must hear the Shaper's words.

The newly crowned Giant-King sat nearby on his own black steed. Tyro was glad Vireon had assumed his normal height again.

The Giant Vireon was someone whose eyes Tyro could not meet, whose massive hand Tyro could not shake. He did not trust the Giant Vireon, the sorcerer who could grow to the size of a mountain. Still, he was glad to have an ally of such power. He must only discover how to bend Vireon's will to his own. The Son of Dairon would not long stand in second place to the King of Udurum, be he Man, Giant, or both.

Vireon showed little discomfort in the torrid heat. Near to him, as ever, stood the blonde Giantess called Dahrima, leaning on her great spear. Whether she was Vireon's bodyguard or lover, Tyro could not say. The blue-skinned witch Varda stood at Vireon's other side. She must represent the Udvorg now that Angrid was dead; even though Vireon was their King, this shamaness would have great power over the Ice Giants. Tyro nearly asked for a blast of her blue flame to cool his mounting fever. However, such a request would only make him look foolish, and she was likely to refuse him anyway. Varda had great skill at healing Giants, but had shown little of that facility with Men.

Sharadza had followed Vireon's lead and taken the size of a human woman. She stood now at the side of the uncouth Slave King himself. That robust man of scars rode no horse, but stood bare-chested amid the northern monarchs, his only garb a kilt of blackened bronze plates, leather sandals, and the seven-pointed crown he had stolen from Gammir. A pack of the eyeless creatures lingered about him always, crouching like apes, horned heads bobbing at the level of his waist. Perhaps forty such creatures, fishbelly pale and grotesquely proportioned, answered to the Slave King's unspoken commands. Three other former slaves stood amid that ring of pale flesh, the Slave King's advisors. Barely more than boys in scuffed black corselets, wearing Khyrein sabres which they likely had no skill in wielding.

A cohort of three hundred Uurzian legionnaires and a hundred

Udvorg stood behind the assembled Kings and their retinues. Beyond the looming Northern Gate, the city with its shattered palace still blazed in places, and the chaos of freedom spilled like angry waters along every street. The houses of nobles had been raided, and many a former high-ranking citizen now lingered in chains alongside former members of the Onyx Guard. It remained to be seen how many would find justice in their new King, and how many would find only slaughter.

A sextet of ships sailed into the harbor now, preceding the bulk of the double fleet. These were the flagships of D'zan and Undutu, flying the Sword and Tree banner and the standard of the Feathered Serpent. Behind each flagship came an escort of two ships each. The remainder of the allied armadas dropped anchor a league from shore, effectively blockading Khyrei and its single port.

Tyro saw D'zan standing in the prow of his lead ship *Kingspear*. The Yaskathan insignia fluttered on the billowing sail above him. The gleam of his silver mail was as brilliant as the scarlet cloak rippling from his shoulders. Tyro recognized the hilt of the greatsword strapped to the Yaskathan King's back. That weapon had served D'zan well during the campaign to take back his throne eight years past. Its seasoned blade had ultimately taken the life of the Usurper Elhathym. Tyro felt a tinge of regret that he would not see that fine blade in action against the forces of Khyrei. He had trained D'zan to wield the weapon and had looked forward to greeting his old friend on the field of battle, once Ianthe's navy had been smashed. Instead they would meet at the table of the Slave King, blades kept firmly in their scabbards.

Alongside the *Kingspear* came the *Bird of War*, forerunner of the Mumbazan fleet. Standing proud in its forecastle was Undutu, youngest of the assembled monarchs, a splendid sight in pearly scale mail, ostrich-plumed helmet, and cloak of white and gold.

His ebony face gleamed handsome and bright beneath the peaked helm. He clutched a royal spear hung with a myriad of brilliant feathers, and the Feathered Serpent insignia coiled across the breast of his hauberk. At his side stood a man in a white robe with a staff of brown wood, an advisor or court wizard, Tyro presumed. His headdress was a mass of crimson plumage that matched perfectly his cloak of feathers. Above the flagships soared a golden eagle identical to the one Sharadza had been yesterday. It glided above the fat sails, heading ever inland, guiding the two Kings' vessels between the black hulls of abandoned Khyrein ships. There could be no doubt that the eagle was Iardu. The Shaper had gone to greet the armada with news of the Slave King's ascension.

Tyro wondered if D'zan and Undutu would be as frustrated with the turn of events as he was. Surely young Undutu had been looking for a chance to prove his manhood in this war that was not to be. As for D'zan, he would be a father soon, so this was his last true chance at martial glory, an opportunity to set his mark on history. In that, he shared Tyro's ambition. The Sword King was certain he could win the southern monarchs to his side as he had done previously. Perhaps the black city would still fall. Vireon was Lord of the Giantlands, but he had no right to decide the policies of Uurz, Mumbaza, or Yaskatha. Now that the bulk of the Khyrein military had been lost or humbled, he would no longer need the Giants to take this broken kingdom.

Let the Giant-King take his Udvorg and march back to his frigid lands.

The flagships dropped anchor and the Southern Kings prepared to disembark, each with a small train of mailed guards. Undutu's feathery advisor walked beside him. Tyro supposed he must be a personage of great power. Then he recognized the dark face with its shrewd eyes. This potentate was none other than Khama, famed wizard of Mumbaza. Tyro had met him briefly on the trek to Yaskatha during the time of D'zan's crusade. Khama dressed like a Lord of Shepherds, but his reputation as a legendary force for peace preceded him. How he must have tried to talk Undutu out of this war. And how pleased he must be that there was so little battle and carnage for his young King to endure. Tyro knew full well that Khama would back Iardu's call to end the war before it had begun. Whatever imaginary enemy the Shaper had dreamed up to take the place of Gammir and Ianthe, the Emperor of Uurz could not guess.

Vireon and Tyro dismounted as the Southern Kings descended the gangplanks of their ships and joined the assemblage on the dockside. Tyro's blood raced like fire in his veins. Here now stood all the Kings of the civilized world. To count the Slave King among them was difficult for him, but he had little choice. This soft-spoken, simple-minded field worker had risen to their level, buoyed by his army of fanged beasts and underfed slaves. The King of New Khyrei had not a drop of royal blood in his body. Even when Dairon had replaced the Old Regime in Uurz, he at least held the honor of being cousin to the old Emperor.

What sort of King would a risen slave be? Tyrant or Fool?

Tyro embraced first D'zan, then Undutu, exchanging his forced smile for their genuine ones. Vireon greeted them warmly, and the Slave King bowed before both of them. The golden eagle dropped out of the sky to perch near Sharadza. A flash of brilliance and Iardu stood where the bird had landed, a blue flame glowing on the breast of his vermilion robe.

The Shaper himself bowed to the assembled Kings. "His Majesty Tong the Avenger, King of New Khyrei, has prepared a pavilion for our meeting," proclaimed the wizard. "While his people labor to extinguish the last of the flames ignited by their liberation, he hopes to honor you with wine and delicacies from his fractured palace."

Iardu guided the procession away from the docks to a great tent spreading high above a long table of cherry wood. It sat heavy with steaming meats, sliced fruits, braised vegetables, green cheeses, and decanters of ancient wine. The King's pavilion stood at the base of the city's northern wall and directly to the east of the main gate. The massive portal stood open to an endless stream of freed men and families. The messy process of redistributing the wealth and goods of an entire city had begun, with little guidance from the Slave King.

The same slaves who had cooked such foods for Ianthe now cooked for the Slave King. Tyro found it nauseating. He shook his head at Tong's lack of language skills. This Man of the Fields knew only the tongue of Khyrei, so Iardu must speak for him. This troubled Tyro deeply, but he said nothing of it. He saw the same worry in the eyes of Mendices. Vireon's face remained mysterious, his eyes like black pearls behind clouded glass. Were they the eyes of a Giant or a Man?

The five Kings and their followers topped a gentle slope and entered the shade of the pavilion. Tyro sighed and sat himself in the nearest of the great chairs. He watched the eyeless ones mill about and was relieved when they did not join their human King at the table. His stomach churned again, and he reached for a jeweled goblet. Sharadza herself responded by pouring his cup full of amber Yaskathan wine, most likely robbed by Khyrein raiders from some innocent tradeship. In any case, it lingered cool and refreshing on his tongue.

The Kings took their places about the board with the Slave King at its head. Directly across from Tong, at the table's opposite end, sat Vireon with Dahrima at his right and Varda at his left. Of course the Man-Giant would choose that place of honor, directly facing the King of New Khyrei. Tyro bristled, held his tongue, and quaffed more wine.

The reign of the Slave King was so new that he had not even a banner to hang at his back. Instead, the ocean gleamed aquamarine beyond the ornate wings of his chair; the crown of obsidian and rubies sparkled on his brow. Unlike his boyish advisors, the King of New Khyrei had been scrubbed clean of soot, grime, and blood. His flesh, touched by the daily sun of plantations, was slightly less pale than the average Khyrein, but his black almondine eyes were unmistakable. He carried silence in those eyes, a quiet wisdom where Tyro had expected to see only insolent savagery.

Tyro enjoyed a broad view of the southern fleets, as well as the crowded harbor. He sat across from D'zan and Undutu. Khama took a seat at Undutu's elbow while Mendices joined Tyro on his left. A pack of the eyeless ones sat on their haunches in a protective crescent some small distance behind Tong the Avenger. His human advisors went off to supervise some function of rebuilding or properly looting the city.

D'zan was the first King to speak. "Well, this was a quick war indeed." He grinned, and others caught his humor. Tyro had no patience for it.

"Yet a long time in coming," said Iardu.

Heads nodded as cups were filled.

"This heat is oppressive," said Tyro, wiping at his brow. "Let's get on with it."

Iardu eyed him curiously with flashing eyes. "I have assembled you Kings North and South here to reveal a great secret. For the first time in history, the rulers of six kingdoms have come together in peace. This is quite an achievement, something your ancestors would have thought impossible. The time for warring among ourselves is past. Old feuds, lingering grudges, and ancient hatreds . . . these are to be cast aside. The world has come together in this place of rebirth. Let us drink to Peace." The Shaper raised his cup and the guests followed his example. Tyro raised his own chalice, but set it down again without drinking.

"You speak what we already know, Wizard," said Tyro. "Tell us now this great secret of yours."

"In good time," Iardu said. "First I would tell you the story of Tong the Liberator, King of New Khyrei. Since he does not yet speak the northern dialects, I will be his tongue."

The wizard spoke of Tong's life under the lash, of his personal tragedy, his flight into the jungle, and his bonding with the Sydathians. Eyebrows raised in wonder as he spoke of the underground city where the eyeless ones kept their own kingdom. He told the Kings of the slave rebellion led by Tong, which spread like hungry flames to a hundred thousand slaves. He spoke briefly of a sorcerous battle with Gammir and Ianthe, which the tyrants lost.

Tyro doubted the truth of Iardu's words when he said they were gone. "Are they *dead*, then?" he asked. "Both Emperor and Empress?"

Iardu responded with a moment of silence before he answered. "As much as sorcerers can ever truly die, yes, they are dead. Yet even if their deceased state does not prove permanent, their grip on Khyrei is gone forever. The black city is no longer theirs. The institution of slavery, which served as the bedrock of their reign and the reigns of those before them, is no more."

"It is plain to see that *you* have done this thing," said Khama, his first words since arriving. The ocean breeze ruffled the gaudy feathers of his headdress, and he waved brown fingers when he talked. "The Shaper has once again influenced the affairs of Men and Giants, molding them to suit his needs."

All eyes fell upon Iardu. "Khama, my old friend," smiled the Shaper, "as an isolationist, I know it must seem that way to you. Yet I did not achieve these ends on my own. Nor are they solely for my own good. In fact, quite the contrary."

"So why have you intervened and stolen this war from us?" asked Tyro.

"Please," said Sharadza, looking at him with eyes like emeralds. "Let him speak."

Iardu took a deep breath and rubbed his silvery beard. "If anything I have merely given your kingdoms the gift of peace. Yes, I worked to achieve certain ends. When you hear what I have to say, you will understand why I have done so." He stood then, walking about the table in a slow and purposeful gait.

"You are the Council of Kings," he said. "You represent the whole of your world, yet you do not know that this world you rule is part of a greater whole."

"Spare us your riddles," said Vireon. His face was grave. Sharadza shot him a glance of concern, and he seemed to soften.

"To put it simply," said Iardu, "there is another world on the opposite side of our own. And it is coming to claim us."

"Another riddle," said Undutu. His black arms had grown thick with muscle. His golden armlets were the very likeness of coiling cobras. Tyro had last seen him as a skinny boy sitting on a throne of opals that was far too large for him. Now the young King was a grown warrior. The calluses and scars of martial training lay upon his knuckles and forearms. His golden cutlass in a scabbard crusted with topaz and pearls was not a thing meant strictly for show. It was a killing tool. His voice rang deep, no trace of the boy remaining in it. "Do you speak of the Southern Isles . . . or the Jades?"

"No, Majesty," said Iardu. "Perhaps Sharadza will explain the true nature of the world."

Sharadza did not stand, but she took a pomegranate from an ivory bowl and held it above the table. She explained that the true world was made in the shape of this purple fruit. That it was a round thing, with two separate hemispheres separated by vast expanses of ocean. "Never have the two sides of this sphere met or mingled," she finished. "Until now."

Her eyes fell upon the pacing Iardu.

"A threat greater than any war in history approaches us," said Iardu. "Only by uniting the whole of your forces can you hope to survive what is to come."

"What is to come?" D'zan echoed the wizard's words.

"*Invasion*," said Iardu. The Kings and their advisors stiffened. Mendices glanced at Tyro. Was that fear or disbelief in his eyes? A little of both.

"You speak contrary to the wisdom of our greatest scribes, historians, and explorers," said Tyro. "Show us your proof of this outrageous claim."

"I will do you one better," said Iardu. "I will show you the *future*. It is within my power to catch a glimpse of What Is To Come." He spread his hands and a cloud of golden mist sprang from his fingertips to hang over the table. "Look hard into this golden cloud," said Iardu. "Look with your eyes, your minds, and your hearts. See the truth of what approaches."

The sparkling cloud shifted and writhed with contrasting colors. Shapes moved and gleamed behind a veil of luminous vapor. All eyes at the table were transfixed by it. Now the golden curtains parted and Tyro felt he stood before a great window, gazing into some part of the world that was far from the shores of Khyrei. Images came clearly into focus as he watched.

Between a wide-open sea of dazzling green and a sky full of scattered clouds, a fleet of strangely made ships moved across the world. Their sharp keels did not touch the waters below, yet the wild winds filled their sails of blue, green, red, and violet. On the sides of each lean sky-galleon, two more sails hung horizontally, wafting up and down like great featherless wings. An unknown sigil, sharp and heavy-lined, lay upon the sail of each aerial vessel.

Men in baroque armor stalked about the decks, faces hidden behind slitted visors, the implements of war gleaming in their mailed fists. Spearmen stood in a shipbound forest of upright shafts, their blades ornate and barbed, the inventions of master blacksmiths. Each of the vast soaring warships carried an entire legion of grim warriors. And there came *thousands* of the impossible vessels.

The host numbered in the millions. Their armor gleamed in the dull silver way that only *steel* can shine. Their swords were man-length affairs of intricate hilts and cobalt blades. The brightness of their shields dazzled the eye, and the sheer numbers of their ranks pricked Tyro's heart with awe and fear. No longer did he gaze into a golden cloud of vapor, but he looked at some very real part of the world whose existence he had never guessed.

Among the sails, the shields, and the glittering corselets, one symbol united the multitude of exotic warriors and their incredible skyfaring galleons: the stylized sigil of a square-jawed face with flaming eyes. The visage of some terrible War God, the sovereign who drove the monolithic armada across the circumference of the world to conquer in his name.

"Zyung." Vireon breathed the name quietly, his eyes still lost in the glowing vision.

Then came a second wave of airborne entities, a flock of winged lizards with tapering skulls and gilded beaks like the prows of ramming vessels. Upon their narrow backs sat more of the armored warriors, these bearing lances and longblades. Twenty thousand flying reptiles at least, each with two clawed legs like those of mighty hawks. They screeched and flapped and filled the bowl of the world in the wake of the great armada.

Tyro tried to swallow, but his throat had gone dry as a bone. His fingers felt across the table for his goblet, and he guzzled wine without taking his eyes off the vision. Here was an invasion force that made his triple alliance seem a boy's collection of toy figurines for playing in his father's garden. Here was a conquering horde that terrified even Iardu in its sheer vastness.

Here was the other side of the world. It was real.

"These soldiers are the Manslayers of Zyung," said Iardu. "More ruthless and ready to die for their God-King than any force in all of antiquity. They live only to serve Zyung and to slay in his name. By their might, second only to his own, Zyung has forged an empire whose size encompasses every realm, province, and island of the far hemisphere.

"The God-King rules half the world, Majesties. And he comes now for the other half. What you cannot see here are the many sorcerers who also serve him. They ride in those skyborne ships, the Holy Dreadnoughts, each of which is larger than our greatest trireme. He is not only King of all the nations he surveys, he is their living God. His empire is built on faith and fear, and it is far older than any of your kingdoms.

"Zyung the God-King is coming to expand his domain with blood, sorcery, and terror."

The vision faded along with the cloud of golden vapor. The Kings sat silent before the untouched board. Even the inscrutable Slave King seemed moved by Iardu's revelation.

Tyro's head swam. Something in the wizard's nature and the reactions of his fellow monarchs told him this was undiluted truth. This vision of the near future was sure to unfold. And when the hosts of Zyung reached these shores, what a war would begin. A war to rewrite history and reshape the world in all its ancient, spherical immensity.

A war like none other.

I wanted war.

But this . . .

Could even six kingdoms united stand against such a horde?

Here was the glory he sought, falling upon him like the shattered towers of Khyrei.

A lingering silence settled over the board. The sun hung low in the sky, a crimson orb framing the sails of Mumbaza and Yaskatha. What had seemed a mighty armada now seemed a pitiful collection of wicker boats.

Tyro's head spun. The heat swelled in his brain. His blood boiled beneath the skin.

"Majesty, are you well?" asked Mendices.

Tyro swayed to left and right, strands of damp hair obscuring his eyes. His fingers grasped at the edge of the table. Swollen beads of sweat dripped from his brow.

"He has the red fever," said Varda the Keen Eyes.

Tyro tumbled out of his chair. His face would have met the ground if the Warlord of Uurz had not been there to catch him. Voices rose about the table, an incoherent babble of alarm. The world faded from view, replaced by a haze of clashing colors.

Someone carried him, dizzy and groaning, through the main gate of the black city. Clouds of smoke and fragments of blue sky swam crazily above him. A mélange of faces and noises he could no longer identify.

Let me stand! he wanted to shout. *We must prepare. We must fortify.*

He could not form the words. They boiled away like wisps of steam from his burning lips. He tried to raise his head but failed.

War falls truly upon us.

A war to shame all other wars.

He breathed one faint word clearly before a sea of darkness drowned him in silence.

"*Zyung . . .*"

22

A Bottle of Red

Between the bastioned wall and the sun-dappled Golden Sea, a second ocean had engulfed the capital of Khyrei; one of armored Men in black and purple cloaks or green-gold tabards. Above the glinting spearheads and gilded helms rippled the banners of Udurum and Uurz. While the black city's new King set about restoring order to his realm, the triple host picketed their vast encampment. Throughout the lines of Men and horses, blue-skinned Giants strolled as if wading through shallows of glittering foam.

Vireon sat at ease in the captain's cabin aboard the *Kingspear*. D'zan had invited him aboard the docked vessel so they might share counsel. For the first time since he awoke at the scarlet jungle's edge, Vireon felt the weight of exhaustion on his shoulders.

In the broad cabin sat a bed, desk, chair, and a cabinet stocked with Yaskathan wines. Vireon's greatsword hung from a peg on the wall, his crown of sapphire and iron beside it. He sat in the padded seat and drank from a bottle of dark red. He did not bother to pour its contents into one of the cabinet's jeweled goblets, instead pulling out the cork with his thumb and forefinger and swilling directly from the bottle's mouth.

Through the round porthole a lowering sun set the horizon aflame; the seven hundred sails of the double armada were cast into silhouette. He was glad that he could not see from this vantage the black ships of Khyrei sitting in the harbor, or the risen city that still smoked and roiled with the chaos of revolution. Such sights would only deepen his mood.

As he brooded over the drink, his memory replayed the vision of Iardu's golden cloud. He doubted none of the sorcerer's words, yet the truth of it all disturbed him. How could two worlds exist for so many ages, yet remain ignorant of one another's existence? It seemed the depths of time were bottomless, full of blood and terror, and mysteries beyond the understanding of mortal beings. He missed Alua fiercely. At times like this she would speak some gentle wisdom to him, quelling the storm of his consternation with tranquil hopes.

A polite knock on the cabin's door broke his reverie. His sister had come to him as requested. "Enter," he called through the oaken door.

Sharadza opened it and stepped inside. She closed the door behind her and smiled in a way that reminded him of their mother. She sat on the bed, her hands smoothing the wrinkles of her amber gown. Her lengthy black hair was tied at the back of her neck with a leather thong, and he saw no jewelry on her person. Not even the splendid wedding ring given her by D'zan.

"How are you?" she asked him.

"Alua is dead," he said. "Killed by Maelthyn."

Sharadza's jaw fell and her brow creased. "What? Little Maelthyn? How . . ." Her green eyes reddened and began to water.

"Maelthyn was never my daughter," he said. The words pierced his own heart as surely as a length of sharp *steel*. Air came thick and stifling into his chest. "She was . . . only a product of Ianthe's sorcery. For seven years she grew among us, feeding on our love, and our ignorance. At last she came for our hearts."

Sharadza came forward to wrap him in a warm embrace. "Oh, Vireon, I am so sorry." She wept quietly, and for a moment he joined her. Then he battled the tears away with the power of the red bottle tipped at his lips once again. He offered it to his sister; she declined.

"You came all this way for vengeance," she whispered.

"No. For *justice*."

She took his big hand, cradling it like that of a child.

Justice had been done. Certainly not by his own hand as he had wished. Yet it was justice nevertheless. He must accept it. He had little choice.

"Why are you not sitting in D'zan's palace," he asked, "ruling his kingdom while he sails?"

She turned away from him, her hands slipping from his own. Now it was her turn to fight back tears.

"Have you not heard the rumors?" she said.

"I have," he said. "Yet I would rather hear the truth from your own tongue. Before I speak with D'zan on the subject."

She faced him now with something akin to fear in her eyes. "No," she said. "I beg you, say nothing to D'zan about this. It's not his fault."

"Is it yours then?"

"Yes," she said. "No! I don't know . . ."

"What are you not telling me, Sharadza?"

She lingered, hesitating to speak at all, while he took another swig from the bottle of jade glass. The wine was strong, a tribute to grapes emboldened by sun and rain.

"It's simple, really," she said. "I could not produce the heir he wanted. So he chose someone else who can do so. I am still Queen of Yaskatha. Yet I must share my husband."

Vireon shook his head. "This is not our way."

"But it *is* the way of Yaskathans," she said. "Some of their Kings have had twenty wives or more."

Vireon sighed. "So you will endure this humiliation to retain the crown and title?"

"I don't know. I came to Khyrei seeking Fangodrel and found him reborn as Gammir. A creature of hate, a drinker of blood, a beast made of shadow. And I have destroyed him. Stolen his kingdom."

Vireon chuckled without mirth. "There are those who would say that a slave named Tong has stolen Gammir's kingdom."

Sharadza gave him a shallow smile, wiping at her eyes. "*Former* slave," she said. "Just as well. It was all a part of Iardu's plan."

Vireon sat up straighter in his chair. "Tell me what you know of Iardu's plans."

"You saw what is coming. The force coming to claim our lands. The greatness of this Zyung. Iardu prepares our nations to defy him. That is my understanding."

"Who is Zyung?" asked Vireon.

"Gammir knew," Sharadza whispered. "He showed me in his mirror of sorcery. Like you, I have only looked upon the image of the Conqueror's face. My guess is that spying on him directly would be far too dangerous. I know only what you and the other Kings know. That he is coming and there will be no making peace with him."

Vireon accepted this. He would speak with Iardu later. The Shaper must know more than he revealed. Such was the nature of sorcerers, sages, and madmen alike. They spoke in fragments of truth, forced their listeners to delve deeply for wisdom. It seemed they thrived on such games of the mind.

"You wear a new crown," Sharadza said. Her eyes fell upon the loop of iron and sapphires hanging on the wall beside his blade. "They say you are lord of both Uduru and Udvorg now."

"This is so," he sighed. "Though I did not wish it. I hold the crown for Angrid's eldest son. Someday it will be his to claim. Udurum is mine by blood. I am content with it."

She smiled again, and once more he saw the face of his mother in her own.

"The world makes terrific demands on us all," she said. Her eyes drifted toward the bloody twilight beyond the porthole. "I would tell you of the terrible things Gammir and Ianthe forced upon me. The killing, the tortures, the carnal crimes ... yet I would spare even the glimmer of these things from your memory. Suffice to say that I was torn apart and rebuilt ... then torn and rebuilt again. I am no longer ... what I was."

"You seem far greater," Vireon said. "Father's power glows in your eyes. You have the strength of the Uduru in your veins. I have discovered this same strength. Father's gift."

"Yes," she said. "Already I have heard the tale of how you slew the Swamp God. How you grew like Vod against the Serpent-Father. I knew you carried this within you. Like it or not, we are both sorcerers, just as we are both Men and Giants. Creatures of two worlds, born to unite them as one."

"Unity." Vireon examined the word. "Perhaps this was Iardu's goal all along."

"I believe it was," she said. "A dream he long held impossible. Now it *must* succeed, or we perish."

"How long do we have?" he asked. "Has the Shaper told you?"

"Days. Perhaps weeks. No more than that."

Vireon took another pull from the bottle. Half empty already. His weary head swam.

"What will you do?" she asked.

"Fight. What else is there to do?"

She had no answer for that, so she only hugged him again.

"How is Mother?" he asked as she pulled away.

"She ages well. The Yaskathan court suits her far more than Udurum ever did. The warm climate enlivens her. She has taken a lover. A master of D'zan's royal vineyards. I believe she is happy."

Vireon smiled. "As she deserves to be. Thank you for taking care of her these past years."

Sharadza shrugged off his words. "She is my mother, and you are my brother. We are all that is left. I will take care of you both, as best I may."

"Only remember to take care of yourself," he said.

She kissed his cheek. "You are weary, King of the Giantlands. Take your rest now. We will speak more later."

Vireon stretched his arms toward the ceiling and moaned. "I had intended to wait here for D'zan and have words with him regarding your marriage." Her eyes widened. "Yet I will honor your wishes and say nothing of it." He stood up, took his great-sword from the wall, then placed the iron crown on his head. "I will sleep among my warriors. Not inside this gilded sea-coffin."

She walked beside him as he descended the gangplank and headed up the sloping lawn toward the first line of Udurum pavilions. Bands of Udvorg gathered about blue fires set by Varda, while Men gathered about their more earthly cookfires: evening meals were being prepared. Provisions from the city were granted to both armies by the Slave King, and the northern forces would soon rejoice at the flavors of fresh beef, roasted corn, black beans, and green cabbages.

Instead of a bloody and devastating siege, they enjoyed a much-needed rest and the unexpected bounty of a rich land freed from tyranny. Some of the Men sought the attentions of Khyrein women, who pleased them mightily, if the cries of passion from the tents were any indication. Already the peoples of the six kingdoms were mingling their bloodlines. Vireon smirked at the lewdness of the observation. The wine in his bottle sloshed as he walked.

Sharadza left him to seek out Iardu and assist in the city's refortification. Vireon wandered through the grassy alleys between the tents of Men, returning their salutes as he passed. When he entered the precinct of the Udvorg camps, he grew almost effortlessly to Giant size again. Perhaps it was the fine wine that dulled the pain of his transformation. Or perhaps he had simply grown used to the magic of change. There were many pains he had grown accustomed to lately.

The blue-skins offered him raw hocks of lizard meat hauled from the swamps and swigs of ale from Khyrein kegs. He refused them all with a smile and a wave, heading directly for the tent of Dahrima. There he found her shield and spear, but not the Giantess. She must be tending to some urgent business of the host. Or perhaps she lingered in the arms of a lusty Udvorg, having finally given in to the ancient call of the flesh. This thought struck a pang deep in his gut, a note of jealousy resounding dimly through his limbs and loins. He dismissed it as a passing phantasm of his fatigue.

He turned to leave the tent and find another in which to sleep. A sudden cool breeze met his face, and Varda the Keen Eyes stood before the canvas opening. Her indigo flesh seemed a deep purple in the glow of dusk. The royal color of Udurum. As ever, she carried her black staff with its dancing blue flame. It was that flame which cooled the tent's interior as she walked inside it.

"Majesty," she said, bowing to one knee. Her black hair, so unusual among the blue-skins, gleamed like polished obsidian. The rings in her ears and nose twinkled in the glow of the azure flame.

"Rise," he told her. "No need for such ceremony. It wearies me." She stood then, her eyes level with his own. Those eyes had been frosted rubies until this moment. Now they seemed to him like warm pools of Yaskathan wine. Their color matched perfectly the contents of the bottle from which he sipped.

"I have explained the Shaper's warning to the Udvorg as best I can," Varda told him. "Yet they would hear it from the mouth of their King."

"They will," said Vireon. "Tomorrow. Let them enjoy a night of peace while it lasts." He tipped the bottle again, letting the wine pour down his throat until there was no more left. He tossed it into the corner of the tent.

When he turned, Varda still stood before him. She did not blink. Her lean jaw was set and her free hand curled into a fist.

"Speak, Witch," he said. He felt her cold anger.

"You are my King," she said. "Yet I would speak with you as Uduri speaks to Udvorg, without crown or court to intervene. Will you allow it?"

"Say what you must before sleep forces me from you." He would have fallen onto Dahrima's furs in that moment, if the mystery of Varda's eyes had not held him standing there like a dimwitted boy. He took off the iron crown and dropped it beside the wine bottle.

She glared at him, blue nostrils flaring. The mounds of her chest heaved as she inhaled. The blue flame at the head of her staff disappeared, and she cast it to the ground.

"I despise you, Vireon Vodson," she said evenly. "You came into the land of my ancestors, dropped your poison words into my King's ears, and brought three thousand of my brothers marching south in a pointless war for your own selfish vengeance. Now you would lead us into the grip of this sorcerer and his mad visions. I fear that you will be the end of us all."

Her words hung heavy as shields of bronze in the gloom of the tent. Vireon said nothing. He considered all that he had done and decided upon the instant that Varda was right. He was no proper King. Certainly no full-blooded Giant-King. He was only a fool who wore a double crown. Yet how could he tell her this?

She lunged forward like an Icelands tiger. For a fleeting moment he thought her nails would dig into his eyes. She would destroy him if she could, she who had given him this crown but did not believe in his right to wear it. He was uncertain of that right himself.

Varda reached out not with icy fingernails, but with pale blue lips that pressed hard against his own. Her arms wrapped about his Giant frame. The chill of her kiss burned his flesh like the touch of the blue flame itself. A storm of emotion and flesh so cold it was searing.

Her weight forced him back and down, onto the waiting furs. His arms wound about her lithe body like vipers, seeking and striking of their own accord. She stripped the clothing from his body and covered his hot skin with freezing kisses. He tore her robe of hides and marveled at the sculpted perfection of her arms, breasts, and hips. She wrapped about him like a winter wind, and he reveled in the wild, thoughtless pleasure of it. The world and its ocean of sorrows fell away from him as he made her body his new kingdom.

The drinking songs of the Udvorg filled the night as King and shamaness coupled in fierce silence, sheltered by the darkness of the tent. Vireon had never lain with a Giantess before now – his stature would never allow it. Yet the stories of the Uduri's savage passion were proven by Varda's paradoxical ecstasy. She raked him and shook him, ultimately conquering the mountain of his manhood.

When it was done, they both lay spent and fading, her indigo arms and legs intertwined with his bronze limbs.

Through a haze of drink and exhaustion he glimpsed a blurred figure standing at the tent's entrance. Golden braids fell across black-mailed shoulders. The light of distant flames cast shadows through the opening. Something deep inside his brain or heart prodded him to rise now, but the call of sleep proved far more persuasive. He dreamed a memory of making love to Alua, lying on a bed of snow at the foot of the White Mountains.

When he awoke at dawn, Dahrima's spear and shield were gone from the tent.

23

A Nation Reborn

In the grand hall of the fractured palace, already the heart of New Khyrei was beating. Tong sat on the onyx throne where Gammir had dispensed judgments of doom and Ianthe had done the same before him. He wore now a robe of scarlet silk to match the rubies in his dark crown. The same sabre he had wielded in the burning fields lay oiled and gleaming across his knees.

Columns of basalt carved in the likeness of tremendous coiling vipers lined the hall, and between them marched the New Khyrein Guard. These former slaves wore the armor of the Onyx Guard and carried their weapons, but their faces were not hidden behind fanged masks. No longer would Tong's people bend the knee to faceless agents of a ruthless order. The time of masks was done.

One by one, or in battered groups, Tong's guardsmen hauled before him the generals and advisors of the Blood Regime. He listened to their pleas of remorse and decided who would be cast into dungeon cells to await trial for their crimes. Those captives who spat at his feet and professed undying allegiance to Gammir and Ianthe he put to death at the very foot of his throne. The New Guard was only too eager to provide this measure of pitiless vengeance. A crew of palace attendants rushed to scrub red blood from the basalt before the next prisoner entered. Those accused who begged forgiveness, hailed Tong as a liberator, and renounced their old loyalties, he most often allowed to rejoin the population. Many pampered functionaries, spoiled by an easy palace life, he cast into the streets or fields to learn the ways of laborers and craftsmen.

Nine out of every ten Onyx Guardsmen chose to honor Tong's reign. Within the space of a single day he added thousands of experienced soldiers to the New Khyrein Guard. The dank cells beneath the citadel grew thick with unrepentant imperialists, or those whose contrition meant next to nothing in the face of long-standing crimes against the people. Not a single Overseer was spared; most of them had died in the night of flaming plantations. As for the rest, their severed heads joined those decorating the blades of tall pikes along the palace's outer wall. Meek citizens walked about those walls constantly, searching for the rotting faces of their former tormentors, and cursing their souls to the darkest of hells.

The Plaza of Slaves was renamed the Court of Justice. A scaffold was built there in a matter of hours, and the members of notorious noble houses were hanged before cheering crowds. Most of the city's fires had been extinguished, yet a new blaze was kindled outside the Southern Gate, overlooking the mass of charred and blackened fields. Here, within sight of their former domains, the dead bodies of hanged Overseers, loyalists, and infamous tormentors were burned without ceremony. The population of the black city cried the name of their new King and praised the Four Gods in his name. In their modest temples the priests of those same Gods hailed Tong and his liberators. In the climate of newfound freedom, their faiths would grow and prosper along with the freed people.

Sydathians prowled the streets and gardens. Most Khyreins had lost their fear of the beasts. They had witnessed scene after scene of the eyeless ones defending innocent women and children against rapacious guardsmen during the revolt. The pale-skinned sniffers were the terror of anyone not allied with the Free People of Khyrei; these lurking individuals they sensed in the way a panther scents its prey. Packs of eyeless ones hunted down fleeing noblemen with chests full of concealed wealth. They broke down the doors of estates where such criminals had taken refuge. There was no hiding from the eyeless ones. They were the living icons of Tong's justice. The Hounds of Vengeance.

A band of twenty Sydathians lingered about Tong's throne, his personal guard. Tolgur and six other freed men stood nearby, splendid now in the garments of noblemen and viziers. Each man clutched a spear or carried a sword at his waist, symbols of their new rank as much as instruments of protection.

Iardu the Shaper waited at the right hand of the throne this day, having arrived the hour previous. He hovered in the patient manner of one awaiting an audience with the busy monarch. Yet at times he leaned in to whisper at Tong's ear, urging him to greater leniency when facing his enemies.

"If you offer the noble families mercy," said Iardu, "they will follow you more faithfully than they followed those before you. Although they were not slaves, they too suffered under the Blood Regime. You would do well to remember this. Let them call you Tong the Merciful."

Tong rubbed his tired eyes. He had grown tired of the killing, but there was much more to be done. Whenever the accused allowed it, by virtue of kind words or public remorse, he spared them. There would be enough justice delivered in the streets, especially for those who escaped official punishment. Iardu was correct: at this early stage of Tong's reign, forgiveness was a quality that would serve him well. It was, in fact, the quality that separated him most from the tyrants who preceeded him. The people would take note of this. With his every word and deed, he established the new culture of his reborn kingdom. It must be a kingdom of mercy and kindness, and only he could make it so.

The burned fields would be replanted and the crumbled structures rebuilt. All by the hands of freed men, who would profit from the sweat of their brows. The vast warehouses full of grain and the fruits of recent harvests would remain in the control of the throne, yet the former plantation workers would supervise and facilitate the portioning, trading, and shipping of such resources. For the coming season the warehoused goods would serve to feed the city; it would be a full season before the plantations were restored. The rebellion had cost Khyrei an entire harvest, eaten by flames, but there was more than enough in storage to avoid famine. Tong set a committee of freed men to oversee the city's agriculture and another body to reform its trading laws. No longer would the devil-head ships spread piracy and death across the Golden Sea. He was determined to make Khyrei a respected trading partner among its former enemies.

He was glad to have the Shaper's wisdom at his disposal. Replacing widespread chaos with a new and just order was no easy task. Somehow Iardu had found the keys to Gammir's deep-buried treasure vault, where lay the accumulated plunder of centuries. Mounds of gold and jewels filled the cellar, along with suits of golden armor, jeweled swords and daggers, priceless jewelry of antique splendor, and coffers full of scrolls writ by the sages of long-dead kingdoms. Tong's mind could not easily grasp this immense wealth. Here were the resources to build New Khyrei into a nation that would make the world forget the Blood Regime and all its crimes. That was a task for future generations, but it must begin now, among the ashes of the old city.

"You must expand and refortify this palace," Iardu told him. "Yet those towers destroyed by the living fire must *never* be rebuilt. The ground on which they stood must be walled off and considered accursed. You may replace the blood-hungry gardens of Ianthe with more wholesome courtyards, but you must never allow anyone to build on – or even walk on – the ground where the central or western tower once stood."

"Perhaps we should demolish the entire palace and build a new one," Tong said.

"A worthy idea," said Iardu. "Yet you must see to the feeding and protection of your people first. Time later for building a new citadel . . . if that is what you decide."

Tong agreed. With the hordes of Zyung approaching, he must prepare New Khyrei for war. Only the alliance with his fellow kingdoms gave him any hope of resisting such an invasion.

Such politics must take priority, even as he began the reconstruction of the shattered city. He was pleased that so many experienced guardsmen chose to pledge him their fealty. The course of history had changed, and most soldiers were wise enough to change with it. They would no longer wear the inhuman masks, but they would still serve King and country. As for those few who remained loyal to the Blood Regime in the face of death, it seemed a kind of madness to him. The mad loyalists died cursing his name.

Now the hour approached for Tong to make his first official address to the People of New Khyrei. He dismissed all but the wizard, his seven human advisors, and the band of twenty Sydathians. The visiting Kings would all be in attendance. Last evening they had dined together and seen Iardu's sobering vision. After the public address, Tong would call a second Council of Kings and begin forming a plan of resistance. Iardu told him the coming war would see an alliance greater than any in recorded history. Yet in the face of Zyung's massive forces, even that did not seem enough.

Accompanied by advisors, guards, and Sydathians, Tong walked the broad corridors of the palace and climbed the stairs to the great pulpit adjoining its western wall. Here a broad forum stood lined with the statues of former Emperors and Empresses; all those marble effigies had been cast down and were now only piles of jumbled rock. The forum itself was crowded with freed men and their families, as well as the bulk of the middle-class city dwellers. Tong's revolt had liberated not only slaves, but also thousands of downtrodden citizens who knew only life in the shadow of terror. Among the common folk of Khyrei there were very few who bore honest love for the Blood Regime. The mass of Khyreins had simply endured tyranny for centuries, an endless parade of sorcerers, witches, and despots stretching back through history.

The multitude cheered as one for Tong when he mounted the high stage of the forum. The thunder of their voices rocked the stones so that he feared the remainder of the black palace at his back might collapse. The morning sun was bright and hot in his face; he squinted to observe the crowd below his vantage. Curious Sydathians milled among the population, sniffing and licking at the grateful and cautious hands of Khyreins. Seeing for himself how these beastlings, so grotesque of appearance, no longer struck fear into the hearts of his countrymen, Tong smiled. Already there was a crude understanding of the eyeless ones and their kindly nature.

Iardu, Tolgur, and the rest of the advisors sat in high-backed chairs behind Tong as he stared across thousands of eager faces. At the last moment Sharadza joined them on the platform. She beamed at Tong with fierce green eyes as she took her chair. He calmed his leaping stomach with a deep breath. At last he raised his arms and the multitudes fell silent.

"People of New Khyrei!" he cried out. "You are free!" His words echoed off the forum's cleverly designed walls so that they were amplified enough to find every ear in the crowd. A convulsion of cheering erupted across the square. Beyond the leaping, shouting masses lay the gleaming calm of the Golden Sea. The sails of the Yaskathan and Mumbazan navies sat at ease there, silent reminders of the great invasion soon to come.

Tong raised his arms again and was gifted with more silence. "No longer will our families suffer and die under the yoke of servitude. The fields of Khyrei belong to all of us. Together we will work these fields, and together we will share in their bounty."

Another round of cheering expressed the crowd's approval. Children bounced on the shoulders of their fathers. Sydathians crawled along walls and rooftops, excited by the fevered emotions. They, too, understood Tong's words, although they did not speak his language. The bond of the Godstone had joined him to their silent brotherhood. It was this understanding that had guided them in the taking of the city. He wondered briefly how many of them had died to make Khyrei a free nation.

"Emperor and Empress are no more," Tong said. "Even now the greatest criminals among us are being brought to justice. They will join our former masters in death. Yet far more of those who served the Blood Regime have chosen to side with us. To become servants of our new society. I welcome them. This day Khyrei is reborn!"

He paused again, allowing the people their jubilation.

"In this New Khyrei, none will go hungry. None will labor without fair wages. None will die to feed the monstrous appetites of their oppressors. None will be consigned to live in the dirt of the fields, banned from the city's comforts. Inside our great wall, every man, woman, and child will live with honor and freedom. All these promises I make as your chosen King.

"New Khyrei forsakes any ambitions to conquer the island nations. We will meet our fellow kingdoms in honest trade, not in piracy. We give up our claims to the trackless jungle and the volcanic mountains beyond. These lands are wild, poisonous, and have little to offer us. Khyrei is no longer an empire. It is a *nation*. A new nation, reborn in the cleansing fires of liberation. *Hail, New Khyrei!*"

As he intended, the cry spread across the forum and into the crowded streets. He allowed his words to sink deep into the hearts of all those present, waiting until the bulk of their noise died away. Waiting for the perfect moment when they longed to hear his next words. Their eyes fell upon him like a million flashing sparks.

"Now I would speak with you regarding our liberators, our allies, our eyeless brothers. Many of you have already met them. All of you owe them your lives. Let every man understand this: without the aid of the Sydathians our revolution would have perished. They have fought and bled for us. They have died for us. They have *saved* us. For this the People of Sydathus have my ever-lasting gratitude. They will forever be welcome inside our walls, for they are brothers to us all. Hail the Sydathians!"

And hail they did. The eyeless ones leaped and twisted with pleasure as the People of New Khyrei honored them. Some of the commoners even hugged their oblong heads and kissed their pink snouts. Children rode upon their backs, grasping their horns like the reins of ponies. Human and inhuman, the boundaries of the two terms were blurred to the point of non-existence. Both Men and Sydathians were now denizens of the black city.

"Although they do not speak our language, they understand our hearts and minds," said Tong. "I have spent time in their city, Ancient Sydathus, which lies beneath the red jungle. I have worshipped their Godstone and seen beyond the barriers of eye and tongue. It is because I joined them in such understanding that they agreed to foster our liberation. We owe them our friendship, our lives, and our freedom. And we also owe them our understanding. Therefore, I am sending a hundred men and women to accompany our pale brothers back to Sydathus. These ambassadors will do as I have done. They will gain the wisdom that only the Godstone can provide. When these hundred return, another hundred will be sent, and another hundred after them. Sydathus and New Khyrei will be brother cities, and thus we will stand as no other nation before us. Our brotherhood with the Sydathians will be the envy of all who visit our land. And it shall be the seed of our new security."

The people roared, and thousands shouted for their chance at ambassadorship. Tong would decide later who to send first. Young Tolgur would be among them, for Tong had it in mind that the sturdy youth should be his chief advisor. In order to earn this honor, he must spend time with the Sydathians.

Tong spoke then of Zyung the God-King and his approaching hordes. His audience grew silent as he described the vision of Iardu and the role the visiting Kings would play in the coming war. "Only together, united with the forces of Yaskatha, Mumbaza, Uurz, and Udurum, can we hope to stand strong in the face of this Conqueror. These nations, formerly our enemies, now join us as allies. Vireon the Slayer, King of Giants and Men, stands with us! D'zan the Sun Bringer, King of Yaskatha, stands with us! Undutu, Son of the Feathered Serpent, King of Mumbaza stands with us! Tyro the Sword King of Uurz stands with us! New Khyrei shall endure!"

He left the pulpit to the sound of their applause and shouts of jubilation. There was much left to do, and little time. The legions of New Khyrei must be assembled and organized. Many slaves-turned-soldiers would require training. Weapons and armor production must increase while the work of restoring streets and fields progressed. Life must go on in the freed city, even as the greatest war in history threatened its existence.

Iardu and Sharadza walked with Tong to share a breakfast of succulents in his council chamber. Outside the vaulted windows, the sounds of excited chatter filled the blackened courtyards.

"You speak with power and grace," Sharadza said. "Your people love you."

"I hope that is so," said Tong. "As I hope I am worthy of their love."

Iardu patted his shoulder. "You are, Tong," said the wizard. "It is why I chose you."

Tong regarded Iardu's chromatic eyes over the bowls of sliced pomegranates and heaped grapes. The cooks and servants of the palace were only too glad to embrace Tong in place of their former masters. He would not demand the use of their flesh for his own pleasure, nor would he drink their blood to satisfy his thirst.

"Since it was you who picked me to guide the rebirth of Khyrei," Tong said, "I must ask this: could you not have prevented the death of she whom I loved?"

Iardu's ageless face lowered. "I am sorry that I could not. Even a sorcerer cannot be everywhere at all times. Even we have our limits. Yet it was this tragedy that set you upon the path I knew you must walk."

Tong considered this as he sipped from a goblet of amber wine. "I would trade all of this to have her back," he said. His eyes swelled. "I would rather live as a slave with Matay at my side than be a King without her. I speak only the truth of my feelings, which I have shared with no one else."

Sharadza regarded him with pity. She reached a hand to cradle his atop the polished table. "Losing someone we love can be our greatest challenge," she whispered. "Yet such pain makes us what we are. Survivors."

He met her green eyes with his own and suddenly he envied the King of Yaskatha. Here was a woman worthy of marrying a King. Beautiful, wise, and possessed of unguessable power.

"Your victory honors her memory," said Iardu. "You must live in a way that would make her proud. You must choose a worthy Queen from the ranks of your freed folk, another who has known the yoke of slavery. It seems only fitting."

Tong did not mention the unborn son that died with Matay. She would greet him again someday, when he was ready to enter the Deathlands. Perhaps that day would be soon, what with the ancient might of Zyung about to fall upon the world.

"Iardu is right," said Sharadza. "You must choose a Queen. Someone to soothe your aching heart. Someone to share your burden."

Tong stared out the southern window. Beyond the plain of blackened fields, the red jungle steamed in the glow of morning. Already groups of freed men worked there, removing debris and detritus, clearing the rows for fresh plantings. The houses of Overseers had been trampled into the earth and would not be rebuilt.

He sensed the truth of Iardu and Sharadza's advice. When a tree falls in that ruddy wilderness, another eventually rises to take its place. This was the cycle of existence. So must he find another Matay, another mother for those children he had yet to father. Among all the new duties of his royal status, this would prove the most difficult.

He squinted at the disk of golden sun rising low in the eastern sky.

The splendid sun that she had loved so well.

Forgive me, Matay, he asked silently.

Forgive me for what I must do.

In time he would claim another wife, provide a living Queen

for his people. She would give him not a single son, but many. Such was the way of Kings, and as a King now he must abide by it. He owed nothing less to the People of New Khyrei.

For all their sakes, he would take the hand of another woman and learn to love her.

One day he would smile at the faces of his strong sons and lovely daughters.

One day he would forget the face of Matay.

Yet that day would not come soon.

24

Shape of the World

The sun blazed high above the azure sea. The *Kingspear* sat with sails furled, the Sword and Tree banner waving silver and scarlet above the wharves. The Mumbazan flagship had sailed out of the bay in early morning to rejoin the fleet. Undutu wished to consult with his admirals regarding Iardu's visions. Khama the Feathered Serpent in his manly guise had accompanied the Mumbazan King as always. The Yaskathan flagship lingered foremost in the bay full of Khyrein vessels.

Tong had offered each visiting King a chamber in the shattered palace, yet none had accepted his hospitality. Something about those barbed towers still reeked of ancient depravity. D'zan remained quartered on the *Kingspear*, perhaps waiting for Sharadza there. He certainly had not sent anyone to summon her.

In the shape of a white gull she soared above the forest of ships' masts, circling the bay in an effort to spot D'zan walking the decks of his ship. Behind the palace walls Tong worked tirelessly to restore order to his city and prepare a new army for the coming war. Iardu had lingered to assist the King of New Khyrei in his daunting task. Tyro still lay in his tent, lost in the grip of fever, and Vireon was nowhere to be found among Giants or Men.

Perhaps he had braved the red jungle for a morning hunt. Yet it was D'zan she must find now. She must face her faithless husband one last time. She did not anticipate kind words and loving reconciliation. She wondered if he would speak to her at all.

D'zan strode across the *Kingspear*'s foredeck to stand beneath the rippling banner. He wore a shirt of silver mail and a crimson cloak bearing the royal insignia. The greatsword with its graven sun sigil hung across his back. His blond hair had grown longer and wilder since Sharadza had fled Yaskatha. A light beard had sprouted across his chin and jaws. He looked older, even from her lofty vantage point. He was no longer the boy who had stolen her heart; he had become a man she no longer recognized. He stared at the black city and the milling legions camped about its walls, then turned to survey the double fleet as if weighing these assembled forces against the host of Iardu's vision. Now seemed as good a time as any to do what she needed to do.

She circled down to alight on the deck a few paces behind D'zan. When he turned at the sound of her flapping wings, she stood already in her human form. A simple gown of white silk hung upon her shoulders. Her feet were bare, as she had always preferred, comfortable against the warm wood of the deck. Her green eyes met his own. His had inherited that color when she and Iardu forged him a new body eight years ago. Except for those emerald orbs, so like her own, everything about him seemed changed. The smiling Prince had grown into a grim-faced King carrying all the worry of the world on his broad shoulders.

"Sharadza." He greeted her with a nod. There was a time when the sound of her name on his lips weakened her knees and set butterflies loose in her stomach. Now it sounded like nothing less than a royal decree. "I have missed you."

She wondered if that were true. "How fares your wife and child?" she asked. Immediately she regretted her biting tone.

"Cymetha is well," he said. "And Theskalus – my son – will soon be born."

She forced a smile. "Congratulations on your good fortune."

He took a step nearer to her, still far enough away that she could not touch him.

"You look lovely," he said.

She gazed eastward at the horizon dotted with white and golden warships. "The time for sweet words is past, D'zan. I've come to say goodbye."

A look of shock spread across his face. "But ... you are my Queen. I *love* you. She is only my Second Wife. Try to understand ..."

"I *have* tried," she said. "I do not belong in Yaskatha. The mother of your child should be your First Wife. I ... will not be returning with you."

He stared at the spreading mass of tents where laughing Giants waded carefully among Men and horses. "This would sadden me more if I believed *any* of us would be returning to Yaskatha. This Zyung may well be the end of us all."

"Iardu and I will help however we can. There is still hope. You must believe this."

"I suppose I do," he sighed. "Or I would sail from here with all speed and never look back. Yet I've always found it best to confront one's terrors instead of running from them."

"Iardu has worked long and hard to make this unity of nations possible. It is the greatest weapon any of these kingdoms possesses."

"Will you be the bride of Iardu, now?"

She laughed. He could be dense at times. "Of course not. He is as old as the hills."

Older. Far older.

D'zan shrugged. "Love is blind, they say. Therefore it must be ageless as well."

"I do not love Iardu," she said. "Not in that way. He is . . . like a father to me."

"Where will you go, Sharadza? Your home is with me. You will grow to accept the ways of Yaskatha. I promise you."

She shook her head, dark locks whipping from side to side. "I will never accept sharing my husband with another woman."

D'zan's eyes fell to the polished boards of the deck. He offered no response.

"Iardu has offered me sanctuary on his island," she said. "I will make a home there. At least for a while."

"I do not like your decision," he said. "Yet I must accept it. But know this: you can always come back. I will leave your chambers untouched."

She gifted him with a warm smile. "You are most kind."

"There is a war council tonight," said D'zan. "Kings and wizards will form battle plans, calculate our strategies. None of us will sleep well until we do."

"The world has reached a turning point," she said. "Nothing will ever be the same, no matter what happens. Be brave, D'zan, as you have always been. Be strong, as I know you are. Remember that you have already conquered death. And call upon me when you need me."

"I will do all of these things," he said. She came forward and kissed his cheek. He grabbed her about the waist and pressed his lips against hers. One last moment of shared passion. She let it run through her body, explored his mailed back with her hands. She pulled away.

"Until tonight," she said. It was far better than saying goodbye again. To do that would only force the welling tears from her eyes. "Farewell, King of Yaskatha."

"Farewell, Sharadza."

His eyes lingered on her as she shifted back into the gull's shape and rose toward the pearly clouds. She flew toward the palace at the heart of the city, looking back once to see him staring after her with those unnatural green eyes.

She met Iardu on a high balcony overlooking the ashes of a palatial garden. Already palace attendants were shoveling the charred remains into buckets while gardeners planted new trees and vines in the dark soil. In a matter of months the splendor of the royal courtyards would be restored, and without those blood-hungry jungle plants so favored by Gammir and Ianthe. The Gardens of Tong would grow wholesome and verdant, a symbol of his reborn kingdom.

Iardu sat with a decanter of red wine overlooking the garden workers and the bustling streets beyond. Occasionally a great cheer rang across the city, the sound of another prisoner executed in the Court of Justice. She wondered how much of the killing here was truly just, and how much was simple vengeance. Yet it was not her place to condemn the long-suffering Khyreins for their actions. She had seen their plight from the inside out; she had participated in it while snared in the grip of Gammir's will. Part of her longed to join the spectators and watch the last of Khyrei's evil stamped out forever. Yet another part knew that these were only empty gestures. As long as Men had free will they would choose good or evil for themselves, and they would not always choose the former.

She dropped to the balcony and assumed her womanly shape once more. Iardu beckoned her into the empty chair beside his own. He poured a cup of the red vintage for her. Perhaps he sensed her uncertain mood, or perhaps he had seen her flying from D'zan's ship. She took the cup and drank deeply. An Uurzian vintage, quite old. It must have come from a ship raided by Khyrein pirates. For a moment she wondered at the morality of drinking away such a purloined treasure, then she considered how ridiculous it would be to carry all the stolen wine in the vaults of Khyrei back to Uurz.

"How is D'zan?" Iardu asked.

"He is well," she said. "Anticipating the joy of a strong son. Yaskatha will have its heir."

Iardu turned from his city inspection to search the shadows of her face.

"You told him?"

"I did."

"You will enjoy life on the island," he said. "There is no more peaceful place in all the world."

"Eyeni called you *father* . . . "

Iardu grinned briefly. "She is one of my many . . . *singular* creations. Beings too gentle to be tossed into the brutal world. They would not survive it. The island is their home as well."

The sound of a cheering mob floated across the city. Another oppressor silenced forever.

"How much more do you know about this God-King?" she asked. "Have you known all along that he existed? Have you visited the other side of the world?"

"So many questions all at once. I have known Zyung since the time before recorded history. Yes, I have visited the other side, but it was long, long ago. Before he had even begun to build his empire. It was a wild and savage place then. As were all places in this world."

"Gammir said Zyung was of the Old Breed. You told me I was of that same breed, as are you. How many more of the Old Breed still live?"

"All of them, I suppose," said Iardu. "You must understand that the Old Breed are primal forces, entities from outside the world who chose long ago to make this place their home. In the early days we formed empires and religions, spawned lesser races to worship us and build monuments to our glory. All this I have already told you.

"Some of the Old Breed grew tired of ruling the world. Others fostered civilizations for ages, only for the joy of ultimately destroying them. Some fell *into* the world itself, becoming part of it, forgetting their true natures. There are several of these Dreaming Ones scattered across both halves of the world. Others continue to manipulate the affairs of Men and their nations. Ianthe was such a one, and you can be sure that she will return eventually. She was the worst of us all, entirely consumed by her own selfish appetites and worldly lusts. There can be no reaching an understanding with someone like her. She can only be confronted and defeated time after time. This is the pattern of her existence, which even she cannot change.

"You are descended from the Old Breed, as are all Giantkind. There are other races descended directly from us. And there are those of us who never forgot who we are, those who continue to strive and shape and guide this world to a place where we believe it needs to go. Khama and I have spent ages doing exactly that. Unlike me, Khama owes his allegiance to one people. He is the ancient guardian of the Mumbazans. That is *his* pattern. I take a broader view, moving freely among the nations. I tell stories, foster legends, and sometimes create them."

"Like you did with Vod," she said. "And now Tong."

"I choose not to destroy but to build, to create, to define. That is *my* pattern."

"What about Zyung? What is his pattern?"

Iardu looked once again toward the busy gardeners below, trying with all their skill to replace death with beauty. He poured another cup of wine and sipped at it before he answered.

"Dominance. Conformity. Order. Constancy. Zyung does not

believe in free will. His empire is built upon the twin pillars of fear and obedience. Those who defy him are crushed without mercy. Only those who recognize his right to supremacy and their own place in his order are allowed to prosper. His is the pattern that drives all tyrants."

"Most tyrants rule from fear," she said. "Is there nothing this God-King fears?"

Iardu looked at the sky, as if searching for his next answer among a flock of birds winging toward the distant jungle.

"Perhaps the word 'fear' is not applicable to one such as Zyung," he said. "What he desires above all is the peace of absolute order."

"*Peace?*" She blinked. "He commands an army greater than any in history and seeks to conquer all free nations. How is this peace?"

"His absolutism knows no bounds," said Iardu. "His empire stands strong in his image because he forged it with blood and iron. All those who oppose him are dead. There are no wars in his empire, no border conflicts, no piracy or rebellions. By uniting every kingdom beneath his banner of total control, he has driven war from his side of the world. There is only one monolithic kingdom, which bears his name and venerates his image. He deems his long work a success because of its vast imperial order. His people thrive until the moment they grow defiant; then they are chastened by his ruthless power.

"Do you see the paradox? Zyung has brought ultimate peace by denying the freedom of his people. He has slaughtered millions to achieve this, and he counts it as no great cost. Each succeeding generation becomes more obedient, as he pulls malcontents from his continental garden like weeds. Now there are no more weeds."

Sharadza savored the tartness of the wine on her tongue.

"So Zyung believes he does what is best for all?"

"He does," said Iardu.

"And he seeks to spread this ultimate peace across the rest of the world. No matter how many Men, Giants, or families he has to murder."

"Now you understand," said Iardu. "Only his ends matter. He cares nothing for individual lives. They are of no consequence to him."

"Unlike you," she said, "who fostered the development of the six kingdoms over the course of ages. Did you never think to conquer them all, like Zyung? To put an end to these wars?"

Iardu chuckled. "Of course I considered it. If I had listened to Zyung all those millennia go, I would have subjugated my half of the world in exactly the way he conquered his own. Then we would unite to form a perfect world. Or so he believed. Yet I rejected this theory."

"Why?"

"All living things have the right to decide their own fate. I nudge them, guide them, whisper wisdom in their ears. Some listen, many do not. But ultimately the individual determines his own role in the universe. This is the essential joy of living, Sharadza, the infinite power of creative consciousness. Sorcerers tap into this more easily than most, but any living being can do the same. Most live their entire lives without realizing this. The ones that do are called wizards, saints, or heroes. To eliminate free will is to destroy the core nature of sentient beings. Zyung and I will never agree on this point."

"So you must confront him, as surely as any of us," she said. "Or bow to his absolute authority."

"These are the choices before us."

"Who is he, really?" she said. Already a spark of revelation had kindled within her.

"Have you not guessed?" Iardu said. "He is what Men would call my *brother*."

Sharadza sat quiet while Iardu drank. It was not easy for him to admit such a secret. She considered its implications.

"You refused his offer a long time ago," she said. "If you had not, the world I know would never have existed."

"Perhaps . . . " His eyes gleamed like prisms; the blue flame on his chest guttered low.

"Ianthe . . . " She hesitated. "Is she also . . . "

"Yes," he said. "All the Old Breed are brothers and sisters, as all Men and Giants are related by a common bloodline stretching back to the primordial mud. Yet unlike these mortal races, our spawning grounds were the gulfs between the stars."

She sighed. "So you spend your life shaping the world in one direction, while Zyung spends his shaping it in the other. A final confrontation was inevitable."

"Inevitable." His voice echoed her word with a heaviness born of remorse. What a terrible weight he must bear, knowing that his own existence was the cause of the coming conflict. Would anything he built survive? Or would the endless legions of absolute control break the world apart and reshape it in Zyung's image?

"You spoke of others from the Old Breed," she said. "We must call them out, wake the Dreaming Ones, convince them to join us against Zyung."

"We must try," said Iardu with a sigh. "And soon."

"After tonight's war council?"

He nodded and drank. Sunlight gleamed on his silvery beard and hair. She could not imagine the true depth of his age, could not even attempt it. He must be older than the Four Gods themselves. She dared not ask him the truth about those intangible objects of Men's worship, whether they were real or entirely imagined. She feared what he might reveal. As long as Men believed in Gods, they served their purpose. She chose to keep that part of her understanding untouched.

"What really happened to Ianthe when you stole her physical form?"

Iardu snapped his fingers. "Her spirit fled. Where I cannot say. It would have emerged in the high tower again if we had not destroyed it. So with Gammir."

"When I held him in the grip of the living flames, Gammir said I had freed him."

"So you did," said Iardu. "You freed him to find another manifestation somewhere else in the world."

"Have you any idea where they will find rebirth?"

He looked at her. "Can you not guess?"

"Can any of the Old Breed be destroyed?" she asked. "Forever?"

Iardu considered the question, rubbing his chin.

"Nothing in this universe is ever truly destroyed," he said finally. "Matter and energy only exchange forms in the endless dance of Being and Nonbeing. What you consider *death* is simply . . . *change*. There is never truly an end."

"What does that mean?" she asked.

"It means that I cannot answer your question."

She sat alongside him on the balcony until they had finished the last of the wine.

Patterns.

Everything she knew, and everything she did not know.

All those who lived, and all those who had died.

All that existed now, and all that would ever be.

Patterns, all of them.

Combining and evolving into the Grand Pattern that was the cosmos itself. There was no distinction between the part and the whole. To be in the pattern was to be the pattern. All of these things Iardu had taught her.

Somewhere deep inside the pattern that was everything there lay an answer for her.

This was her duty: to seek and to find that answer, before the pattern itself crumbled, only to be replaced by a new one. If Zyung reshaped her world into his own image, would she even miss the old one? Or would the emerging pattern swallow her and everyone else into its ineffable weave?

Like Iardu, she had no answer. But perhaps questions mattered most.

Questions led to wisdom.

Or to death, which was itself a kind of wisdom.

The wisdom of change.

25

A Decision and a Name

His dreams were bloody infernos, hordes of howling foes, a rain of blades hissing at his skin, the skulls of dead men crunching beneath his boots. Winged shadows fell from the sky to pluck eyes from living faces. Flames consumed the earth on every side, and his enemies rushed from the fires, eager to spill his guts and trample them into the bone-littered earth. His blade was an extension of his right arm, as it always was in the murderous chaos of battle. He hacked a path through the flames, splitting open faces and bellies and chests. He killed until he was sick of killing, and the battle continued. The great, stony face of the God-King hovered in the black sky, flaming comets dripping from its eyes. Its vast mouth was open, pouring forth an endless stream of armored Men and blazing Giants.

After a restless eternity of battling phantoms, he rose from the morass of nightmares into the quiet gloom of his tent. His eyes fluttered open. The muted sounds of camp life drifted through the canvas walls, and the terrible heat of Khyrei lay heavy upon his chest. The blankets on which he lay were soaked through with sweat, as were the bandages about his arms, legs, and torso. The silhouette of an Uurzian spearman stood outside the tent, sunlight casting a golden aura about his shield and corselet. Tyro called to the guard, but his voice was no more than a hollow croaking.

Water. He must have it now or die. Black ashes filled his chest, as if his interior organs had burned to cinders. He no longer saw the flames of his nightmares, but still he felt their merciless heat licking at his flesh.

Someone stirred in the gloom and a new figure moved into view. The sharp-nosed face of Mendices leaned over him with a chalice of sparkling fluid. His hand slipped beneath Tyro's head and he raised it so the Sword King could drink from the cup.

Water, cool and perfect. He drained the cup.

"More . . . more . . . " he moaned.

Twice more Mendices filled the cup and twice more Tyro drained it.

He fell into a deeper sleep then, dreamless and dark.

How long was it until he awoke again, the sun still hanging high above his tent? He might have lain here for days or weeks, so oblivious was he to the passing of time. Mendices once again walked out of the tent's shadows and gave him water.

"Hungry . . ." Tyro mumbled.

Mendices grinned, his pockmarked face suddenly feline in aspect. "Good," he said. "Hunger is a good sign, My Lord." He sliced apart a ripe pomegranate and placed a few tangy seeds into Tyro's mouth. Tyro sucked the sweet flesh from the seeds, then crunched them between his molars. A sudden wash of strength fell across his limbs as he devoured the pomegranate. Then quickly it fell away again, leaving him exhausted on the crude couch.

"How long?" he asked.

"Less than a day," said Mendices. "You fell ill last night. Now is just past midday."

"Where is Vireon?"

"With his Giants," said Mendices. The look on his face was one of deep worry. "Tonight the Kings meet once again for a war council."

Tyro inhaled the hot air. "I must go," he said, and strained to bring himself into a sitting position. His head swam crazily, and he fell back to the cushions. His arms and legs seemed made of lead. He lay helpless before the only man of Uurz he trusted completely.

"Rest easy, Majesty," said Mendices. "Sixty men have died from this red fever already. Gods of Earth and Sky willing, you will not join them. Let the fever run its course."

"I have slept too much," said Tyro. "I am done with nightmares."

Mendices moved a chair near to Tyro's couch and sat himself upon it. He wore a corselet of boiled leather over a green tunic. His swamp-stained boots had been replaced with easy sandals. A longblade hung at his side, the same one he always carried. Its pommel was carved in the likeness of a hawk's head with tiny garnets for eyes. They glinted at Tyro as he lay powerless and listened to Mendices' words.

"Iardu has given you some concoction of herbs and sorcery," said the Warlord. "It has done you well. The first stage of the fever passed quickly. Your head is cleared, your skin cooling. It will be a while still before your full strength returns. You must be patient . . . "

Patient? The greatest conquering horde the world has ever known is bearing down on Uurz and its allies, and Mendices wants patience?

"I will represent the throne of Uurz tonight in your stead," said the Warlord. "So speak, Majesty, as best you can. Tell me your mind so I may convey it to the Kings."

Tyro blinked and managed to raise a hand to wipe his damp brow. "You speak eloquently, but I know your mind," he said. "When you have something to say, you take on the aspect of the keenest listener. Out with it."

Mendices grimaced. His dark eyes glanced toward the tent's entrance. The blurred shapes of Men and horses passed by. Somewhere in the distance the gravelly voices of Giants were raised in song. "You know me too well, Majesty." He stood and paced between the couch and the far tent wall. Tyro's gilded breastplate hung upon a wooden stand, alongside a new shield bearing the Uurzian sun and a freshly polished spear and broadsword. He coughed and waited for the Warlord to speak his mind.

"You saw what happened to Vireon," said Mendices. "How he defeated the Swamp God."

Tyro nodded weakly.

Mendices turned toward him, lowered his face to stare directly into his King's eyes. "You saw him standing tall as a mountain, tossing towers into kindling with a single step. Never will I forget the sight of it . . . "

"Aye," Tyro mumbled. It was a miraculous tale he hoped to tell his grandchildren someday. The legends of Vireon the Slayer were built on a solid foundation of truth. He was every bit the legend his father had been.

"With Angrid's death, Vireon adds the might of the Icelands to that of Udurum. In this southern clime he rules two thousand Udvorg. How many more thousands must lurk still in the Frozen North? Vireon now wears the crown of a true Giant-King. He wields the mightiest force in the world. And this force is not human.

"I have seen him walking about the camps at the height of his Giants, as if he is now one of them. And I have come to realize that he is indeed more Giant than Man. Why, taking Angrid's throne has made him Emperor of the North. He might declare himself so at any time!"

Mendices grew silent. He poured a fresh cup of water for Tyro, and a goblet of amber wine for himself. He helped Tyro swallow a few sips before he continued.

"I fear him, Majesty. Vireon's might is beyond our ken. Now this sorcerer shows us a vision of Zyung and his approaching hordes. I know you feel the weight of this vision, as I know it to be true in the depths of my heart. The Shaper would not lie about such things. Our situation is dire, My Lord. We came south to conquer Khyrei and it has been done for us. Stolen from us, one might say. What more will we lose if we stay here?"

The words rolled like hot stones about the confines of Tyro's skull. His head hammered, but he would not yield to the pain. He would vanquish it, as he vanquished all foes.

"What would you have us do?" he asked.

"Return to Uurz," said Mendices, his voice a whisper. "Bring our legions together and fortify our walls for the long siege that is sure to come. Let Vireon and his Giants lead the defense against these invaders. Let Yaskatha and Mumbaza, and this New Khyrei, take the brunt of Zyung's assault. The war that falls soon upon us will be deadly beyond mortal reckoning. Let our enemies humble Vireon and his newfound power, while he weakens the ranks of the invaders. By the time Zyung reaches Uurz, he will have faced an army of Giants and several armies of Men. We will have the advantage of unspoiled legions and the strength of our unfailing walls."

Tyro lay silent for a while, staring at the yellow canvas above. Already the heat consuming his body seemed to have lessened. Yet strength eluded him.

"I have been foolish," he said. "I sought glory in the conquering of Khyrei and the deaths of the sorcerers who ruled it. I was angry that this glory had been stolen from me by Iardu and Sharadza ... and this risen Slave King. Yet it was all a ploy to bring me here that I might see the truth of what is to come. Iardu is but the agent of that truth.

"Now I understand where the true glory lies. The greatest war in history sails toward us on the wild sea winds. Only by facing what comes can a warrior know the truest taste of glory. Only by abandoning ourselves to death can we truly know what it means to live.

"You ask me to run, Mendices. You would have me flee this coast and leave my allies to face the terrors that I will not. These are not the words of a Warlord. They are the yammerings of a coward."

Mendices lowered his eyes. Whether anger or shame or some mixture of the two stole across his face, Tyro could not tell. He sat in silence for a long while.

"Forgive me, Lord," he said at length.

Tyro forced his hand over the lip of the couch and placed it on the golden bracer encircling the Warlord's forearm.

"Let us speak no more of it," said the Sword King. "We will consult with the Kings, we will support them, and we will fight with them. There is no greater honor. And if we die in the coming storm? Well, if we die we become something far more than Men."

"What is that, Majesty?"

"*Legends.*"

Mendices nodded and rubbed his tired eyes. "Do you still hunger?"

"I crave meat," said Tyro.

"Very well." Mendices left the tent and returned with a hock of roasted pork, part of the provisions given to the Uurzians by the Slave King. Mendices fed it to him in small bites. Tyro reveled in its delicious flavor. How long had it been since he tasted such solid fare? Mendices urged him on with every bite.

When the meal was done, Tyro drank a cup of wine. He managed to hold his head up and bring the glass to his own lips. Mencides was pleased.

Now came the difficult part. Tyro gathered his breath for an ultimate effort. The muscles of his belly contracted beneath the white bandages, and he pulled himself into a sitting position. He breathed in ragged gasps, sweat dripping from his wet locks. He sat now with elbows upon his knees, and looked at Mendices, who stood before him.

"Iardu's potion has done its work," said the Warlord. Tyro's head resounded with the clanging of unseen shields. The heat seemed to rise once more inside his skull, as if his brain were immersed in boiling saltwater. He ignored it.

Mendices brought him a ewer of cool water and a sponge. With painstaking slowness, Tyro himself washed the sweat and grime from his body. He lay back down while Mendices removed his bandages, washed his wounds, and replaced them with fresh strips of linen.

The face of Talondra drifted into Tyro's mind as he sat up a second time on the cot. It had been long weeks since he felt her hot kisses. Too long since he took her lithe body in his hands and enjoyed the sweet embrace of her womanhood. He missed her so. By now her belly must be growing round; not huge yet, but noticeable. He smiled when he thought of her hiding the lump beneath costly gowns. She would disguise the loss of her slim figure until the child came. Such was her vanity, and the vanity of all highborn women. Still, she took great pride in bearing his son. The Priests of the Sky God had ordained that Tyro's first-born would indeed be a boy. He had never known them to be wrong about such matters.

For a moment all thoughts of glory and war left him. Perhaps Mendices was right. Perhaps his place was in Uurz with his wife and son. Yet he could not leave his friends and allies to fight a war for him. There was no honor in it. Better the honor that death provides than the shame of retreat. If he died, at least his son would live to take the throne of the green-gold city.

"Mendices," he called. "Find parchment and quill. I wish to write a letter to my wife." Mendices nodded and left the tent. Tyro forced himself to stay sitting upright. No matter how weary he felt, he would be at tonight's war council. He would not let Mendices make any great decisions without him. The other Kings would see it as weakness if he missed a second gathering. The path to glory was long and hard, and he had barely set his foot upon it.

Mendices returned and arranged quill, ink, and parchment on a makeshift desk. Tyro spoke the words aloud while the Warlord inscribed them on the paper.

"Dearest Talondra," he began. "May the Four Gods guide this letter so that it finds you whole and healthy. I miss you dearly. We have come to Khyrei, where the seeds of revolt have sprouted before us. Emperor and Empress are vanquished, though not by my hand. The city's slave population has risen up and toppled the regime. In this noble feat they were aided by the hand of Iardu the Shaper. Although the humbling of the black city was our goal, we know now that we have been called here to face a far greater threat . . . "

He went on to tell her of Zyung the God-King and his approaching hordes. He spared her the details of aerial ships and flying lizard-beasts. It was enough to tell her that a force of millions would soon descend on the world from across the Golden Sea. He explained his decision to stay and fight together with the Kings of the known realms. He even shared his hope that they would survive the coming of Zyung and see a new age of peace and prosperity born from these historic alliances.

"I know not how many months or years will pass until I hold you in my arms again. Or when I will see the face of my son. Until that day I carry both of you in my heart. It is my fondest wish that you name our first-born after my father. Let him be called Dairon the Second. If I am to perish in the coming war, raise him to understand why I stayed here and fought with my brother Kings. Let him know the deeds and honor of his father and grandfather. Raise him to be a fearless warrior and a wise ruler. I know that you will serve him well, as you serve all of Uurz." He finished the letter with the customary call for the blessings of Earth, Sea, Sun, and Sky.

"Find a strong rider, uninjured and quick-minded," he told Mendices. "Bid him carry this scroll to Uurz and deliver it to the hand of the Queen herself."

"It shall be done," said Mendices. He rolled the parchment, stuffed it into a capped leather tube, and left the tent to find a suitable messenger.

Dairon the Second.

A fitting name for the boy who would one day rule the Stormlands. And if Tyro never got the chance to read Lyrilan's book, let young Dairon read it and learn the history of his name-sake.

Tyro forced himself to stand with no little pain. On his third try he succeeded in walking seven steps to the entrance of the tent. He stood there looking past the shoulder of the sentinel, scanning the sea of sun-kissed bronze and *steel*, the simple tents of legion-naires, the clusters of soldiers tending to mail and blade with oil and hammer. The towering forms of Udvorg stumbled across the crowded encampment; beyond their shaggy white heads the black walls of Khyrei stood strong as ever.

Near to that wall, in the place where the first Council of Kings was held, a parade of attendants was already setting the board for this evening's summit. Out beyond the double armada, the sun sank at its own steady pace toward the sparkling mirror of the sea.

Tyro turned back to the cool interior of the tent.

"Guard!" he called. The man turned and stepped respectfully inside. "Come and help me with this armor."

The warrior was only too glad to assist his King. When Mendices returned, he was shocked to see the Sword King arrayed in all his finery: golden breastplate, sunray cloak, jeweled sandals, and the golden helm with its intricate wings. Tyro buckled the wide belt that held his broadsword in its scabbard.

"Majesty!" Mendices huffed. "You should be resting still."

Tyro swayed on his feet. His scalp was damp with fresh sweat. Like an ancient tree caught in a windstorm, he stubbornly refused to fall.

He was the Emperor of Uurz. He was the Sword King.

"I am done with resting," he said. "We have a war to plan."

Mendices lowered his bald head, expressing his disapproval in silence.

Let this Zyung come. The world stands ready to meet him.

Tyro plodded from his tent into the humid purple twilight.

26

The Apotheosis of Shadow

The fountain sat amid a ring of palm trees and beds of blooming lavender. Some sculptor from a previous century had carved it whole from a massive block of white marble. It was not an overly large pool, nor any deeper than a man's knees. A mosaic of finned and scaly Sea Folk decorated its outer rim: mermaids and mermen, gliding squids, graceful mantas, and swirling eels all brought to life from inert stone by the sheer skill of a single man's obsession.

At the fountain's center a dais rose from the cascading waters. Atop the dais stood a trio of white stallions, sculpted as if rearing on their hind legs. From the sleek backs of each marble horse spread a pair of pearly wings, each feather evoked by minute tools and infinite patience. The mouths of these winged steeds spewed arcs of water into the air, and each arc fed the bubbling waters in the basin.

Lyrilan sat on a padded seat in the dappled solitude of the Yaskathan garden. The pinnacles of the palace rose high beyond the palm trees, while close-set hedges and cypresses blocked the rest of the courtyard from view. The rhythmic sound of ocean beating against the strand reached his ears. A legion of tame birds sang melodies from the branches of southern oaks, myrtlewoods, and willows.

He bent forward to study the fine lines of the fountain mosaic, then stood to admire the stone stallions' musculature and exquisite wings. *Patience*. Yes, that was the key to creating a great work of art. He saw the marks of patience in every curve and detail of the fountain. The laughter of its waters joined the symphony of mingled birdsongs. Here was a day to define Yaskatha, a golden paradise growing ripe beneath a cloudless sky.

A robe of checkered black and white hung loose on his thin frame, tied at the waist with a sash of crimson silk. A matching necklace of twelve rubies hung about his neck. Volomses had helped him relearn the importance of a proper appearance. His long black hair was entirely gone, shorn from his lean skull in a symbolic show of rebirth. He enjoyed the feel of warm sun on his bald head. The ocean breeze soothed his skin and brought the faint scents of brine and seaweed into the eastern gardens.

He sat now with hands in his lap, eyes closed, enjoying the song of the fountain and the warbling refrains of birds, soaking in the wash of sunlight. His recent studies had taught him, among other things, how to embrace the moment. Nothing else existed beyond this fountain, these trees, and this garden. If he listened long enough, he might understand the deeper meanings of the birds' language. He might hear the wind whisper secrets from faraway lands. The fragrance of blossoms might deliver to him the secrets of the ancient cosmos. He might wear the sun and stars as his crown, King of the world and all its petty intrigues.

He might have sat thus forever, yet no solitude endures. The shuffling of sandaled feet on the jade path told him that Volomses approached. He knew the sage's awkward gait, the sound of one leg perpetually lagging behind the other. Victim of an old riding wound that never truly healed, Volomses always favored his right foot. So Lyrilan knew that his request had been seen to by the old man.

"Majesty," said Volomses. The fabric of his burgundy robe rustled as he kneeled. Lyrilan opened his eyes to see the sage poised on one knee, a shuttered box of rosewood in his brown hands.

"You found it? All of it?" asked Lyrilan.

Volomses stood and offered him the box. "I faced many difficulties, but everything is here."

Lyrilan took the modest box and sat it on his lap. "Very good," he said, staring at the casket. "You never fail me, old friend. You may go."

Volomses blinked. "But . . . My Lord . . . shall I not stay to assist you?"

Lyrilan met the sage's rheumy eyes. "I will be fine."

Volomses nodded and left him once more alone in the garden. Lyrilan opened the lid and scanned the coffer's contents. The eyes of an eagle, brought down by a skilled archer in the High Realms; they lay on a velvet cushion like two tiny topazes with ebony centers. A small vial of aged Uurzian wine spiced with the venom of a camel spider. The fingerbones of a dead King, purloined from the deepest crypts of Yaskatha. To be caught with such remains would earn a death sentence from the Yaskathan authorities, but Volomses had hired only the most discreet of burglars. Finally, a short-bladed dagger newly forged of purest silver. The mark of a local smith lay upon the base of its blade, and the pommel bore a single black onyx as its only decoration.

Lyrilan carried the open box to the fountain. He walked slowly about its circumference, singing a low song of the Vital Tongues. When he reached the place where he had begun, completing the circle, he started the song again and dropped the eagle's eyes into the fountain waters. They hardly disturbed the swirling flow.

As he circled the fountain a second time, he poured in the

entire contents of the vial; poisoned wine swirled like blood in the foamy water. He scattered the fingerbones into the fountain as well, each one sinking to lie still on the bottom like pale pebbles. When his second circuit was complete he cast away the empty box, stopped his walk, and held the silver dagger in his right hand. He began the song a third time and placed the utmost tip of the dagger to the tip of his left index finger. A tiny drop of crimson sprang forth, swelling into a minute red sphere. He touched the water of the fountain with this bloody finger, and his touch turned the clear water black as pitch.

Stars gleamed in the black waters now, although the sky was blue and bright overhead. Lyrilan began a second incantation and waved his hands in precise patterns above the benighted water. An image swirled to life, replacing the darkness with the daylight of a distant kingdom. Mighty Uurz reared its towers into a roiling sky heavy with gray clouds. The first thing he noticed was the steady rainfall. The long drought of his homeland was over. He sang on, and the vision in the fountain pool shifted. The great palace loomed above streets of green and muddy gold, an assemblage of forested terraces, blooming roof gardens, jeweled domes, and gilded spires. Sentinels walked the walls beneath green banners bearing golden suns.

Again the vision changed, and Lyrilan stared through the water into the throne room of Uurz. There, on a jeweled seat worthy of a King, sat Talondra, Empress of Uurz. A throng of courtiers in the bright silks and baubles of their station filled the hall, every face turned to heed the words of Tyro's wife. In his absence she was the Ruler of Uurz. Lyrilan had no doubt that she would rule the city with an iron fist. There could be no more effective plotter or strategist than this Sharrian with the soulless eyes of a Serpent.

He smiled as he spoke the final syllables of the incantation. This living vision of Uurz and Talondra was proof that he had mastered a modicum of Imvek's wisdom. He anticipated the emergence of a far greater proof very soon.

Last night's conjuring was long and painful and exacting. He had yet to see the fruits of his nocturnal weaving. Yet for now it was enough to spy on this murderess who wore the crown.

So Lyrilan watched.

Patience is the key to crafting any great work of art.

Talondra enjoyed her lofty view from the throne of Uurz, yet little else pleased her on this day. The faces of the fawning courtiers looked up at her with a mixture of jealousy, fear, and desire. No woman could be more intoxicating to a man than one who held utmost power over him. The females of her court were scheming fools, and she had already removed her greatest rivals from the palace. It was easy to create imaginary crimes and enforce very real penalties for those who defied her. Yet those who remained were only hypocrites. Her spies knew the secret blasphemies whispered behind the doors of noble houses. She forgot nothing and forgave less.

How could the burdens of an Empress be so worldly and mundane? She was called to judge a string of cases involving theft, slander, and murder. Each man hauled before her claimed his innocence, shouting it to the very rafters of the Great Hall; each accuser claimed his own veracity with equal fervor. Both sides unfailingly invoked the Four Gods in their pleas and protests, as if the Gods had anything to do with the fates of Men and their tiny lives. Still, she must judge and deliver the Emperor's justice in his stead. For a fleeting moment she wished Tyro were still here to handle these unpleasant verdicts, instead of conquering Khyrei.

These pitiful cries for justice never seemed to end. This morning alone she had sent two men to the dungeons, another to the headsman, and ordered the hands removed from a woman infamous for stealing palace loaves. And still there were the tax advisors waiting, the masters of the granaries, the lords of the vineyards, and the ambassador from Mumbaza would arrive any day now. Preparations for this southern dignitary's visit had consumed the better part of a week. There would be daily feasting and nightly entertainments, all for the benefit of Undutu's favorite cousin and his humorless retinue. She did not look forward to the Mumbazans' stay. They were a singularly humorless people.

She played with a jeweled bracelet at her wrist and listened to the latest accuser, a smith who stood at the bottom of her dais and condemned his apprentice for stealing silver.

She sighed. "How many ingots were stolen?"

"Five, Majesty! Enough to make a fine chalice."

She turned to the sooty face of the smith's apprentice. A lanky boy of no more than fifteen, he looked as if he had never eaten a whole meal in his entire unglamorous life. Such poverty created thieves, as surely as rain caused the grapes of the field to grow.

"Five ingots of silver," she repeated. "Guards, remove five of this boy's fingers."

The smithy and his ward cried their protests at the same time. No matter what decision she gave, there was never much satisfaction among the parties involved. The people of Uurz were ungrateful, spoiled, and worthy of little but her contempt.

She missed the fine lords of Shar Dni and their splendid daughters. The games and dances and contests of her youth were nowhere to be found in the green-gold city. Here a royal steward put together various entertainments for her nightly distraction. Yet more often than not he missed the mark. Off-key minstrels plucked from the muddy Stormlands roads, motley fools who tumbled and leaped like trained monkeys, even contests of skill where swordsmen and knife wielders fought to the death. All of these desperate spectacles left her restless and bored.

She rubbed the gentle swell of her belly. In another month the last of her lithe figure would be lost beneath the growing bulk of her pregnant stomach. This was her only source of joy. She missed Tyro's strong arms and his savage lovemaking. He had been the source of all her pleasure in Uurz; without him she would rather travel to some distant land and find new ways to spend her time. Yet her duty was here. She must run the Stormlands while Tyro ended the threat of Khyrei. When the Sword King Emperor returned, his son would be healthy and strong, a worthy heir. Now Sharrian blood would one day sit upon the throne of Uurz; she shuddered with quiet glee when she mused upon her son's future reign. Then her ennui always returned, mixed with a painful longing for her husband's touch.

The ladies of the court told her not to fret, for pregnant women were often besieged by stormy moods and periods of clinging sadness. She supposed they were correct, but she seemed to have lost the joy of golden Uurz without Tyro at her side. She had only the birth of her son to anticipate in less than seven months. The little Prince growing inside her would transform her life, as he would one day reshape the Stormlands and the world.

Sentinels dragged away the displeased smith and the weeping boy. Talondra declared an end to the proceedings. "I will hear no more cases today," she announced. "The rest of you must wait until tomorrow. My condition causes me to tire easily. I am sure you understand."

The assorted courtiers, advisors, and petitioners nodded, smiling to conceal their disappointment. Nobody in the palace ever spoke honestly or revealed his true thoughts. She admired their skill in these courtly games, but since Tyro's leaving these too had grown to annoy her. All of the courtiers were so predictable. She might ban all spoken word from the palace, and still she would know the exact thoughts of every man and woman who entered her presence.

A train of twelve maidens accompanied her from the great hall to her private chambers. There she slipped free of her bejeweled robe and the crown of silver and opal. She lay naked across the bed where Tyro used to work his magic on her willing body. She slept for a little while, then awoke to thirst and hunger as the sun sank low and thunderheads rumbled across the purple sky.

A light rain fell outside the arched windows as she dined on candied fruits, rare legumes, and slivers of braised swordfish. Instead of wine she drank warm goats' milk blended with honey and sprinkled with cinnamon. One of her maidens plucked at the harp while Talondra ate, and another girl sang in high, clear tones. She crooned the story of a valiant knight gone off to war, and the dreams of the faithful girl who awaited his return.

Talondra caressed the singer's cheek. "You always pick the loveliest and saddest songs." She gifted the girl with a soft kiss from her red lips.

They dressed her in an evening gown of maroon with gold stitching, trimmed with an abundance of white lace. The hairdresser wove a matrix of silver wire and diamonds into her hair and set twin rubies dangling from her ears. She walked barefoot across the western wing of the palace to meet with her private guests.

The Lords Ymbrand and Adacus had arrived last evening. Although they had called Udurum their home for the past seven years, they were both loyal Sharrians, and Talondra's eyes and ears in the City of Men and Giants. Before the fall of Shar Dni both lords had enjoyed the lives of Merchant Princes, yet both had successfully transferred knowledge and experience into profitable ventures north of the Grim. Since the fall of Shar Dni, the population of Udurum had tripled.

Talondra ate very little as the two lords devoured the bulk of a roast piglet and washed it down with some of her finest Uurzian wine. "It is true, Majesty," Ymbrand told her. He was a portly man with terrible taste in clothing. His gaudy robes were more suited to a court fool than a master of jewelcraft and royal intrigue. "A true Man sits upon the throne of Udurum. Ryvun Ctholl, they call him, and damn me if he doesn't have some Sharrian blood. Got the green eyes, you see."

"Go on," she urged. Finally a topic of interest. How did the City of Men and Giants endure without its legendary King? Especially when there was no longer a Queen to rule in his stead? And why pick a human to rule? The Vodson must trust this Ctholl to an immense degree.

"Vireon declared him regent as long as the Khyrein War lasts," said Adacus. "The Udurumites are quite fond of him as well. His reputation is built upon loyalty and fairness. Not a bad choice for regent, if you ask me." He lifted a bunch of black grapes and shoved them into his mouth six at a time. Thin as a ship's rail, Adacus nevertheless ate with all the manners of a pig.

Yet he was a useful pig.

"How many Giants are in the city?" she asked.

"None," said Ymbrand. "Only thirty Giantesses."

"Uduri," clarified Adacus. Grape juice dripped from his chin onto his crimson doublet.

"You saw no signs of unrest? No whispers of revolt?"

Ymbrand's tiny eyes narrowed. "If any there are unhappy, they must keep it to themselves," he said. "In fact, I'd say the Men of Udurum are glad to see one of their own on the throne for a change. For we who remember the glory of Shar Dni, it reminds us of our lost monarchy."

"Fascinating. What else can you tell me?"

"Mmmm." Adacus struggled to swallow a mouthful of cheese. "They're building . . . a great statue. A new one . . . for the Avenue of Idols."

Ymbrand nodded, swilling the expensive wine. "A bronze effigy of Vireon the Slayer to stand alongside the great image of his father."

"So Vireon continues to enjoy his people's love, even while long absent."

Her informants nodded. "He remains ever the hero of Udurum," said Ymbrand. "Before he departed, he called the Ice Giants down from the White Mountains. No one has ever done such a thing. Bards are still writing lays about the Son of Vod. No doubt he will return from Khyrei with a whole new host of legends."

"No doubt," Talondra said.

Ymbrand's eyes looked nervous. "In the company of Mighty Tyro, of course," he stammered. "*Two* heroes for the northlands! It shall be a glorious day indeed when the northern Kings return."

She left them to finish their meal and ordered a pair of palace courtesans to share their beds tonight. They were simple fools, but she would continue to employ them as her agents in Vireon's realm. A shrewd ruler must know everything about her allies as well as her enemies. Knowledge was ever the gateway to power.

She returned to the great hall and watched two brawny Uurzians wrestle for the prize of a splendid yellow opal. The courtiers enjoyed such blood sports, yet Talondra found them taxing. Two oily brutes pounding at each other's faces and trying to squeeze the life from each other. She lingered long enough to see one warrior break his opponent's neck. He beamed at the cheering of those who had wagered on his prowess. More duels were scheduled for the evening, as well as a contest of throwing knives and a display of archery. Yet she had no appetite for them.

She excused herself and returned to her bedchamber. The songs of her favorite maidens lulled her to sleep while a golden moon rose into view beyond the bay window.

She lay on her side, one hand cradling the small lump of belly that was her gestating son. She dreamed of Tyro's face emerging from a wall of flames and rattling bones. He screamed a warning at her, but his lips made no sound. She woke in the darkness after midnight, chilled by a sudden breeze blowing in through the casements. The rain had ceased, but its coolness had dispelled the warmth of the Uurzian night.

Raising her head from the pillow, she would have called for a heavier blanket. Yet the dark silhouette that caught her eye made the words linger in the back of her throat. A man stood on the terrace, wrapped in a loose black cloak. No, it was not a man at all. The cloak rustled like a pair of leathery wings, and spread out to hide the moon and stars.

Inside the black folds was no man, but the coiling mass of a bloated viper. Its diamond-shaped head hovered above the shifting coils. Its eyes were identical flames, bright as blood.

They caught her, those eyes, and she lay transfixed in their ruddy glow. The viper slithered across the floor. The wings wavered and twitched, joined to its coils just behind the pointed head. She could only watch it glide, her breath and her voice frozen, as it neared her bed. Two spearmen stood outside her door as always; they might as well be in Khyrei with Tyro, so far were they from her side.

She scrambled across the bedcovers toward the door, saw the golden gleam of torchlight that limned the rectangle, and tried again to cry out. But she was mute, terrified into silence.

A frigid coil slipped about her left leg, pulling her back toward the bed. She coughed and vomited and struggled as the black viper encircled her entire body, squeezing and hissing. Its red eyes flamed, and now she felt the heat of them singing her face. She expected the pungent smell of reptile flesh, but there was no smell at all. Only the tangy ocean air that filled her nostrils yet refused to enter her lungs.

She lay helpless at the heart of the tight glistening coils, and the serpentine face hovered above her own. The black wings cast her world into shadow. The fiery eyes glowed like mad stars. A forked tongue darted out to lick her cheek. Tears welled in her eyes and ran across her face. The tongue licked at them curiously. She lost control of her bladder, and her water ran across the marble floor. She trembled in the iron grip of the devil-shadow.

Her eyes studied its fangs, long as daggers and dripping amber venom. Drops of it burned her flesh when they fell upon her neck and breast. She quivered and stared against her will into the dancing flame eyes of the beast.

Now those strange eyes grew familiar. The winged reptile grinned, and a voice that she recognized spoke to her softly.

Lyrilan's voice.

You did this.

The horrid mouth yawned wide. Twin fangs sank deep into her eyes, and her bones snapped inside crushing coils.

Lyrilan stood by the fountain long after sunset. In the enchanted pool he surveyed the grisly pulp on the floor of Talondra's bedchamber as the winged shadow withdrew. It slithered out the high window, flapped its wings, and soared into the night trailing strands of blood.

What lay on the marble floor could no longer be called a human being. A mass of flesh and jagged bones, even the skull had been crushed to splinters. There was no trace of the second life his servitor had claimed. Its fetal remains must lie somewhere among the heaped entrails and minced viscera of its mother, but he did not care to look any longer.

He waved a hand and the lights gleaming in the fountain pool faded. Darkness rushed to fill the water beneath the trio of winged horses. He longed to call up an image of Ramiyah and explain his vengeance to her. Yet he had already tried reaching beyond the grave. It was not to be.

Finally he understood the Apotheosis of Shadow, the underlying principle of Imvek's Fourth Book. Here was definitive proof of it. Conjuring this foul thing from beyond the living world showed that his grasp of the Vital Tongues was strong.

The Incantations of Night were now his own.

He inhaled the brisk nocturnal air. A fine night for stargazing. He sat himself on a padded chair and considered the blinking constellations. He thought of Tyro, marching or fighting or sleeping somewhere beneath these same stars. The Sword King could not know that his wife and son were gone now, like his exiled brother. Yet word would soon come to Tyro on scrawled parchment carried by a red-eyed rider from Uurz. And he would know at last the weight of the pain his brother had endured. The scales had been balanced.

Lyrilan was wise enough to know that he was no true sorcerer. Yet he stood well inside the gateway to a storehouse of ancient knowledge that would forever separate him from his fellow man. He spoke enough of the dead languages to understand their power. He had grown adept at singing these ancient songs of blood, death, and wisdom.

He was no longer Lyrilan the Scholar. He was Lyrilan, Son of Dairon. Soon he would be Emperor of Uurz. He was no sorcerer. He was only a man who commanded some small portion of the knowledge that other men had owned long before him.

He left the scented garden and retired to his private chamber, where the final two *Books of Imvek* waited heavy with secrets.

Epilogue

The Pale Carriage

The sands of the desert were white as powdered bone. Sages in distant lands claimed these sands were indeed the crumbled bones of Men and monsters, ancient hosts whose ceaseless warring drained the land of all its green and growing things. The name of these wars and the nations who fought them were lost in the sunken hollows of time. Only the desert of white sand remained, forever burning beneath the unforgiving sun.

Near the center of the white waste lay the rotting stones of a city older than memory. It shared the pristine hue of the desert, stubs of towers and fragmented walls sprouting from the dunes like pallid fungi. Alabaster domes sat cracked and empty, while rivers of dust filled the streets and drowned the prehistoric plazas. Monolithic columns stood scattered and broken, jagged teeth knocked from a God's roaring mouth to lie in ash. A few soaring effigies of forgotten Kings still stood in the smothered city, their faces worn to blank masks by eons of wind and driving sand. Colossal temples lay in jumbled piles of rock. Somewhere in the midst of the devastation the curving ribs of a great baroque palace rose from the dunes, a skeletal memory of what was once a glory upon the face of the earth.

The winds sang wordless refrains of loneliness and death. In crypts beneath tons of sand, the mummified remains of the city's former masters lay in the grip of eternal peace. The world had died and been reborn twice over since the Princes and Princesses of the nameless city walked beneath the stars. The shards of broken magnificence lay among the toppled ramparts of the bone-white city, which lay at the heart of the bone-white desert.

Yet today there was movement among the stillness of ages.

From the direction of the ruined palace an odd conveyance glided through the sandy streets. It resembled a carriage in which the nobles of antique kingdoms might ride. Its four great wheels and oblong body were conglomerations of bleached bones, welded together by some obscure artistry. Jawless human skulls sat upon each of its four corners, and at the center of each spoked bone-wheel.

The skeletons of four once-great horses pulled the carriage, their naked bones glittering in the sunlight. The tack and harness that held them to the carriage were likewise formed of interlinked bones. The fleshless horses ran without instinct, fatigue, or hunger. They were dead things, products of an elder world that would never rise again. They had lain in the vault of a disremembered King whose favorite steeds were buried with him long before scribes began to record the movements of history.

The skeleton stallions pulled the pale carriage rattling from the ruins into the blinding glare of open desert. They ran throughout the day and did not once pause, not even when the sun had set and blankets of frost settled upon the cacti and rocky crags of the wasteland. The carriage sped across the dunes by the light of a silvery moon. When the sun rose to bake the white plain again, the unliving steeds did not slow their pace.

There was no window set into the walls of the bone carriage, only a single door which never opened. Nor did the carriage stop for food, drink, or any other comforts. It flew like the wind itself across the sea of white sand, between forests of tapered obelisks, between the walls of winding ravines, on and on across a realm of everlasting heat.

After many days the carriage rolled to the summit of a weedy ridge, then down onto a green and yellow plain. Far to the north a ridge of sharp mountain peaks gleamed purple and gray, but the carriage of bones raced eastward without a moment's pause. The hooves of the equine skeletons ate up the soft ground and sent clods of earth flying above its churning wheels. It rushed toward a wide lazy river; the bone horses galloped across the warm water as if it had frozen to solidity. Later the plain began to sprout herds of wild oxen, flocks of crimson waterbirds, and isolated copses of trees heavy with wild fruits. The carriage did not stop for its passengers to pick fruit or bathe in the gentle waters of brook and stream.

It rolled on, constant as death.

Next the conveyance passed through a pleasant land of farming villages. None of the field workers or shepherds at their flocks noticed the passing of four skinless horses, or the strange burden they pulled. Following a day and a night of traveling through green and fertile valleys dotted with hamlets, the pale carriage came to a broad road, unpaved yet well maintained. This road led to the gates of many a walled township where simple folk worked at wells, gardens, orchards, and shops. None of them saw the carriage or the horses, unless it was glimpsed like a swift shadow in the corner of an eye. It moved through each community like a chill wind, leaving no traces but for a coolness on the skin, a shudder in the bones of the living.

At last the walls and spires of a great city rose to dominate the horizon. The pale carriage raced on toward the massive gates. The road was now paved with millions of six-sided flat stones. The dead steeds hurtled across the centuries-old roadway toward the purple stones of the steaming, smoking metropolis. Spires rose from the city's outer wall, which was so great in circumference the carriage might have traveled a whole day about it. The wall stood taller than the mast of a great warship, and so thick that each of its eight gates opened upon a long tunnel lined with platforms full of armored guards. These voiceless legions held spears of ornate design, and visors like the beaks of hawks disguised their faces.

In the shadow of the purple walls camped a great host, millions of warriors moving about in precise formations. The constant glinting of spear, shield, and mail gave the city the semblance of an island surrounded by a sun-kissed sea. Yet the true sea lay some distance away, at the end of the green river flowing through the city's eastern quarter.

The legions of soldiers looked not at the bone carriage when it passed among them, nor did the galloping horses take any note of the various banners, standards, and nationalities that comprised this greatest of hosts. The carriage rushed like an icy wind from the ancient west.

It sped through the nearest gate in the early light of morning, the first of any vehicle to pass that way on this day. The gate's sentinels did not see the skeleton horses or the mélange of ancient bones that was the coach itself. Their eyes saw instead the splendid chariot of some wealthy landowner, flowing with dyed silk pennons and pulled by a team of spotted draft horses. Some lordling on his way into the city for a day of trade, dining, and business, followed by a night of revelry.

The brown-skinned folk of the city walked proudly about their flat-topped pyramids, their ziggurats of jade and granite, their ivory towers sculpted fine and delicate as the bodies of women. The carriage rolled alongside broad canals where riverboats carried their goods to market stalls and crowded bazaars.

Mastadons with gilded tusks lumbered through the streets with steepled pagodas of silk and gold upon their backs. Warrior maidens drove chariots pulled by spotted leopards, and trained gorillas carried barrels and crates for merchant lords and their companies. Two-legged Serpents carried mailed warriors on their hunched backs, fangs held in check by leathern hoods and the clever prodding of their masters. Most men of the city carried slim swords at their belts, straight of blade and patterned with precious stones. Noble folk reclined aboard slave-borne palanquins; they wore horned and gaudy headdresses above painted faces.

In the sky great galleons hovered like floating mountains, sails spreading from the sides of each hull as well as the mainmasts. They moved in constantly shifting patterns, gliding in unison from north of the city wall, coming in low to skirt the summits of spires and temples. From these ships launched winged lizards bearing human riders; they jousted with wooden poles between the summits of towers. These flying reptiles found perches on the tops of high turrets. Air galleons docked between those pinnacles as well, sending men up and down their hanging rope ladders.

The greatest of all the city's wonders stood near its center. Grander than any palace or temple alone, it served the purpose of both. A massive eminence of pearly stone, nearly as white as the distant desert, rose from a labyrinth of cloistered gardens and orchards. Its walls slanted inward, yet instead of a pyramid's point or a series of terraced gardens, the structure culminated in a massive face of pale stone, square-jawed and with stylized flames about the eyes.

Here was the carven face of Zyung, whose name was also the name of the city and the empire that stretched across an entire continent. The temple-palace's lower regions were a mass of bridged towers and rosy domes. Phalanx after phalanx of warriors marched about its sheltered grounds. Here was the home of the God-King, standing tall and majestic as an ice-crowned mountain. Yet no mountain ever bore a visage like that of Zyung, whose great stony eyes overlooked hundreds of tributary kingdoms.

Zyung, whose high house was the center of the world.

Along the winding courtyard roads of the palace rolled the bone carriage, the dead steeds slowing their pace at last. Servants and soldiers wandering those gardens heard the beating of hooves where no horse or other mount was visible. Yet those who peered from the upper windows of the citadel, priests and sages and sorcerers, saw the rattling bones for what they truly were. Soon their warnings spread to the very heart of the temple-palace.

The carriage drew up before a gate of jeweled iron fronting the structure's grand entrance. The ceaselessly beating hooves finally came to rest on the polished pavement, and the pale carriage rattled to silence. From the shelter of flowering trees and sculpted hedges, slaves, laborers, and strolling courtesans peered now at the strange conveyance.

Its single door of melded bones opened without a sound. From the shadows of its dark interior came a white panther tall as a war horse. It stalked patiently in a ring about the carriage, purring low and deep. Next, a black wolf exited the carriage and followed at the heels of the panther, sniffing the air for stray wisdom.

When the panther ceased its prowling about the carriage, the conveyance crumbled at once into a clattering pile of bones. The four dead horses reared their heads one last time and fell into dust. Soon there was only a pile of white sand lying before the open gate of the temple-palace. The wind picked up and began to blow the sand away. Before the sun passed beyond the city's imposing wall, there would be no more trace of the pale carriage or the bone steeds.

Warriors marched forth from the gate, spears and shields at the ready, but they did not confront or hinder the white panther or the black wolf. The troops only stood facing one another in double row, and the two beasts walked beneath a row of crossed spears into the vaulted hallway.

Panther and wolf peered about the columned recesses and ivory galleries, the first with eyes like black diamonds, the second with eyes of liquid ruby. Palace servants hid behind corners or ducked into niches to avoid those hungry glares.

Eventually the pair of beasts came into a throne room vast as a hollowed hill. Jewels sparkled like constellations on the walls and ceiling; a forest of pillars stood carved from agate, emerald, and onyx. Panther and wolf followed a long carpet of intricate design toward a dais of nineteen steps at the hall's far end. There sat a grim Giant with a face to match the greater face atop the temple-palace. Warriors and advisors stood like tiny gamepieces in orderly rows about his massive throne, a chair carved with unmatched skill from a single colossal diamond.

The face of Zyung expressed an abiding calm to rival that of his stone effigy. The fires of his eyes simmered low now, but the heat of them fell across the two beasts as they came to lick at his black boots. One of his hands, each large enough to cradle or crush a living man, lowered to stroke the glossy pelt of the panther, then the rough fur of the wolf.

Panther and wolf licked his tree-thick fingers. When the God-King drew back his hand, the beasts paced about his throne and settled into place like complacent hounds. The white panther lay to the right of the diamond throne, the black wolf to the left. Red tongues lolled between their fangs. Their devious eyes remained open, darting about the spangled hall, searching for easy prey.

Zyung raised his other hand now, and a great horn blew somewhere in the hall.

A second horn took up the golden note and passed it to another, and another, until a thousand such horns echoed about the ramparts of the temple-palace.

The God-King spoke three words that rang like thunder across his realm.

His eyes blazed, twin suns that would scorch the world clean.

Let it begin.

Acknowledgments

In addition to the wonderful people I thanked in the First Book of the Shaper, I'd like to add these fantastic folks. They helped make *Seven Kings* possible, and I owe them all a huge THANK YOU:

Tom Bouman, who came onto the series as my new editor and helped me to make it the best book possible.

John Harter, who offered me friendship, moral support, tons of great comics, and nonstop encouragement. Waterfront Comics in Suisun, CA.

Tom Serene, who shared his friendship and his terrific historical insight. Viva la Revolution!

Frederic S. Durbin, a fellow author and dreamer whose fine work speaks for itself.

Brian McNaughton, for the *Throne of Bones* and Seelura.

Clark Ashton Smith, for his gorgeous vampires, fearsome wizards, and exotic landscapes.

EVERYBODY who read *Seven Princes* and helped spread the word.

extras

orbit

www.orbitbooks.net

about the author

John R. Fultz lives in the Bay Area, California, but is originally from Kentucky. His fiction has appeared in *Black Gate*, *Weird Tales*, *Space & Time*, *Lightspeed*, *Way of the Wizard*, and *Cthulhu's Reign*. His comic book work includes *Primordia*, *Zombie Tales*, and *Cthulhu Tales*. John's literary heroes include Tanith Lee, Thomas Ligotti, Clark Ashton Smith, Lord Dunsany, William Gibson, Robert Silverberg, and Darrell Schweitzer, not to mention Howard, Poe, and Shakespeare. When not writing novels, stories, or comics, John teaches English literature at the high school level and plays a mean guitar.

Find out more about John R. Fultz and other Orbit authors by registering for the free newsletter at www.orbitbooks.net

if you enjoyed

SEVEN KINGS

look out for

THE HERETIC LAND

by

Tim Lebbon

Chapter 1

betrayals

After six days at sea, following a storm that almost swamped the ship, a waterspout that toyed with them for half a day, and an attack by sea scorps that left three crewmen swelling until their skin split and bones ruptured, it was the food that almost killed Bon Ugane.

'I mean it,' the woman said. He'd noticed her before, emerging from the second hold with other prisoners and walking the deck during exercise periods. He could hardly *not* notice her. But they had not spoken until now. 'Don't eat it. I've cooked flatfish all my life, and that one is diseased. The colour of the flesh, the texture . . . ' She shrugged.

'There'll be nothing else from them today,' Bon said. His stomach was rumbling, and he'd already lost weight from hunger and sea sickness.

'So go hungry.'

He looked down at the meagre meal their guards had presented him with, watched and listened to the other prisoners chomping down on their fish, lifted it close to his nose to take a sniff, then tipped it over the railing.

'Here,' the woman said. She held out her plate to him. She'd already eaten most of the good meat. 'Go on.'

Bon scooped up the thin fins in one hand and stared at them. The woman paused in her chewing, offended. Bon smiled and ate, nodding his thanks as the stringy, spiky fins came apart in his mouth.

They'd been allowed up out of the holds to eat today. The sea rolled as waves clashed from two directions, colliding with thunderous impacts, flinging spray skyward to be caught by the easterly wind and blown stinging across the ship's deck. Wave tops rolled white, and flying fish drifted through the spray as they hunted unsuspecting prey. The sky was a deep, threatening grey, and far to the west the clouds had burst, rain falling in silent sheets. They'd only seen one spineback today, and rumour had it the last reported sighting of a deep pirate was a hundred miles east of here. This was as calm and safe as the Forsaken Sea ever was, and the crew's good cheer had filtered across to the usually gruff, hard guards.

The dozen guards leaned against the railing or strolled the deck in pairs, casual, chatting, weapons sheathed. They were recruited from the Steppe clans that lived across Alderia's central regions, where the Harcrassyan Mountains and Chasm Cliffs ravaged the landscape and effectively divided the continent in two. The tallest, strongest people on Alderia – with stocky limbs for negotiating slopes, and vicious teeth for catching prey whilst clinging to rock faces – through the years those generations that left their challenging hunting heritage behind had naturally found their way into the military. Most worked for regional armies or the prison ships, and those few that excelled might even find their way into the Spike, the Ald's own expansive personal defence force. Bon had always found an irony in Alderia's ruling elite requiring their own guard, when they professed to encourage freedom and peace for all.

'What's your name?' he asked after he'd managed to swallow the remains of the fins.

'Name?' the woman asked. 'Oh, so we're straight onto the formalities. Name, where am I from, what did I do that put me on this ship? Life fucking story. But I left all that behind. We're all heading for a new life.'

Perhaps she saw Bon's face drop a little, because her rant faded almost as soon as it had begun.

'My life's been this shit for years,' he said. He smiled, not to show that he was joking, but that he could live with it.

The woman smiled back. 'Lucky you. Head start.'

'And I know where you're from,' Bon said.

'Is it so obvious?' She held up one splayed hand, the thin webs between her long fingers almost transparent.

'I thought your sort might just jump overboard and escape.'

She looked at him for some time, expressionless, eyes never

leaving his face. He glanced away first, and when he looked back she was still staring.

'My sort?' she asked at last.

'Amphys,' Bon said.

'Well, at least you use the polite name. Most just call us floaters.' She glanced around at the other prisoners sat across the deck – one woman had tried standing when they'd first been brought up, and had been kicked back down by a guard – and she and Bon shared a silent moment. It was strange. He had not felt truly comfortable in a woman's presence since his wife's death, and now he was sitting with this amphy stranger and feeling more settled than he had since they'd left Alderia's coast on their journey north towards banishment. Maybe it was her straightforward manner, her easy way of talking. Or perhaps it was the hint of exoticism that all amphys held for him, and had done ever since his parents had first welcomed an amphy friend into their home thirty years before. Many people hated them because they were different, or more graceful than most, or often simply because hating came easy to some.

'Lechmy Borle,' she said, holding out her hand palm up. 'Leki to my friends. Haven't got many of those on board, that's for sure.'

'Bon Ugane,' Bon said. He pressed his hand to hers, and they pushed against each other. It was a formal greeting, but their smiles diluted some of the formality.

'I can't just jump and swim,' Leki said. 'A distant cousin of mine was arrested and deported seven years ago. He jumped ship a day out and was never seen again.'

'Maybe he swam along the coast, made a new life for himself?'

'He's dead. The bone sharks got him, or some other wildlife. Or the deep pirates. They come that far south, sometimes, if pickings are thin to the north. Or more likely he drowned.'

'Drowned?'

'We're good swimmers,' Leki said. 'I can hold my breath for a lot longer than you. But we're not fucking fish.'

Bon chuckled. It felt good, and he thought it was simply because he was talking to someone like a person for the first time in days. Other prisoners had engaged him in conversation, but it was always light, and rarely developed into anything more than cautious platitudes. The disgraced Fade priest in his hold seemed immune to anyone's efforts to enter into conversation. Bon wondered what the priest had done to deserve this, and how he had offended Alderia's official Fade religion. But when Bon had approached, he had not even lifted his eyes. The guards spoke sometimes. But even those who were more fair and reasonable would not grow familiar with the prisoners, because they knew what was to become of them.

'They say it's two more days to Skythe,' Bon said.

'And the worst of the storms are always closer to the Duntang Archipelago.'

'Great. I think I've already vomited everything that's not tied down.'

Leki laughed silently. He watched her as she glanced away, eyeing her up and down. The amphys had always fascinated him, and it went way beyond their webbed hands and feet, and their wider chests that contained the larger lungs. It was the less obvious differences that he found more compelling. They were all blue-eyed, a trait unique to them. They were usually taller than the northern Alderians, and though their limbs were streamlined, they were much stronger. They wore clothing only out of water, and they were always loose and flowing, their natural grace matching the swish of cloth. Their favoured material was sea-spider silk, shimmering with a rainbow of colours from the natural oils. Waterproof, strong and light, their clothing was one of the amphys' main exports from Alderia's three southern states.

Leki was dressed in a dirty, shapeless jacket and trousers, with a heavy belt and clumsily stitched leather boots. She'd probably lost her own clothes the moment she was arrested.

Bon was intrigued, but he had no wish to be pushy. If her story came naturally, he would be interested to hear. If not, it made little difference. He was simply grateful that she had spoken to him at all. It almost made him believe he had a future.

'They'll be putting us back in the holds soon,' Bon said. 'Maybe we should try—'

'Spineback,' Leki said softly.

'Where?'

'About three miles to port.'

'Must be big if you can see it that far out.' He stretched up to see past Leki, out over the port railings and across the angry grey ocean. He spied nothing, and feared she was teasing. He didn't know her.

Then one of the three lookouts up in the skynests sounded his horn twice, and the deck erupted into chaos. Crewmen dashed back and forth, and the guards started urging the prisoners back towards the two ladders leading down into the holds.

'It *is* a big one,' Leki said as she and Bon stood together. 'But don't worry.'

As they were parted and shoved towards different ladders, Bon turned to look past his fellow prisoners and their animated guards. He spotted the shimmer of weak sunlight on a spineback's slick skin, and seeing the upright spikes along its back from this distance meant they must be taller than a man. The huge beast was cutting through the waves towards them, and occasionally it reared up, revealing a wide head and heavily toothed mouth. *How can she tell me not to worry?* he thought.

'Get a shift on!' a guard growled, and Bon obeyed. The fear was palpable – prisoners hurried, guards shouted, and the activity across and above the ship's deck was frantic. Harpoon guns were uncovered, and heavy, glass-tipped harpoons were loaded, the guns' steam mechanisms pumped and primed. Sails billowed, booms swung, rigging creaked and whipped as the ship turned to face the threat, offering a narrower target for the spineback to tear through. The crew started singing a strange song in their own seafaring language, a bastardisation of Alderian blended with the ancient languages found written in western coastal caves. The song beseeched Venthia, the Fade god of water, to help them. Bon did not believe in Alderia's Fade religion and its seven deities, and yet he found great irony in this – the crew prayed to a god which even devout Faders contended had vanished from the Forsaken Sea at the time of the Skythian War six centuries before. Sending criminals across such godless waters was the Ald's favourite way of getting rid of them.

Silent, resigned, Bon caught one last glimpse of Leki as she was ushered down into the second hold. She was not looking his way. That gave him a surprising stab of loss, and his heart was in confusion. On the ship until now, he had given no thought to his fate. Life for him was over.

The hold grating slammed shut, locking them inside. Excited, frightened chatter filled the shadows. The roar of the approaching giant sent shockwaves through the sea and against the prison ship's hull. The Fade priest sat silent and motionless. And as he waited for the end, all Bon could think was, *I want to see her again*.

Bon's hold was not completely dark. Many of the prisoners

had brought candles, and the fifteen other deportees down there with him listened to the chaos with flickering flames reflected in their wide, frightened eyes.

Crewmen shouted, waves thudded into the ship as they swung booms and changed direction, harpoons hissed and whistled as they were fired, and three times something immense struck the vessel, impacts knocking Bon and the others down, wood creaking and metal bracings shrieking. The attack did not last for long, but Bon was far more afraid than he had expected. He was thinking of Leki in the neighbouring hold, and when after the second impact someone shouted that they'd been breached, he heard water hissing in and the cries of those drowning, and Bon dashed across to the separating wall. Banging on the wood, he shouted her name. Screamed it. It was only as an old man grabbed his arm to quieten him, and he pressed his ear to the wall, that he realised the hull had not been compromised at all.

Later, a guard opened the hatch and threw down several bags.

'What happened?' someone asked. 'Did they kill the spine-back?'

'Kill it?' the guard scoffed. He slammed the hatch, laughing, and the prisoners went about sharing out the food.

As Bon ate he looked around at the others. Before today he'd had little interest in them. But the closer they drew to the huge island of Skythe – a hundred miles from east to west, and its northern limits unknown – the more he began to wonder. Some would be political dissidents like him, banished by Alderia's rulers, the Ald, for questioning their word and the tenets of their rule. Others could be religious exiles sent away for being too vocal in their own beliefs; some fringe religions were allowed, but if they actively challenged belief in the Fade they had gone too far. Perhaps there were murderers, rapists, or terrorists. He would not ask, and few people seemed willing to betray their crimes. They might all be classed as criminals by the Ald, but in many cases that would be all they had in common.

In one corner he saw several people praying to the seven Fade gods, changing position, prayers and tone for each deity. Bon felt what he always felt when confronted with such a scene – a faintly painful nostalgia for his childhood years when his parents had made him pray, and a vague sense of disgust. He knew things that, if proven, would expose the Fade for the lie it was. *Many* people knew. His crime was in believing them.

He glanced again at the Fade priest, hunkered beneath dark robes and staring down at the deck between his knees. The man was quite young, handsome, but his face was etched with bitterness. One side of it was bruised, his lips split and scabbed. He rested his hands on his bent knees, and the finger on his right hand that should have borne a priest's Fade ring was missing. The stump was roughly bandaged. The wound was recent.

Bon crawled across closer to the priest. Even as he moved he berated himself, because he had no wish to become involved with anyone down here. *Except Leki*, he thought.

'Fuck off,' the priest said. Bon paused and sat back against a heavy timber brace.

'Not a typical greeting from a priest,' Bon said. He sighed and leaned his head back against the bracing. He could feel the impact of sea against hull transmitted through his skull, and each shiver or thud brought Skythe close.

'I used to believe,' Bon said, softly, quietly. The priest did not respond, and Bon felt that he was talking to himself. 'It's traditional. You're brought up that way, and my parents never gave me any cause to doubt. Seven gods of the Fade, each of them watching over us, demanding prayer and fealty in return for wellbeing . . . it sounds so attractive. So comforting. I had no reason *not* to believe.' He snorted. 'How stupid. I'm so glad I saw the light.'

'And in that light, darkness,' the priest said. His voice was gravelly, older than his years.

'No,' Bon said. 'Enlightenment.'

'The Fade provides,' the priest said, intoning a familiar prayer. 'From before time, the Fade has watched the world for us, and now watches over us. All hail the seven gods.' He lifted his hand and kissed the space between fingers where the missing digit had once resided, his eyes closed and his face almost serene.

'But you're here,' Bon said.

'You think because I'm a priest I must have been banished for betraying my faith. Which means you're as much a fool as anyone else on this damned vessel.'

'Then why are you——?'

'Every moment, I pray to the Fade to send a deep pirate to take us down and consume us all,' the priest said.

'You must have done something terrible,' Bon whispered, staring at the man's mutilated hand.

'Fuck off,' the priest said again. 'Take your heathen heart away from me.'

Bon wanted to protest, and argue, and tell the priest what a fool he must be for still believing in a religion that had done nothing to save him. But the priest closed his eyes and breathed in deeply, praying and finding comfort. Alone, Bon crawled away and sat in the shadows. He had only his own company for the rest of that night, and as usual he found it wanting.

They were not let out for another exercise session that evening. They could hear some pained crying from far away, and Bon guessed that some of the crew or guards had been injured in the spineback attack. It was said that the creatures were infected with poisonous, fist-sized parasites, which were known to infect some of those vessels they came into contact with. As darkness fell outside, occasional shouts, running footsteps, and the sound of crossbows firing seemed to bear out that tale.

Bon bedded down. All but one candle was blown out, and in the darkness he heard the sound of a couple rutting, and someone else muttering insane words as the Forsaken Sea rocked them into sleep.

The silent priest was comforted by his gods.